OF STONE AND SKY

'An enthralling mystery, family saga and
Sunset Song-esque ode to the land'
Herald

'Full of connection and mystery . . . with the backdrop of
the beautiful Scottish Highlands, this is a story of
love, wisdom, and wit'
Scottish Field

'With the most wonderful blend of stark and sharp plot
lines mixed with richly descriptive detailing, this is a
beautifully readable novel. Merryn Glover has an evocative
pen, the descriptions sing, the sense of place flowed into my
awareness and I found I couldn't stop reading.
An unexpected novel, echoing the past and asking
questions of the future, it really is a truly lovely read'
LoveReading

'Glover writes with a poet's clarity and economy . . . each
of the pieces of the jigsaw is compelling in its own right
and interlink to create a picture of considerable beauty
and power . . . exceptionally touching'
Scottish Mountaineer

'This complex, exquisitely written and meticulously-
structured work covers almost a century. It deals with love,
community, family, the legacies of the past; but also with
alcoholism, tragedy, betrayal and loss. It's immensely
readable – and overflowing with grace'
In

Of Stone and Sky

Merryn Glover

Merryn Glover

Polygon

First published in hardback in Great Britain in 2021 by Polygon,
an imprint of Birlinn Ltd. This paperback edition
published in Great Britain in 2022 by Polygon.

Birlinn Ltd
West Newington House
10 Newington Road
Edinburgh EH9 1QS

www.polygonbooks.co.uk

9 8 7 6 5 4 3 2 1

ISBN 978 1 84697 608 7
eBook ISBN 978 1 78885 376 7

The publisher gratefully acknowledges investment from
Creative Scotland towards the publication of this book.

ALBA | CHRUTHACHAIL

British Library Cataloguing-in-Publication Data
A catalogue record for this book is available on request
from the British Library.

Typeset by 3btype.com
Printed and bound in Great Britain by Clays Ltd, Elcograf S.p.A.

for Sam and Luke,
who call this place home

BOOK I

BOOK I

Eulogy

We are gathered here today on the shore of Loch Hope in the presence of God, in the worshipful company of birds and beasts, on the hallowed ground of the Earth, to give thanks for the life of Colvin Munro. We do not know that he is dead, and without certainty and without a body we cannot perform last rites or lay him to rest. But we must release him and we must lay ourselves to rest. There is a time to bind, and a time to let go.

But where to begin when it goes back so far, and where to finish when there is no end? In truth, this is the story of us all, for we knew and loved Colvin, and we drove him away. Ah yes, we have been haunted by that fear, haven't we? Was it me? Was it my fault? And through these years you hoped I would say, in soothing pastoral tones, 'No, of course not. It was nobody's fault – certainly not yours. Be at peace.'

But we could not find peace, could we? Because we were hiding behind shame and half-lies when what we needed was to get to the heart of the matter: the truth, if you will. And I do not presume to know the whole truth, but I do know this story. I know it for I am part of it and because you have told me your parts. Slowly, painfully, in these seven years since Colvin disappeared, you have spilled your tales, mainly over drinks at the Ferryman, swilling sorrows into your beer, sighing regrets on whisky breath, confessing sins in the sipping of wine. And as the truth has come out, like bits of shrapnel from a wound, I have tried to piece it all together, to understand. Some of it will never make sense this side of the Promised Land, but of one thing I am certain: Colvin Munro is still alive.

Sign 1: Knife

The day Colvin disappeared, I found his knife. It was lying in the in-bye field, where the May grass is rich and speckled with flowers, and old dry-stone dykes form the rectangles of a sheep fank. On one of the gates, a length of plastic twine flipped in the breeze where Colvin had tied a ewe by her horn so he could check later if the lambs were feeding well, as her teats were so large. She was the last to birth and he had made two cuts in her horn. As every shepherd round here knows, ewes that are barren or need help with delivery get one cut, and if either event occurs another year, a second. But big teats warrant two cuts straight away, and two cuts mean a difficult mother not worth the effort. She will be sold for mutton. This particular ewe – now marked for death and perhaps resenting it – must have broken free from her tether and stormed off, her two frantic lambs chasing that bursting bag, while Colvin must have forgotten his knife. A sharp snap-blade with a bone handle, it had been made by his Traveller grandfather, handed down to his mother and then to him, and he carried it everywhere. So strange for him to leave it behind.

Birth

He was born on the farm, in the shed, on a cruel night in April 1955. Aye, without a doubt the cruellest month, April, wooing you with her bright face and warm breath till you are in her arms, puckering for a kiss, and she slaps you. Hard. Never more cruel than in the Highlands, neither, where our daffodils can be slashed by hail or our Easter eggs buried in snow. A Pentecostal month, if ever there was one, swinging from ecstasy to exorcism at the spirit's whim.

The night of Colvin's birth was wild with sleet as his mother, Agnes, struggled out in the field with a bulky jacket over her nightie and a torch strapped to her head. She was helping a ewe. The wretched beast was caught in a barbed-wire fence and bleating into the storm. Agnes pulled her father's knife from her pocket, cut away the tangled fleece and guided the ewe into the shed, laying her on her side. Pushing a hand into the tight wet of the birth canal she came at once on the hooves of a lamb and drew them down slowly, feeling for the head, tugging and twisting, till the slimy creature squeezed forth, trailing afterbirth. With a scruff of fleece from the ewe's flank, she wiped his black face, put him to the mother's nose, and as pain surged up her own belly, reached in again. The second one came quicker, sliding onto the straw with a sneeze and a dribble of bloody waters, his useless legs tucked under him, face smooshed to the floor. While the ewe lumbered to her feet for the first lamb to suckle, Agnes rubbed and prodded the second one till he tottered to his mother's face and also got a welcome slurp. Our shepherdess then lumbered to her own feet, stomach tightening like a belt of steel, and after washing her hands in the freezing water at the corner tap, she made a cut in the ewe's horn. The storm outside was a blizzard by now, blocking any return to the house, so she lit a fire in an iron trough and stomped around to keep warm and fight the pain.

She was a practical woman, Agnes: Traveller's daughter, shepherd's wife, angel unawares. Her jacket pockets held not just the knife and matches, but also twine, a fresh hanky, work gloves, some pegs, hair pins, a couple of nails, a pen that didn't work, one that did, shop receipts, scraps of paper, a small telescope, a letter from the council, coins, a dog whistle, dried-up sprigs of heather, a mouth organ and a crumbling bit of flapjack. While waiting for the baby, she cut a length of twine, sterilised the knife in the fire and set them down on the hanky. Her own family had never gone to hospital for anything and she had helped with several of her mother's deliveries, as well as years of lambing; she was calm and breathed deep, groaning through her teeth, till she finally brought our Colvin into the world on a bed of straw. There were no singing angels or visiting kings, and the only shepherd – apart from herself – was snoring in his bed, pickled in liquor and dead to the world.

Ahh, Colvin, what a time to be born.

When he slithered forth head first and howling, she cut his cord and tied it off with the twine – struggling with frozen white fingers – then rubbed the hanky over his face and burrowed him inside her layers of clothes. He was slippery, warm and wriggly, snuffling as his jaw worked the ripe swell of her breast. Touching her finger from her tongue to the top of his head, she murmured in Gaelic. *A small drop of water to encompass my beloved, Meet for Father, Son and Spirit.* The rhythmic tug of his feeding and the sounds of fire and suckling lambs finally pulled her into sleep, where she dreamed of a Traveller's tent with rain pelting the canvas and her father singing.

It was the cold that woke her: the sharp iciness of her feet in their wellies, the draught around her head, the ache of her limbs. Breathing in Colvin's womb-dark smell, she wound him in her scarf and tucked him beside the lambs, then scooping the straw and afterbirth into the trough, rekindled the fire. Warming her hands on the blaze as the wind scuttled the roof, she wondered how on earth she would manage lambing, a newborn and a drunken husband.

Another child was born that night. Fifty miles up the road, in the clean delivery suite of the Inverness hospital, bum first and blue, half-strangled by her cord and blighted with a cleft lip. She too lacked a loving father pacing outside, as he was, coincidentally, also drunk in his bed. In this case, however, our man didn't care one jot that he had sired a child, since children had been the last thing on his mind at the time and because he had already washed his hands of the whole silly business. When the mother, little more than a child herself, had told him she was pregnant, he'd just laughed and said she couldn't prove anything. And, he had added, that if she so much as squeaked to the kitchen mouse she would regret it for the rest of her life, would never work again, and probably never marry. Presumably he would see to it himself. Two cuts in the horn. She'd bitten her lip and carried on till she could no longer fit into her maid's uniform, and the house keeper – a fearsome Mrs Duggins, who will enter our tale soon enough and plague it for far too long – sent her packing.

Once the baby arrived, however, the girl decided three things:

1. She didn't want to get married.
2. She bloody well would work. In fact, she would get rich.
3. She would pass this deformed baby back to its father and never regret it.

And that was how the baby's fate became inexorably tied to Colvin's, though at that precise moment, while he snoozed happily beside the lambs, *she* was fighting to breathe.

That baby was me.

Strath

Colvin and I were, as it happens, conceived in the same valley, though perhaps not on the same night (parish records not extending to such detail). I was swiftly returned from Inverness, and ten years later, brother Sorley arrived, completing the triangle. It is this strath that cradled us (though *cradled* is perhaps too gentle a word) till each, in our own time, took flight.

Two of us are back.

And Colvin? Our dearly departed. We have waited so long for his return, but now we declare it, once and for all: *You will not come back.* And the strath is lost without you.

It is a valley of the vanished.

I learned its story from Dougie MacPherson, mountain man and ecologist, who knew this place so deeply it was engraved within him like an inner map, summoning him daily to walk its ways. Oldest friend of the Munro family, he confessed to me at the bar of the Ferryman Inn – white head bowed over his Glenfiddich – that he was *a thorn in their side*. As well as in the ribs of his only son, Fachie – best friend to Colvin and head keeper of Rowancraig Estate. But such is the price for a prophet in his own land.

And what a land! Lying high in the heart of Scotland beyond the fortress gates of Drumochter Pass, the strath unfurls like a green carpet. Its basin is marshy floodplain, but the soil either side so rocky and weather-whipped that few crops grow and only hardy animals thrive. Thus it has raised a tough breed of farmer – like Colvin – who turn the other cheek to the wind and their hands to a labour of love. But for all its stubborn stones and capricious skies – its flood, fire and famine – the strath is full of beauty.

Its artery is the Spey. Winding down through forests and fields, lochs and rapids, this old, old river passes below mountains so ancient they are half worn away. The rounded humps of Am Monadh Liath – the Grey Hills – rise to the north-west, their memories reaching back three billion years, while to the south-east, are Am Monadh Ruadh – the Red Hills – younger and higher. And though both ranges change colour with the shifting light, only this one has changed name. We now call it the Cairngorms: a pile of blue stones. (I sympathise with the changing of names, for I have had three.)

From each hill, cold springs tumble down into burns that become rivers of their own – Truim, Feshie, Nethy and Dulnain – and lose themselves in the Spey. As she swallows their momentum and their names, her lovely face hides dangerous currents till, wide and swift, she spills into the sea. She is revered for her gifts of pearls and salmon and whisky and feared for her curses of flood and drowning. And whisky. She giveth and she taketh away.

The great hills that rise at her sides, in all their colours, stand barren now. We still argue about why, and even dispute the word *barren*, for heather and peat is full of life, but most agree it's not what it once was. Five thousand years ago, the fabled Caledonian forest spread across these slopes, harbouring bears and wolves, boar and aurochs, beavers and lynx. All are gone.

And the people – we who call this valley home – are hungry as wolves, stubborn as sheep, and surviving, like the few wildcats, as a remnant. And though we are ruinous and stiff-necked, yet we are marked by beauty. For ours is the strength of the river, the endurance of the mountains, the bond of the strath.

Ours is this place.

Exile

My name is Sorley MacLean Munro and I am the shepherd boy made banker. I am the younger son, with a hand on his brother's heel. And I admit the exact nature of my wrongs.

It is 2009, August, Thursday afternoon. Stepping onto the pavement outside the office block I am nearly blinded by the sun as it bounces off the windows across the Thames. *You!* It says. *You failure! You no longer belong here in the towers, the onwards and upwards of glass and steel, the radiant and rich. Get out.*

I stand blinking, holding my briefcase and archive box: the flotsam of ten years in this office and twenty years climbing to it. My keys I have just given to the liquidator, a tall thin man with grey trench coat and crooked nose, hands like claws.

The first day he came, he stalked around the office scribbling on a wad of papers, eyes darting. 'Leave all the paintings.'

'They're mine!' A nude with vast breasts, a cityscape in slashes of black and orange, a digital creation of dots. Strident and expensive, I gloated over them.

'Not yours any more, I believe.' He tapped the inventory and slid his gaze to me. 'Now partnership property.'

I walked away. 'I AM the fucking partnership.'

'The only distinction,' he said, so low I could barely hear him, 'is that we can't sell you.'

Today, now it's over, I just wanted to give him the keys and go, but he insisted on sifting through my archive box, examining the papers, setting the pens aside like surgical instruments, holding my rams horn letter opener aloft like it was infected. When his vulture eyes rested on the photograph of Annabelle, I pulled it back.

'Not for sale.' I laid it in the box and slapped on the lid.

'Oh, I wouldn't be so sure,' he whispered.

Outside, I lower my eyes from the sun and try to breathe. A gust of wind lifts the flap of my jacket and sends a paper cup scudding past on the terrace where seagulls stalk the railings. I move the letter opener and photo to my briefcase, then walk across and throw the box in the river. The lid and a sheaf of papers take flight, scattering across the water and backing up onto the terrace where the seagulls shriek. Someone yells.

I walk away – past offices and banks, my usual cafes and bars, shops with dead-faced mannequins and handbags, past people lost and looking and lying in wait. I walk across littered parks and through arcades, turning corners, crossing roads, not knowing where I am going, not caring where I will stop.

The Bull and Bear, one window boarded up, stains on the pavement. Never seen it before. In the jaundiced light and cooking-fat smells, faces turn to me and colours ricochet around the jukebox. I order whiskies and sit in a corner. Waiting for oblivion, I think of Annabelle.

Her beauty and bell-ring laugh are all I have left. Stalking the London catwalks and splashed over magazine covers, she became my obsession. I reeled her in with theatre trips, gallery lunches and gifts. She was twenty-three, Texan, a dancer before she took up modelling, a lover of film and fashion, though not a reader, or a thinker, as it turned out. But I wasn't looking for that. Nor was I just looking for sex, as that was readily available for money or none. At forty, I was drawn to her youthfulness and her childlike sense of everything being possible and promising. I hoped it might rub off. That through her I might find dreams that would come true rather than turn stale. I certainly had no intention of ruining hers.

That was in the heyday of the mid-noughties when we were building our castles in the air and fooling everyone. Even ourselves. We were trading fortunes like football cards, banking on debt, investing in lies, and I played it faster than anyone I knew. In thirteen years I'd built my hedge fund, Winglift Capital, from my flat in Kensal Green to a billion-pound business on Canary Wharf with over thirty traders and a dozen staff. Wheeling and dealing the moment my alarm went off, I had a sixth sense for the market and could clinch a deal before anyone else saw it coming. By the end I could earn enough in a day to buy a sports car, enough in a week to buy a yacht, enough in a month to buy a mansion.

But I could not earn love.

God knows I tried. I even got married. Twice. The first one was misery for both of us for all of its eighteen months. Thank god there were no children. The second one didn't even last the reception. The whole thing was a drunken bacchanal in somebody's country pile in Yorkshire and my new wife left with the band. I didn't even realise till I woke up the next morning on the floor of the billiards room with a pair of antlers tied to my back.

Others came and went. Some for months at a time, some for little more than a fuck in a lunch break. And with each one there was that moment of ecstasy when I believed – even for a second – that I could be loved for ever. Wrong every time.

Until Annabelle. It's been nearly two years and she's still with me, in the two-floor riverside apartment on the Southbank that she helped to choose. I worried that her loyalty was just because of the money, but when I told her about the financial crash last year and things looking shaky for Winglift, she wrapped herself around me and said she loved me no matter what and was absolutely certain I would see us through. So was I. At first. Believing I could pull it back from the brink, I kept borrowing from the bank and making personal guarantees, mortgaging to the hilt. I didn't tell Annabelle that. But as the months went by and more of the fund's investments fell away and clients pulled out, I hinted that things were tough. She stopped my nervous talk with a kiss. When we started laying off traders and staff and reducing office space, I didn't confess that all my personal savings were now in the fund or that I was selling the extra cars, or that I was up every night sweating and pacing and drinking: I just suggested we cut down on holidays.

'I'm absolutely certain I'll get us through,' I lied. 'It's just for now. Till we steady the ship.' I wrapped myself around her. 'And anyway, we love each other no matter what, right?' I pushed my hand under her blouse.

'Right,' she sighed.

I'd known today was the end but I hadn't told her. I'd said I was flying to New York to negotiate a deal that would give us a whole new lease of life. I'd be back Friday evening and take her somewhere special for the weekend. A surprise. I had no idea what I was going to do when the weekend came. I still don't. All I know is I can't face her.

And so, I drink.

Habit of a lifetime. A bloodline. A legacy.

Sign 2: Hip Flask

The day after Colvin disappeared, a mountain biker found his heirloom hip flask on the hill behind our village. She brought it straight to me, Mo, the almost-sister.

An Sgiath, the name of the hill, means wing or shield in the Gaelic, perhaps for its curving ridge, or because it rises to the north and shelters us from the coldest wind. On bright days in late spring its treeless flanks glow in a mosaic of browns and greens, broken by a grey patch on one side where the heather has been burned. Sheep trails run like veins across the slope, worn by generations of flocks hefted to this grazing, and the biker had been slogging up one of them. When she got to the summit cairn and flopped breathless against the stones, she saw the silver flask. Engraved with the letters 'GM', it was shining in the sun, worn smooth, and empty.

The funny thing about the hip flask is that Colvin never took it anywhere. He hated it.

Highland Games

There was somebody, however, who had treasured the flask and carried it all the time – joined at the hip, as it were – but was reckless enough to nearly lose it one summer's day a long time ago. We are, after all, a people of loss; it runs in our blood, washes down our rivers. *A bunch of losers*, according to the young Sorley Munro, when he took off at seventeen, kicking the dust and sheep shit off his feet.

Further up the Spey from our small village of Briachan with its 500 souls, is the bigger village of Kirkton, where we do our shopping, send the kids to school and catch the train. While we have a handful of windy roads and farm cottages, it has a proper high street with heavy old buildings and a clock tower. It also has a history of doomed attempts to draw more tourists: the Crochet Clan Map (now sagging), the MacMagical Maze (full of midges) and the Giant Haggis (misappropriated by hen parties). Its true distinction, however, lies not in these half-baked gimmicks but on the outskirts of town, where a large field draws devotees of the local religion to perform its rites. I speak not of the Church, which draws hardly anybody, but of shinty, a kind of hockey, but wilder. These days, all the novitiates wear helmets – and even some of the high priests, I'm told! – but when Colvin and Sorley and I played, there was no such nonsense as we sacrificed teeth and skin, camans flailing at the hard ball, bodies smashing into each other, blood mingling. One thing about the shinty remains the same, however: no other event sullies its hallowed pitch except for the Kirkton Highland Games the first Saturday in June.

It was at these Games in 1939 that Agnes encountered the hip flask and the man who was to end up in a drunken stupor as she delivered their son. She was fifteen and had come with her Traveller family to sell the pots and baskets they'd made. Her job was to walk to and fro with a barra hawking her wares, but she was easily distracted. Down one side of the field, a row of marquees flapped in the breeze, while in the middle, a roaring man hurled a hammer and another tossed the caber, his neck as thick as the log he threw. She joined the cheering crowd and banged a spoon on a pan, then stopped to watch the girls in tight buns dancing and tip-tapping over a platform. Eyeing their black jackets and shiny buttons, the matching tartans of their sashes, kilts and socks, she straightened her own shabby clothes and scanned the field for her father. He was standing with the pipers, nothing in his straight back and full Highland dress hinting that he had emerged that morning from a packed and smoky tent. She blew him silent prayers for luck. If he won the pibroch, they would get five pounds and eat their fill. And it seemed a lucky day, with its clear blue sky and an arrowhead of geese moving north, their calls like rusty hinges.

As she passed the events sign-up stand, Agnes couldn't help notice a striking young man in the queue, thumbs hooked into his braces, cap at a rakish angle. He couldn't help notice her either, as she was quite the beauty, with her dark hair, apple cheeks and full-blown figure. Calling her over, he pretended to be very interested in tin strainers and pegs, all the while catching her in the spark of his blue eyes. She felt like a trout flipping on the end of his line. When he told her he'd joined The Queen's Own Cameron Highlanders, and was just waiting for the call up, she felt his excitement and a little swell of pride.

'I haven't a penny on me,' he confessed at last, handing a pot back to her. She blew out in disgust. 'But I will by half three.'

'And how's that, then?'

'I'm going to win the hill race.' He pointed up at the brooding hulk of Ben Bodach behind them. 'The prize is three pounds and I'll buy all your pots for my good mother.'

'And how can you be sure to win?'

'Cause it's the only way I can be sure to see you again.' He winked. 'Meet me at the finish line and my prize is yours.'

'Bet you won't win.'

'What will you bet?'

'Nothing. I don't gamble.'

'Ah, but you just did. Here's the deal.' He pulled the hip flask from his back pocket and gave it to her. It was a bit dented, but polished to a bright shine. 'If I lose, you keep my lucky charm – my grandfather's whisky flask. See, "GM" for Gideon Munro – I'm named after him, though most call me Gid.'

'And if you win?'

'I spend all my prize money on your wares.'

She studied the flask in her hand and squinted up at him. 'Sounds like you lose both ways.'

'No, cause if I win . . . you gie me a kiss.'

'Never!' She shoved the flask back at him and trundled away with her barra, a hot glow on her cheeks, the sound of his laughter behind her. She had got away, but a barb from his hook was in her side.

When the men lined up for the hill race, she peered round the edge of a marquee to watch. Sure enough, he was in the front row in his shorts and vest, flop of blond hair bouncing as he trotted on the spot. A farm boy, she thought, looking at his lean, muscled limbs and brown neck. As the lads jostled one another and teased, he threw back his head in a yelp of laughter and she wondered if the joke was about her. It made her both cross and excited.

At the gun, he was away like a hare and she felt her blood leap, transfixed as he broke free of the group with a loping stride and disappeared into the trees. For the next half hour she kept glancing up at the hill, catching glimpses of small figures and sometimes thinking it was Gideon at the front, but never sure. Finally, their route took them round the back and she forced herself to turn away.

'C'mon, Aggie!' her mother barked, as she got back to the family cart. 'What you been doing aw day?' She pointed at Agnes's barra, still half full.

'There's no good Traveller will want you!' chorused Aggie's younger sisters, erupting into giggles.

'Well, that's good, cause there's no Traveller I want!' she retorted, loading up more wares.

Her mother shook her head. 'If you cannae hawk and sell, you cannae get a husband! Girl your age should be praying for one. Just gone fourteen when I married your father and he just a tad older. Started the family straight away, we did.' Agnes knew these lines so well she mouthed them at her little brother as he passed baskets from the cart.

The family had grown to seven children, not including the two who had died and the one on the way. Travellers did nothing to stop the flow but let nature take its course. As the oldest, Agnes had spent her life looking after nature's bounty and though she never wished any of them gone, had decided that her own life would not be left to the whims of nature or the traditions of Travellers.

Unlike her siblings, she loved the six winter months of each year when the family pitched their bow tent near a town so the children could go to school, and her hunger for learning was stronger than the taunts of the local kids (*dirty tink!*) or the nagging of her mother to quit reading and dae summat useful. Kind teachers loaned her books to take on the summer travels, while farmers saved newspapers and one crofter passed on precious paperbacks full of swashbuckling on high seas and heroines in shawls. Agnes supplemented the evening tales and songs round the fire with news reports from far-flung places, chapters from *Kidnapped*, or poems, most of which she memorised. Her brothers and sisters listened with huge eyes, her mother with mingled fascination and disapproval, her father with furrowed brow. They knew they would lose Agnes, but to whom or when, they couldn't guess.

That day in June, she was on the far side of the field, hot and tired with her heavy barra, when a shout went up and she whirled around. A runner was appearing through the trees. Shoving the cart behind a tent, she scrambled to the edge of the track. But the man's stride was short and strained. It wasn't Gid. Despising her disappointment, she took hold of herself with crossed arms. Then another runner burst from the forest and people started yelling. She squinted into the afternoon sun as the first runner staggered over the stile for the final lap, his pursuer flying down the path. When he vaulted the fence and the crowd roared to its feet, she saw it was Gid. There was a gash under his knee and a slick of blood on the white shin, but he bore down the track like flame, legs long and loose, arms pumping. The crowd brayed, Agnes screamed, and the lead runner pushed harder, face contorted with pain. But as they hurtled round the last bend, Gid drew up beside him, and in the final paces to the tape, edged past and threw himself across.

As he collapsed, the crowd exploded, whoops and hats rising like dizzy birds above the field. Agnes saw men carry him to the first aid tent and she pushed through the crowd, arriving to glimpse through the flaps uniformed women washing his wound and offering water. His face was white, hands shaking. She hovered outside for a while, trying not to gawk, and sure he'd forgotten her. *Indeed,* she scolded herself, *he'd have forgotten you no mair an five minutes after you huffed off with your barra.* The barra! She turned to scoot back for it, but the sound of his voice made her stop.

'Hey, Gambler Girl!' He was standing in the entrance to the tent, knee bandaged, a tweed jacket over his whites. The colour was back in his face, the spark in his eyes.

Her guts catapulted.

'You stupid thing!' she hissed. 'Look what you've done to yourself.'

'I won,' he said, a grin rising.

'And so you did. Well done for that. But they'll no be wanting you in the army with a gammy leg, now will they?'

'Ach, shame, shame. Just have to find someone that does want me, then.' He winked.

'Good luck with that!'

'I'm having a very lucky day, Gambler Girl.'

'Doesn't look like it!' She pointed at his knee.

'Och, but it is. If you'd seen where I fell, that bash should've been on my head and I should no have finished that race alive, let alone first. So, a lucky landing, for one. But even better, a lucky meeting with the bonniest lassie at the games.'

She snorted, folded her arms and blushed.

'Will you make it a hat trick, Tinker Tess? Will you give me that kiss and make me the luckiest man alive?'

There was a spluttering from her and a wild looking about. 'What? Here?!' she demanded, forcing her eyes to meet his and slain by their sheer blueness.

'Anywhere at all,' he said softly.

And so it happened, right there and then, because she couldn't resist him when he took that hobbling step closer and drew her in, the brief strong smell of his sweat and wool jacket, his lips cracked and gentle. The insides of her soared like a kite.

A time to embrace.

We have to hold that picture of Gid, bright and fleet of foot, for he was not always what he became.

Gideon Munro, Gideon That Was, Gideon the Good, set a record for the Ben Bodach hill race that day that was not broken for another forty years till Sorley, seventeen and the image of his father, shaved two seconds off the time. He did not bash his knee, but by then so much else was bashed up that neither Agnes nor Gid, nor Colvin nor I were there to cheer him at the finish. All he had left was the prize money, enough for the bus fare away.

Inheritance

One night at university in Edinburgh, after I won the students' race up Arthur's Seat, I went out to celebrate and the city glittered against a smoky sky and friends shouldered me in and out of crowded pubs and a girl with pink hair kissed me and I felt free and immortal and maybe even a little bit happy, so drank till the lights began to spin and the buildings collapsed and the street rose up to punch my teeth.

Next day I remembered nothing. Waking in a cell, I was charged with drunk and disorderly behaviour, brawling and threatening a police officer. Walked home alone through early morning streets of a city fagged-out and grey, tramps bundled in doorsteps like rags. Looking in the mirror – all bruises and a cut lip – I wondered how my father could have been a drunk for so long yet still have a face.

The Ferryman Inn

Gid, as it happens, perfected the art at the Ferryman Inn.

Ah, the dear old Ferryman. Heart, hub and hellhole of Briachan village life, it holds many a tale. So many, in truth, that despite listening to everyone's yarns and spinning a few of my own over the years, I'm barely scratching the surface.

You see, in the beginning – oh, way back, when drovers were herding cattle down this strath – it was simply the house of the ferryman, for there was no bridge over the Spey here. The building was a one-room hovel with a byre at the side and a pier at the front.

The first ferryman recorded (in 1759, in the journal of a travelling aristocrat) was a Charlie MacPherson, the venerable forebear of our own Dougie. The tourist pronounced him *'a wild brute with neither English nor manners and costume rough and reeking as cattle hide'*. He added a sketch to prove it. Charlie was indeed strong and knew the unpredictable currents where Loch Hope narrows into the Spey, but he was no savage and knew a good wife when he found one. She was Maggie Dallas, who distilled whisky (quietly) and cooked broth and bannocks (noisily) and began selling them to the passengers, first at her hearth and then in an extra room they added. Their son Murdo, famous for singing as he plied his craft, started taking in overnight guests and the inn bulged and grew, adding rooms and upper floors over the generations till Queen Victoria herself stayed overnight on her scouting mission for a holiday shack. It was a lean time for the incumbent MacPhersons and not knowing their guest was royal, the hospitality was spartan. She wrote in her diary that *'there was only tea and two starved Highland chickens! NO pudding and no fun!'* Needless to say, she did not pick Briachan.

She did, however, change the course of its history. Of the entire Highlands, in fact, for she fell in love with it. Despite her predilection for desserts and evening entertainments, she was a tough breed, staring down a hoolie with a straight back and turning a stiff upper lip to the driving rain. Indeed, she seemed to enjoy it. So she bought Balmoral and in a stroke turned the Highlands from a barbarous backwater into a fashionable holiday destination. Thus it wasn't long before a bridge replaced the ferry, bringing stagecoaches and buggies, and not long after that, the next MacPherson built a granite hotel on the site with bay windows, reception rooms and an attic for maids. He also served pudding.

Then the railways came and there was no stopping them. Nobility were joined by flocks of the aspiring classes in the great summer migration north, where the plumage changed to tartan and tweed, and the mating rituals and dominance displays entailed much strutting across moors with guns, in and out of dinners and across dance floors. The Ferryman Inn flourished. There was a pianola and a billiards table, a piper heralding evening buffets, and no surface spared from antlers, potted palms, doilies and porcelain shepherdesses. Better still, it had the best views in Briachan. Looking over Loch Hope to the Cairngorms, its perfect angle on the osprey nest on Small Isle was enough to reduce even dignified ladies to squabbling over the telescope. By then, our beloved oak tree in the garden was already very old, and nationalists of a romantic bent claim it was planted during the first Jacobite rebellion by a local MacPherson chief. Why he diverted energies at that critical moment from uprising to gardening I cannot fathom, but it has played a part for our current cast of characters over the years and was, indeed, about to become very important to the lovely Agnes.

Winner's Return

She wrote to Gid away at the war and sometimes he wrote back, but his letters gave little of the bright, mischievous boy who'd stolen a kiss and forgotten to buy any of her pots. (Well, I shall be charitable and say it was a lapse of memory. In the heady excitement of winning the race and the girl he apparently forgot the terms of his wager and spent the money on rounds of drinks at the Ferryman. We are a funny people that way, so closely tying our successes to our ruin.)

His handwriting was a struggle and stunted his sentences, forcing him to keep things short: 'Leaving S'ampton for France tomorrow. Don't like sea.' She longed for more: descriptions of how he lived, the army way of things, his thoughts and passions – but he didn't give it. He did say, however, that her letters gave him courage, so she wrote every day. She told how her family walked with their cart and horse across the moors to the crofters in the west, who called them the Summer Walkers and welcomed their wares, their news of other villages and their labour on the farms. How they pitched their bow tent in all weathers and washed in streams, pausing beside the big rivers as her father and brothers caught fish and hunted for pearls. How they sat round the fire at night naming the stars and sharing their stories and songs that went back hundreds of years. How her people were the knowers of land, the tellers of myth, the keepers of faith.

Though there could be several days' walk between post offices, she kept writing every day, even when his letters dwindled and stopped altogether. That was in June 1940, and as her fears rose, the news finally trickled back of the battle at St Valery-en-Caux where many of the 51st Highland Division had been killed and even more taken as POWs. No one knew Gid's fate, except that he was not listed among the dead, and

Agnes swung between pleading prayers and grief. She had nowhere to send her letters, but she still wrote and kept them safe, waiting.

At seventeen she joined the Women's Timber Corps and found herself back in Strathspey, felling the giant pines in the Caledonian Forest at Glenmore. The lumberjills were crowded together in wooden huts with no electricity or running water and just an outside shack with a hole for a toilet. In the winter mornings they woke to frost on their blankets and ice stiffening their clothes, and Agnes got up first to revive the fire and get water on for tea. She was tougher than the others, who came from cities and factory jobs, but she did not scorn them. They were noisy in their protests at stiffness and cold, but also in their laughter and ribald tales and their embracing of her. *Whit a braw wee trooper! Look at they muckle great airms, ye've got! Ach and you're a bonnie yin, so ye are. Gies a sang, Aggie, gies a sang!* There was no '*dirty tink*'. At night she wrote her letter to a disappeared beloved and held the image of him, fragile as the candle flame, as full of hope.

Finally, it was all over: victory declared, soldiers returning, home fronts and Land Armies disbanding. Agnes got work at a dairy farm on the north-east coast of Caithness where the flat, low country seemed as endless as her waiting. Demob stretched across agonising months till in October 1946 she overheard a conversation in a grocer's. It was a girl from Briachan, now a scullery maid at Dunrobin Castle, who was talking about some of the lads from home coming back and a village dance in the offing. *Who? Who?* Agnes couldn't help pulling her sleeve. There were a few names and then the only one that mattered: *Gideon Munro.*

Begging the Saturday off, Agnes caught the train to Briachan on the Friday afternoon under a sky cloud-heavy and damp. As she travelled south from sweeping farmland to coast and firths, through towns and forests and over rivers, up mountain passes and down again into the strath, darkness fell. Outside the carriage everything was vanished and unknowable; inside, she studied her face reflected in the window, and it seemed as much a mystery. By the time she got off at Briachan, a lone figure on the small platform, it was well after nine and the village was dark and silent as the bottom of a loch. She walked down to a deserted Ferryman and wondered about slipping into an outhouse for the night if there was no welcome at the Munros'. Music struck up in the distance and turning towards it, she saw lights through the trees. Pulling her coat tighter, she walked along the road towards the village hall where a ceilidh was in full swing, music and light spilling from the arched windows.

She peered through at the people swinging together in a steamy glow of warmth and laughter, the musicians on squeeze box, fiddle and piano, the men scrubbed and shining, the women in floral dresses with lipstick and set hair. She cringed at her own worn clothes and cursed herself for coming. Why was she here? There had been no invitation and the raw truth was she had not heard from Gideon in these six years. He had forgotten her. She was a fool.

But turning away to investigate the sheds at the Ferryman, she saw him. He was wheeling down a Virginia Reel, a steely energy in his spin and turn, sweat glistening on his skin and sticking the shirt to his back. His hair was blunt short and showed every contour of his skull, so much thinner now and harder, as if chiselled from stone. And there, on the right side of his face like a chunk broken from sculpture, was a patch of white flesh where his eye had been.

Agnes stood watching, then pushing her fingers through her hair and licking her lips, slipped into the back of the hall. The air was thick with the fug of perfume and Brylcreem, cakes and tea, sweat and breath, and as the reel ended and grinning people fell away and jostled back to seats, the band struck up a waltz. The young men scooped the pretty girls into their arms, the farmers took their wives and the kids shot through to the buffet tables in the next room. She stood inside the door, scanning the hall, sick with fear.

'Agnes!' a voice cried. She turned to see a tall woman in a pink crepe dress and blonde hair with a cigarette in her hand. 'What you doing here?' It was Beulah, Gid's younger sister. Agnes had met her a handful of times before he left for the front, and occasionally during the war when the lumberjills at Glenmore came into the villages for a dance. Beulah was a parlour maid at Rowancraig House, the mansion on the local estate that owned the Munro sheep farm and thirty thousand acres of moor, but she swanned about like she owned the place. She'd also been possessive of her brother and scornful of Agnes – *Gaelic speaker, vagrant, tink*.

'I came for Gideon,' Agnes said.

Beulah lit up her cigarette, took a long, deep draw, then blew out a blousy cloud of smoke. 'Seen him yet?'

'Yes.' Agnes lifted her chin. 'Through the window just now.'

Beulah eyed her. 'He was hit.'

'I know.'

There was another hard look, then Beulah puffed out a breath of smoke and shrugged. 'God knows he could do with a bit of fun. He's in there.' She pointed with her cigarette to the buffet room and swept off.

Entering, Agnes recognised Dougie MacPherson, as he also had spent the war serving the Timber Corps in the strath and they had met at the dances. His face lit up at the sight of her and he nudged Gid, who was standing with his back to the door. When he turned, the rawness of the scar was a shock. She made herself smile and look deep into the remaining blue eye. He stared back, the flesh around his wound blanching, till he finally gave his plate of sandwiches to Dougie and brushed his fingers on his trousers. As he hesitated, she moved forward and took his hands.

'Welcome home,' she said and stretched up, kissing him on the scarred cheek. His hands gripped hers and then he caught her in a tight hug and she felt how all the boyish excess had been stripped away. His smell was stronger, his hands sinewy and his voice, when he finally spoke, was darker.

'We won.' The words were harsh. She understood, but believed this bitterness would pass. Time would heal, love would heal, *she* would heal.

Right now, it was a time to dance.

And so they did, for as long as the band played, Gid holding her like he feared she might disappear, and when he had to release her to swing with another man, catching her back again with a fierce pull. He and his friends had already been drinking at the Ferryman before the dance, and every now and again he whispered to her that it was time to pay old Moothie MacDram a visit, and he would draw her out the back door to the beech hedge where he'd hidden a half-bottle of whisky. For each of his slugs he insisted she have a sip as well, and while the fire of it hurt her throat, she saw how it brought a softening to his limbs and face. By the final waltz he was holding her so close it was long past decent, but she had no reputation here to lose and he, she could tell, didn't give a damn.

Afterwards, he walked her down the road to the oak tree behind the Ferryman where he pressed her against its gnarled trunk and kissed her hungrily, his breath heavy with alcohol. Giddy herself, she met his kisses with all her sweet power, opening her mouth to him, running her lips across his face and brushing them over the scar. And when he tugged at her blouse she helped him, undoing buttons and bra so her breasts fell freely into his hands, till the wanting and needing peaked, and they welded in a clumsy rush against the dark tree.

Her head reeled, eyes stung; she was a good girl. She had wanted this, but not now. It seared her, a branding that would tie her for ever to him and his land, binding her – whose family walked the whole Highlands – to him, hefted like his fathers to one farm.

'Marry me,' he said, kissing her softly across the forehead, still joined at hip and breast.

'I just have,' she whispered.

And so it was.

Union

By that accounting, Gid had already married several times. The giggling barmaid in the Southampton pub; the ladies of the night in France; the whores in London on the way home. But he did not count them. It's what war did to you, he believed – indeed, what it *owed* you. Flesh for flesh, an eye for an eye. For all that, none of it compensated; not a thousand good-time girls could balance the scales. He never confessed any of it to Agnes and she never asked, not even about the gossip in the village after they married, the drunken fumbling at the Ferryman, the hook-ups away on market days or the maid at Rowancraig who had to leave.

Instead, she gave herself only to him.

Colvin was the same: the wild goose that partners for life.

Sorley, on the other hand, as he freely confesses, played the field. Sowed his wild oats. Was a Cassanova, a Lothario, a Don Juan. By what other glorified titles shall we name him? Playboy, Stud, Stag?

If he was a woman, he would merely be a slut.

As for me – Mo the Maid (ha!) – never.

Though I came very close.

Once.

Loser's Return

Don't remember leaving the pub or anyone putting me into a taxi or a driver putting me on the front step of my place on the Southbank, or how they worked out I lived here. Did I speak? Did I pay? Sure he wouldn't let me go free, must have gone through my wallet, peeled out cash. Only know I've woken up cold and stiff with head pounding and face in a puddle of vomit. I moved here so I wouldn't have to meet people like this.

Not wanting to wipe sick on the sleeve of my suit – pure wool French bespoke – I stand up slowly, bending forward, the worst of it dripping to the ground. Grubby sun leering at me through the morning cloud, I look at my watch – something past seven. It is Friday morning, still August, still 2009. My hand is shaking. I fumble in trouser pockets. My mother gave us a clean hanky every day and even when I couldn't remember her, I kept up the habit, like a lucky charm. But the hanky isn't there. Somehow its loss hits harder than everything else. I push my hand over my slimy face, wipe the mess onto the red brick wall and unzip my briefcase – leather Pierotucci – now smeared with vomit. Cursing my trembling hands, I pull out keys, struggle unlocking the security pad, type in code.

Wrong.

Wrong again.

I lean my head against the wall and think hard – slow – think – one – *think* – button – *think!* – at a time. Buzz! *In!*

The lift has mirror walls so I close my eyes, fire burning in the sockets, then shuffle down the carpeted hallway. Opening the door of our apartment, I hear Annabelle yelp.

'Sorley?!' From our bedroom upstairs.

'Yep.' Move towards the downstairs bathroom.

She yanks open her door. 'What are you doing here? I thought you were in New York!'

I look up, her pacing along the gallery, pulling dressing gown around naked body, face still made-up, hair round her shoulders. She gasps, hand flying to her mouth. We eye each other.

'I know,' I mumble. 'Plans changed.' I go into the bathroom, lock the door behind me. She'll be here in a flash, hammering, demanding explanations. She isn't. There's running back along the gallery above and footsteps in the bedroom. Splash cold water on my face and watch orange and yellow bits swill around the sink and hear more footsteps. Wrong footsteps. Heavier, slower, coming down the stairs. Push a towel over my face and open the door.

A red-haired man is standing there, shoes in his hands.

'Morning,' he says, a little nod, and steps out the door.

Sign 3: Hanky

Two weeks after Colvin disappeared, a surveyor found his hanky. He was from Glasgow, sizing things up for a wind farm in the backhills of the Monadhliaths and saw the fabric caught in a gorse bush. It's a vast wildness up there – an ocean of browns and greys, of peat bogs, scree and grass – and it's a battlefield. The wind blows waves of light and dark, clouds mount armies and rain pelts down like arrows, till finally the sun breaks through and rainbows arc across the warring sky: a truce is called, a time for peace. Colvin's hanky flapped there in the gorse: a white flag on a galleon of gold beside a black bog. It was torn and stained, but unmistakably his because of the 'CM' in the corner. Agnes used to embroider them and put them in the boys' Christmas stockings. Even I got a few. I'd no idea Colvin still had one of those old ones, and the strange thing was, the hanky wasn't just snagged in the bush, it was *tied* there.

Church

The night before their wedding, Agnes gave Gideon a snowy handkerchief on which she had embroidered his initials, and told him to keep it in his pocket with dried heather for luck. She still believed in it then, twined together with her quiet faith. Both were handed down by her family who walked miles every July to camp near the Free Church in Lairg for Communion. They believed the Gospel never rang so true as when read in the Gaelic, nor the praise so pure as when it was the Psalms alone, lifted by voices alone, with no worldly stanzas or instruments to sully the sacred. And so it was a grief to her people that Agnes married a settled man from the Church of Scotland where the old language had died on the tongue and there was an organ and hymns, not to mention an unholy alliance with the state and the landowners. But they didn't speak of it. And so it was that Agnes and Gideon were legally wed in the little stone church above Loch Hope.

The Church – if you will forgive the digression, for it is a topic close to my heart – is another character in our tale though she has, over the centuries, descended from dramatic heroine to sleeping with the enemy to relegation in the dusty wings with an occasional walk-on part. Not that she's silent, mind. A remnant still gather round her knees backstage to warble the sweet songs and hear again the great lines from a dog-eared script. Indeed, the faithful know them so well they can recite them. But what I learned as a minister is that even when the message is new and there is dialogue and action fit for centre stage, most of the audience doesn't hear. They stopped listening long ago. Which is why I stopped trying to coax them into the wings and went out to find them – in the stalls and the streets.

The pub.

The Pub

Our beloved Ferryman had fallen on hard times. The last of the MacPherson line sold up during the Great War and it went through several new owners, each running it down a peg or two till the palms and doilies were replaced by greasy tablemats, and the haunch of venison (like the distinguished guests) had vanished. None of this stopped the local men gathering to drink – indeed they came more than ever – swapping tales or sunk in silence. And as women's liberation stole quietly, eventually, up into the strath, the lassies were free to come to the bar as well, just as free to have a laugh and let their hair down, to waste their money and weep in the toilets, to find love or lose it.

Marriage

The wedding was in February 1947, and the loch was frozen over, grey and hard as the sky. The ducks and swans had fled to the coast and the bare trees were shivering. Those that remained, that is. Thousands had been felled through the war (by Agnes and Dougie and others, who had loved what they'd had to destroy), an ancient army slain and carried away. Glenfeshie, Rothiemurchus, Abernethy, Glenmore – the great forests reduced to acres of stumps in a trampled ground. Gid had returned to yet another landscape of loss. Little wonder he took hold of Agnes as the only thing left from a stolen youth.

In turn, she received him as a gift of grace. The beloved lifted from death and brought home, wounded and shell-shocked, now entrusted to her care. No task meant more, no calling higher.

She made her own outfit for the wedding – a trim skirt and jacket in deep green wool that would serve her for every church service or fancy function for years to come – and tamed her heavy brown hair into a roll of curls at the nape of her neck, topped it with a little hat and spent precious savings on stockings and lipstick. Too poor for flowers and bereft of wild ones in winter, she carried a small Gaelic Psalter, given by her mother, and clipped a sprig of holly to her lapel.

In turn, her Traveller family begged and borrowed clothing coupons, scrubbed themselves raw and polished every last button, brooch and shoe, for even if it killed them, they would be a match for the settled respectability on the other side of the church. Beulah, however – as self-appointed bridesmaid and flaunting a dress of apricot silk – barely looked at them and stood in the front row with her nose in the air. Gid, ungainly in his new suit, didn't seem to care a whit about anyone else, fixing Agnes with his one eye and gripping her hand as he promised to love and to cherish, his vows laced with the vapours of the previous night at the Ferryman. Agnes tried not to breathe too deeply.

Later, at the wedding dance in the village hall, half of her family did her proud playing such winsome tunes on fiddles, whistles and accordion that none could hold their seats, while the other half of the clan, like her father and uncles, made her cheeks burn as they drank their way into glassy-eyed stumbling. Worse, her Gid spent much of the evening slipping off into the side room where there were men and whisky and bawdy laughter, and Agnes felt her first flicker of doubt.

She hadn't seen much of him in the months between their passionate reunion and the wedding, as she was still bound to the dairy farm in Caithness. They'd met a handful of times, but usually with other people present, and though she could see he was shadowed and quiet, she assumed he was still recovering from the war and that the old spark would return. Why, she would rekindle it! What she hadn't seen, till the wedding night, was how the only thing that seemed to light that flame again was liquor.

But, shoving this uncomfortable realisation to the bottom of her mind's drawer like a bill that cannot be paid, she joined the labour of the farm with every sinew of her body, burning herself up to prove a Traveller's daughter could make a shepherd's wife. She rose early and worked alongside Gid and his father, preferring to be outdoors rather than stuck in with her mother-in-law, Phamie, who regarded her as little better than a vermin invasion. Agnes was quick to learn and slow to tire, tuning her ear to the shepherding language and biting her lip when Gid criticised. She had to bite hard for growing up she'd been headstrong and fluent of tongue, whereas now she was guarded. As was he. It seemed a shutter had slammed down and he was both trapped and lost at the same time, with more than just an eye left on the battlefield.

At first the passion of their love-making was thrilling to her and the only time she seemed able to get behind the shield and recover the old Gid (the *young* Gid). In those moments she was swift to flood him with tenderness, cradling his thin body in her strong brown arms, summoning out a vanished spirit of joy. Once, on a midsummer full moon, when the air was still warm from the sun-baked day, she pulled him outside and up the wooded gully behind the farm. There the burn forms a pool beside the empty forester's hut they called the Green Bothy. She coaxed him to swim with her, and they stripped naked and splashed and teased in the cold water and made love on a wide rock, and when he climaxed with a shout, Agnes felt triumph. She was winning him back.

But victory was short-lived and bliss rare. Most often Gid was dark, speaking mainly in half-thoughts and mumbles, only raising his voice to swear at the dogs, his one eye flaring a hot blue, the empty socket clenching. He didn't run any more, claiming the limited vision threw his balance, but Agnes saw him chase the sheep and knew there was still speed and power. She tried to persuade him to enter the hill race at the Kirkton Games that first summer, but he turned on her with such venom that she never asked again. At night he sat by the fire with his fingers pressed against his white scar, as if blocking the memory of its advent. Agnes did not know how it had happened as he wouldn't speak of it or, indeed, anything from the war. She knew only that he was wounded at St Valery, kept as a POW for four-and-a-half years, then forced to join The March across Europe in 1945, nearly dying of cold and starvation. Most of his friends had. They were seven years stolen from his life, and with them, it seemed, the pleasure of everything that came before and the hope of anything to come.

The Munros of Briachan

Unexpectedly, she found solace in her father-in-law, Donald. Tall and dignified in his tweeds, he had eyes that crinkled at the edges and a musical voice. Like her, he was more comfortable outside than in, and he explained things with patience, gave encouragement and never rebuked.

'It's all in the bond,' he said once, kneeling in a field as he wrapped the skin of a dead lamb around an orphan. 'See?' He set the overcoated creature beside the ewe whose lamb had died, and watched as she nuzzled the fleece of her lost child. 'Even if they don't start together, they can believe they belong, like.' He glanced up at Agnes and smiled.

She saw the way the dogs flowed around his feet, watching and waiting, how his slightest gesture made them ripple, a whistle and they were off. They were held to him with invisible threads and when they flopped back at his feet, a rough pat was sufficient prize. Gid, she noticed, could make them obey, but it was harder; the tie had been cut and the reknotting rough.

Taking the sheep up to the summer pastures that first year, Donald told Agnes the story of the Munros. 'We've been the shepherds here for generations.' They paused at the top of An Sgiath and waited for Gid, rounding up stragglers on the slope below. It was a morning in late May and the land was unfurling in warmth and fragrance, Loch Hope full of colours like an opal.

'A much bigger farm at the start,' Donald said. 'From that forest to the north, down to the crags there, and from the loch to way back in the hills.' He pointed his crook, a long stick of hawthorn topped with black horn. His hand was shaped to it, gnarled fingers curling around it like tree roots. 'Thousands of sheep when my great-grandfather was in charge, and a good herd of cattle, least half a dozen men working for him. Been chipped away ever since.' Anchoring the crook under his chin, he looked across the fields. There was a silence and Agnes waited, watching his face. 'Price of wool dropped middle of last century, see, and like most of the lairds up here, the old Lord Mackintosh saw all the money in the shooting. Started clearing the sheep to make way for the deer. And then the grouse. That was my father's time and he had no rights. So after that, the forestry came and then the quarry, and we just got herded off to the sidelines. Never owned a blade of it, but it's where we belong. Nowhere else to go.' The strong light made him squint. 'Except the Promised Land, of course, and when the Lord takes me, who knows? Can't even be sure to pass the tenancy to my son.'

They looked at Gid, approaching at the brow of the hill, snarling at his dog. As he paused to catch breath beside them, the crook fell loose in his hand and the good eye was empty as the stolen one.

Together they herded the flock high up in the Monadhliaths where the grasses blew russet and a golden plover pierced the air. Donald pointed his crook at the sheep, their fleeces tangled with bracken. 'They don't need fences up here. Each hirsel is hefted to a hill and the daughters follow their mothers' footsteps. Passes down the family line.'

She witnessed his bond. To the sheep and the dogs and the land, to the seasons and the weather, to the neighbouring shepherds in time of need, but mainly to this solitary walk; this ancient herding windblown way.

Running

After red-haired man leaves I stand there and wonder if life is still real or if I've entered some absurd cosmic joke. Am I still drunk? Dreaming? This time last year I was one of the hottest fund managers in London – sought-after party man with a model girlfriend. Now I'm bankrupt and cheated on. Fucksake.

Take the stairs slowly, wrecking ball in my head. Annabelle in her bathroom having a shower, door locked. Bed's a mess. Shuffle into my bathroom, hands twitching as I undress, struggling with the strap of my watch – gold-plated, diamonds at each hour. At the shirt buttons, I feel like a leper with stumps and yank, ripping it apart, buttons pinging against tiles. Slump onto floor of the shower, smells of vomit and drink and money washing down the drain.

Much later, after turning the water to a blast of cold and dressing, I go downstairs. Quiet. On the marble breakfast bar, a note.

You ASSHOLE! Just found out what's going on! You fucking liar! How dare you?! Will text before I come for my stuff coz I never want to see you again! Fuck you!!!

Read it several times, then toss it into the bin. Head throbbing and nauseated, battered by exclamation marks, I fumble in a corner cupboard for co-codamol and gulp them down with milk. Hands won't stop shaking. Pick up the stack of yesterday's mail on the table and take it to the sofa with its views across the river. Post is predictable. *Yachting Monthly* (Annabelle claimed seasickness and we didn't go much), Royal Concert Hall programme, Mutual Provident annual report, charity begging letters. And all the bad news. Eye-watering credit card bills, mortgage statement and the builder's invoice for the Italian villa.

Stare at wet clouds mustering on the edges of a metallic sky clamped over London like a trap. The river is heavy, slapping against its banks and churning at the bridge posts. I think of the unwritten bills for the recreational drugs and old boys' deals, the entertainments that the Royal Concert Hall would never provide.

Can't pay any of it now.

Hands are steadier but headache is a spear in my right temple. Fingers press into my closed eyes. Just need a plan. A next step, a door. Fast.

It was only a few weeks ago I finally got over the denial and accepted I couldn't save the fund, then it was like falling down a black hole. Life consumed with liquidators and lawyers and I barely spoke to anyone else. Didn't know what to say. Couldn't look anyone in the eye.

The bills and brochures slide to the rug as I get up and shuffle to the door where my briefcase is dumped. Pull out my laptop and the framed photo of Annabelle. Why I kept this I don't know, as the apartment is full of her photos. I dig in the bag for the ram's horn letter opener and take it with the laptop to the refectory table. Bought off an antique dealer in Fitzrovia. Poor old Benedictines would be spinning in their graves at the decadence of its latter years. Rest my fingers on the keyboard. What now? Bit of tapping and clicking and a CV appears. It's from fourteen years ago, when I moved back from Australia, makes me sound like God's gift to the financial sector. Thought I was. But useless now. In the upper floors of the money towers these days, no one cares what's on the CV. It's the stuff they dig out themselves that matters: track record, connections. Don't know what mine are any more. Yes, I was bloody good at buying and selling money, but those weren't bags of gold we were trading. They were promises of gold, and bags of debt, golden promises that could not be kept and debts of gold that could not be paid. Did nothing illegal, strictly speaking, but I was a master at finding the loopholes. Now the beanstalk is cut and the castles in the air are crashing down, what does that make me? Unlucky? Unwise? The culprit?

All three?

Sick as I feel, I go back upstairs and haul on my running gear. It's the only way I can think. Out on the street, I run without my usual earphones and music, giving myself over to the pounding and the panic. I take the path along the river, but can only move slowly, keep having to retch bitter gas. Running has always been my survival, since school days when I was in the cross-country team and entered Highland Games. Back then it was escape from home and venting of rage. I'd take off up An Sgiath and run and run till I was exhausted and could barely limp back. Way out there on the moors I saw red deer and hare and buzzard, ran amongst heather and thorns and clumps of juniper, pushed through wind, rain, sleet and snow, and on good days ran through ringing light and into the arms of the sky. And each time I was a little bit healed. And each time I had to go back into all that harmed.

So I left home soon as I could, and everywhere I go, I run. Every day. And drink. Several times a day. But no matter how much I run – or drink – something in me is never spent and nothing in me is ever filled.

Bound

Gid's mother disliked Agnes and did little to disguise it. She and Beulah shared the conviction that he could have done better and that it was only his scar that made him settle for a tinker.

'Don't know why he was in such a rush,' Phamie said once, at the kitchen table while Agnes scrubbed clothes in the wash room next door, hearing everything.

'If he'd only waited a little longer,' Beulah agreed, pouring the tea. 'Everyone would have got used to his face.'

'Aye. No decent woman would have noticed, far less minded.' Phamie sloshed milk into the cups.

'They'd have forgotten it in no time, Mother.'

'Like we have.' Dumps of sugar, clackety stirring, tinging of spoons on rims.

'Could have had his pick of the strath,' Beulah concluded and they sighed in unison, daughter dunking her biscuit in her tea, mother snapping hers in chunky fingers and eating noisily, a small shower of crumbs dusting her chin and the front of her pinny.

Beulah, as it happens, got the pick of the strath soon after, by netting a stocky Yorkshireman, Archie Duggins, who came to be gamekeeper at Rowancraig. Lord and Lady Mackintosh of Mackintosh, owners of the estate (and a town house in Russell Square, a holiday cottage in Cornwall, sugar plantations in Jamaica and numerous other business and banking interests), splashed out by giving them a bottle of champagne for their celebrations, a Royal Doulton jug and three days off. Agnes was not invited to the wedding as she was 'in the family way' and though nothing was visible or known outside the family, Phamie and Beulah were agreed that her presence would be indecent. She could, however – if she stayed well back in the kitchen – wash up after the buffet.

The truth was that, despite her scorn, Beulah was jealous. Agnes had a fresh beauty that outshone any face paint or set hair and her kind spirit drew people. They unburdened themselves and asked advice. No one had ever asked Beulah's advice on anything, no matter how often she gave it. Worse, Agnes had other gifts that Beulah and Phamie grudgingly recognised, though would not admit out loud. She could sing and play her mouthie, spin a good yarn and fix things. She read the sky like one divining the future, knowing from the taste of the air if rain or snow were coming and from which direction and how hard. She knew bird calls like the voices of friends, and detected the passage of animals from a soft print or a snag of fur. The forest was her storehouse, giving of its berries and mushrooms and wild garlic for her pot, from leaves and bark the medicines she made. She concealed these preparations, and the old prayer charms that accompanied them, from everyone but Gid, knowing the suspicions about her knowledge, the distrust of her skills. Imagine Phamie and Beulah's triumph to expose her as a witch! Ah, the cackling and libations! Though her love was for wild things, she found a rough affection for the sheep and learned to commune with the dogs, especially as the years passed and Donald died and she carried more of the work.

The baby that had relegated her to the dish water at Beulah's wedding miscarried at four months and was not mentioned again. It was the way then, as if a pall of silence would hasten healing. Indeed, healing was not deemed necessary for no wound acknowledged. Twice more she conceived and lost the child, and each time she named it as she placed a stone on the cairn at the top of An Sgiath. *Go home in peace, Thou child of my love.* She wondered how many of the stones marked a loss, the hill's quiet tribute to sorrow. Were she a ewe, it would have been three cuts in the horn, but being a woman, it was three to the heart.

After the first, she kept each pregnancy and miscarriage to herself, not even telling Gid, for she didn't want him to feel her loss or, worse, to know and not to feel. There had grown between them a silence that she couldn't always read. Sometimes it seemed a deep union, like when they spooned together in the warm dark of bed and listened to the wind, or when, on a cold hill at dusk, he reached for her hand. But other times it was a gulf and they did not know each other. She still sang when she was out working but not so much in the house, for Phamie complained and Gid said nothing in defence. In the evenings by the fire when she made and mended, stifling her humming, he sat in his late father's chair, hand on his scarred face, and never reached for her.

Most Friday and Saturday nights now he stayed late at the Ferryman, and when he crawled into bed, was too drunk to make love, but lay snoring and stinking, still tangled in half his clothes. On the nights when passion flared, his kiss was a bite and his entry into her a battering; he kept the one good eye closed and once, when she yelped in pain, he hit her.

After Donald's death, the new law of 1949 meant Gid had inherited the tenancy, but though he went through the motions of keeping the sheep, he no longer had the gift for it. He sold the cattle, but the loss of their dung gradually depleted the soil till it turned sheep-sick and sour; he made useless efforts to save money by repairing machinery himself; he stored bales of damp hay that fermented, caught fire and burned down the barn. Failure dogged his every step and fear of it devouring him drove him through dark mornings and bitter winds to keep a farm that had turned from proud legacy to millstone. And so the heirloom hip flask, that had once gone everywhere as an empty talisman now always carried whisky, and was topped up whenever he could scrape enough for a half bottle.

All the while, Phamie lived on with them, getting fat, whiskery and curdled. Of course, everything was Agnes's fault: the fate of the farm, the lack of grandchildren, her own poor health. At sixty she announced she was on the brink of death and took herself to bed, not rising for four years save to lumber on and off the chamber pot. Her afflictions – by her own extensive testimony – were multitude, and the family were fortunate she'd lasted this long, though she did not entrust herself to fate alone and repaired to her deathbed with a little service bell. It was always Agnes who brought the trays of food and emptied the stinking potty, secretly glad the woman was at least confining herself to one room. Beulah visited every Sunday – her day off – but Gid rarely put his head round the door.

'He'll be so busy,' Phamie would say, hiding disappointment, as Agnes bathed and changed her. 'Works non-stop, my lad.' Agnes never argued.

Her mother-in-law finally died choking on a chicken bone. By the time they heard her fall and ran up the stairs, her face was already blue, and despite them pounding her back and even excavating her throat with a crochet hook, there was nothing for it. With a final gasp, she collapsed across Gid's lap, a white-haired whale in a flowery nightie smelling of talc, urine and sage-and-onion stuffing.

When the undertaker took the coffin, Agnes felt a boulder lifting off them and looked to Gid for signs of change. Perhaps he could be free to find his way, to once again be proud man of the hills. But it was as if his mother's death meant nothing to him – neither loss nor gain, neither here nor there – and the way he found was not the shepherd's trail, steep and narrow, but the wide and well-worn path of drinking more and living less.

If it were not for the conceiving of Colvin and the unaccustomed feeling of a baby growing strong and big in her belly, Agnes might have slipped away, back to her Travelling folk and the summoning sky. But the baby was here now – nuzzled against the lambs, licked by a welcoming ewe – and with a torrent of love, came the certain knowledge that just as fiercely as she was bound to Colvin, he was bound to the sheep.

Basket

And very soon, he was bound to me. Mo. Growing up, we joked we were twins, though looked nothing alike apart from both being ugly sods. He had inherited more than his fair share of grandmother Phamie's doughy features and had ears like barn doors. As for me, the surgery on my cleft lip was botched and pulled my nose and upper lip to one side and I have heavy bones, always looking male and mis-aligned. But we didn't care because we had each other. We swapped sandwiches at lunch time, raced each other home from school, worked side-by-side at clippings and shared every secret and story and silly joke. I did most of his homework and he fought to have me on the boys' shinty team. I did half his talking and he did half my chores. I never called him stupid (like a lot of people) and he never called me smart arse (like a lot of people). We held everything in common, even Agnes. It was only from being abandoned by my first mother and spurned by the second that I got her, and am eternally grateful. The Lord works in mysterious ways.

But I digress, again. (It was one of my many failings as a preacher.) I have not yet told you how I ended up back in the strath after Our Lady of the Unwanted Conception arrived at her three conclusions in the Inverness Hospital. The details of my transfer, like the identity of my father, were not revealed for a very long time.

To set the scene . . .

Before I was conceived, Beulah had wasted no time in transforming her husband's Keeper's Cottage on Rowancraig Estate from a contented bachelor pad into a bastion of domestic strife. Marital Blitz. Should Archie Duggins have been unaware of any of his faults, he was swiftly brought to full comprehension; should he have imagined he could decide where he might put his possessions or when he might visit his

47

mother in Yorkshire, he was relieved of such delusions with equal speed; and should he have harboured any hopes of affection or admiration or even undivided attention, he was soon enlightened. Unsurprisingly, he found ever more reasons to be out.

Over time, the only emotional territory they shared was the wish for a child. For Beulah this had more to do with keeping up with her friends than anything else. Most of them had popped several bairns by now and Beulah feigned interest, till she found she couldn't have a conversation without a toddler squalling or a scuff-kneed boy butting in, and decided she disliked children. Alarmingly, it did little to dent her determination to have her own. No doubt she believed hers would be different. They would neither cry nor soil nor spoil anything and in fact, under her management, would soon be making life easier. God knows she needed it, what with working at the Big House all day and then tending to a great loafing oaf at home.

For Archie, who would have been quite happy not to be tended, the longing for a child was simply that. He wanted to bring his own little being into the world and to raise him well (for he imagined a son). Indeed, he imagined a whole life in which this little fellow was his constant companion across the moors, in the stables, and in his shed where he would teach him to carve lovely things from horn. As for schooling, Archie would sit patiently and help him with sums and spelling and swell with pride as the lad grew in stature and the ways of the keeper. None of these wistful visions included Beulah, which demonstrated an admirable fortitude of mind, but he did foster a frail hope that a baby might soften her and unite them. He still believed in love, and more than anything, that was why he yearned for a child. He simply wanted someone to love. Beulah had offered that tantalising prospect in their whirlwind romance and he had fallen for her vivid personality and looks, her big laugh and flirty ways. But it had been a hard fall with a painful landing and he had never quite recovered.

The only place he found dignity was on the hill with Lord Mackintosh and his guests. Out where the air was clear and cold, where the patchwork of heather harboured grouse, and the ridges revealed stags, Archie swelled to fill his boots. His was a good nose and he'd come to know the land like his own body and the beasts better than his family, and striding the moors with his gun and dogs he felt lord of all he saw.

So it burned him that within his own home he was treated as a fool. Beulah ridiculed and blamed him. Especially for their infertility, though how she could uphold such a charge when she had moved him into the spare room and only summoned him on the two nights of the month she deemed propitious, he could not fathom. On these appointments proceedings were conducted in much the matter-of-fact fashion of a plumber fitting a new pipe and it was a wonder to Archie that he could perform at all. But though he did, every time, as instructed, he was still blamed.

Eight years passed without a flicker in Beulah's womb, her only comfort Agnes's equal childlessness and her own promotion to house-keeper at Rowancraig. But when the silly new maid managed to fall pregnant at barely fifteen after just one lascivious romp (though she had described it in rather different terms) Beulah got mad and sent her packing. And then, to cap it off, Agnes had the temerity to grow round as a beach ball and Beulah's jealousy reached boiling point. It was all so bloody unfair!

'Do something!' she shrieked at Archie, though quite what he was supposed to do was a mystery. His timid offer to make a few more visits to her bedroom was met with such ferocity he never mentioned it again, and when he suggested adoption, she let out a sharp hack of a laugh and rolled her eyes.

'If that's the best you can do,' she said and stabbed out her cigarette. He took that as permission.

Social Work came and Beulah, who had insisted they wear Sunday best and put a copy of *The Times* on the coffee table, hosed them with tea and chuckling charm and her tales of baby-minding for friends, helping at Guides and loving wee bairns to bits. Fairy tales. Every last one of them. But Archie just smiled weakly, kept his knees together and sipped from the Royal Doulton cups that Beulah had 'borrowed' from the Big House. Approval was swift, a letter sent and their names added to a list. It wouldn't be a long wait, they were told, as there was no shortage of irresponsible young women.

'You can say that again,' said Beulah. Archie didn't say anything, but shot her a look. Had she forgotten their own feverish couplings in the Rowancraig barns well before the wedding? He certainly hadn't. 'Like that little slut we had here,' she went on. Nellie Pegg, the housemaid. Archie hadn't forgotten her either. Soft in shape and voice, with thick auburn hair and full mouth, she used to come into the stables in the mornings with the shooting guests' lunch to be packed in the pony baskets, and she always smiled shyly and called him Mr Duggins. He wished he knew what had happened to her.

As it turned out, he did not have long to wait.

A week after Colvin was born (catapulting Beulah into a poisonous temper), Archie slipped out of Keeper's Cottage in the early morning and into the stables to ready the hill ponies. It was roe buck season, and despite the recent blizzard, the shoot was going ahead. Lifting one of the baskets down from its peg, he was astonished to find a bundle inside. And not just any bundle, either.

Wrapped in a shawl covering the face up to the closed eyes, was a baby. Archie's breath raked. He lowered the basket to the floor and, drawing down the shawl, saw a ragged opening from nose to mouth. Something in him broke as he lifted the child and kissed the soft forehead and found himself praying he could keep this gift.

The baby, of course, was me.

Pinned inside my blanket was an envelope containing my birth certificate naming Miss Eleanor Pegg as my mother but no one as my father. This, she explained in the accompanying letter, was only because the Registrar could not, by law, include him as he was not present to acknowledge paternity. In the young mother's view, however (expressed in no uncertain terms), since the man had done everything necessary to *initiate* paternity he was now honour-bound to follow through. She had thus given his surname to me and me into his care. Farewell and good riddance et cetera et cetera. Archie read all of this in the musky dimness of the stable, motes of dust circling in the early light, and started to tremble. Beulah must never see this letter.

But she must be persuaded to care for the child.

He carried me home, claiming he knew nothing of my origins, and let Beulah pronounce that I was Nellie's and that the father must be some local farm-hand. He also let her choose my name, which is how I was saddled with Maurabelle Donaldina Euphemia Duggins. The middle two names were in honour of her parents and the first after the heroine in a romantic novel she was reading at the time, one of many cheap and ghastly paperback fictions that littered the house and our lives with their impossible plots. All my life I failed (in Beulah's opinion) to live up to my namesake, who was beautiful, sweet-natured, hounded by suitors and ultimately won by the brooding, wealthy aristocrat, who was, in my opinion, the worst of the lot. But as it happened, almost everyone apart from Beulah called me Mo.

To her credit she did not reject me on the grounds of my disfigurement; perhaps her brother's scar had taught her something, or perhaps she was just desperate. Either way, she seized upon me as her pride and joy and paraded me around in frilly caps and ribbons, briefly glowing with saintly adoptive motherhood. Very briefly. Within days she was worn out by a hungry baby who couldn't suck or settle to sleep but could project vomit to fifty paces. She rapidly tasked Archie with the night feeds. He found a way of getting enough milk down me and spent half his nights sleeping in a chair with me upright in his arms, and I swear I remember the feel of his wool dressing gown under my cheek. Gradually, he also took on the bathing and dressing and would often come home to find me screaming in my pram outside the door while Beulah sat inside smoking and flipping furiously through a magazine.

'How long's she been crying, love?'

'Oh, just five minutes.' It was always five minutes no matter how red and tear-soaked my face or soiled my nappy. 'She was about to settle,' she would add, as if he'd spoiled everything.

Then he noticed scratches on my body, then bruises, and when a burn mark appeared on the side of my head he went straight to Agnes. They spoke quietly in the kitchen at Shepherd's Cottage, where a chubby Colvin beamed and gurgled as she kissed the top of his downy head. Archie looked from him to me – the scrap in his arms, bald and blighted by that cleft, always crying – and his heart ached. When he confessed his fears, Agnes lifted me with a musical sigh and with her hand resting on my head, spoke to me in Gaelic. *The love of your creator be with you, My own blessing be upon you, The peace of the life eternal keep you.*

I believe her words encircled me and mark me still.

She told Archie to drop me round to hers for a wee bit every day, and though Beulah sometimes came too (to offer a professional housekeeper's advice) she soon gave it up and my times at Shepherd's Cottage grew happily longer. When I was six months old, Beulah announced she was returning to work at Rowancraig and Agnes must have me all day and that was that. Payment was unnecessary, apparently, because Beulah had done her bit by taking me in, and now everyone else needed to step up. Archie, however, quietly passed on wild game and leftovers from the Rowancraig kitchen, and Agnes accepted them with thanks. And so it was that she became my third mother.

Third time lucky, is all I can say.

The Walk

Archie died when I was seven and with him went the only joy of Keeper's Cottage. For a long time I lay in bed at night holding him in my memory: the bristly morning kisses, the smells of peat and game on his clothes, the cracked hands. By day I sought his spirit in the old shed where he'd done his carving from horn, building on what he'd taught me till I could make my own buttons, spoons and letter openers. There were some precious photographs: Archie in uniform, the wedding, even one of him holding me a few weeks after my first mouth surgery at fifteen months – we were both grinning. But too quickly the memory of him was fading. My father was gone, and though his presence had been only the bookends of my day, his absence filled it.

I didn't know then about Nellie Pegg or my arrival in a basket. No one had said anything on the matter so I had assumed that Archie and Beulah were my real parents, and when he died, had felt I'd been served a rum deal. I sought refuge at Shepherd's Cottage. But even that was a house of conflicting currents with Gid sometimes offering a lopsided smile and a pat on the shoulder, but more often cutting us with harsh words, the scar of his missing eye pulsing. Most of the time he was silent.

Colvin and I kept largely out of his way, easy enough on a farm with miles of open space. We roamed the hills shooting crows, poaching rabbits and vying to spot foxes and birds of prey. In the forested gully where the Green Bothy slid quietly into disrepair, we made tree houses, built dams in the burn and lit fires. Agnes taught us the Traveller way, cutting out a circle of turf with a snap-blade and returning it once the fire was doused, and if ever she gave us sausages to roast, we felt rich as goblins.

When we had to come inside, it was always to the kitchen where she would catch us up in her bread-making hands, leaving a speckling of white across our heads.

'So tell me the wonders,' she would say, going back to her kneading, flour rising in little puffs around her wrists. And we told her of the stag and the hare and the eagle we'd seen and she told us their Gaelic names, and if we begged and did our chores well she might tell us a story.

'Let me see,' she would murmur. 'I might just have one in my pocket.' And she would pull open the drawstrings of the little cotton purse that always hung round her waist and we would hold our breaths as she rummaged. Then her empty hand would appear, her fingers snap and she'd say, 'Got one!' as if it had nearly escaped.

There's a stag on the hill turns into an old grey man at nicht and in a high wind you can hear him roar.

If we were really lucky, she might sit down for the telling.

Ah, the hare. Now the hare is a beautiful woman trapped by a jealous queen. A long, long time ago, there was a king . . .

Sometimes I caught sight of Colvin's face lit with delight, mouth moving in unconscious mimicry.

Haw, and the eagle! Are you sure it was an eagle and not our dear old friend the buzzard?

We weren't, but pretended we were.

Because there's an eagle that flies over our strath once a year on the shortest night. He's as old as the sky and never lands. When he sets his claw to earth, the world will end. Mark my words.

'Naw, Auntie Aggie!' I would giggle. 'That's no true!'

'Ach, aye it is,' and she would wink. 'The faeries of the forest told me, and the *shin* never lie.'

We loved the story-telling for it was a rare moment when she was all ours and we hers, a magic spell that bound us together. Apart from that, she was always working; be it for house or farm, village or church, inside or out, she never stopped. And no matter how hard she worked, nothing was ever finished. The farm was always a shambles of burst hay bales and broken machinery and beastly muck; the house higgledy-piggledy with muddy boots and piles of mending; the kitchen a ceaseless clutter of cooking, cleaning and creatures (the house dog with annual puppies, the cats, the orphan lambs, the invading chickens, the mice, bugs, beetles and flies). Gid struggled under the weight of it all, barely managing much beyond the sheep. Agnes, on the other hand, shouldered the lot with her earthy blend of Highland stoicism and Traveller poetics. You just had to get on with it, and all the better with a song. She was always moving; even during a meal she would be jumping up and down to get the salt or stir a pot or bang on the window to scare the crows. Gid would sit gnawing on his mutton, that burning blue eye following her round the room, till he snapped.

'Will you just sit, woman!'

'Oh aye,' she would sigh, slipping into her chair. 'Just a wee sit.'

The only time she truly fell still – like in church – she fell asleep.

We never saw her speak back to Gid but she could be stern with us. With no tolerance for insolence or laziness, she had no qualms about a wallop on the bottom, and once, when she heard Colvin swear, she frog-marched him to the sink.

'I'm no having that kind of language in my house or in the mouth of my child!' she barked, holding the back of his head down and using her other hand to wash his mouth with soap. 'D'you follow me, son?' He did and kept his swearing out of her earshot from then on. She was a little softer on me, though not shy of a fair telling-off. 'Where's your manners, young lady? Not heard a please or a thank you aw day!'

I forgave her. She held me in the centre of her big heart, her untidy home, her greasy hugs, and I adored her.

But the happiest times and the best stories were out walking. Life on the farm was so relentless there was little opportunity, but whenever she could, she stole away with us. It was partly her Traveller blood, but also the need (never spoken but shared by us all) to be away from Gid. Sometimes she only had an hour to slip off to the Green Bothy where she gathered wild garlic and mushrooms in the woods as we splashed and swam. Sometimes a whole sweet afternoon to take a jammy piece up An Sgiath where she always laid her hands on three of the stones. Sometimes, very rarely, an overnight.

On the longer trips we nearly always went with the MacPhersons, the Munros' nearest neighbours and dearest friends, though Gid always made excuses about the sheep and never came. Their son, Fachie, our shinty team goalie and a keen shot on his air rifle, was Colvin's best buddy (after me, of course, though everyone thought of me as his sister). Margaret – Mrs Mac to us – was short and tubby, surprisingly fit and a legendary baker, while Dougie – Mr Mac – could name every tree and flower, bird and beast. He bored us with his elegies for the lost forests and the devastated land, and it was years before I learned to pay attention, but back then he just smiled sadly and shook his head as we interrupted him or scampered off.

Both he and Agnes loved the Cairngorms, and though he was often in their lower reaches for his forestry work, she could rarely do more than gaze at them across the valley. The year Colvin, Fachie and I were nine, they took us for a longer walk than we had ever ventured before. *Higher up and deeper in!* was Mr Mac's rallying cry as the maps were spread across the table at Shepherd's Cottage. It was September, and we set off early in the cold dark, bundling into the MacPherson's Land Rover in our coats and hats, squished in beside canvas rucksacks and their dog who panted hot breath on our knees. We drove through a thick pool of mist, over the bridge and on to Glenmore forest where we started walking in the grey dawn. The woods smelled of damp earth and pine, the ferns spread with cobwebs in lacy pavilions. We steadily gained height through the cloud, the path getting steeper, the trees thinner and our chatter falling away as our packs grew heavy and our breath short. Mr Mac told stories of the wartime foresters who came from Norway, Labrador and Newfoundland, those who had married and stayed, and those who still wrote to him. Agnes told stories of the Green Fairy Dogs and the Raven's Stone and the Old Grey Man of Ben MacDui. Mrs Mac just chuckled and passed round the shortbread.

And then, without warning, we stepped above the cloud and into sun. I'd never seen the like of it before – the great white sea filling the strath below while we stood on a height of glory. We whooped and laughed and cast off our packs, startling a hare and causing a herd of deer to lift their heads. Joy was our companion for that walk, up, up into the corries and high passes, the wind-blown ridges and the summits of stone and sky. At rushy burns where dragonflies hovered, we drank the clear cold water and, stopping for lunch, gathered the last of the wild berries and skipped stones across a shining loch. Higher up, we saw dotterel scampering so close they made us laugh and a raven pass overhead with a dark croak. We knew we had wandered into the plains of heaven and would never want to leave.

That night we built a fire in a mountain bothy and fell like wolves on Agnes's stew and Mrs Mac's fruit cake and the hot chocolate from Mr Mac's kettle. We sat long in the glow and crackling of the fire, listening to their stories and songs and giggling as he started snoring. The women had such a light in their eyes and a rose in their cheeks that I couldn't stop looking at them and hugging such happiness inside me. What I didn't know was that Agnes was hugging a happiness inside herself, too. A tiny mote of life drifting into the delta of her womb, already sensed by her, already named Sorley.

The next morning, the wet air was shot through with rainbows as we took a steep trail up beside a waterfall to a green lochan, held in a high bowl at the foot of cliffs. By now the sun was risen full and strong and the adults laughed as we paddled our feet and squealed in the cold. Last of all, we climbed Angel's Peak above, a triangle that thrust like the prow of a ship into the ocean sky, and there we fell still, gazing across the land in its hush and holiness, all of us transfigured.

Knee-Woman

The day Sorley was born – the following year in the summer of 1965 – Agnes ploughed through her chores as usual, feeding the chickens and the dogs, pegging out sheets and chopping veg, while humming in short, quivery bursts. It was a Saturday, and Colvin and I, both ten, were playing in the burn up beside the Green Bothy, while Gid was away clipping on another farm. When we came in for lunch, Agnes's face was red and sweaty, and in the middle of serving soup, she dropped the ladle with a gasp. We stared, hunks of bread half way to our mouths.

'Awright, Mum?'

She couldn't answer for a moment, then breathed out in a great rush. 'Aye, son. Just fine.'

We said nothing as she set bowls of cock-a-leekie on the table. But instead of sitting, she walked about clearing the benches, a fixed look in her eyes, gripping tightly to pots and utensils. I stirred and blew on my soup, while Colvin did not lift his spoon or take his eyes from her. Then she clutched the sink and leaned forward, a strange moan blowing from her like a horn.

Colvin jumped up. 'Is the baby coming?'

There was a longer space now where she couldn't talk and I shifted on my chair.

'Mum!'

'Aye, son. That's the baby,' she said at last.

'Who shall I call?'

'Mrs Mac, love. She said she'd—' But another moan cut her off.

'You look after Mum,' he commanded me and shot out the door.

I sat frozen for a moment, then took the abandoned bowl to Agnes, still leaning against the sink with her eyes shut.

'Want some soup?'

Short laugh. 'No thanks, dear.'

In between contractions, as she finished clearing the kitchen, she sent me to fetch an old sheet, some fishing twine and a sharp knife and asked me to lay them all out in her bedroom upstairs. The furniture was dark and too big and still spoke of her mother-in-law's taste and temper, though it smelled of Agnes and Gid. A chair by the wall was piled with his clothes, the bottom of the bed with hers.

'Wash your hands with soap!' she rasped, coming up the stairs with one hand on her belly and the other gripping the banister. 'Really scrub now. Right to your elbows.'

I scuttled into the bathroom, my hands fumbling under the cold blast as I heard her pacing and panting. Back in her room, I stood twisting my damp fingers as she took the clean sheet and spread it on the carpet and then, to my horror, reached up under her skirt and pulled off her pants. They were grey, misshapen things and soaking wet. She tossed them into the corner of the room, angled Gid's chair around as if making the man turn his back, and took hold. A terrible cry came from her and my eyes smarted as I patted her arm helplessly and wished Mrs Mac would come bustling in.

The next moment, Agnes leaned herself back against the bed and with a deep, sonorous moan, pushed herself into a squat. As she did, there was a slipping, squelching sound and I sneaked a look. Below her mass of dark hair and against her white, veined thighs was a goblin's face. Blue, folded with fat and topped with black slime.

I squealed.

She laughed. 'It's the baby. Hold its head and . . . when I tell you . . . pull.'

I stared at her.

'Come now,' she growled. 'No different to a lamb needin a hand.' I knew about lambs – we kids often helped with deliveries – but was I going to have to push my hand inside Auntie Aggie? Her face was turning purple, eyes screwed up, and she was making the biggest, loudest moo like an angry cow. 'PULL!' she bellowed.

I dropped to my knees, gripped the slippery head and pulled. There was a moment when it seemed nothing would give and then a sudden release and the baby began to move. As I drew on him, he came faster, till with a rush of waters, he spilled onto my lap. My hands and arms may have been scrubbed raw, but the shorts and knees he landed on were filthy.

All thoughts of hygiene were swept aside, however, in the tide of this wet hot bundle in my hands, a throbbing blue cord snaking from his tummy back to Agnes. I stole another glance at that sagging, watering, black-haired place and felt my cheeks burn. She didn't seem to care, but leaned forward to inspect her baby.

He wasn't breathing.

Swift as you like, she took him by the ankles, swung him upside down and whacked his back with a cupped hand. No sound. Just a heavy weight hanging from her hands, blotched and bruised. I felt an inner howl: *God, let him live!* She whacked him again, but still no sound.

Unbidden, my own hand flew out and thumped him on the back.

'Live, live, live!' I yelled, whacking.

There was a splutter and a sneeze and a thin wail – Agnes whooped and I burst into tears. Then she rested him back across my lap as she wiped his howling face with a hanky.

'There, there, my laddie,' she said. 'That's you breathing now. Enough fuss.'

I thought she might take him then, but instead she opened her dress and unclipped her bra. My baptism into womanhood was only getting worse. A vast white breast burst forth, streaked with pink marks funnelling towards the nipple as if to say Suck Here, and at last she took her yelling baby, born across my knees, into her arms.

'All the rest will come away soon enough,' she said, gesturing below as she held him, his black head pillowed in her elbow. I prayed I wouldn't be needed for that process, but Agnes seemed to have forgotten about me anyway as she looked down at the little fellow, his noise faded into snuffling as his jaw worked and a tiny hand rested on her.

'So it's yourself, Sorley MacLean Munro, so it is,' she murmured. There was a watery smile on her face and tears on her spider-veined cheeks. 'I knew it was you.'

The Letter

It's not long before I give up on the run and walk back to the apartment, legs trembling, mouth scummy. More mail in the box and I look through it in the lift. Porsche brochure, bills and a hand-addressed envelope. I know the writing and the postmark and it makes my guts lurch. My brother's wife.

Inside, I pour a vodka and seeing my letter opener on the dining table, I use it to tear along the envelope. A quaint old-fashioned habit, like carrying a cotton hanky, it's a rare vestige from my childhood. On yellow paper bordered with her wild designs, the handwriting is almost unreadable with its swishing letters, loops and curls.

Our Sweet Sorley, Hermanito,

How are you, distant one? We always miss you and wish you would come. Summer is dancing on our hills in her bright green and demands to know where you are. Has he forgotten his home? His people? His blood? No, no, I tell her, he is just heartless. He knows how much we love him but he doesn't come, he doesn't care. Made of nails.

Ha, ha, you see, you little scoundrel! Others may 'respect your privacy' and 'give you space' but not me! I was not brought up to this cold British way. We Bolivians believe in family and we don't let our loved ones disappear, we chase them till they are forced to come home. Ha, ha! You see? There is no escape from me, hermanito.

What news? Tess is growing too fast, too pretty, plus too independent. She finished school and wants to be a musician, though how she will make a living I cannot dream. But she does.

She dreams all the time and thinks she can live on songs. Alex is away to himself with only his birds for friends and I can never find him. Colvin is same as ever.

Sorley – Rowancraig Estate is up for sale and the farm is almost lost to us.

Please come.

Liana

Clipping

Everybody gathered at the Munro farm on the appointed day, from distant hills and glens, down rutted tracks in squeaking four-wheel drives, holding hope against rain. Far-flung folk coming together on a summer's day, shepherds and a smattering of keepers and stalkers, some hardy women, a herd of kids, and me – the grafted sister – all hungry for company. Though he was a forestry man, Dougie always came too, and it was different then to what it has become, with the hiring of contractors. Back then the clippings were always neighbours from the strath helping each other. I will always remember that one in June 1970, because it was the last of its kind. The last with Agnes.

She was at the heart of it, working with Mrs Mac in the kitchen, peeling tatties, stirring big pots of soup and stew and getting scones out of the oven, while the rest of us fanned out and circled back, not aware that she held it all together. The quiet farm was erupting with noise as the hundreds of sheep bleated and bayed, vehicles rumbled up the drive, doors slammed, gates clanged, boots stomped and men laughed. Gid gave everyone big clapping handshakes and seemed twice his size, the one eye bright as he led them across his property.

Sorley was five and fit to burst, scampering from house to sheep fank, in and out of pens, over and under fences and on and off his brother's back. A quiet hulk at fifteen, Colvin suffered it with patience till the clipping started, when he shooed him away. Most of the older men still used shears, but Gid had hired in some electric clippers and Colvin and I were learning how to use them for the first time. The only woman clipping and competitive as ever, I proved myself up to the task, which included swearing as much as the men (so long as Agnes wasn't nearby).

The warm June air gradually filled with fluff as beast after beast was hauled by its horns to the clipping stool and rough-handled this way and that, till they cantered away shorn and disgusted. As each fleece fell, one of the older men twisted it into a tight bundle and tossed it into a large bag on a frame. When it was about half full, Gid lifted Sorley into it and the boy stomped backwards and forwards, pressing down the wool, repeating with each new layer till the bag was sewn up and laid flat on the others in a pile of taut mattresses. Then Sorley jumped up and down on them till Gid barked and pulled him off and he scooted back inside to Agnes.

By noon, she and Mrs Mac had lunch laid out on a trestle table near the fank and everyone downed tools to get soup and a roll, followed by tea and cake, till a dram was passed out to all the men and a crate of beers set down. Agnes gave Colvin and me her usual fierce gaze in the presence of alcohol, but when she went inside, Gid tossed us each a beer and we drank and swaggered like the best of them. Gid took a whisky and a beer back-to-back and then another beer, with each drink getting quieter and smaller, eye blinking. His grip on the shears loosened and his pace slowed, and there were knowing glances between the other men, tight lines on Agnes's face, worry on Dougie's.

Mid-afternoon, the sky was threatening rain and there were still sheep left, so we all sped up. Agnes and Mrs Mac set up the stew and treacle pudding in the barn and glanced from their watches to the clouds. If we got the sheep finished in time, everyone could linger over dinner, tell a few tales and share a song till finally wending their way home in the green night, a little boozy and a great deal blessed. But already Gid was wavery in his walk and trembling, not saying much apart from cursing the sheep, who were now stronger than him and resisting.

Then there was a man-and-beast howl and everything stopped. Gid's shears were on the floor and his right hand was gripping his left, blood seeping between the fingers. Locked between his boots, a ewe jerked and squealed, its pure white flank spurting red.

Where God Lives

A few months later, I was washing up at Keeper's Cottage after Beulah's lunch of shrivelled fish and peas when the phone rang. It was Colvin and I knew something was wrong. Not just the usual Gid in a rage or wee Sorley gone AWOL or Agnes hurting herself. She was always doing that – burning her wrists on the oven, skewering herself on fencing wire, banging her head. Dappled with bruises and sores, she laughed them off and refused medicine. *The body heals itself!* But if it didn't, she applied her own remedies of herb poultices or nettle tea. *Nature knows best!*

Colvin's voice was strangled. All I could make out was: *Come.*

Abandoning the dishes and Beulah, I ran for my bike. It was a clear October day, the afternoon sun firing the hills as I pedalled down the track, the cool air whipping my jumper. I threw the bike in the dirt at Shepherd's Cottage and pushed inside the kitchen door.

Colvin was leaning against the bench, ashen. 'It's Mum.'

Sorley piped up from the table. 'What's wrong with her?' Five years old, his cheeks were smudged with jam, blond hair tangled.

Colvin just shook his head and put his fingers to his lips, struggling to summon a sound.

'What?' I said.

He waved an arm in the direction of the sheds, opened his mouth and seemed unable to breathe. Then his hands flew to his face and he started shaking. I hurled myself at him. I knew she was dead.

'What's happened?!' Sorley demanded, eyes like saucers. 'Where's Mummy?'

I caught him up between us, sobbing as he started wailing. Slowly, in broken bits, Colvin told us.

She'd been mending the roof of the barn and fallen through a weak skylight. Fallen through a shower of glass to land hard on the stone floor, scratched and cut, neck snapped. The ambulance had come and gone, police had come and gone, her body was gone. Gid had appeared when there was nothing left but her blood.

We were stood there clutching each other, a three-headed torrent of grief, when Beulah arrived. At first she patted backs and put the kettle on and said *wee souls* and *terrible, terrible*, but when her ministrations failed to stem our weeping she told us to pull ourselves together and have some dignity. It was not the first time, nor the last, that I nearly hit her. Then she gave us a volley of instructions and set off to find her brother. Mrs Mac came with tears and hugs and a tub of soup, and others came and went, and Gid came and went upstairs without a word, and the minister came and sat with us at the table for a long time. I don't remember what he said, but there was none of the nonsense about Agnes being too good for this earth or God needing another angel.

At some dark hour, when Agnes's hankies were sodden clots in our fists, I realised Sorley had fallen asleep on my lap. I changed him into his soft pyjamas and as I folded him into bed, he reached up and I slipped in beside him. There in the deepest dark I held him close, inhaling the smell of his hair and skin, feeling his hands curled against my ribs and his little knees on my thighs. When his breaths finally came slow and warm on my collarbone, I let tears fall again and promised Agnes I would look after him for ever.

I cannot forgive myself for breaking that promise.

People began to arrive several hours before the funeral, walking quietly through the ancient graveyard into the little white church above Loch Hope. Agnes's family came, as scrubbed and polished as they'd been for her wedding but looking like everything inside had been ripped out. The old farmers and gamekeepers came, in their tweed jackets and uncomfortable shoes, hair combed down hard, calloused hands folding and unfolding. And the women in dark coats and hats came, their faces knitted with worry for the Munro boys. Beulah, however, had decided that Sorley was too young to attend and that I should look after him at home. Incensed that she could bar two of the people who loved Agnes more than anyone, I came up with my own plan. Dressing Sorley in his smartest clothes – corduroy trousers and an Agnes-knitted jumper – I took him to the shoreline below the church where we could hear the tolling of the bell and the singing, and I gave my own eulogy for his mother, imprinting memories in his mind like the pebbles I pressed into his hands. Then I pointed out the ducks and geese and the empty osprey nest on Small Isle.

'Every year the mother goes first, then the father, and finally the grown chicks go too, flying all the way to Africa, alone. We don't understand how they know the way, but they do, and every year they come back.'

'Is Mummy in Africa?'

'No.'

'Where is she?'

'She's . . . in the Promised Land, where God lives.' I didn't know that for sure, but couldn't bear to say anything else.

His chin jutted forward. 'She said God lives here.'

'Yes.' I had to make things up fast. 'God can live here and there at the same time, but we can only be here first, then there.'

'Why?'

'Because we're human. He's God.'

His face was brimming with questions, all fighting to be first to break the surface. Finally: 'Will she come back?'

'No, Sox. She can't.'

'Why?'

'Because it's one way. You go and . . . the door closes.'

'Can I go?'

'One day you will. We all will. When we die.'

'I want to die.' He was squeezing hard on his stone.

'No, darlin, don't say that. You have to live. For me and Colvin and Daddy. For Mummy, looking down.' I was battling tears. 'She wants you . . . to live.'

He stared up at the sky, then turned his gaze on me, blue eyes huge with incomprehension.

At the end of the funeral, I took him up a trail through the trees to the edge of the churchyard. I wanted him to see all the people who had come to honour his mother, all the people who would gather round him. But I regretted it. We arrived at our hiding place behind the wild raspberry bushes just as the coffin was carried out of the church. There at the front, opposite his father and bearing his mother to her grave, was Colvin. His fifteen-year old body was awkward in a suit and bent as he tried to match Gid's lower stature; his hands on the casket were white, his face frozen to a numb grey. Gid's face was a strange and twisted mess. All of it was crumpled and clenched in reddish blotches, but while half of it streamed with tears, the other was dry as a stone.

The Kirk

If I had known then that I would one day be minister of that kirk, would it have stilled my weeping?

Or would knowing its story only make the sorrow worse?

It sits on a knoll above the loch, Scots pine rising around it like a company of worshipful giants, waving their arms in the wind, hushing and swishing through the hymns of the sky, leaning quiet to the earth's prayer. Birch and larch are gathered amongst them, rowan and aspen, oak and yew. A choir of rooks cry out as they beat their silk black robes and circle and roost. Some of the graves in our churchyard are so old the names are lost under lichen, others so new the soil yet lies wounded. To step here is to enter the sacred. It is one of the *thin places* they say, where the veil between heaven and earth – between spirit and flesh, above and below – is slight as a bee's wing. The ancient ones worshipped here, to which spirits we know not, but they left a tall stone wedged in the ground. And then the Celts came from Europe, trailing their gods of war and goddesses of fertility, their druids and dark sacrifices, their own dealing with the divine and the dead. From their root grew the Picts and a line of kings who fought over these lands, but feared spiritual power greater than their own and kneeled before it here. By which power I cannot say, but they did repel the Romans who came clattering up through these glens in the first century, and despite the invaders' pleas to Jove and Mars et al, had to go clattering back. They left no sign of their prayers on our sacred site, but there is a story that their 9th Legion disappeared in the mountains of Caledonia. There are other stories. Such is the way with loss that we must fill it with stories of what is vanished and why – our people, our trees, our treasure – but no matter how many stories we tell, be they our longings or our lies, we know that deep down, we seek what is true.

Much later, a monk of the new religion came. All the way from Ireland in a wave-washed coracle to the island of Iona where the rock is ancient and the air, they say, is thin. He carried a story five hundred years old and performed miracles (so the story goes) and planted the new faith. A new power! Though he said it was the oldest of all, from The Beginning, and the greatest of all, to The End. He was Columba, *the dove*. With little more than his staff and his guiding Spirit, he walked the north of Caledonia and drew followers – like the Pictish king of this strath – and left monks in stone huts to carry on the work, summoning worshippers with a bell. One of those huts was on our hillock above Loch Hope and we still have a bronze bell. Some say it cannot possibly be so old; others insist it is and tell stories of it crying out and flying home when stolen. Some say it has the power to heal. I know of no one healed by it, but I know of people who would rather pray to a lump of bronze than bow to any god.

The Celtic church gradually won the Highlands, but eventually gave way to the higher power of Rome at the seaside Council of Whitby in 664. *Nae bother*, said our small band of believers at Loch Hope, praying the same words as before and paying the same old tithes in butter and lambs. So too, when Reformation fires burned from pulpits and stakes further south and the new Church of Scotland came north. The locals were pragmatic, hammering up a wooden screen in the kirk so the old worship could carry on in the chancel while the new struck up in the nave. All were united in not knowing Latin or English or, indeed, what all the fuss was about. They kept their Gaelic blessings that filtered through every day and all deeds of life, regardless of the outsiders' liturgy or law.

> *Be the sacred Three of Glory*
> *Aye at peace with me,*
> *Aye with my horses, with my cattle,*
> *With my woolly sheep in flocks.*
> *With the crops growing in the field,*
> *On the machair, on the moor.*
> *Be the sacred Three of Glory*
> *Aye at peace with thee.*

Just as Reformation dragged its heels up here, so too did loyalty to the Protestant kings, especially after the crushing of the Jacobites in 1746 on Culloden moor. Fearing backlash in the Highlands, the King (he they called *Mad George*) wielded the Kirk to strengthen his hold, ordering more churches, manses and ministers. Thus our old sanctuary above Loch Hope was torn down and a new one erected in the 'parliamentary' style. The altar gave way to the pulpit, the priest was upstaged by the preacher, and the Mass swallowed by the Word. And it was a Word approved by the powers that be, for the ministers were paid and appointed by the lairds.

There was no escape. Everybody had to go to church and if you didn't, it came to you. The Kirk Session was local government, and busied itself barging into homes to hear the catechism, bundling lepers and lunatics off to asylums, and battling *the sins of the flesh*, of which there was no shortage. Lest there be any doubt, before Communion Sundays they decided which members of their miserable flock were fit to come to the Lord's Table and went door to door, issuing tokens. Those fortunate few, now torn between relief and the fear of sinning by pride, must hand them over to get the bread and wine. Reformation fathers would have spun in their graves.

And so to the Clearances, that curse that fell over the Highlands when landowners forced thousands of peasants off the land. In the face of such a scourge, did the Kirk defend the poor and the homeless? Did it rise up and challenge the Pharaohs in the name of justice and mercy? *Let my people stay!* No. Ach, to be fair, there were a few prophets and eventually the protesters who formed the Free Church, but most of the ministers at the time were less servants of God than servants of the lairds. So they preached obedience to the authorities. Some even taught that these misfortunes were Divine punishment for sins and should be borne in penitence. And so the spiritual Shepherds stood by and watched as their flocks were herded over the cliffs, as wolves devoured and fires burned.

And that is my heritage.

These are my fathers.

This is my Kirk.

Music

After Agnes's funeral, there were more people in Shepherd's Cottage than I'd ever seen before; they crushed into the front room, filling the kitchen, shouldered through the hallway, sat on the stairs. Plates of sandwiches and cakes and cups of tea kept appearing and flowing through the crowd like a Feeding of the Five Thousand, and Beulah – in rare New Testament mode – seemed to be the fount. All the women of the community had rallied, bringing food, slicing, pouring, heaping plates, serving, clearing, ushering, scraping, bumping hips, talking all at once and plunging work-worn hands into the sink.

Then, at last, everyone was gone. Sorley was tucked in bed and Gid asleep in his chair by the fire, head cricked to one side, a wheezing snore rising and falling. I looked at Colvin and hoped for talk; it was our only moment alone together that day. But he just said 'Night' and turned up the stairs. My father's death was so long ago I had forgotten how grief axes into life and can cut everyone apart, throwing us on lone trajectories of pain like birds that have lost their bearings. All I knew was the world had gone dark and I was not sure where I belonged.

I slipped out into the night, wind hauling clouds across a fragile moon and blowing cold on my head. I could not bear going home to Beulah, so I went to the Ferryman, making my way down the track by memory and foot-feel, aching with sadness. Someone had said there would be Traveller music, so I slipped in the back to a shadowy corner to listen. There were plenty of dark nooks back then, the place having deteriorated into a spit and sawdust joint, reeking of cigarettes and old carpets. For a long time the only music was a man on a squeeze box, and the tunes drifted in and out like gusts from a swinging door. Then a younger man brought out a whistle and played sweet lines that curled around the accordion, and a heavy woman twanged and buzzed on a

Jew's harp. A lad joined in on the guitar and, as the songs gathered strength, a lanky woman in a long dress added a mouth organ and someone passed spoons to a blind man who rattled and rocked in his corner. Finally a tiny, wizened woman with a grey plait all the way down her back untied the string round a battered case and pulled out a fiddle. It gleamed like golden syrup in the firelight and seemed to waken as she tuned. For a moment she rested it under her chin and listened, eyes closed, foot tapping. Then she hit the bow on the strings and the music soared. The people tipped and swayed, the musicians shaking their heads as her tune pulled them together in a sad, fierce sound; it rose and rose above the dusty dark, filling the air and flooding our heads, till on a wild climax of unbearable pitch, it stopped. There was hush. A long, thick silence.

Then a voice whispered, 'Gie's a sang, lassie!' and they nudged a lovely woman with a sleeping baby on her lap. The guitarist picked a few notes, his eyes on her, and she began to sing. Her voice was high and held all the clarity of the north light, the cry of birds. I didn't understand the Gaelic, but I knew it must be a lament for the dead, for by the end they all had tears. I also knew this was Agnes's sister and that the grief was not just for a woman lost but for a way of life. None of them travelled any more.

Fleece

Reading Liana's letter, I laugh at her passionate claims about Bolivian family values. She has never once gone home since arriving in Scotland. Never had a visit from any of her people. Never spoken of her family except to say they were all killed when her village was swept away by a landslide. She alone escaped by being in the city at the time. Full stop. End of story. Whether Colvin knows more about her background, I don't know, but the landslide has conveniently wiped out an entire childhood. I get it. I have wished for landslides, but they don't happen on the ancient, hard-gripping rock of the Highlands. Instead we have gales and blizzards and freezing and floods, and for all the ruin they cause, they have so far failed to wipe out my childhood, my village or my people.

And now Liana is one of them. A startling arrival from the most foreign land, wildly out of place yet hopelessly tangled in like a vine up a native tree. A seed blown in on the wind, now rooted deep, laden with fragrant flowers and forbidden fruit.

At the bottom of her envelope is a tuft of fleece. She always sends something. A leaf, a feather, a sprig of gorse, as if these fragments from home might tempt me back. They do not. But she . . . she. Her letters arrive once or twice a year and I would let Annabelle see them and laugh. Then I would send a brief reply by postcard, several weeks later, giving very little of my life but hoping she would give more. I never used text or email for Liana as I didn't want that kind of reply with all its immediacy and mundane details of family and farm. Not from her. I preferred the long wait and the not knowing. The sudden jolt when these vivid letters arrived, stirring something dark and dangerous.

Before Annabelle was on the scene, Liana came to London once. It was just over two years ago, with Tess, who was fifteen at the time.

A flying visit for the pair of them to see a show and cram in as many of the London sights as possible in three days. Of course I insisted they stay with me, but it turned me upside down and left me sleepless. Tess was easygoing and there was always an impish spark in her eyes, a brimming laughter. London and its people were an endless source of amusement. How fast they scuttle to their trains, how silent when squished together, how stupid to pay so much for a flat! I wondered what hilarious stories she would tell of me when she got home. Did she know how much I paid for a bottle of wine? Would Colvin laugh?

Liana, meanwhile, was all intensity and passion, speaking fast with hands flying, searching me with those wild eyes, tormenting me by her sheer proximity. I couldn't say how much was sisterly affection or how much was seduction but I knew what I wanted. By day, I had to force myself to look at something else, and not the arc of her collarbone or the tendrils of black hair that curved around her neck. By night I craved.

And now this letter. This is the first time she has directly asked me to come. I lift the fleece to my nose and smell the beasts and the barns, the heaps of fresh-clipped wool, the steamy warmth of new lambs. And with it, the straw and dung and piss, the fermenting silage, the reek of alcohol that soured my father's breath.

I look at the vodka in my hand, raise a silent, bitter toast to him and drain it.

He is long dead now, but I still don't go back. Only once – for Colvin's wedding – and it left me raw like a carcass on the hill with the wind stinging through and the crows plucking out my eyes. Except I wasn't dead. I was home.

With my brother, and his new wife.

And Mo.

Migration

As we moved into that winter of grief – Colvin and I still fifteen, Sorley five – I moved into Shepherd's Cottage. Nothing was discussed or decided; it just happened. Sorley needed me to settle him to bed and half the time I fell asleep wound around him. On each visit I brought another bundle of my things shoved into an old canvas bag of Archie's, and Beulah did not resist this migration, as we both suffered from the unholy blend of my teenaged wilfulness and her just being her. She couldn't move in herself because she always had a lodger and I sensed it was a welcome excuse. Colvin she could tolerate (quiet, serious, hard-working) but mischievous Sorley jangled her nerves and she was quick to skelp him round the ears if she got the chance. And for all her loyalty to Gid, if she was around for too long, they bickered. So holding life together at Shepherd's Cottage fell to me.

While Colvin was paralysed by loss, I was galvanised. I couldn't bear the emptiness, so I filled it with action, steering the flood of casseroles and soups into an orderly queue that I labelled, froze, heated and served as needed. As the stream slowly dried up, I replaced it with my own cooking, fairly stodgy fare at first, but improving, and since no one else was going to do it, I took on the washing, and then the cleaning, exhausted by all of it on top of school, but finding purpose in being Agnes's hands and feet. Gid moved about in a shuffling daze and it was impossible to tell if he was numb with grief or drink, or if it had blurred into one. But despite the alcohol, he was always up and dressed at breakfast, his clothes buttoned and belted, chicken-flesh skin shaved. He was so accustomed to my being around that he didn't seem to notice I was doing all of Agnes's housework, except when I burned the dinner or moved something he couldn't find, and then he turned on me with a hiss and that angry eye. For a long time there was no thanks, no smile, but I didn't expect it. His world had gone black. All I cared about was that he let me stay.

Because most of all I wanted to be with Sorley. I remained in his bed, which he'd shared with Agnes. She'd moved out of the double room when he was born, claiming she needed to be near him and that his night crying would disturb Gid, but she never went back. The room was crammed with their joint possessions all jumbled together, shoved under the bed, dumped in sliding piles on the bedside unit and dresser – a tender tangling of their lives.

Those first nights I wrapped Sorley in her dressing gown and gave him her nightie to hold, swathing him in her softness and smell. But after the funeral, Beulah chose the first day we were back at school to go through the room like a dose of salts, taking all of Agnes's things to a charity shop or the dump. We got home to find it stripped. The wardrobe was empty, Sorley's clothes were folded into two drawers, and a couple of children's books sat squarely on a shelf.

'What a state it was in!' Beulah said. 'A midden! But all done now. Spotless from top to bottom.'

I could have killed her.

Instead, I lived at Shepherd's Cottage for nearly three years, juggling schoolwork with housekeeping and mothering Sorley. Had to give up shinty and seeing friends, but I was so busy and tired I barely noticed. What I did miss were the walks with Agnes. None of us had time or energy for going far and I yearned for that wandering outdoors as she unfolded the world to us. A year after she died, the MacPhersons moved to Aberdeen for Dougie to do a PhD in Ecology, leaving Fachie as a trainee keeper on a nearby estate, father and son already arguing about deer and trees. Most of the time, the only outdoor peace I managed was a short break at the Green Bothy with Sorley, sometimes dragging Colvin along. Soon after Agnes died, he left school to work the farm, giving Gid company and a sure hand where his own was uncertain.

We built a life of sorts together, slowly finding our way out of the valley of the shadow of death and I was proud to lead that walk. Gid sometimes recognised my efforts, and there might be a quiet nod or a pat on the shoulder, even a kind word. By the summer of 1973,

Colvin and I were eighteen and our sweet Sorley a knobbly-kneed eight-year-old who was already winning all the races at school and everyone's hearts. They all said he was the image of Gid and I knew it was a compliment, though saw little to match the vibrant child to the shrunken father, always smelling of booze and defeat. They were an incongruous sight, angelic Sorley curled in Gid's lap as they listened to the radio, or holding hands as they trudged out to the fields. Meanwhile, Colvin grew broad and strong, driving the tractor over lumpy ground, walking hill tracks, filling the shepherd's boots and finding himself on the farm. I, on the other hand, was torn. I wanted to be a teacher and had an offer at university, so long as my final results were good. But I couldn't bear to leave Sorley.

'You have to go,' Colvin said. 'He'll be fine – we'll be fine. You're wasted here with these dumb sheep, like' – he snorted – 'dumb people.'

'No!'

'You've got a life to make.' He looked at me hard. Colvin, who never told me what to do. 'That's the thing about this place: anybody with brains has got to leave.'

Beulah, of course, had her own sweet take. 'University? Who do you think you are? How can you leave poor Gid to run the house by his own and wee Sorley with no mother? What about Colvin? What about *me*? You so high and mighty to think you're better than the rest of us?'

Gid just gazed at me and rubbed my arm, as if I'd confessed pain. 'Do what's right,' he said, finally. Which wasn't any help.

In the end I never knew what was right and never really had a choice. I didn't see my exam results or Sorley running at the Kirkton Highland Games or Colvin's tup winning first prize at the Inverness Show. On a clammy June day, with a basket of washing on the table and a pan of burnt bacon on the stove, I fled.

Sign 4: Letter Opener

A month after Colvin disappeared, a couple of archaeology students found his ram's horn letter opener in a stone circle. It was the summer solstice and they had turned up with cameras and laptop to observe the patterns of the rising and setting sun on this 6,000-year-old site of worship. It was in a field at the northern end of Rowancraig Estate where sheep graze and where, in the spring, great flocks of geese land to rest. Beside it, a forest of birch rises up the hill, the trees lithe with silver trunks and bright leaves, brushing their fingers against rowan and bird cherry, goat willow and shimmering aspen. As one of the students inspected the tallest stone, facing east, she saw the letter opener wedged into a crack. Begun by Archie and finished by me, it was the one I had given to Colvin for his eighteenth birthday, just months before I left.

Bastard

The night I fled, I ended up at the Glasgow City Mission, where I barely slept. I believed I had killed Gid, and it was just a matter of time before the police would come. Every knock on the door made me panic. But there was no police visit, no news, no nothing. It was as if Briachan had vanished and I no longer existed in the same universe. I didn't know what had become of them, what Colvin and Sorley had been told or what they believed. I was sure Beulah could not possibly have told them the truth.

I finally got the courage to phone one night, but heard her answer and put the receiver down. The next time it was Colvin, but my voice seized. When he rang off I wept. The third time, Sorley picked up and I knew, with a crushing certainty, that I could not begin to speak to him because I could neither tell him what had happened or a lie. Hearing his sweet, frightened voice so close in my ear was torment. Aching to speak to Colvin, I tried again the next day. This time it was Gid. I hung up, shaking with relief and nausea.

Now I knew: he was alive and it was me who was dying.

I could not go back. But I could not simply vanish and leave my brothers with nothing but fear and questions. I tried writing a letter. But where to begin? What to say? I tore it up and wrote another, and another and another. Finally, this:

My Dear Colvin,

I had to go. I can't say why. I wish more than anything that I could be there to help, but I can't, I'm so sorry. I love you and Sorley more than anyone and always will. Be strong for him.

Mo

I heard nothing. So in the end, despite everything, Colvin's loyalty had lain with family. Whatever Beulah and Gid had said, he must have believed them. I was the bastard – I had just discovered it – and I was banished.

I existed in a kind of oblivion for years, working all the hours I could: cleaning, waitressing, typing, shelf-stacking. I lived in tiny grotty flats, walked city streets, breathed fumes. The Highlands were lost to me: the strath, the river, the hills; the birds and the beasts; my home. My family. And who the hell were my family, anyway? I was progressively losing them and left to wonder about the miserable couple who had started the whole thing and ridded themselves of it as soon as bloody well possible. Bone-weary, I had no free time and no friends in an overloaded half-life that I thought of ending many times. The only thing that stopped me was the memory of Agnes passing five-year-old Sorley into my lap just a few days before she died.

'There you are, Foxy Sox,' she'd said. 'I've got to get the tea on. You sit with MoMo for a whiley. She'll take care of you.'

And he had given me one of his monkey hugs, winding his arms and legs around me, burrowing his face into my neck and squeezing hard. Then he'd sat up and kissed me on one cheek saying *Love you, MoMo*. And then on the other – *Love you, MoMo* – and then again and again and again till we were all helpless with laughter, our cheeks damp, and he collapsed against me and I could feel his giggling right through my ribs. If I could ever have that feeling again, I could live.

Branding

And so we lived. Our severed lives, our separate stories.

This was theirs.

An uncertain April. By turns fragile and fierce, days shifting between mizzle and sun, nights curled up in cloud or naked to frost. The land is only half awake. Still a little crushed by that hard husband winter and not yet dreaming of summer, it heals slowly to the touch of spring.

Colvin was first up, dragged by a jangling alarm from his bed of unwashed sheets to the heap of unwashed clothes and down to the unwashed kitchen. Since Mo had left last summer, dust had settled on every surface, grime built up in crevices, mould spread. He had never known where to start or finish and Gid was no help and Sorley – so young and bewildered – little better. Eventually, Colvin had just given up the fight.

But he couldn't give up on the farm. The sheep. They pulled him out in all weathers to be fed or gathered or lambed or rescued. Some days he cursed and wrangled with them like demons. Other times he felt protective, fond, even proud. A mix of Cheviot and Blackface with strains of Texel, Border Leicester and Swaledale, some of the ewes had bloodlines going back to the beginning of Rowancraig sheep walk two hundred years before, and in his grandfather's time they'd been the prize flock of the strath. But that was history.

As Colvin stepped outside, the air was cool, the sky laden. Snow clung to the higher hills, but the ground on the farm was trodden mud. Last year's lambs were pushed together in the fank, butting and bleating. On the far side of the pens, Gid was lighting a coal fire in a rusty five-gallon drum. Hunched over in his stained jacket and cap, with spidery red cheeks and lined face, he looked older than his fifty-three years and weary. Smoke rose in stinging plumes around him, making him cough and swear as he poked four irons into holes at the sides. Nearby, Sorley swung on a gate. His clothes were grubby, wellies split, his upper lip raw from constant colds, and he wiped it on the sleeve of his sweatshirt. No one put clean hankies in his pockets any more.

Colvin pushed through the sheep on the inside of the pen, the smells of damp wool and droppings rising to him on the waves of noise. Everything smelled of sheep: the house, his clothes, his hair and hands. He hauled the nearest hogg up against the fence, clamping it with his body and laying its right horn over a rung.

'Here we go!' Sorley yelped. He was like that. Bringing voice to the day's work while Gid and Colvin said little. It was not companionable silence, but avoidance – a skirting around of the painful, unacknowledged things at the centre of their lives. The women. They did not speak their names or venture the reasons for their departures for fear of what that might reveal. They just carried on. And Colvin – now nineteen – carried his anger and grief like concrete in his lungs.

As for Sorley? Colvin saw that he was fed and clothed and sent to school each day, with something for lunch. A clumsy piece with jam, or a margarine tub of leftovers. At bedtime, he knelt beside him to hear the prayers that Agnes had taught and Mo had upheld.

I lie down this night
With the nine angels,
From the crown of my head
To the soles of my feet;
From the crown of my head
To the soles of my feet.

The head was a tangle of unwashed curls, the feet filthy, the angels nowhere to be seen. Colvin would hug him – feeling every rib under the flannelette pyjamas, the twiggy arms – and wait for the questions he could not answer. Till eventually they dried up and there was nothing in the hug but heartbreak.

Gid – who got up each day and went through the motions of the farm like a prisoner on a chain gang – drew an iron out of the fire and pressed it into the hogg's horn. There was a sizzling moment and then the same again with a second iron. R4. *Rowancraig, 1974*. Branded now, they belonged, and would stay on these hills to breed for five years. Unless they died, or got barren, or difficult, or broke their teeth, when they would get marks in the horn and be sold for slaughter.

Sorley jumped off his gate and herded the branded hoggs into the next pen. 'Whaw! Whoosh, whoosh!' He clapped and glanced up at his brother and father. Nobody smiled. When the branding was done, Gid left his post at the fire drum and moved round to the side of the dipping trough, full of a stinking swill of chemicals to ward off scab, lice and tics. As Sorley released them down a run, Colvin ushered them through metal gates and, one by one, shoved each hogg into the dip. Though it wasn't necessary, he kicked them in. Gid then pushed them under with a long-handled broom and they surfaced a moment later, scrambling out of the trough, wet-brown and bleating.

Baptism by full immersion.

Death

Gid finally killed himself.

Not deliberately, but by drowning in drink and shame. It was early 1987 and I dreamt about him for the first time in years and woke with my face wet, tears down my neck and in my ears. I wept then for Colvin and Sorley, my brothers lost to me. A few enquiries and I learned that Gid had died three days ago. It was fourteen years since I'd left Briachan and never been heard of again. For much of that time I wasn't heard of anywhere. It was as if my tongue had been cut out and I couldn't speak of my life. But in my silence I began to hear the voices of those around me. People spoke to me and slowly, slowly I learned to listen. It was the beginning of my pastoral training, though I didn't know it then. I did know, soon enough, that others had suffered far worse than me and there was mystery in who was ruined and who redeemed.

I wandered across the British Isles, in and out of jobs, mainly hotels. Something about their transience appealed; their temporary shelter for the sojourner; bed and board for those far from home. Like me. I was permanently away and always alien. But I knew I had chosen that life, that it was an act of mourning, of penance perhaps.

One morning after I'd finished my shift as the night manager of the Green Oak Hotel in York, I stood on the front step watching the sun steal across the river and the old city stirring to life. Near me, a bent man threw bread for the pigeons and sang. He was there every day in the same worn suit with a shirt and tie, his brogues old but polished, his wisp of white hair lifting in the breeze. I recognised the lumpy purple nose of the alcoholic, the scars and missing teeth, but his gait was steady and his eyes clear as a child's. As the birds flocked around him, he cast the bread like a blessing, his voice rising and falling in its tuneless quaver, his face shining.

How lovely is Thy dwelling place, O Lord of hosts to me. My soul is longing and fainting, the courts of the Lord to see. I recognised the song. *Even the sparrow finds a home where he can settle down. And the swallow she can build a nest where she can lay her young.* An old hymn that Agnes had loved, though he rasped through it badly. *Within the courts of the Lord of Hosts, my King, my Lord and my God. And happy are those who are dwelling where the song of praise is sung.* When his paper bag of bread was empty he looked over at me and smiled. I felt embarrassed to be staring and turned to go, but he came and reached out a hand that was gnarled and nicotine-stained; on the knuckles were the letters H.A.T.E. I held it and listened to his story, and that was the beginning of the end of the old Mo.

A year later, at the end of the beginning, he lifted me up from the waters of my baptism and it was his other hand that took mine. On its knuckles were the letters L.O.V.E. I tell you the truth – the dead can live.

So I went back to Briachan for Gid's funeral and slid into the back pew. The church was two-thirds full. Even though his life had narrowed over the years, this loyal community had not forgotten him. I could see the MacPhersons and a few other old family friends, and all the shepherds and farmers, keepers and estate workers and villagers, even the postman. Colvin stood at the front, bulky and pinched in a grey suit. The last time I'd seen him in a suit, equally uncomfortable, was his mother's funeral. There was no sign of Sorley and I felt a terrible fear that he had died. Beside Colvin, a figure in a black velvet coat and matching hat could only be Beulah.

Now I was a Christian I had to forgive her. And Gid. And myself. Again. And again. Seventy times seven. I did not know how to make it hold.

Colvin and Fachie and some other local men carried the coffin to the grave, where a pile of earth had been heaped over Agnes's side. I didn't like the thought of him beside her but I knew she wasn't there anyway. Nor indeed was he, but I could not imagine him in heaven nor summon the hope of it. No, I still wasn't a very good Christian.

It was January, the sky bolted over us, the wind low and chill. We stood around, our faces white as bone, while a young and nervous minister made a hash of things. Drizzle seeped from the clouds and people began moving back to their cars, Beulah on Colvin's arm. Her face was raw, mascara leaking into the folds under her eyes, lipstick smudged, chins wobbling. My disgust gave way to pity and I seized the moment.

Father forgive her. Maybe she didn't know what the hell she was doing. Forgive me.

Everyone else at the funeral went back to the Ferryman, but I headed straight for Shepherd's Cottage. It was my first time there since I'd run away at eighteen, and I watched it from a distance, memories rising and falling like waves. Colvin got back around seven. It was dark and he walked slowly from his Land Rover to the spot that looks over the in-bye fields and across the strath to Loch Hope and the Cairngorms beyond. All was black except for a scattering of lights in Briachan. Above, the sky had cleared and the stars were bright, a slip of moon dangling low and luminous in the west. Colvin heard my footsteps on the gravel and turned.

'Who's that?'

'It's me. Mo.'

He didn't move, and I could only see the dark shape of his body twisted towards me. Even as I came close, I could not read his face.

'Mo?'

We stared at each other till, with a rush of breath, he pulled me to him.

In the days that followed we told each other the truth of that summer: what had happened between Gid and me, what Beulah had said. He showed me the letter I'd sent – with no return address. I never knew that in my distress at the Glasgow City Mission I must have forgotten to include one and there was no way for him to find me. We spoke of our lives since, and hearing about theirs, I cried. He held me and patted my back, stroked my hair roughly.

'Aye,' he murmured. 'But we survived, eh?'

I asked if he knew anything about my birth parents and he said no. Had only found out I'd been fostered after I left. He made me tea in a stained mug and put in extra sugar instead of milk, because it was off. In the fourteen years the house had sunk under layers of filth and disarray, and stank of male excretions and Gid's smoking. Everything was broken and I grieved for our home.

There'd been nothing from the estate, Colvin said, nothing repaired or renovated. After I'd left, Beulah had helped in the house a bit, but soon retreated. The MacPhersons had visited from Aberdeen when they could and other folks had pitched in for a while, but you can't expect it for ever and Gid was too proud anyway. So it had just been the three of them. And a thousand sheep.

Colvin ran his finger around the chipped rim of his mug, nodding softly as he spoke, gnawing on his lips. His eyes lifted to me for a moment, then squinted out the window.

Sorley had . . . Well, Sorley had done okay. Done great in school, in fact, and gone to Edinburgh University at seventeen – economics – come home a bit, but mainly stayed in the city working. After graduation six months ago, he'd set off travelling. In Australia just now, where Colvin had tracked him down with the news of Gid's death. A phone call. Colvin had not asked him to come home and Sorley had not offered.

So there it was.

He stared into his mug, then pushed back his chair, tipped the dregs into the sink and went out to feed the dogs.

There was an address for a hostel in Darwin, but no sense of how long Sorley would be there or where he might go next. I wrote a long letter, then put it aside and wrote another one, and then another. I'd been here before. *Where to begin? What to say?* All my explanations for leaving Briachan just sounded like excuses and blaming others. I didn't know what he felt about any of it, what he understood or what he wanted. I didn't know who he had become. So I just said I was back and there was a long and sorry tale (if he ever wanted to hear it), but more importantly, I had missed him every day and hoped we could be in touch. I desperately wanted to write *I love you* but it sounded cheap and hollow. Everyone says it to everyone these days. For him now, after everything, would it just feel like a slap in the face? It was too important, too true to risk.

At Colvin's request, Beulah came to see me. She was still in dramatic black and so distraught by Gid's death – she claimed – that she couldn't really think of much else.

'Grief erases *everything*,' she said, eyeing me warily from her perch on the sagging sofa, tea cup in hand. 'Nothing else matters.' She took a bite of shortbread (brought by Mrs Mac) and chewed noisily, crumbs catching in the powdered hairs on her chin. 'No one else.' Lest there be any doubt.

As it happened there was quite a lot else and quite a large number of people who mattered to Beulah, though entirely outside her family. She talked at length about Lord Mackintosh – the son of the lord who originally employed her and Archie – and the New Year's house party at Rowancraig House, where she still worked as housekeeper, and all the grand ladies and gentlemen who were there and the dinners and dresses and days out. I managed to establish that the guests had moved on but his Lordship was staying for a few days to deal with estate matters.

Little did he know those matters would now include me.

An Old Family

I made an appointment with Lord Mackintosh by claiming I was a developer wanting to discuss diversification opportunities. He certainly needed them. The estate was haemorrhaging money and he was always casting about for new schemes. In fact, in his efforts to get rid of one tenant, he had constructed a legal argument asserting his 'poverty'. The courts were still inspecting the evidence. It wasn't till I was shown into his study at Rowancraig House, offered a chair and given tea that I explained who I really was. Mackintosh nearly choked on his Lapsang Souchong. He was early fifties, with bony features and hair silvering above his peaked ears. Although not at all handsome, he carried himself with such entitled ease I could imagine women finding him attractive. I did not.

'I'm here on behalf of my brother, Colvin,' I said, settling back into the Regency armchair. 'Though he doesn't know it.'

'He's not your brother.' Mackintosh fumbled in his pockets for a hanky and dabbed at the spots of tea on his jumper and splashed across his desk.

'A cousin, then, and in some cultures that's the same thing.'

'Not even a cousin, *technically*.' He eyed me over the rim of his Royal Doulton cup and risked another sip.

'No. I don't know who I came from but I know who has cared for me, and that's what matters.'

'Yes, terribly good of Archie and Beulah, but—'

'I wasn't talking about Beulah. It was Agnes that raised me, so Colvin is my brother.' I took a draught of my own tea. I had requested bricklayer's: strong, sweet and milky.

'Yes, yes, whatever, it doesn't really matter.' He stretched out his legs. 'Your family ties are neither here nor there to me, but if Colvin has an estate matter to discuss he should do that himself, and with Gregor Pickett, the estate manager.'

'He's tried. Your man is full of promises but never gets a damn thing done. And all Colvin's requests to meet with you have been refused.'

'I don't have time for tête-à-têtes with all my tenants, Maurabelle—'

'Mo. Please call me Mo.'

'If you wish. What I'm saying is that I'm not here long enough to keep track of the detail. That's what Pickett is for.'

'How many working tenants do you have? Five. And you don't have time to meet with each of them, even once a year?'

He looked affronted. 'I host the estate Christmas party every year—'

'Hardly a time to discuss business, though, is it?'

'And what business do you wish to discuss?' He leaned forward and put down his cup. 'Let's get it on the table, shall we?'

'The list of outstanding issues with Colvin's tenancy is longer than your driveway, Lord Mackintosh—'

'Oh, call me Edgar, please . . .' He waved his hand as if at a passing fly. 'And do stop exaggerating. Just get to the point.'

'All right then, *Edgar*.' I put down my own cup. 'The critical thing is the state of Shepherd's Cottage. The estate has done nothing in Colvin's living memory and it's barely habitable.'

He raised his eyebrows. 'Well, I'm terribly sorry to hear that and I shall mention it to Gregor.'

'That achieves nothing.'

'Are you suggesting that I am ineffectual with my own employees?'

'No. Just that things will only happen if they matter to *you*. So, with that in mind, I've called the paper to take photos of the house for a story about the appalling treatment of one of Briachan's oldest families.'

Mackintosh eyeballed me across the desk. 'You really don't have to be so underhand, my dear. I have given you my word.'

'I don't want your word, Edgar. I want your money.'

A moment's silence, then he burst out laughing and stood up. 'Join the queue!' Moving to the window, he looked across the valley.

'Well, this isn't really *your* money, is it? It's Colvin's. The money you legally owe, as landlord, and are long overdue in paying.'

He turned to me. 'Dear lady, I have been entirely unaware of this and will speak to Pickett at once. One can't get embroiled in the nitty-gritty of plumbing and decorating in every estate cottage!'

I stood up. 'Let me be clear – put it on the table, so to speak. If I don't see a builder surveying that house by noon tomorrow, the paper will publish.'

We eyed each other like boxers.

Then he laughed again. 'Well, that's wonderfully clear then, isn't it?'

'I hope so.'

'Goodness, it's not such a big problem after all.' He stalked back to his chair, scribbled something with a fountain pen and signed with a flourish. 'I shall send a chap round first thing and work will commence as soon as possible thereafter. You really don't need to come in here with all guns blazing. A polite request would have been quite adequate.'

'Your tenants have tried good manners for donkey's years, Edgar, and it's got them nowhere. But they're afraid to be pushy because they don't want their leases threatened.'

A sharp laugh. 'Your Colvin has a secure heritable tenancy. There's bugger all I can do to get rid of him.'

'You know that's not true. You have taken back chunks of his land for other uses and even sold bits of it under his nose. You know he has not registered his right to buy with the Land Court because your Mr Pickett threatened him with higher rent. You know you can make his life so difficult that he could relinquish his tenancy out of sheer desperation. Don't pretend otherwise.'

'Oh for pity's sake!' He threw down the pen and dropped his head into his hands. There was a long pause. Then he said my name quietly.

'Yes?'

'I'm afraid we've got off to a bad start, you and I. Let's begin again.' He raised his face to me and I was surprised at the sadness.

'Yes. Of course.' I sat down. 'I'm sorry I tricked you. I had to see you, by hook or by crook. But it's not my usual way. Been an emotional time.'

'I understand. Gideon Munro's passing, of course.'

And the rest. At least Mackintosh had shown the decency to attend the funeral.

'My condolences, by the way. He was a father to you after Archie, I suppose.' He leaned back and crossed his legs.

'Not really, no.'

Mackintosh studied me over his steepled fingertips, then spoke quietly. 'I barely knew my own father, you know. It was always nanny in the early years, then he was an officer in the war and by the time that was all over I was at boarding school. Packed off at six. It was Frederick he doted on – my older brother. Or the girls. I was the spare and I don't think anyone believed I would ever be needed.' He got up and walked back to the window, bony hands clasped behind him. Snow was blowing in gusts and spirals outside. 'But poor Freddy was killed in a car crash. And suddenly, at thirty-one, I'm it. Father never recovered from the shock, treated me with this nasty mix of disappointment and suspicion – as if I'd somehow planned it. It was utterly ghastly, the whole thing.' He stood still, staring at the darkening valley. 'Then, four years later, Father died and I'm lumbered with all this.' He threw open his hands.

'Lumbered?'

'Oh, I know it's wealth and privilege and all that.' He turned back to me. 'But it comes with a lot of strings attached and a shed load of bloody hard work, and most of the time, frankly, it runs at a loss.' He moved to the fireplace, where a blaze crackled in the grate and a portrait of his young son hung above. Leaning an elbow on the mantel, he shoved his other hand in his pocket and studied the fire.

'So why not sell it – even give it away?'

'Not as easy as that.' He fiddled with something in his pocket.

'Surely easier than all these strings and sheds you have to bear.'

'But it's not just mine, is it?'

'Exactly.'

'What I mean is, when you inherit an estate like this, you take on a family history, a responsibility to all who came before you and' – he paused – 'to those who come after.' He did not look at the picture and I knew why. I knew what had happened to the boy, his only child, and that his wife had died soon after.

His voice was fragile. 'We are a very old family.'

I watched him. He watched the fire. (Oh, if only he'd known what documents had been committed to that fire, so many years before, by his very own father! If only I had known.)

'What do you mean?'

'Our genealogy can be traced back as far as any records in Scotland go.' He drew a letter opener out of his pocket, carved from horn. It caught my breath. 'We are there at the beginnings of Clan Chattan and further back amongst the great northern kings. As for this land, my ancestors were the earliest known chiefs in this area—'

'Back when the land belonged to everyone,' I said, staring at the letter opener.

'No, it didn't.'

'It was clan land. The chief was like a father with a large family and a communal property.'

'Not communal. *Technically*, legally, he owned it. We have the ancient title deeds to prove it. And, anyway, if the chief was a good father, it really didn't matter.' He shrugged, flicking the letter opener.

'Except they weren't, were they? Come on – you know the history! Once the clan system was crushed chiefs morphed from father-figures to landlords.'

'Well, some maybe—'

'Started pushing their own clansmen off the land for sheep. And then for the shooting. And then the shepherds got pushed around, didn't they, Edgar?'

'No!' He snapped the letter opener in half. 'I utterly reject your crude and biased version of the history and I resent your insults to me personally. My family have always worked hard to care for this land for the benefit of all. We maintain proud tradition and heritage, we make business from barren moor that is good for nothing else, we bring income into the local economy and ensure the Highlands remains a world-class tourist destination, without all of which the whole goddamn place would go to the dogs!' He threw the bits of letter opener into the fire – there was a snap and flare – and stalked back to the desk. 'I will not be lectured by some finger-wagging socialist who invests nothing in the place and has just swanned in for the weekend. I think our interview is over, Miss Smith.'

'Mo.'

'Why don't you bloody well accept who you are?'

'I do!' I stood up. 'You say yours is an old family? All that means is that you have a long history of privilege, so you were written about.

94

It doesn't make your family any older or more important than anyone else's. In fact *my* people go all the way back to the beginnings of the race, but it just so happens I don't know their names. I don't even know my own mother or father. What I do know, Lord Mackintosh, is that – despite how distasteful this must be to both of us – you and I are from the same family. Good day.'

I should like to say I swept out, but *bumbled* is more the word, tripping as I did en route on a leather pouffe.

Purging

We gutted Shepherd's Cottage. Anything worth saving – which wasn't much – we carried into the barn, heaving wardrobes and beds down the stairs, toing and froing with seats, bumping out with shelves and chests of drawers. A few cardboard boxes of important papers and precious things we kept, like the collection of letters Agnes had written to Gid during the war, but never posted. They were all still sealed and neither of us felt fit to open them. Most of the house went into a row of skips: the soiled mattresses, the curtains and rugs heavy with dust, the battered pots and moth-eaten blankets. The entrails of a rotted home.

Fachie MacPherson and others came to help and they were all uneasy around me. I don't know what folks had really believed about my disappearance but, according to Colvin, there had been rumours and wild speculation. Most of the stories had included the same kernel of truth: that I'd had a run-in with Beulah. Indeed she had put that round herself as much as she could, perhaps to deflect from the fact that it coincided with Gid's run-in with a cow and subsequent days in hospital. People must have put two and two together, but as time had gone on and the Munros stayed tight-lipped, I had slipped down the gossip charts till I was relegated to the growing heap of unexplained events in the community. Life had gone on.

But now I was back, the memories resurfaced. Of course everyone wanted to know what had happened and why I'd left, but couldn't ask. All I gave were a few off-hand comments about my various jobs and that I was managing a boutique hotel in Edinburgh but had a couple of weeks' leave.

My pressure on Mackintosh had ensured that Colvin could stay in one of the estate holiday houses during renovations, close enough to his beasts and barns to maintain the daily round of feeding in the changing weather of January. Apart from that, he and I laboured for most of every day clearing out Shepherd's Cottage. It was filthy work – a protracted exorcism.

'Some things just need to be burned,' I said, as we carried Gid's armchair outside and set it on the gravel. It was lopsided and sagging, the upholstery ripped and stained so much the pattern was obliterated, cigarette burns peppering the arms, stuffing erupting through the cushions like pustules.

Colvin shot me a look and nodded. 'I'll get the axe,' he said. When he returned from the shed I was still staring at the chair, gripping my coat around me. He started first. Strong, clean blows that broke its back and sheared off the legs. Then he paused and offered the axe to me. I swung it high above my head and brought it down hard right into the seat. I did it again. And again and again till the whole thing was a butchered mess.

Colvin watched quietly till I threw down the axe. Then he held me as I wept.

Once

At the end of my waitress shift at the Highland Tea Room in Kirkton, I whipped off the frilly white apron, slung it on a hook and shot out the back door to my bike. It was a muggy June day in 1973 and as I pedalled home a quick spurt of rain made my gingham uniform cling to my skin. I hated dresses and couldn't wait to change to shorts and T-shirt. It was Friday lunchtime and I'd managed to wangle the afternoon off to watch Sorley compete in the school sports day. Colvin was away clipping and Gid supposed to be as well, but he'd been complaining of a cough and pounding headache for some days and stayed home. He was in a bad patch, smoking a pack a day and drinking himself to sleep at night. Half the time he fell asleep in his chair by the dead fire.

Even before I got through the kitchen door I could smell burning. A pan on the stove was spitting and smoking, the bacon in it shrivelled to crisps. I ran across and shoved it off the hot plate and started opening windows. The rest of the kitchen was a mess – breakfast dishes still on the table, unwashed porridge pot on the stove, an overflowing basket of wet washing on a chair.

'Gid!' I yelled. 'Gid?!'

I went crashing through the house. He was in the front room, a place none of us ever went during the day, as it was north-facing and cold. The curtains were partly drawn and the place reeked of fags and whisky; in the gloom I saw him sunk in his chair, a trembling cigarette in one hand, tumbler in the other. I'd never seen him with a dram at this hour before. There were papers on his lap and some had slipped to the carpet. He turned his one eye to me and shook his head.

'What? What's happened?' I moved across and gathered up the documents.

There was a letter on heavy embossed paper with a watermark and the insignia of Rowancraig Estate, signed by a Mr Gregor Pickett, Esquire. I'd never heard of him. The other pages were legal documents. Coughing and muttering through the smoke, Gid told me the story.

Seemingly, when the old Lord Mackintosh died the previous year and his son Edgar inherited Rowancraig, he set about making Improvements. The estate needed to be profitable. *For the good of everyone that lived and worked on it*, the new laird had been eager to emphasise. The first Improvement was to accelerate the 'retirement' of the old factor, a local man who knew everyone and was often at the Ferryman playing darts, and to appoint this Mr Gregor Pickett to the newly created post of estate manager. According to his letter, there was need for a significant increase in rent. New lease documents enclosed, signature required within twenty-eight days et cetera. Mr Pickett had delivered the papers in person and was, apparently, every inch the suited, booted and polished figure one would expect of an Estate Manager and Esquire. He probably didn't play darts.

When Gid finished, he ground the cigarette into the crowded ashtray and pressed his fingers into his scar. Gripping the tumbler, he drew in a gurgling breath, then spoke on the outward wheeze. 'We can't do it.'

I watched him from my spot, kneeling at his feet. 'We'll find a way.'

His fingers pushed harder, his head moving in a slow, small shake. 'There is . . . no way.'

I put my hand on his knee. 'Let me see all the accounts, Gid. I'm good at maths, I'll work something out.'

His hand dropped down over mine and the one, watery blue eye locked onto me. 'You . . . are going to uni . . . Mo.'

There was a sudden heat in my hand, sandwiched between his palm and his knee and I didn't like it. But that eye was beginning to leak.

'I don't have to go,' I whispered.

He stared at me, his gaze dropping down my damp dress to the place where my thighs appeared. The Highland Tearoom uniform was already too short when you were standing up, but kneeling, it barely covered my knickers. He put his tumbler down and shifted forward.

I went to pull my hand back. He gripped it tighter.

'No,' he croaked. 'You don't have to. You could stay . . . and help us.'

'I could . . . but—' I tried to wriggle my hand free.

'We need you . . . *I* need you . . . please!' He leaned over and grabbed my other arm, his face inches from mine.

'I . . . I need to think.' I looked down, starting to sweat. 'I don't know what to do.'

'Marry me,' he breathed.

I gaped at him, a shock in my limbs.

'You're the woman of this house . . . You've earned the right to be the wife.'

'No . . . no . . .' I was mumbling.

He lunged for a kiss and I pulled back, but being on my knees and with his grip so tight, I could only stumble half way up, and he tipped towards me.

'No!' I cried. 'Stop it!'

He fell to his knees, clinging to my wrists, tears wetting that one cheek. 'Please, Mo! I need a woman! Man can't be . . . alone! I need—'

He threw his arms around me, burying his face in my crotch.

'Get off!' I pushed his head away but he began clawing at my thighs and pushing up my dress. His nails were jagged. He yanked at my pants.

I yelled and kneed him in the chin, snapping his head back, but he came for me with a howl, making me crash backwards onto the old sofa with him gripping my thighs. We struggled, him biting and tearing at my clothes, me writhing and kicking him. Hard. He recoiled and I got free, but kept on kicking. In my panic I kicked him again and again till he was doubled over and retching.

'You disgusting . . . drunken . . . idiot!' I was hysterical. 'I'm your flesh and blood!'

So I believed.

As if on cue, blood spurted from his mouth.

Flight

I jumped on my bike and fled. Past skittish sheep and rabbits and a buzzard on a post. In that silly gingham dress. I didn't think or decide, I didn't know where else to go, so I raced to my childhood home and crashed through the door.

Beulah was there, frying mince. The smell turned my stomach.

'Call an ambulance for Gid!' I ran for the phone.

'What's wrong?' She was at my elbow as I gave the garbled message. Drunk man . . . fifty something . . . coughing blood.

She gripped my arm. 'What happened? Why didn't you phone from there? Why did you leave him?'

'Because—' I couldn't find words. I burst into tears.

'Oh, my dear, what is it?' She took hold of my other arm and looked at me with those terrified eyes and I thought she cared. About me.

Stupid me.

I should have told her any crazy story. Anything. Anything at all, but the truth.

Because when I did, in a torrent of sobs, she refused to believe me. Said I was making it up so I had an excuse to leave for uni. *Why? Why would I make it up?* I wailed and showed her the scratches on my thighs. *Why would I leave my uncle bleeding on the floor?*

She ran for her handbag.

'God knows why,' she spat, fumbling for her car keys, 'but if anything happened, it would a been your fault. Must have led him on.' And what's more – she pointed a key at me as if taking aim with a dart – if I dared to tell that dirty little story – dirty little *lie* – to anybody, she would take Gid's side. So would *everybody*, she went on, for he was a loved and respected member of the community from a long-standing family and I was filth. She yanked open the door.

'How can you say that to your own daughter?' I cried.

She paused on the step, then turned, very slowly, to look at me. 'Because you're not my daughter. You were a botched-up bastard, dumped by your slut of a mother, and we were good enough to take you in. Wish we'd never done it.'

Silence.

'You're lying.'

'I most certainly am not. Ask anyone old enough to remember. Your mother was a maid here at Rowancraig, Catholic scum from the gutter, she was. Got rid of you soon as she could and has never been heard of since.'

She stomped out to her car, me following.

'I don't believe you, I don't believe you.'

'Ask *anyone*.' She opened the door. 'You're the only fool who doesn't know.'

I grabbed her arm. 'Who . . . who was my father?'

'God only knows. She had her cock-and-bull story, right enough, but I'm damn sure she was making it up cause truth is she whored herself round this whole village and looks like you're doing just the same.'

I slapped her. She fell back against the car with a yelp, head jerking, handbag hitting the dirt. There was a horrible pause, then she snatched up the bag and clambered in.

Just before slamming the door, she turned to me, her cheek burning red. 'Away with you! You don't belong here, you little bitch, and you never bloody did!'

So I left.

As she roared off to Shepherd's Cottage, I ripped off my Highland Tea Room uniform and changed into some of Archie's old clothes. That was the last time I wore a dress. I walked in a daze to the main road and when a couple heading for Glasgow gave me a lift, I told them my name was Mo Smith.

Marking

Liana's letter lies on my lap. An invasion from another life, as if someone has cut the partition to a parallel universe and the stuffing has burst through. I turn the ram's horn letter opener in my hand: smooth, grey, sharp as a knife. It once belonged to Mo. Spearing the tuft of fleece on it, I hold it up to the light.

I am fifteen and full of rage. We are in the barn, damp and cold, even though it is late May. Colvin stands on one side of a high bench, in a narrow pen packed with lambs. At twenty-five, he is a giant with hands and feet like shovels, a missing tooth and a bent nose from a shinty blow. But he doesn't have time for shinty any more. I'm the only one who plays now, mainly so I can hit something really hard and feel a savage joy.

Dad and I stand on the other side of the bench with our tools. His eye is glazed, hands shaky. Colvin lifts a tup lamb, holds its back against his chest and grabs its legs so it can't kick and its balls are laid bare. It's the first big day out for these suckers, who just yesterday were still skipping the fields like the world was a happy place. How wrong can you be. Dad pulls the furry black balls through the opening of a castrator and releases a tight band. Welcome to the world, wee lamb. You didn't make the grade for breeding so now you're a wedder and set for mopping up ticks on the grouse moor. Or for the butcher. Swapping to a lug marker, Dad cuts nips in the ears, two triangles on the right and a slit on the left: the mark of Rowancraig Farm since it all began. A thin spray of blood speckles our macs.

As he works, I use a knife to dock the tail, tossing the woolly end into a bucket. It's Mum's knife – Colvin carries it with him every day, just as he carries her memories. I have none. In the past ten years they have seeped away till I am left with fragments of stories and blurry photos and a hole inside that is sometimes flooded with longing, or frozen hard, or slowly distilling to a dark anger. More than the loss of Mum, it is the leaving of Mo. The sudden taking-off without warning that was brutal as an axe. I remember that time so clearly it still takes my breath away.

I'd got home from school with my sports day medals, all cross that she hadn't come to watch me run. There was no sign of her at home, just a neighbour cooking a meal. Dad was in hospital in Inverness, she said – kicked by the cow! – but he would mend and be home soon. Colvin was up there now with Auntie Beulah.

And Mo?

Neighbour hadn't seen her. Must be there too. She chattered and hummed as she fed me and tidied up, then finally put me to bed, as the others were still away.

Next morning, only Colvin was back. Said Dad had broken ribs and a punctured lung, but he'd get better.

Where's Mo?

He said she'd stood in for Auntie Beulah at Rowancraig. Big party of guests, fancy dinner and Mo joined the serving team so Auntie Beulah could be at the hospital. Back today.

But his face was full of clouds.

She didn't come back that day.

I heard Colvin on the phone to Auntie Beulah. Voice raised. Not like him.

Where's Mo?

He didn't want to talk. Just said Mo had gone to friends for a few days but back soon.

What friends?

Each night I touched her clothes, strewn across our room, and her books, her clock, the ram's horn letter opener. It was her most precious thing, made by her father, she'd told me. Why hadn't she taken anything?

Every day Auntie Beulah came to help in the house. She and Colvin were always stomping around, crashing things, arguing, but they always stopped when I walked in.

I asked again and again, *Where's Mo?*

Back soon, back soon.

Dad came home from hospital. Hobbled round the house in blankets, coughing, spitting yellow slimy stuff. Didn't know where Mo was either. *Don't ask me about her ever again – you hear me?*

Then one night Colvin came in, found me hunched in the corner of my bed holding her pyjamas. He stood there, big and gawky.

'Awright, Sox? Bedtime.'

'I want Mo.'

He sat on the end of the bed. 'She wrote to us. Today.'

'Where is she?' I leapt forward. 'She okay?'

He raked his thick fingers through his curls. 'Yeah . . . she's fine.'

'Is she? But where? Why? What happened?'

All he would answer, to all my questions, was he didn't know.

'She coming back?'

'I don't know, Sox.' His huge hands lay on his jeans. Like dead animals. 'I don't know.'

I started to cry and he pulled me into a hug and I clung to him, sobbing.

His voice in my hair whispering, 'She said . . . she loves you.'

But she never came back.

We go on with the castrating, lug-marking and docking of two hundred beasts. Blood drips where the tail is severed and sometimes the lamb craps or pees or both. By the end of the morning, we are stained with all of it, sticky with wool, smelling of blood and piss and straw. And Dad's breath.

I hate it. All of it.

Empty

When the house was completely barren, carpets pulled up and wallpaper stripped, we piled Gid's clothes on top of the hacked chair and set fire to it. At first, a stench rose from the flames as artificial fabrics curled into black blots and the varnish on the wood sizzled. But slowly, the fire burned them away and Colvin began throwing pine branches onto the blaze and the fragrance of sap and bark lifted to us.

And there it was at last: the laying down and the letting go.

We stood a long time in the cold January night, hugging ourselves and feeding the flames in a vigil of silence, till everything of Before was burned to ash and the only thing left was Now.

And then something rose out of the fire, a soundless voice that spoke my name. A call on my life.

I hid my face.

Shepherd's Cottage lay empty for three days and three nights and we left all the doors and windows open for the wind to blow through.

Then the workmen started and I went back to my job in Edinburgh. I phoned Colvin every night and returned on every day off to hover like a hawk as the place was renewed, from roof slates to floorboards. Every time there was a delay or the work was below par, I badgered Mackintosh till he got so sick of me he upped the builder's wages to get the thing finished quicker and better. It took six months, but finally everything was completed and I came back in the August to help Colvin move in. The place was pure as a convent: every wall white, floorboards polished, new carpets the colour of wheat. Colvin had sold all the old furniture and replaced it with second-hand things or stuff passed on from friends. A new start.

'I don't need much,' he said with a shrug, looking around the bare house. The one new thing was a big leather chair by the fire – a gift from me – and I had to teach him how to stretch out on it with back reclined and feet up. Seeing him marooned there made me laugh. 'You bloody deserve that,' I said. On my last day, we walked together up into the hills above the farm where the sheep were dotted across the slopes and the bracken a vivid green. Mistle thrushes foraged for rowan berries and the last of the golden plovers pierced the air with their high-pitched cries. The sky was a billowing sail above us, the vast moor flooded with light. On the way back we stopped at the Green Bothy.

We'd often played in it as kids, though there was still glass in the windows then and doors that closed. Later, it had become a teenage hangout with fags and booze round the fire and a few of our friends creeping off into the undergrowth (neither of us, mind: lack of interest on my part and lack of confidence on his). But after Agnes died all that had stopped. Colvin and I had stopped drinking, for a start. Our friends soon found other hideouts for their clumsy forays into adult vices, while the two of us were too worn down by grief and work to join in. But we kept going to the Green Bothy. On our own, or just the two of us, or most often taking Sorley so he could play with all the noise and joy of a kid and not be shouted at. It was our refuge.

Now it was a hive of life. Once the makeshift home for wartime foresters, the forest had taken it back, colonising its single wood-panelled room in quiet victory. Ivy grew up one wall and over part of the roof; an oak thrust its branches through a window; a silver birch rose through the floor. Birds had nested in the chimney and mice burrowed in nooks behind the splintered panels; a red squirrel scampered along a beam as spiders hung in their veils. We stepped inside and fell silent.

Walking home, I gathered pine branches and wildflowers, feathers and river stones, and brought them back to the house, putting them on window sills and in bottles, as Agnes had done. I'd hoped I would leave Colvin free, but he was far from it. Though released from Gid, he had inherited the tenancy of a struggling sheep farm and years of debt. And he was alone. Neither of us had heard from Sorley. I could not bear to admit how deeply that hurt or how much I suffered at leaving Colvin. I'd offered to stay, to get a job in the area and live at Shepherd's Cottage, helping out with house and farm, but he had refused. He repeated what he'd told me years before: 'Go to university. This is your time.' He cannot have heard the call from the fire and yet somehow he knew.

On my last night, I put a Bible on the living-room bookshelf and spoke an old blessing that Agnes had taught.

> *God, protect the house, and the household,*
> *God, consecrate the children of the motherhood,*
> *God, encompass the flocks and the young;*
> *Be Thou after them and tending them,*
> *What time the flocks ascend hill and wold,*
> *What time we lie down to sleep;*
> *What time the flocks ascend hill and wold,*
> *What time we lie down in peace to sleep.*

BOOK II

Neverland

It is late 1989 and I arrive at the Devlins' Sydney Harbour mansion just as the evening sun turns its western windows to gold. The street is already full of extravagant cars: Porsches, MGs, Alfa Romeos, even a little black Lamborghini that I stop beside. It's sleek as a panther and I reach out to stroke it, stopping myself just in time as I realise it will have an alarm. My car is an old Ford Fiesta, parked a full block away.

Tonight is important. Tonight I move from being just Carrick Devlin's personal trainer to his friend. I've spent precious cash on new clothes and the most expensive bottle of wine I've ever bought. Been to the barber this afternoon for a cut and shave and I know my breath is fresh and my body giving off a seductive scent. I researched this fragrance at the men's grooming counter in David Jones where I reduced the middle-aged assistant to schoolgirl giggles as I insisted she sniff behind my ears or at my throat with each new trial.

I trip lightly down the steps towards the house. It is white, modern, split across three levels on the hillside and flanked with glass. I catch glimpses of elegant people milling through open-plan spaces; there are trays of champagne, art and antiques. Everything glitters and I am drawn like a moth.

Carrick's wife welcomes me with kisses on both cheeks, coos over the wine, and propels me into the room. She is forty-something, perfectly made-up and well served by her aerobics instructor and her plastic surgeon. There are more greetings and kisses with equally sculpted women, pert breasts and buttocks pushing against little cocktail dresses, eyes shooting harpoons at me. I play them all to perfection – a soft hand on an arm here, a subtle leaning in to hear that remark – and they open to me like tropical blooms.

But the men are just as essential to this game, so I manoeuvre my way amongst them with equivalent charm, talking property prices and politics, cars and cricket.

'Hey, everyone, meet Sorley,' Carrick says, leading me out to a group of overweight men on the sun deck. 'This kid is what you lot need. The best personal trainer in Sydney – Australia, probably.'

'Yeah, cause that's what it takes to work on you, mate!' one of them says and the others laugh.

'Dead right,' says Carrick and puts down his beer. 'Look at this.' He lifts his arms, does a slow twirl and pulls his stomach in and out three times. There are cheers and whistles and cries of *Encore! Encore!* and *Now do that with your bum!*

'Lost twenty kilos, guys, and ran my first half-mara last week.' He smacks his stomach. 'Going for the full caboodle in July.'

More whistles and back slapping.

'What's your secret, Sorley?' someone says.

'Oh, just a bit of good old Presbyterian finger wagging and chasing after him like a sheepdog.'

'Shouldn't be hard to catch *him*,' a voice pipes up and there are more guffaws.

'Yeah, but you've got your work cut out trying to make a Presbyterian out of this lapsed Catholic bastard.'

'Lapsed?' Carrick says. 'Liberated, more like it! Live for now, not the Neverland!' And he raises his glass.

More cheers and clanking of glasses and cries of *For now! For now!* And *Fuck the Neverland!*

'So, you're a Scot,' a bald man says to me. 'Where from?'

'Grew up on a sheep farm in the Highlands, south of Inverness.'

'Oh, right. My mother's family comes from Scotland.' The man swigs his beer and narrows his gaze into the middle distance as he tries to remember. 'Little town called Struay, I think. Know any Peggs from Struay?'

Never heard of Struay nor do I know any Peggs, but I make a good show of interest in the man's fragments of Scottish knowledge. Some uncle had played the bagpipes and there are distant cousins somewhere.

I've not been back in over three years, not even for Dad's funeral. I was in Northern Territory at the time, working in a Darwin nightclub and partying hard when I got the message from Colvin. It made me hit the road again, just me and a backpack hitchhiking down through endless miles of scrub, walking myself to a skeleton, riding with strangers, sunburned and fly-bitten. At night I collapsed under the vast sky and stared at the stars and remembered everything I'd wished to forget. It was months later in Adelaide that an envelope found me, with a copy of the funeral service and a letter from Mo. Where to begin? What to say? I had no answers. Time passed and it was all too late.

I try not to look back any more.

As I banter with the men, my eyes rove across the sweep of terraced gardens to the swimming pool and the spread of Sydney Harbour beyond. It is dusk now and all the lights of the city are winking on, the windows of skyscrapers flashing in the last rays of the sun. The floodlit bridge is a gleaming span and the opera house shines pearly white, echoed in the tiny sails dotted across the water. In the garden below, people lounge on deck chairs, sip champagne, laugh.

I promise myself that one day, all this will be mine.

Sign 5: Fountain Pen

Two months after Colvin disappeared, a Czech woman found his notebook and fountain pen lying in a fishing hut on the River Spey, a few miles north of Briachan. It was a clear July day, the sunlight sparkling on the water, sand martins flitting in and out of the banks. She had turned up that morning to clean the place before the next set of paying guests, and saw his things on the table, his name written in childlike block capitals on the front of the small scuffed book. Inside were his scribbled notes from the daily rounds of the farm: numbers of lambs marked, address of a feed supplier, price of a champion tup. The fountain pen had been dismantled and lay tucked inside the notebook in pieces. Silver and expensive, it was in fact not Colvin's pen, but – as the lettering on the side so clearly spelled out – the property of Rowancraig Estate.

Hogmanay

Colvin stepped out alone into the cold morning. It was New Year's Eve, the last day of 1990, and though he was only thirty-five, he felt old. It was still dark and the stars were blacked out by cloud, the air so icy it cut. His breath misted around him as he walked to the byre to get the dogs. Today he must bring the tups in from their six weeks of serving the ewes and he prayed for no rain. As soon as his footsteps sounded on the cobbles, the dogs started barking, and when he snapped on the bulb, they leapt in their cages.

'Hush! Down!' he growled at them, and they dropped to their stomachs, eyes fixed on him. His favourite, Rum, was nearly ten now and closer to Colvin than his shadow, reading him like a book and hearing his whistle from miles away.

With his binoculars in the pocket of his jacket, he walked out to the fields. The sky was shifting slowly from a heavy charcoal to grey, and a mean breeze haggered around his ears and shook the naked branches of the trees. He rarely wore gloves, the skin on his hands so toughened that he could bear both freezing winter and scalding water without flinching. Years ago he'd lost half the ring finger on his right hand in a clipping accident and it was the missing bit that seemed most sensitive, prickling with cold and itching with heat aches. He often scratched the stump and even bit it in frustration, but still the pain of what was absent nagged him.

The sheep were in the in-bye fields today, and rounding them up would be easier than when he'd brought them down from the hills in November. Even that task was easier than it once was, now that their territory was bounded by deer fences and forestry plantations. In his grandfather Donald's time they roamed far off into the moors and some got lost in distant corries and glens. But so much of that land was gone now as Lord Mackintosh had sold off more and more chunks of his estate. Then he'd sacked the detested Gregor Pickett and handed over the direction of Rowancraig to Reginald Spinks, a land agent from the London property firm, Grevilles. Mr Spinks visited the barbaric north only to shoot things and conducted most of his transactions from the comfort of his Mayfair office.

Colvin had never met the man, but had received numerous letters on his crisp stationery that nearly always arrived with a sheaf of legal documents. They joined the plague of paperwork already piled up on his desk: records of Veterinary Medical Treatments, grim statements from the bank, inspection reports from *Scotch Assured Cattle & Sheep* and so on and so on. Reports, Regulations, Requirements, Records. He was cursed by all of it. Couldn't get his head round it or a handle on it, so mostly ignored it. He tried to pick up what he could from the shepherds round about and relied a lot on Fachie. Now Mackintosh's head gamekeeper, his old friend kept his finger on the pulse and regularly briefed Colvin.

Together they'd examined a particular piece of paperwork from Spinks this year: a proposal for Colvin to relinquish his tenancy of Rowancraig Farm in exchange for a Limited Partnership Agreement. The wily Mr Spinks knew Colvin's secure, heritable tenancy might give him the right to buy his land one day, whether Mackintosh wanted to sell or not. The idea that he might ever have the money was laughable to Colvin, but clearly Mackintosh was taking no chances. If he was forced to lose any more land he wouldn't have enough moor left for the field sports that were, apparently, the whole point of a Highland estate. Fachie had spelled out the losses and risks of giving up the tenancy, advising against it, but Colvin had lain awake night after night counting his debts, so when Spinks had offered financial incentives to take on the Partnership, he felt there was no choice.

But now, as he looked across the land through his binoculars, there was an ache in his ribs. Though the Munros had never officially owned the land, there was always a sense that it belonged to them, or, at the very least, they belonged to it. He was still there, but his hold was slipping. And what of the tenant farmers that had fought for the rights of all? For secure tenancies and protecting the bond? This felt like moving things backwards, like betrayal. But what else could he do? He worked harder each day and went to bed poorer each night. Sometimes he wondered why he carried on but the answer was always the same. *Where would I go? I'm a shepherd. As hefted to this hill as my sheep.*

Sending his dogs out to skirt the first field, Colvin sensed a shifting in the air and a drop in temperature. The rain of the past few days had stripped most of the snow and left white rags on the hillsides and in the hollows. The ground was sludge-brown, the undergrowth anaemic, the trees standing around empty-handed. The snow queen had once again turned into an ugly hag.

As the dogs gathered in the tups, the first drops of rain blew in on the wind. Just a sprinkling at first, but coming sideways and fast and soon laced with ice. Colvin pulled up the hood of his jacket and shouted at the dogs to work faster, but the tups were stubborn. By the time they were all heading back to the field behind the barn, the rain was driving, getting right into his neck and pelting his bare hands and cheeks. The long coats of the collies were plastered against their bones, their faces grim as the sky.

As for the tups, six weeks of chasing ewes through sleet and gales had worn them out. With fleeces ragged and balled with snow and their flanks skeletal, they were a miserable lot.

'Don't worry, lads,' Colvin murmured, 'you'll get a rest and some good feed now. Done well.'

By the time he'd fed tups and dogs and stumbled back into the kitchen, it was dark and he was cold and starving. At times like this he wished he'd thought ahead and put a casserole in the oven, or even got a pie in from the butcher. He rooted around in the fridge, pushing past old packets of cheese and curling ham, hoping for some sausages or even eggs. Nothing. Auntie Beulah brought the occasional ice-cream tub of soup, but it was always over-boiled and consisted more of cabbage and grease than anything else. It was that same smell that clung to her, that steamy, soggy odour that had seeped into her clothes and furnishings, and even rose from her skin. On this night, though, Colvin would have welcomed even Beulah's soup.

He had an invite down to Fachie and Glenda's for a Hogmanay dinner, but he knew they would drag him on to the ceilidh in the Briachan hall and he just couldn't bear it. Quite apart from being knackered, he hated these events, with everyone whirling around in manic displays of happiness when half of them were miserable and sick as rabbits. He wasn't one for gossip but he knew what went on. And he never knew what to do with himself at ceilidhs, as he was a clumsy dancer and didn't drink. While all his friends knocked back pints and drams, he felt a fool with his Irn-Bru and always had to leave before they got drunk. The sight of them sliding into buffoonery and ugliness twisted him up inside. So, after a shower and a tea of baked beans on toast (again), he settled on the leather chair by the fire and watched telly.

He was woken by the sound of banging on the back door and shouting. The clock on the mantel said nearly 1 a.m. Rubbing his foggy head, he shuffled to the kitchen in his socks. By now he could tell it was Fachie out in the sun-room entrance, full of cheer and drink. First-footing, damn him. Colvin hesitated. Should he pretend he was asleep?

'C'mon, pal!' Fachie bellowed. 'Got a surprise for you!'

Colvin's heart sank.

Then there was another voice. Soft, high and swift. He couldn't make out the words, but it was clearly a woman. He felt panic.

'Oh, aye, he'll be asleep,' Fachie was saying to her. 'But he won't mind. I'm his oldest pal. He'll be pleased to see me. COLVIN!' He hammered on the door and the woman laughed – a birdlike sound.

Colvin yanked open the door and the pair jumped. He snapped on the light and saw Fachie in a kilt and down jacket with a small figure at his side, in a black shawl. Fachie squinted in the brightness while the woman laughed again and held out an impossibly small hand. Colvin stared. Little more than a girl, she had black hair and eyes, a delicate face and perfect teeth. In fact, he had never seen anything so delicate and perfect in his entire life.

'Greetings from Bolivia,' she said, in a strange accent. 'I am Liana Perez Fervola and I am looking for work.'

Stray

I did not trust her. I thought she was trying to use Colvin for something. But what? She found out pretty quickly the farm was struggling and he owned little more than some beat-up tractors and the family debts. Colvin promised her nothing but relentless hard work and penury and she accepted it. Embraced it even. Finally, when I saw her beside him on a sleet-driven day, kneeling in the mud with her thin arm inside a ewe, I had to accept that she must love him.

And I felt ashamed. How could I, who claimed to love Colvin more than breath, doubt that someone else might be capable of it? But he was ugly and poor and twice her age, while she was astonishingly beautiful with her whole life ahead of her. Why Colvin? Why Briachan? Why a blighted sheep farm in Scotland? It was a long time before I learned what Liana had endured in her short life to make this marriage in this place a kind of paradise.

The summons to me from Gid's bonfire was to the ministry. I had resisted at first. Who am I to preach or pastor? What do I know? But the call never left me, the Presence. Not so much a booming great voice or a pillar of fire, but more like a stray bird that turned up and wouldn't leave. A wing-ragged scrap that was always in my garden or pecking at my window. Finally I gave up. *What? Whaddaya want?* So I listened and followed its sweet song to a Divinity degree and the Church of Scotland. There wasn't a lot of choice back then for women and I felt a kind of loyalty to the kirk Agnes had embraced.

I had an urban job in South Lanarkshire first, visiting Colvin regularly and observing, without comment, how Liana colonised the house. She was never offered 'my' room (which had also been Agnes and Sorley's), but it wasn't long before she moved from the camp bed in the spare room to share the double in Colvin's. My discomfort at that migration was tempered by secret happiness, that at last he was held at night and knew passion and joy. More obvious signs of her dominion were the jugs of flowers and the colourful fabrics she picked up second-hand and turned into cushions and throws, not to mention the changing fortunes of the walls. The kitchen was painted turquoise, the living room a chilli red, their bedroom in swathes of hyacinth and pink. Everywhere she added patterns: vines, flowers, birds and fish. She dressed like a gypsy, wore dramatic make-up, sang loudly and cooked dishes with wild names and even wilder flavours. Colvin seemed a bit lost in it all, but disarmed with wonder. Nothing like Liana had ever happened to him before, or indeed to the whole strath.

It made me tetchy. This was my Shepherd's Cottage and my Colvin and she was turning the place into some kind of Carnival and him into a fool. But dammit if she didn't win me, too. She called me *Momo* or *Mamo* or *Mamá*, showed off her creations like a child, asked my advice on everything, giggled a lot and hugged me. Most of all, she adored Colvin. What more could I want? By the time they asked me to conduct their wedding in the summer of 1991 – a mere five months after her arrival – I was truly happy.

And then terrified. Because Sorley was coming back from Australia. We hadn't met since the day I fled Briachan nearly twenty years before, and I'd received no reply to my letters.

On the night before the wedding, Colvin met him at the station and brought him straight to the lochside for the rehearsal. Liana had insisted on a ceremony outdoors because she never set foot in a church, but that May evening it was raining and we were all shrouded in waterproofs and umbrellas. As I watched the brothers approach, I thought the dog-mad lolloping of my heart would split my ribs. Sorley was twenty-five now, but recognisable by his clean, loping gait and the lift of his head. Colvin introduced him to Liana first, then brought him to me. He was insanely handsome, like an advertisement for beach holidays or aftershave, but when his blue gaze fell on me, it hardened. He extended a hand, brisk and unyielding, and with a curt nod said, 'Mo. Long time.'

'Yes,' I squeaked. 'Too long.'

He looked away and said nothing more to me for the rest of the wedding. Every time I hovered near, he moved away. Though he was full of charm with everyone else – and how they loved to have young Sorley home! – he was closed to me. By the end of the reception my face was a ghastly mask, my chest burning. I barely slept those two nights in my bed at the Ferryman (having given Sorley 'my' room at Shepherd's Cottage, which was, of course, 'his' room and, once upon a time, 'our' room). I prayed desperately for a reconciliation.

The day after the wedding I arrived at Shepherd's Cottage for the family lunch we had planned: a short time for the four of us together before Sorley went home and Colvin and Liana left for their honeymoon. Walking into the kitchen, I was glad of the flowers and gifts in my arms that hid my shaking. Colvin took them and Liana embraced me, so lovely in a green velvet dress with her hair swept up. I looked around, trying to find a place for my hands.

Then I saw the table. Set for three.

'Sorley?'

Colvin looked at me sharply.

'He not tell you?' Liana cried. 'He have to catch early train.' She threw up her hands. 'Gone already!'

Onwards and Upwards

Carrick Devlin collapses into my arms and bursts into tears. All 100kg of him thrown against me, hot and soaked with sweat. It's the end of his first marathon and I have run beside him every agonising minute of the six hours. The park in Sydney is teeming with people in shorts and singlets, hobbling, hugging and wiping tears. In the gum trees above us, the birds are cackling.

'I did it!' Carrick wails, his slimy face in my neck. 'I fucking did it!'

'Aye, you did, pal, you did.' I am staggering under his weight and try to keep him walking, but he slides to the ground and kneels with his face in the grass, arms outstretched. His whole body is heaving.

'Blessed Mother of God, thank you! I'm still alive!'

It's several minutes before I can persuade him to keep moving. As I take him through the stretches we have done together a hundred times, he can't stop the laughter or the tears streaming down his cheeks.

'No, it's you that did this, you beautiful sonofabitch!' he says, leaning on my shoulder as he wobbles on one leg, stretching the other thigh. 'Used to lose my breath just getting out of bed, but now—' He shakes his head.

'You put in the effort, Carrick, you put in the miles.'

'Aww, but I've been trying gyms and shit for years and nothing's worked till you, mate. You've got fire, Sorley, you don't give up.'

'Onwards and upwards – that's my mantra. Faster, higher, better.'

'If only everybody in my office took that view. Bloody waste of space, most of 'em. No drive, no work ethic.'

'Maybe life has been too easy.'

'Got it in one, kid. Everything handed to 'em on a plate – never had to struggle, never had to escape anything. You and me, though – we know what poverty is.'

Carrick had started out as the ninth child of thirteen in an overflowing Irish immigrant family with a father who did railway work and a mother who nearly starved herself to feed the kids. He'd taken an interest in my story and quizzed me a lot about my maths skills and economics degree.

'Listen, Sorley – got an idea.' Carrick has built his empire on keen intuition and relentless work. 'I reckon you've got everything it takes to be an investment banker. I'm always looking for a bright new kid to train up. Wanna give it a go?'

I'd been wanting nothing more for a long time. Prepared the ground and planted the seeds, watered and waited.

'Hey, yeah! I've been thinking about that. No better person to learn from.'

'Good. Then give notice to all your desperate housewives and fat bastards like me and let me know soon as you can start.'

'Be ready for that in about a fortnight, I'd say. Thank you, Carrick!'

'Course, you gotta keep on as *my* personal trainer. Not letting you off that easy!'

'Didn't think so.'

I wonder how long I can keep on as his wife's lover, too.

Minister

When Tess was born and Colvin laid her in my arms, it was like holding the baby Sorley again. The same shock of dark hair, the dimples, the face of infinite wisdom, and I felt an avalanche inside me. Meanwhile, Liana never left her newborn for a second, strapping Tess between her breasts, talking and singing to her, sleeping with her, and feeding her so often the poor thing was forever writhing with wind or puking. Liana herself got thin and ragged and slightly unhinged, while Colvin was worried but helpless. I visited as often as possible and tried to bring Liana down off the ceiling, while she, mercifully (and somewhat miraculously), trusted me with Tess. But three years later when Alex arrived, colic-ridden and defying sleep, I sensed Armageddon. In another miracle, the church in Briachan became vacant, I got the job and moved – all before Alex was six months old. It happened so fast and I was so focused on holding that beloved family together that I didn't have much time to think about other things. Like Beulah.

Let me tell you, if I wasn't a Christian I would have cheerfully turned my back and never spoken to her again. Or murdered her. There's plenty of precedent for that sort of thing round here. (The back turning, I mean, not the murder, though I was willing to kick things off.) Her horns were invisible but I was quite sure they had several cuts up both sides. Very Difficult Mother who should have been sold for mutton long ago. But, for my sins, I had to put my money where my big wonky mouth was and love my enemies. Walk the talk, as they say. Live the sermon. It was trials like these that made me regret being a minister in my home village, but in exchange for Colvin and his precious, crazy family; for my little flock; for a landscape of soul-rending beauty – I got Beulah. The cross I had to bear.

Little and often was the only way to survive her, so I would whiz up to Keeper's Cottage once a week on my bike.

'Why didn't you tell me you were coming?!' she'd address me like a rat advancing across the linoleum.

Because whenever I did give warning, she would bake rock-hard scones and get out the wedding china and make us sit on the lumpy chairs in the 'sitting room' with the gas fire ticking to life and smelling of burnt dust. Then she would talk about Rowancraig and how lavish her retirement party had been and how sad it was that Lord Mackintosh had given up a permanent staff and resorted to hiring in for his visits (too few and far between, in Beulah's opinion) and how she popped up to the house most days just to 'keep an eye'. She never once asked anything about me, though did not spare her opinions about the Briachan church, which was, apparently, going to hell in a handcart.

'It used to be so good. And packed, absolutely packed.' *How would she know? She never went.* 'Lots of folk have stopped going since you arrived,' pursing her lips with satisfaction. *Which folk?* 'Lots of the old-timers saying what a shame it is.' *What exactly?*

After sitting through that agony a few times I made it a policy always to turn up unannounced, to decline a chair and lean against the kitchen bench, swinging my helmet in my hand, ready to bolt. I rarely lasted more than ten minutes and straight afterwards had to retreat to the Ferryman for emergency resuscitation.

Old Tavish was always behind the bar. He looked like a beagle with his sad brown eyes and drooping jowls, greasy hair hanging like ears past his chin. I swear I'd never seen him smile. The place had been on the market for years, but he couldn't get a buyer; it was rot-ridden and his first asking price was too high. But even though he dropped it every six months there was very little interest and anyone who dared view the place was treated to dire warnings.

'Can't run a successful pub hotel these days,' he would tell them, and pick at something in his teeth, long and yellow like old piano keys. 'Not up here where we don't get tourists for several months of the year and the weather's terrible and the locals are tight-fisted. Even the summer's plagued by insects – midges, ticks and our very own Briachan birch fly. Not to mention all the regulations and that.' Then he would lean close, as if divulging a particularly nasty conspiracy. '*Health and safety.*'

His cockney wife Pat got fed up waiting and took off to the Costa del Sol with an old flame. Tavish's gloom sunk deeper and the Ferryman's fate with it.

'You know I'd buy the place in a flash,' I told him once, sipping my fizzy orange. 'Only problem is I haven't got a penny.' I lived in the manse and what savings I could scrape together I gave away. *Store up treasures in heaven*. Hey ho. I should have just joined the Poor Clares and been done with it. Poverty and chastity came naturally: obedience was a different matter. But it's the Church of Scotland that took me in when few other denominations would have women – and mouthy ones at that – so that's where I stayed. Till then, anyway. New millennium had come and I had an itching to leave. Not that I'd lost my faith or wanted to leave Briachan. More that I had a growing sense that I belonged with the sheep outside the fold. And Briachan, you see, had left the church.

And it wasn't my fault, despite what Beulah would have you believe. The village was long gone before I came. When I got here in '95 there were about six old ladies and a crusty gent who were regulars. I was charged with building it up again but felt like some hapless creature shut in a locked tower and told to spin gold from straw. And there were no Rumplestiltskins or Prince Charmings bursting in to save the day, either. The old folks dearly wanted more people. But no change. So I just kept their antiquated 11 a.m. service going with Mrs MacClatchy plunking on the organ and Miss Dysett making her intrepid journey from the back of the church to read the Intimations and Mrs Gregson rustling sweetie papers and Mr MacDonald sitting poker-straight and fast asleep. I kept them there, quietly pickling in last century's vinegar, and turned my energies elsewhere.

New wine, new wine skins. I prayed hard and started an evening service instead, in the village hall. I persuaded a local musician to play guitar, found a Quaker and some former Baptists and a family of charismatics who somehow got along together. Friday nights I ran a youth club called Fireworks that played Demon Volleyball, and Sunday mornings hosted Breakfast Beat and served pancakes. People started rocking up, and because I was rubbish at lots of things, they had to help and it grew. We did Alpha courses and Christianity Explored and Christianity Explained (I'm onto Christianity Exploded now, according to the Presbytery) and The Most High came down and stuff happened. Even some of the old folk from the 11 a.m. service said they preferred the evening gig and, hey, who knew Mrs Gregson could flip pancakes or that Mr MacDonald had played volleyball for Scotland? Or that Miss Dysett would get down on her arthritic knees every night to pray for the young people?

Colvin's Tess adored Breakfast Beat and Fireworks and worked her way round all the jobs in the church from passing the offering bags to playing her fiddle. Alex came now and then, but he was usually a dark little thundercloud in the corner. *I don't like PEOPLE*, he clarified, several times. Liana flatly refused to come to anything. *I don't like God, Mamo. No – I HATE God*, she told me, *because he hates me*. It was a very long time before she told me why. Colvin never came to anything churchy and his excuse was always the sheep.

So we had our Briachan mini-revival and I got pats on the back from Church HQ and cheers from some local ministers (jealous, suspicious comments from others) and we kept growing. For about five years. And then it slowed down. And then it stopped. We'd been level for a couple of years, a few folk coming, a few folk leaving, but nothing else changing. (I was beginning to get a whiff of vinegar.) And what I noticed is that most of the people out there who are hungry and thirsty for life do not look for it in a church. They believe this well dried up long ago. Or claim it never was a well, just a deep, empty pit that needy people fall into and can't escape.

But who needs a well when you have a loch and a river and clear springs rising from the mountains? The water of life is not hidden down a dark hole but running free and wild and open in the land. The Kingdom of Heaven is among you.

Night of the Long Knives

It was 2 February 2003 and a snow storm swept across from the west. Colvin and Liana were out in it all day and half the night checking the pregnant ewes, bringing them into the stalls on the hill and some into the barn. The snow blew in whirlwinds like a plague of white moths stinging their faces, and nothing could be seen beyond outstretched hands, the dogs' barking torn away on the wind. The children – eleven and eight – were out helping till the afternoon when Liana took them back home, Tess to heat soup and Alex to light the fire.

All of that day was a white blindness that turned to black at three. Colvin and Liana were ghosts, stumbling with head torches, as they accounted for every beast and battened down the hatches of barn, byre and shed. At last they crashed into the house after nine, streaming water onto the kitchen floor and pressing themselves against the warm oven, devouring food like wolves. Tess had laid the table and was pouring out bowls of thick Scotch broth with the efficiency of a dinner lady while Alex had disappeared to his favourite place behind the sofa with his bird books, the fire long gone out, his fingers white as wax.

Once everyone was fed, Liana ran a deep bath, dipped the kids through it, then left Colvin wallowing in the milky warmth as she tucked Tess and Alex in bed. Back in the bathroom, she found him asleep. His shaggy head lolled to one side, brown hair spiked with grey, skin mottled with moles and broken veins. Yet he looked like a child, the way his lashes rested on his cheeks and his mouth was parted, the rise and fall of his breath so gentle. She watched the soap bubbles popping in the hairs on his chest as she peeled off her damp clothes and dumped them on the floor. Then, taking his head in her hands she kissed him – on his forehead, on the tip of his nose, on his lips – and climbed into the bath on top of him.

When they finally fell into bed, they were dreamy, aching to the bone, skin humming. Colvin felt Liana curl into him, nudging her head under his chin, her hands into his armpits and feet between his thighs. These parts of her were usually iced fish in his tenderest hollows, but on this night, every tip and touch of her was warm as they folded together and floated to sleep.

Outside the storm blew wild.

At a quarter to midnight there was a honking horn and then a banging on the door. It jolted them awake and they yanked on dressing gowns and stumbled downstairs, barefoot and bleary. Colvin pulled open the door to find his friend.

'Fachie! What brings ye? There's trouble?'

'One way of puttin it.' Fachie stomped his feet on the mat. 'Come in?' He held a briefcase. It was a strange sight, as they'd never seen him – nor any gamekeeper – carrying a briefcase.

'Aye, c'mon in pal.' Colvin stepped back and took Fachie's coat, snow-blown and damp despite the short walk from his vehicle. 'Must be serious if you're out in this.'

Liana put the kettle on and took out a tin of fruit cake. Fachie didn't sit down, but opened the case, took out typed papers and spread them on the table. There was the slightest tremor in his hands and he gripped them behind his back. Colvin looked from Fachie to the papers and back again. Liana put mugs of tea on the table.

'Sit, Fachie, *mi hermano*,' she said, patting his shoulder. 'Sit down.'

He sat and put three spoonfuls of sugar in his tea and stirred hard, making it slosh over the sides.

Colvin did the same, but slowly, not taking his eyes off his friend.

At last Fachie put down his spoon and spread his hands on the papers. They were working hands, ridged and pockled with red-blonde hairs standing out on their backs. There was a pale circle on one finger: the wedding ring gone, Glenda gone. She had moved in with an environmentalist from Edinburgh, into his new eco-house in the village, and the kids moved back and forth, baffled and sullen.

'Mackintosh sent me,' Fachie said. 'These papers . . .' He ran his hand over his mouth. 'This is notice to quit, Colvin. Termination of partnership.'

Silence. They stared at Fachie. Colvin's face went grey. His lips were cracked and there was spit pooled in the corners of his half-open mouth. At last his brows bunched together and his head shook slightly. As if he'd forgotten something, Fachie suddenly rummaged in the briefcase and pulled out a pen. It was a silver fountain pen, smooth and spotless as the polished briefcase and the starched white papers. Fachie uncapped the pen and held it out.

Colvin didn't take it. 'Fachie? Is this 'cause of the new bill?'

'Aye.' The pen was still there, sticking into the air between them. 'Mackintosh's land agent told him to end all leases that he could. In case tenants get absolute right to buy.'

'Now?' There was an edge in Colvin's voice. 'At quarter to midnight on a night like this? You get me out my bed to tell me to get off my land?'

'Don't shoot the messenger, Colvin. Mackintosh got *me* out of *my* bed! I've bloody risked my life driving up here in this blizzard. Says it has to be done before midnight, like, before the new bill becomes law. Nothing to do with me.'

Colvin glowered at him. 'Except you've still got a job, long as you keep doing his dirty work.'

'Steady!'

Colvin stood up, knocking his chair over backwards. 'Since when is this gamekeeper's work?' He jabbed a finger on the papers. 'Stalking tenants? Shooting them with fountain pens?'

'He's my boss, Colvin.'

'It's not an army, Fachie.'

'Still my boss.'

'He doesn't own you. He's no right getting you out your bed at this hour, no right risking your safety or making you stab your oldest friend in the back. You're not a slave, Fachie – stop bloody acting like one!'

Then Colvin scooped up the papers, tore them in half and walked out.

Fachie and Liana sat in silence. Outside, the blizzard howled, rattling the roof and clattering the doors. At last she got up, put the lid on the cake tin and poured the untouched tea down the sink. Then she leaned against the kitchen bench, arms folded across her old dressing gown and stared at her feet. They felt like blocks of ice on the bare floor.

Fachie capped the pen. His hands trembled as he gathered up the torn papers and put them back in the briefcase, clipped it shut and stood up.

'You cannot go home in this, Fachie,' Liana said. He didn't reply. 'Use the spare bed. Wait till morning.'

'Can't stay.'

'You have to. No point killing yourself for Mackintosh, *hermano*. Do as I say.'

But he shook his head and left. She heard the front door close and a few moments later the grumble and wheeze of his vehicle as it crawled down the drive. The pen was still lying on the table.

They found him the next morning, half way down the track, snowed in and near frozen to death. Bundled him back to Shepherd's Cottage and kept him wrapped up by the fire till he thawed out. For that day and night he was holed up in the spare room as the blizzard raged on and the snow locked them in. He and Colvin did not look at each other.

Mackintosh never phoned to find out if Fachie was all right. But Reginald Spinks phoned promptly at nine on the 3rd of February to check that Colvin had received all the paperwork and understood it.

Yes, Colvin told him. He understood perfectly.

The Gift

The Lord works in mysterious ways. How did it come to pass that a teetotal celibate minister of religion ended up running the local den of iniquity?

'Maurabelle!' the Presbytery Clerk said, slapping his meat-steak hand on the table. How I hate that name. Only Beulah and people who don't know me or don't like me use it. 'Stop making excuses. Your deviations from church law are now legion. You have allowed – nay, *encouraged* – lay people without any training to lead worship and even to *preach* in Briachan church. Your kirk session includes people who are not even members of the Church of Scotland, let alone Elders! You allow lay people to administer the Lord's Supper in their own homes and even, last Sunday, *in the church*. You regularly fail to turn up at Presbytery meetings and when you do come you have never fulfilled any of the action points assigned to you. I have been keeping a record!'

'Thought you weren't supposed to keep a record of wrongs, Wilbur.'

'I am duty bound, by church law, to keep a record of proceedings in this Presbytery, Maurabelle, and it's just a terrible pity that you do not seem to be constrained by any similar sense of duty to your God-given calling.'

'On the contrary. I give my life daily to God's call, but He told me to act justly, love mercy and walk humbly with Him, to make disciples and baptise them, to care for the poor, the hungry, the sick and the imprisoned, to love Him above all else and my neighbour as myself. I don't recall the bits about ticking off action points on Presbytery Minutes. Is that in Romans?'

'Maurabelle, my friend,' Wilbur said with a deep sigh and a shake of his head, as if addressing a child.

'Mo. Mo! How many times?'

'Mo, then. Your inspirational little list is the call placed on *every* Christian. Do I need to remind you that by taking office as an ordained minister in the Church of Scotland you have committed yourself to certain duties that are *particular* to your post?'

'No, you don't need to remind me, Wilbur, my friend. It's just that I believe growing the church is more important than controlling it and getting everyone involved is more important than getting them branded on the butt with a Church of Scotland stamp.'

'Well, if that is your view of Church of Scotland law, I would encourage you to consider your place in it.'

'Believe me, I consider it every day.'

'Come now,' said the minister of a cluster of little churches further down the valley and a beacon of grace. 'Your concerns are noted, Wilbur, and I'm sure Mo will make every effort to keep within the guidelines now.'

'Are you?' I said. ''Cause I'm not. In fact I'm quite sure I'm not going to make any effort whatsoever.'

I stormed out of the meeting, slapped on my bike helmet and took off down the road. I might have been swearing. (Precious God, I know I shouldn't, but after my misspent youth, these things still escape.) That Presbytery meeting was the last straw, especially when my mind was preoccupied with Colvin, who responded to Mackintosh dissolving the partnership by lodging an appeal with the Land Court. This was going to be long, painful and expensive.

Back at the manse I kicked off my shoes, threw the folder of Presbytery paperwork into the recycling box and whacked on the kettle. On the kitchen table was a small stack of post. A Co-op flyer, *Life and Work* magazine and a stiff white envelope printed in the top left corner with the Dorset address of Messrs Hogget & Skully, Solicitors. Interesting. I poured my tea and started chomping an apple as I settled into a chair and opened the letter.

May 2003

Dear Ms Smith,

We are instructed by our client to inform you that they have recently purchased for you an establishment in the village of Briachan. They understand that you had expressed interest to the current proprietor in owning *The Ferryman Inn* and have accordingly instructed us to register the property in your sole name. They have also instructed us to pay you the sum of £100,000 in order to fund necessary renovations and a cheque in this sum is enclosed, drawn in your favour. A condition of these gifts is that the Inn may not be resold for five years or converted to any other purpose and the renovation fund may only be used for said purpose. Our client has also specifically requested that, as a condition of your receipt of these gifts, you do not attempt to discover their identity or make contact. Please acknowledge safe receipt of this letter and the enclosed cheque.

Yours sincerely,

Timothy Hogget
Hogget & Skully Solicitors

Water to Wine

There is a time to gather in and a time to go out. So I had no choice but to accept the gift and use it as intended, wondering often about my secret benefactor. It could be almost anyone. I had met so many people in my hotel work, some of them incredibly wealthy, all of them glad of a listening ear. Or it could have been one of the numerous visitors to our little white church above Loch Hope – beautiful and never locked – and folks often leave donations. American tourists are especially generous, as are the dying. I cannot thank my benefactor, so I thank the Lord and ask for His blessing on 'them', whoever 'they' are, and on all who come to the Ferryman.

For many come.

The keepers and stalkers with the far sweep of the hills in their eyes. An ageing hippie in her home-spun hemp. A big guy who stacks shelves by day and plays computer games by night. An Olympic skier, a fish farmer, a girl with Down's who dances to the jukebox, a statistician. They all come and rest against this bar, my confessional. Young and old, able and weary, strong and afraid. And I, who will not touch a drop, pour out beer and spirits, whisky and wine, and watch them drink.

Believe me, I am plagued by doubt.

Sign 6: Binoculars

Nearly four months after Colvin disappeared, a photographer found his binoculars, an old pair that Alex had cast off and Colvin used for spotting sheep. They were hanging on a low branch of a Scots pine in the woods at Glenmore, one of the few pockets of ancient Caledonian forest that survived the felling in the war years. Its trunk was massive as a tower, red and creviced, with branches that spread in a fragrant canopy above carpets of ling and blaeberry. The photographer had come to capture the elusive capercaillie in the soft light of that September dawn and had spotted the binoculars through the lens of his camera. They still bore Alex's name and address on a little tag.

Bird Boy

Colvin and Liana's boy never liked school. The wee primary in Briachan had a big overgrown garden and two kindly teachers, but he only consented to attend because Tess was there looking after him. She coaxed him through the day, whispering and nudging, talking for him, sitting by him at lunch and shielding him from the bullies. When Tess moved up to the high school we all worried. He didn't like it and didn't talk to the teachers and didn't hang out with the other kids, but he went most days and struggled through. Oh yes, he'd had all the health visitors and GPs and educational psychologists looking at him with puzzling eyes and scribbling pens. Dyslexia? No. Dyspraxia? No. Intelligence? High here, low there. Autistic spectrum? Maybe. Attention deficit? Yes. But hyperactivity? No. Definitely no hyperactivity. In fact, he was slower than most kids, often completely still. Usually because he was watching something. A trail of ants, a twitching cocoon, a spider dropping on a line of silk.

Or birds. He was always looking at birds. He gazed at them with hunger, as though they possessed what he was missing, as though he belonged with them, not us. Whenever he was allowed, he was off walking by himself with his binoculars and bird books; while at school he topped up the feeders every day and kept records in notebooks of his sightings. *Chaffinch, siskin, blue tit.* By the time he was twelve he could name all the birds he saw, whether on hill, in field or by water, and tell you if they were male or female, young or old, common or rare. *Crossbill, lapwing, goldeneye.*

In his final year of primary school his class followed Flora, a golden eagle. She had a tag, and they drew lines on a map of the Highlands wherever she went, wrote stories and poems about her, painted pictures and made a dance for the music festival. Alex, of course, would not dance and was a pest on the sidelines because he kept saying the other kids didn't look anything like a golden eagle. They were just stupid.

But then I would see him all alone on the sloping field behind Shepherd's Cottage, running with arms stretched out, soaring and dipping, wheeling and waiting. Once he stood so still – arms wide, head tilted – he looked like a crucifix. And then I saw his fierce eye raking the ground, a lift of the heels and he was down scooping a rabbit. A pretend rabbit. But he crowed for joy and took it back to his eyrie on a boulder, and squatted there, biting and tugging on it, sidestepping around, arranging twigs, feeding chicks. After a few minutes, he stepped again to the edge of the rock and cocked his head, looking to some far-off point before leaping with a cry, arms flung out, face wild.

Back at school he started every day at the computer, checking Flora's flight path and recording all the details in his jotter. One Monday morning he yelped and ran for the teacher, who was sitting with a reading group.

'Come, Miss. Come! You have to see.' His face was chalky. Alex rarely spoke to her unless in reluctant answer to a question and he certainly never touched her, but on this morning he was yanking on her sleeve. She went with him.

'Look!' He pointed at the screen. She ran her eyes over it, flustered. 'What's happened?'

'She hasn't moved, Miss! Not since yesterday morning!'

He insisted she immediately phone the countryside ranger who was leading their eagle project, and could not settle while they waited for his response, constantly rechecking the computer and pacing around the classroom. At last the message came, in the afternoon. Flora had been found dead. Poisoned. On Logie Estate to the south. When the teacher told the children, there was a collective cry of shock. Some of them burst into tears, one kicked a desk. Alex lurched from his seat and ran outside to the trees at the end of the playground. When the teacher found him, he was hunched with his head between his knees, fists over his ears, keening.

Meeting

Our dear Lord Mackintosh finally lost enough of his ill-gotten gains that he had to put Rowancraig Estate up for sale. It was January 2009 and I had come to know him quite well over the years in my self-appointed capacity as Official Thorn in the Side, frequently reminding him of his landlordly obligations and our rights of access across his land. He grumped and growled and suggested I should focus on the planks in my own eyes and tending to my flock. I pointed out that, although my planks were certainly in need of daily removal, they had little to do with owning excessive land and its incumbent responsibilities and, furthermore, he *was* one of my flock.

'I don't do religion,' he sneered. 'Haven't you read your church history, woman? If it's abuse of wealth and power that bothers you, look no further.' He was right. Though, that said, our little ecclesiastical outpost in Briachan no longer had either. So I badgered and he baulked and we bickered, but, strangely, slowly, I think we came to like each other. We got past the prejudices and grudgingly acknowledged that the other loved this place too. Somehow, we also sensed that something was shared in us; being rejected by parents left us fighting a familiar demon. And I had to hand it to him: he still put up with Beulah. The staff occasionally called me to extract her, as it kept slipping her mind that she was no longer housekeeper, but Mackintosh was invariably kind. Perhaps because she was the only living person who had always adored him.

But despite his best efforts to hold on to the family heritage, fate and the financial crisis trumped him. I surprised myself with mixed feelings. It was the end of a long clan connection to Rowancraig, the end of a story. But who's to say how much better that story could have been had old Chief Mackintosh not taken title deeds for himself way back in the 1600s, declaring that the land belonged to just one thread of the clan, rather than the whole weave?

Believing in better stories, I organised a community meeting at the village hall to discuss the future of the estate. Worried no one would come, I sent a press release to the paper, notes through the school bags and slapped posters on anything that stood still. Then I talked it up at the Ferryman and appealed for home baking. Even I was astonished when, by 7.30 on the Thursday evening, the hall was heaving and we were sending folks to nearby houses for extra chairs and pints of milk.

Overjoyed, I got up to the mic and coughed, holding up one hand in Pope-like blessing. It took a few minutes, but hush fell.

'Dearly beloved . . .'

They laughed. Despite my reputation within the kirk – Mo the Mad, the Maverick, the Menace – I was still ordained. Had not been *defrocked*, so to speak. (That happened when I ripped off the Highland Tea Room uniform nearly forty years ago.) I nearly wore my dog-collar, though, because it felt like that sort of event, a shepherd rounding up the flock. A prophet, even, calling them to the Promised Land!

'We are gathered here today to begin our walk to freedom.'

Cheers. Applause. I grinned. Frowning faces and tut-tutting from certain quarters.

'Okay, okay, a little OTT, but we are here to decide if we want to make the biggest change in this area since the Clearances. As you all know, Rowancraig Estate is up for sale.' Dramatic pause. 'Do we, as a community, want to buy it?'

There were snorts and exclamations, head waggings and head noddings. Half way back, Liana beamed and gave me a thumbs up. Next to her, Colvin sat with arms folded, the fingers of one hand on his mouth.

'Can we *own* the land,' I went on, 'and work together so the estate benefits those who live here, rather than ignoring – or worse – exploiting, them?'

'With what money, like?' It was Fachie.

'Ah yes, I'll come to that. But, for example, can we ensure that Rowancraig nurtures the environment?'

'Aye,' muttered a gruff voice from the front row. He was head stalker from Logie Estate to the south. 'So long as you pay no attention to the environmentalists but listen to the locals who work the land.'

A German accent piped up. 'Some of the environmentalists *are* locals who work the land.' A member of Strathspey Eco-Warriors, she had lived here for over thirty years. There was a rustling across the room of under-the-breath voices and shifting seats.

We weren't getting off to a good start. I knew most of these people and the groups behind them, the complex web of organisations, ideals and agendas that crossed paths and swords in our precious strath. I saw our man from the Cairngorms National Park Authority taking notes in a large jotter, but knew he wouldn't say much. It didn't matter what the Park said about anything, there would be outrage.

'Before we start the customary brawling,' I joked, 'let's have a look at this presentation from Community Land Scotland.' I handed over to a young lassie whose PowerPoint jammed on the second slide, but nevertheless spoke with passion about the buy-out of her home in the Outer Hebrides.

'We make the decisions now,' she said in her breathy lilting accent. 'Not the laird or his estate manager, who never lived on the island, anyway. We know the place and we love it like no one else; now it belongs to us.'

After her talk, I got everyone into discussion groups, but despite my efforts at engineering a diverse mix, all the birds stubbornly flocked to their own feather and chirped in unison. I slipped among them, listening.

In one corner there was a brood of farmers, one in his eighties who still tended his own prize-winning Blackface sheep and Highland cows. Turning a worn cap in his hands he was talking about the Outer Hebrides project. 'I heard most of the Trust committee are incomers – English, like.'

'Aye,' another replied. 'And it'll go that way here, too.'

'It's locals should make the decisions.'

'Right enough. The families that have done the donkey work for generations.'

Across the room, the scruffy young guy who ran the water sports centre on Loch Hope was chatting with his outdoor instructor friends. 'Who's a local?' he said, a toddler squirming on his lap. 'I'm born and bred in Briachan and Mum's from down the road but Dad's Polish. Do I count?"

'And what about me?' his Kiwi wife piped up, bursting at the seams with their third child.

In a group of gamekeepers nearby, Fachie was cracking his knuckles. 'Problem is, these environmental organisations are more interested in trees and animals than people.'

'Aye,' another replied. 'Always out to get farmers and field sports, but these industries employ most people round here.'

'Yeah, yeah. And they pick their animals, too.' A third voice. 'All in favour of eagles and some three-eyed bat-leech, but they don't give a damn about sheep.'

'Or deer,' said Fachie bitterly. 'What they do to deer is positively criminal.'

'Too much culling, aye.' His friend nodded.

Just in earshot was a group of articulate, professional-looking types, including the man who had taken Glenda from Fachie. He worked for Scottish Natural Heritage.

'We're plagued by environmental crime!' he said to his circle, counting on his fingers. 'Burning the moor; killing birds of prey; over-grazing; putting up fences and pushing deer populations so high that, come winter, they can't get food or shelter and they *die*—'

'I'm not listening to this shit!' Fachie muttered from a few feet away and stood, his chair tipping back onto a startled Mrs McClatchy. What should have been a dramatic exit rapidly degenerated into farce as he had to squeeze and fumble his way around the groups, with people tugging their chairs this way and that, pulling bags and kids out of the way.

'Right with you, pal,' someone murmured. Others looked embarrassed or wouldn't meet his eye. His father, Dougie, rose to speak to him, but Fachie just stormed past.

It wasn't much better over coffee at the end. Most folks stuck to their familiar clots or to polite avoidance.

'Weather's been that crazy the day, eh?' Chomping a cupcake.

'Oh aye.' Sip of tea. 'Cannae make its mind up.'

But the minds of the people were very firmly made up.

'Sheep are on land that's good for nothing else and deer belong here!' It was a solicitor, who owned law offices across Scotland and lived nearby in the Duchess of Bedford's old house. He'd moved up for the field sports.

'Yes, but the problem is over-grazing,' the Eco Warrier tried to explain, proffering her vegan cakes. 'Sheep and deer prevent regrowth of trees, and though deer are native, they belong in forests—'

'Who needs more forest?' The solicitor spoke through a mouthful of coconut quinoa slice. 'We've got enough trees! People love the Scottish moors and mountains the way they are. Cover it with forest and you can't see a damn thing and you won't get the tourists.'

'Actually, in Norway they get more tourists—'

'We're not friggin Norway and we don't want to be! This mystical magical forest that you lot keep trying to bring back never existed. Utter mumbo-jumbo!'

'I beg—'

'Okay, maybe in darkest prehistory there were a lot more trees but the reason we have open moor today is because of natural climate change. And we're not in the business of going back to the Stone Age, anyway, for godsake! We live in the modern world.' He slipped the remains of the quinoa slice into a paper cup on the table.

'Yeah, right,' the Kiwi lass murmured to her hubby on the other side of the table where she was mopping up the toddler's spilled juice. 'That'll be why they dress up like Victorians and prance round the hills in their archaic shooting rituals, then.' He nodded with a smirk and pulled the child's hands out of a bowl of crisps.

Out in the car park I heard voices raised among a group of old-timers.

'The real problem is all these hill walkers and mountain bikers trampling the peat.'

'And where's the People's Trust?' an elderly woman cried. 'Hill shepherds are a dying breed, crofters on the brink of extinction. Who's going to protect them?'

'But that's what community ownership is for!' I appealed, walking over. 'That *is* your People's Trust!'

'Ah, but can you trust the people to run it?' The solicitor strode past me, tossing the remark over his shoulder as his BMW winked to life.

'Long as they're locals,' someone said.

I stood there in despair. *What have I done to displease you, Dear God, that you put the burden of all these people on me?* It was like those church meetings when I opened the floor and let folks share their views. *Did I conceive them? Did I give them birth?* Always the same voices saying the same old things, but most folk too perplexed or loyal to pipe up. Till it all comes out with a vengeance in private. Or the local paper. *Dear God, why do you tell me to carry them in my arms, as a mother carries an infant?*

'So much for your community buy-out, *Momo*,' Liana said back inside, as she helped me stack the chairs. 'There is no community.'

Community

Who are we?

What makes us a people? Is it simply that in this moment in time we share this place? We don't share it very well. We just live here. Some of us by choice, some by chance, some by luck, some by lack of it. For one it is Eden, another Egypt, for others a kind of Babylon.

One day our cradle, the next our cross.

After the meeting, a small group of people joined me in a steering group to explore the options for a community buy-out and present a proposal. But we didn't get far. The wrong personalities signed up; the chair was cheerful but useless; the secretary muddled the minutes; people didn't do what they said they would do; people did what they said they wouldn't do; there was gossip and squabbling and dropouts. Three brave souls carried the torch a bit further, but in the cold deluge of government paperwork, it was doused.

The Red Sea came crashing in.

The people stayed put.

Sign 7: Penny Whistle

Five months after Colvin disappeared, an upland path builder found Tess's old penny whistle from school days. It was on the shore of Lochan Dubh a' Chada, a small pool in the treeless lower slopes of the Cairngorms, lying at the foot of the forbidding ridges. Its name means The Black Lochan of the Narrow Pass, but that October day its water was the electric blue of the sky and ridged by wind. The path builder saw sunlight bouncing off something in the pebbles and discovered the whistle – a sticker on the back bearing Tess's name. When he blew on it, the sound rang high and pure in the cool air.

Whisky

The Ferryman was lit up that night, that August night of 2009, the year – indeed the weekend – when everything changed. But we didn't know it then, and for that moment the place seemed bathed in a kind of innocence, a pre-lapsarian, pre-Fall glow. That night my pub was brimming with people and flooded with light, floating on laughter and music and the generous tides of food and drink. Because, you see, the Briachan men's shinty team had beaten Kirkton today; it was David felling Goliath, and they were all there, glistening with sweat and thumping backs, awash with beer and disbelief. The women were there, too, chattering, drinking, rejoicing. The kids swarmed though the melee, spilling crisps and glasses of Irn-Bru, tugging on their parents' elbows and chasing each other out into the green night. Being late summer, there were tourists as well: a Dutch family playing cards at their table, three men with beards and backpacks, a young Canadian couple gazing at the scene in wonder.

Liana and I were behind the bar, spinning like dervishes – the Dancing Girls I called us – reaching up for glasses, pulling pints, whipping round for peanuts. I dug her in the ribs, and she laughed, and I loved how that sad face lit up. She was always beautiful, Liana, with her Latin looks, the river of black hair down her back. I'd never seen her without make-up and I teased her about being the village tart. She'd never seen me with make-up and called me the village tomboy. Toad, more like, I would say, and she would shake her head furiously and hug me.

'One day, your prince will come, *Mamá*' she insisted. How she could still think I wanted one amazed me.

'One day my king will come,' I would say. How I could still believe in God amazed her.

Over in the corner, Tess was tuning her guitar. She looked so much like her mother it was uncanny, except she had Colvin's blue eyes and her hair was caramel and wavy. She'd been playing the Ferryman since she was a skinny kid with a whistle, then a fiddle, scratching out 'Scotland the Brave' to charmed tourists and patient regulars. And then when I bought the place she asked if she could play her guitar instead, and sing. She'd never done it in public before, so I gave her a wee try-out one rainy afternoon, Liana and I sitting opposite her on bar stools. She was shaking and told us to close our eyes.

'Can't ask my punters to do that, baby. Why don't you close yours?'

So she did and her voice rose and swelled and lifted us out of the stone walls and into the trees and the sky, higher up and deeper in, and when she finished and opened her eyes, there were tears in ours.

After that she performed here every Saturday night until bookings started to come in for other gigs and we were lucky to get her. Most of what she sang was her own stuff, bittersweet songs, too knowing for one so young, too close to the bone for a local pub. Sometimes Liana flinched and sucked in her breath or wagged a finger, but then Tess just sang some old favourite of her mama's and all was forgiven.

That night, Tess was wearing a dress the colour of wild blaeberries, yellow Doc Martens and a pheasant feather stuck in her hair. She was seventeen, but still looked seven to me.

'One, two, three, four!' she barked into the mic and launched into a driving rhythm on the guitar.

A moment later, the door opened and three people slipped in. A tall South Asian man, handsome and greying a little at the temples, a woman with a sculpted blonde bob and a young man, whom I guessed was their son, being such a perfect blend of their colouring and features. Squeezing past a clot of people, they made their way to the bar, taking in the scene with alert interest. They watched Tess finish her song and I could see the lad's face, captured and alight.

There was applause and cheering and a few whoops from the shinty boys and the visitors turned to me. The man flashed a smile and ordered a red wine for his partner and a Guinness for the lad. His accent was North American, warm but sophisticated, with the lilting precision of his Asian roots.

'And I think I'll have to try a little of the local Scotch,' he said, nodding to the bottles on the wall. 'What do you recommend, sir?'

'Well, first of all –' I leaned my elbows on the bar – 'I recommend you call me Mo.'

His face blanched.

'Short for Maurabelle,' I whispered, 'but never, *ever* use that name.'

'I apologise.'

'Nae bother,' I said. 'Happens all the time. Comes in handy when the queue for the ladies is too long.' He winced. 'As for the whisky, our closest is Speybridge, up the river, but my favourite is Bowmore, a peaty island malt with a real kick at the end. I have a very expensive bottle, 1983, fifty quid a dram.'

'I'll have both, and try to guess which is which.'

'You're on.' I winked at Liana who ducked under the bar to hide her smile. We loved American tourists; they were entertaining and they tipped well.

He turned his back and watched Tess as I poured. She was now singing a lonesome little tune about lost love, which always amused me as I didn't think she'd ever been in love. Not, mind you, for want of effort on the part of the local lads, but because she'd never been satisfied. They were all just yokels with no dreams, apparently. She'd fancy them for a bit, hang out here and there, then get bored and give them the old heave-ho. And then write another song about her broken heart and make me laugh.

'You just exploit these poor buggers for material,' I told her once, and she rolled her eyes.

'That's ART,' she said, in her smug tone, and shot me a grin.

At the end of her song there was a final twang on the guitar, a moment's silence full of every heartache in the room, and a stampede of applause. A few folk gave her an ovation. The Asian-American lad hitched up onto a bar stool, sipped his drink and didn't take his eyes off her. She looked up with a smile, dimples appearing in each cheek, and as she nodded and murmured her thanks to the room, she saw him. I caught that look between them, that moment when a silent bolt shoots across my pub and I know that everything is about to change.

The man turned back to me and eyed the two tumblers gleaming on my polished bar.

'Visiting?' I asked, offering him the Speybridge.

'Yes.' He sniffed, took a sip and closed his eyes. Held it in the mouth and swallowed. 'Hmmm . . . that is very good. Yes, we're . . . on vacation.'

'Sample B.' I pushed the second glass towards him, clocking his large expensive watch and understated, elegant clothes. 'Where are you from?'

'Malaysia first and then Boston, but my wife's British, so we're this side of the pond quite often.' He closed his eyes and sniffed again, sipped the second malt, his eyebrows knotting together. Then he swallowed and the brows shot up. 'Ahhh . . .' He breathed out a long, knowing sigh. 'That, ma'am, if I'm not mistaken, is the Bowmore. Very fine, indeed.'

I chuckled. 'Dead right. But I thought I told you to call me Mo.'

'In America we like to show a little respect.' Then he smiled sheepishly. 'But sometimes we get it wrong.'

'Yes, like health care,' his wife said, leaning in to put her empty glass on the bar. 'And gun laws. And foreign policy.' Her many rings caught the light in constellations of diamonds, sapphires and emeralds.

'Don't get her started.' He grinned and put an arm around her. 'She's never forgiven me for dragging her to the States.'

'Oh I have.' She stroked his chin. 'It's staying there for ever I won't contemplate.'

'And you won't have to. We are the Aggarwals, by the way,' he said, extending a hand to me. 'Kirat and Vivienne. And that's our son, Rahesh.'

'Welcome to Briachan.'

His hand was warm, smooth, strong. Hers was sinewy, with blue veins pushing through at the back.

'You been here for long?' she asked, circling a manicured finger, tone casual but a sharp look on her face.

'Brought up here.'

'Oh!' she said, eyes widening. 'Really?'

'And what's it like?' Kirat asked.

'Desperate,' I said, enjoying their alarm. With a sweeping gesture round the pub, I continued in my best Wee Free pulpit voice, clamorous and quavery at the same time. 'A seething den of depravity, an abyss of abomination! Why, a Babylon that Beelzebub himself is afeart to visit!'

The Note

Tess finished playing about 11.30. For her last song she got everyone singing 'Caledonia' and at the end there was wild cheering and whistles and stamping feet. She grinned and bowed her head – *thank you, thank you.* Then she glanced towards the bar. Rahesh was still there, perched on the stool from which he hadn't strayed, though his parents were gone. Tess met the boy's eye and blushed and busied herself packing her guitar in its case and gathering up the tips from her hat. As she pulled her gypsy-patterned bag onto her shoulder, he slid off his stool and started towards her.

I could see her face glowing, but just before Rahesh got there, local boy Charlie MacPherson jumped up and gave her a hug.

'That was byootiful, byootiful, my gurl,' he said, thumping her on the back. Fachie's son, he'd been her buddy since they were kids.

'Thanks, pal,' she said, trying to look over his shoulder.

'Better than anybody that's ever played this pub,' he went on, scooping her off her feet and spinning her round.

'This week, anyways,' said another lad and there was raucous laughter when somebody pushed him off his seat.

'Put me down, you numpty!' Tess said, pummelling Charlie's back, but as soon as he did, somebody else hugged her and she was pulled down to sit with them and offered drinks and undying love.

By the time she'd wriggled free to look for Rahesh, he was gone.

He had chatted with me a bit through the evening, asking keen questions, showing more interest and insight than the average tourist. He had a gift for drawing you out, making you talk about your life without you realising or regretting, which was a funny reversal for me, as I'm used to doing most of the listening here.

Before he left, he offered me twenty pounds.

'That's a tip for Tess.' He glanced across at her, in the middle of the boozy group hug from the shinty boys. 'She is incredible. Has she recorded anything?'

'Not yet, but that's definitely the plan. The dream, I guess.'

'I'd buy her stuff. Buy it for everyone I know.'

'Why don't you tell her?'

'She looks a bit . . . busy just now. But maybe . . . Hey, have you got a scrap of paper I could borrow, and a pen?'

'Sure, bud.' I passed a waitress notepad and pen to him, watched him think, write, think again and write some more. Then he folded it, set it on the counter with the twenty-pound note and put his empty beer glass on top.

'Thank you, ma'am.'

Then he left and a moment later Tess wrestled free from her bevy of suitors and looked across, her face falling at the sight of the empty bar. She came over and drank her customary ginger beer on the house as she waited for Liana, quizzing me about the visiting family. I was vague and dismissive, she was probing and irritated.

As they left, nigh on midnight, I slipped the tip and the note into her bag, and in the quiet of my empty pub, stretched out my legs by the fire and sipped my peppermint tea, wondering and praying about what would happen next.

Of course I had read the note.

Tess, you are beautiful and your singing has bowled me over. (I'm the guy at the bar who couldn't take his eyes off you.) Would you, by some miracle, meet me here early tomorrow morning? I have an appointment with my parents at 9 and then I'm back to the US. Outside, under the big oak at 7, if you want to make me a very happy man. I will wait for you. Rahesh Aggarwal.

Osprey

Before the light, Alex was up, slipping slow and silent through the dark to the loch. The osprey chicks would fly for the first time today, he knew, he knew. He had studied them every day, perched on the edge of the nest as their father circled the loch in protection, swooped like an arrow for fish and brought it back, settling on a branch nearby to keep watch. Alex knew the little ones were ready and he would watch over them with their father.

When he got to the lochside, the dark sky was beginning to glow, turning green like a mallard's feathers, green like the walls of Tess's room, green like the inside of his head when he closed his eyes. He sat at the tree foot and watched till the black bulk in the loch became the island of trees and he could make out the nest, till the sun rose behind the mountain and the father bird rose from his roost. And he watched through his binoculars, heart leaping, as the two little ones fell from the tree and rose and fell and rose again. And he was alone with them and drank the air and fed on the light and breathed the smell of trees.

And in his listening and in his stillness he heard another thing. A wrong thing. There were people coming. Not quiet and slow like Bird People, but talking and laughing and pounding their feet.

And he was angry and then confused because one voice he knew and one he did not. He peered round the tree. It was Tess. With a man. She was holding his hand and looking at his face and the man was looking at hers and Alex didn't like him. He was different to anyone here and his voice was like the American TV shows. Then they stopped and looked across to the ospreys and pointed and talked and Alex was going to run out and hiss at them to *Be quiet!* but saw something that froze him.

They did go quiet. They looked at each other's faces again and stepped together and wrapped arms and held very still. Then their faces moved closer and closer, so slowly, till their mouths touched. And they kissed. Then they kissed again, slower, longer, and again and again till everything of them was pressed together and they were kissing and holding and kissing and pressing and Alex was sick to death of it.

Rowancraig House

Later that Sunday morning, Rahesh went to meet his parents as arranged.

Kirat drove the hired BMW up the track, wincing at the ruts and stones and swearing at wandering sheep. From the back seat, Rahesh laughed.

'Be patient, darling,' Viv said. 'This is the Highlands.'

As they rounded the last curve in the drive, she glimpsed grey stone walls and a turret behind the Scots pines, then a view of bay windows and steps sweeping to an arched portico. Her pulse quickened. But as they parked, she noticed the steps were chipped, the front door a bit squint and a side window covered in board. They walked across patchy gravel towards a silver Fiat from which a young man was unfolding, tugging on his suit.

'Welcome to Rowancraig House!' he said, pumping their hands. He had flaming orange hair and pale skin peppered with freckles. 'I'm Jason Storkey from Grevilles, the land agents acting for Lord Mackintosh.' Handing them the glossy schedules with touched-up pictures and ecstatic prose, he licked his teeth and gave a nervous laugh. 'On a good day, you've got a glorious scene before you.' He swept his hand towards the river valley, hidden by fog. 'Most days are good!'

Kirat raised his eyebrows and Viv laughed.

'Scotland's famous for its sunshine,' she said, winking at Rahesh.

'And Scots for their positive thinking,' Kirat added.

'You'll love it here, then.' Jason's freckles flared. 'Such an ideal location . . . there's been settlement on this site since the beginning.'

'When was that?' asked Rahesh.

Jason wafted a hand. 'Oh, about a hundred thousand years ago.'

'Or maybe . . . ten thousand years ago?' Viv drawled. 'But hey, what's a zero?'

'Nothing at all,' said Kirat. Rahesh and Viv snorted with laughter.

'Slip of the tongue!' Jason blushed. 'But fabulous history, never-theless. The estate boasts a Bronze Age chamber, a Neolithic stone circle and, in the walled garden, the remains of a Pictish fort!'

'Hey, that's awesome,' Rahesh said.

Jason warmed up, leading them back to the house. 'Then the Mackintosh chief built a keep in the twelfth century – destroyed in clan battle – and finally this house in 1783. Much extended and renovated over the years, of course, and now a fine example of Scots neo-gothic baroque.'

The hinges of the front door squealed, revealing a dark entrance with mail and damp boots. Jason quickly led them through to the main hall.

The guests exclaimed. A vast, airy space, it rose two floors with a wide staircase, a gallery floor and red walls hung with paintings, stags' heads and weapons. The parquet floor was dotted with Persian rugs and at one side stood a grand piano and at the other, a fireplace. But the light gradually revealed grime, moth holes in the stuffed animals and cracks across the mirrors. Viv sat on the wobbly piano stool and began to play, the keys yellow and chipped as old toenails, their tuning little better.

'Mind the piano!' a voice yelled from above. They all started. A bulky old woman was shuffling along the gallery, one hand gripping the railing, the other a white handkerchief.

'Mrs Duggins!' Jason cried. 'I thought Lord Mackintosh said you would be with your daughter today?' He checked his paperwork. 'Mo Smith?'

'Can't go gallivanting when I'm needed.'

'But we're managing just fine!' He pulled out his phone. 'Shall I call her?'

'No use calling that besom.' In a grubby house coat, rumpled tights and slippers, she steered herself down the stairs, teetering on each step. 'Who are these foreigners?' she exclaimed as she reached ground level.

Jason's freckles glowed again. 'Oh, I did explain, remember? The family viewing the house? Mr & Mrs Aggarwal, Rahesh – this is Mrs Beulah Duggins, *retired* housekeeper of Rowancraig House.'

'Ach, you don't retire in this job!' She chuckled. 'Been a widow for forty years but still married to the house.'

Kirat and Viv exchanged glances.

Jason cleared his throat. 'Such commitment, Mrs Duggins! But as the house is now for sale—'

'For sale?' She looked aghast.

'Yes! As I explained. Now if you'll please excuse us—'

'Oh, don't worry,' Viv said, putting a hand on his arm. 'I'm sure Mrs Duggins has a wealth of stories to share. Do join us, Mrs D.'

Jason opened his mouth but too late.

'Surely!' the old woman said. 'But you mustn't touch anything—'

'Nothing to worry about! Follow me, everyone!' Jason quick-stepped into the drawing room, trying to out-talk Mrs Duggins as he pointed out the antiques and paintings. 'The front rooms all face south-east. Drenched with sunlight and warmth for most of the year!'

'Except when the wind's blowing,' she said. 'None of the windows are double-glazed, you see. It's a deathly blast.'

'Not at all!' Jason protested.

'That's why we got wool carpets and lined drapes. Chose all the decor here, so I did,' Mrs Duggins said, gazing around her. The room was hung in muddy purple and black. 'That Lady Clarice Mackintosh hadn't a clue!'

'All the fitted carpets and curtains are included in the sale,' Jason struggled on.

'Can't be! Cost a fortune, those drapes—'

'Don't worry,' Viv said. 'Lord Mackintosh is welcome to them. They need replacing anyway.'

'They do not!' Mrs Duggins flared. 'That's quality stuff, that is. Made to last for years.'

'As indeed they have!' Jason clapped his hands together.

'Much like Mrs Duggins,' Kirat murmured to Rahesh.

Jason marched them into the dining room, which was dominated by a vast table with twenty-two seats and silver candelabra on the tartan cloth.

'You're not having the candlesticks,' Mrs Duggins said, shuffling behind them. 'Or anything in here. All family heirlooms.'

'I think you'll find,' Jason said, 'that the schedule lists a number of items included in the sale or available for purchase. Most of the contents of this room, for example.'

'The candelabra are cursed.'

'Oh, really?' said Rahesh. 'How?'

'From the 1800s these are.' She pulled one to the edge of the table.

'Laird's son got a young maid in the family way, then sacked her. On her last day, she raged and cursed him and his people for forty generations and cause she was polishing these candelabra at the time, the curse has carried through them.'

'What a story,' Viv said. 'And what's the curse?'

'Every firstborn son of the owners of the house will die before he's forty.'

'Yikes!' said Rahesh. 'And has it come true?'

'Of course not!' said Jason. 'Old wives' tale!'

Mrs Duggins impaled him with a dark stare. 'Since the curse, every firstborn son has died young.'

'But why did they keep the candlesticks, then?' Viv asked.

'They didn't know they had,' Mrs Duggins rasped, her bug eyes wide. 'Maid hid them in the attic, and it was only the minister – back thirty year ago – who worked it out. He was a proper minister, so he was, had a sixth sense and knew the place was haunted. So he chased her with his Bible and made her confess her secret before banishing her to hell.'

'My word.' Viv's eyebrows arched.

'They don't make ministers like they used to,' Kirat said.

'That they don't.' Mrs Duggins pointed her hanky at him. 'Dead right there, son.' Jason winced.

Rahesh inspected the other candlestick. 'So, when they discovered it was the candlesticks, why didn't they get rid of them?'

'Because it was *too late*.' Her voice was a low whisper now and they all leaned in to hear, even Jason. 'Edgar and Clarice Mackintosh only had one child – a son – and he had *just died*. The minister was here to plan the funeral, because the wee laddie had fell the day before from a window. An *attic* window.'

There was electric silence.

'No!' Kirat breathed.

'Aye. So then they asked me to get the candlesticks melted down and cast into the loch, but as there was no other child, I didn't see the point. I hid them, only brought them out when Lord Mackintosh shut the place up three years ago. There's been no son since.'

Everyone looked at Rahesh, who swivelled his eyes from one to the other in mock horror.

'Run, Scooby!' Kirat yelped.

Viv burst out laughing and Mrs Duggins gave her a baleful stare.

'Oh it's a house full of stories, that's for sure, Mr and Mrs Aggarwal,' Jason chuckled. 'Very entertaining, very entertaining indeed, but shall we move on?'

They left Mrs Duggins rubbing the candlesticks with her hanky.

'The master bedroom!' Jason opened a door off the gallery. A four-poster bed, dressing table and wardrobe were set against the three internal walls, all of a dark wood carved with pomegranates and palms. The outer wall had a bay window, the murky green swirls of its curtains matching the bed hangings, the wallpaper and even the carpet. The effect was oppressive, like the captain's quarters of a shipwreck.

'Decorated this room, too,' said Mrs Duggins, appearing at the door, breathing heavily.

'You're full of surprises,' Viv murmured.

'But there was no pleasing that Lady Mackintosh. Wanted it all white!' She gave a small incongruous hoot. 'Would you believe? Told her I'd be cleaning all the days God gives, so—'

'Mrs Duggins,' interjected Jason, 'I was just about to tell the Aggarwals about this stunning suite of furniture.'

'I can do that. Could give you the tour of this whole place with my eyes shut.'

'Ah, but can you do it with your *mouth* shut?' he muttered. Kirat stifled a laugh.

'It's all here in the schedule,' Viv said, tapping hers. Mrs Duggins scowled at the offending document.

Jason quickly started to read. 'The suite in the master bedroom dates from the late eighteenth century when Captain William Mackintosh was plying the trade routes to the Spice Islands. He brought them back from Malaya for his new bride, who gave birth in it to all of their nineteen children. It thus came to be known as the Blesséd Bed.'

'Oh,' sighed Viv, running her hand down the ornate post. 'What a wonderful story – and from Malaysia, Kirat! How perfect. What a beautiful, blesséd bed!'

'Aye,' said Mrs Duggins, folding her arms with satisfaction. 'Lady Clarice died in it.'

Foreigners

Mercifully, Beulah didn't come to the Ferryman very often. But she was there that Sunday night *bearing news*. She always came when she sniffed gossip to be heard or, better still, had some to tell. Then she summoned Colvin to fetch her. Sometimes she'd ask Liana, or even me if she was desperate, but getting her out had become such a palaver, what with having to stop her sallying forth in her slippers, or with wig skewiff, that only he had the patience.

She heaved in, eyes gleaming. Colvin looked weary. 'You'll never believe it,' she announced to the room. A few folk glanced up. Fachie was at a table with some keeper friends, computer game guy on his bar stool, some lads playing pool, and a couple on a leather sofa were staring into the fire.

Beulah moved across to an armchair opposite them and banged her military-issue handbag on the coffee table. Now everyone looked across.

'You'll never believe it,' she said again, triumphant.

'What is it, then?' someone asked.

Fachie shot her a twisted smile. 'Prince Charles been to visit?'

Beulah never could resist detailing the great and the good who had come to Rowancraig, although there had been none for the past three years.

'No, but there's an Indian going to buy it.'

What? Which Indian? Who?

'Going to take it off the Mackintoshes, who've had it hundreds of years!' Beulah folded her arms.

'It is for sale,' I pointed out, setting a raspberry lemonade on the bar for Colvin.

'But why would an *Indian* want to live here?' someone asked.

'Because if you live in a house like that and own the whole estate, you've got it made, haven't you?' A voice from the pool table. A few laughs.

'You've got trouble on your hands, that's what you have,' said Fachie. 'Look what happened to Mackintosh.'

I glanced at Colvin. The person in the room most affected by the fortunes of the estate and the fancies of its owner was the least likely to say a word.

'Oh, he didn't lose his money because of the estate.' The man on the sofa stretched out his long denim legs. 'The estate lost money because of him.'

'Never!' Beulah said.

'But we've got enough foreigners taking over the place as it is – this is ridiculous.' Another keeper.

'And his wife's English,' Beulah went on, as if that only made matters worse (and as if she'd forgotten her own husband, which I think she had). 'Thought she was quite the madam, so she did.'

'Ohhh,' I said. 'Oh, I see. Was it that couple who were here last night? What was their name?' I clicked my fingers. 'Kirat and Vivienne Aggarwal! That's it. Was it really them?'

'Yes, and their lad.'

I knew the lad had met our Tess at the oak tree that morning and walked off down the lochside with her; I had spied on them from my upstairs window.

'Kirat said he was from Malaysia and Boston,' I clarified. 'That's interesting. Said they were on holiday – never mentioned looking at Rowancraig.'

'Dishonest, you see,' said Beulah.

'Just a canny businessman, I suspect.' Fachie downed the last of his beer. His son made a perfect shot at the pool table, the balls clicking softly.

'Last chance for the community buy-out?' I ventured. A few folk laughed.

Fachie shook his head. 'Wouldn't work.'

'What buy-out? What community?' Beulah demanded.

'Could be amazing,' the woman on the sofa said. 'Just so difficult, though.'

'Yes.' I spread my hands to the pub. 'Freedom is difficult.'

Fachie rolled his eyes. Colvin gave me a sad smile.

The Ache

'Oh, darling, it's perfect!' Viv gushed the moment they were back in the vehicle. Her menfolk laughed.

'It's a wreck,' Kirat said.

'Oh, it's not going to stay like that! We're going to transform it!' She looked back at the house and waved excitedly at Jason on the front steps, drained and pale, as Mrs Duggins heaved into view behind him.

'That's what I feared,' Kirat said, lifting a hand in salute as he drove off round the circular drive.

'The place is crying out for a complete overhaul and we're the people for the job! Oh, do say yes!'

'I'm a businessman, Viv. I never say yes to anything without a lawyer and a contract.'

'You do to me,' she purred, resting her hand on his thigh. 'And I *adore* you for it.'

He chuckled as they turned onto the A9 and headed north to Inverness airport.

'But seriously, darling, it's spot-on – astonishing history but a recent lull that gives us freedom.'

'*Lull?*' Kirat said. 'Nice euphemism for "dire neglect and financial ruin".'

Rahesh laughed.

'I know, I know, but you know what I mean,' protested Viv. 'We don't have to inherit stuffy old expectations and stick-in-the mud staff and—'

'Looks like you'll inherit Mrs Duggins,' Rahesh said. Kirat roared.

'Oh God, please, no. What a troll.' Viv clutched at her hair.

'I felt a bit sorry for her, actually.' Rahesh looked out at the barren hills to the north. 'Living for a past that doesn't exist any more.'

'Bet she's harboured a life-long passion for Mackintosh!' Viv pressed her fingers to her breastbone. 'He's probably selling the place just to get rid of her.'

'Ooh, plot twists!' Kirat said. 'Maybe she murdered poor old Lady Clarice!'

'In the blessed bed,' Viv breathed.

'With the revolver,' Rahesh chimed in.

'No, no. That would have made a mess! She'd have to scrub for days. Better with the lead pipe.'

'Or one of the cursed candlesticks!' said Kirat.

'Of course!' Viv crowed. 'Yes, yes! We *have* to stage murder mysteries at this place. What fun!'

'We can wheel in Mrs Duggins at the climax, with a tray of eggnog!' Kirat lifted a finger from the wheel. 'Utterly terrifying.'

They laughed until Rahesh broke in, pointing through the window. 'Hey, that must be the shepherd's house. Up on the slope there in front of the trees.'

It was a misshapen house with dormer windows and haphazard extensions, a bright yellow door and window boxes full of flowers. Sheep dotted the fields around, bundles of scraggly white with black faces and legs.

'Ah, yes,' Kirat said. 'He'll be an estate tenant. One of the jobs for the lawyers – finding out the state of play there. Scotland has fiendish land law.'

'Hmm,' mused Rahesh. 'I'm interested to look into that.'

Kirat wasn't sure he would be much help. Twenty-four years old and a law graduate, Rahesh's recent masters was in human rights law and it seemed to have translated into a polemic on his parents' human wrongs. He'd got in with a particular lecturer and his fan club of neo-socialist, save-the-world eco-hippies and had been awkward company ever since.

'The singer last night?' Rahesh said.

'Oh, wasn't she *gorgeous*!' Viv swivelled round in her seat, beaming at him.

'She's the shepherd's daughter.'

'Oh.' Her smile dropped.

'And the woman at the bar with long dark hair?'

'Now, *she* was gorgeous,' Kirat said. Viv smacked his leg.

'The shepherd's wife.'

'Really?!' Viv asked. 'She didn't look local.'

'No. Bolivian.'

'My god, how extraordinary. And how do you know all this, pray tell?'

'I talked with the other woman at the bar. Mo. Owns the pub and knows everything and everyone. Really interesting. Interesting place.'

'Absolutely!' Viv said, triumphant. 'It's a *fascinating* place and we are destined to become a part of it. We start by gutting the house, then renovating *everything* – top to bottom!'

'Perhaps I could sell a few factories in the Far East to cover that?' Kirat raised his brows.

'Don't be such an Eeyore! There'll be grants available for restoring a heritage building.'

'Surely they don't give them to rich people,' Rahesh said.

'Oh, in this country they do!' Viv giggled. 'That's why I'm coming home.'

'Well, that's a disgrace. How on earth does that work?'

Kirat smiled at him in the rear-view mirror. 'Lots of ways, if you're clever. Farm payments from the EU, tax breaks for forestry, and you can run a sporting estate without being charged business rates.'

Viv wafted a ring-heavy hand. 'And we'll probably set up a company or trust or something to own the house and manage the estate, register it offshore and get investment.'

'Easy as that?' asked Rahesh.

'It is for your father.' She plucked a grey hair off his shoulder. 'Isn't it, darling? And you've been hankering after a Highland estate since you were at school!'

'But this shambles wasn't quite what I had in mind.'

'I know, but just think! You could buy any old thriving estate tomorrow and keep it ticking over, but there's no challenge in that, is there? No adventure! Here, you can take something on its knees and turn it into something really quite marvellous. You've been itching for a new project, and what's more, we can do it together!'

'That's the bit I'm worried about.'

She swiped at him, grinning.

But Kirat knew Viv was right. There was a yearning. What she didn't know was that it wasn't new. That ache was his oldest companion, and though it had never been satisfied, he had to credit it with making him who he was. As a kid in Kuala Lumpur he'd thought he had to outdo his older brother to earn his father's approval, so he'd worked harder at everything till he beat him, even earning a scholarship to Lugano Academy in Switzerland. But his father only seemed annoyed at the wrong order of things and the ache deepened. At school he longed for acceptance amongst the top tier of boys – the Saudi sheiks and American business heirs, the British aristocracy – and he learned their sports, their accents, their dress and swagger till he got invited to parties, weekends at home, holidays. At university in St Andrews and throughout his MBA at Harvard Business School he longed to impress lecturers and girls – and mostly managed it, being intelligent, handsome and hard-working. But still the ache.

He had thought winning Vivienne might put a stop to it. She was, after all, from a wealthy and well-connected family with roots going back into powerful dynasties in every corner of the British Isles; she was strikingly good-looking; and her love of art, her bohemian flair and her lack of snobbery attracted him. Half his friends had courted her, wanted her, even slept with her, which had disturbed and galvanised him with equal measure, but she'd chosen him. And promised the promiscuity would end. He never knew for sure if it had and the not knowing kept fear and desire twisting inside him like a rope. And so he pushed on, building the family empire, buying companies and companions, binding to himself the possessions and people for which he had longed, but which never gave him peace.

Even Rahesh had not dispelled the ache. The only child, the first-born son – the pinnacle of his heart's desire. If anything, his presence only goaded Kirat all the more, to be better than he was, to make more of himself, to create a legacy greater than wealth. But what could it be?

'Well?' Viv broke through his thoughts. 'Are we going to proceed? Instruct a full survey and a legal search?'

He tilted his head.

'Whatever you guys decide,' said Rahesh, 'I trust you'll do it with integrity.'

Sign 8: Wallet

Seven months after Colvin disappeared, a new recruit on a RAF training expedition found his wallet. It was a brutal December day with sleet whipping in spirals, clouding vision and numbing the face. The small party took shelter in the ruins of an old shieling hut on the lower slopes of the Cairngorms, and she spotted the wallet wedged between the stones. Brown Italian leather, with a few credit cards, bank notes and scraps of paper, it was the one given to Colvin, many moons before, by Sorley.

Home

Sunday evening. August 2009. Same weekend. The clock on the dash says 19:07 when I turn my Porsche off the A9 and onto the farm road at Rowancraig Estate. Within seconds the tarmac gives way to a cattle grid and then dirt track and I bump up it for a few minutes, cursing every rock and pothole and myself for bringing this car. Sheep stand in the tussocky grass on all sides, most with their heads down, till a stout ewe with curly horns and ragged coat strides into the middle of the road. I brake hard and she holds her ground, staring me down like a queen. Hit the horn and she starts running up the track in front of me, till finally skeetering off. Then a closed gate. The sprung latch is rusty and stubborn, and when I manage to drag it back, it pings free again and catches my finger, slicing off skin. *Fuck!* I yell at the fields. Yes, I remember all this: the rutted roads, the stupid sheep, the old gates. All the obstacles and never getting anywhere. Just the drudgery as the scars and scabs spread across your hands.

Hanky wrapped round the bleeding finger, I drive through the gate, climb out again and shut it. The rest of the track is worse and I hear an ugly scrape on the bottom of the car. Welcome home, Sorley. Welcome bloody home.

The house is the same clumsy shape, an old cottage with bits added and hammered on over the years, and beyond it a garage and the satellites of sheds and outbuildings. I see the marks of generations of my family and sense the footfall and fingerprints across every surface. There at the back is the big barn where my mother fell to her death.

Grabbing jacket and a shoulder bag, I walk to the house, then hesitate. Do I go round to the sun-room entrance at the kitchen, where everyone goes and the door is never locked, or to the front? At the front door, I press the doorbell and wait. Why the hell have I come? There is no sound and I press again. Then I knock. Like a stranger.

Behold, I stand at the door and knock . . . An unexpected memory of a picture that hung in my childhood bedroom. Jesus with a lantern at a dark door. Mo had said it was my mother's, so it remained, enshrined. I glance up at the window of my old room. Picture's probably still there, covered in dust.

Footsteps. And then a lot of scrabbling as keys are turned and latches scraped back.

'Just coming!' a voice calls and the door is hauled open.

'Tess?' I say. 'It's Sorley. Your uncle Sorley.' Makes me sound ridiculous and old. In front of her, I feel it.

'Sorley!' she cries. 'What you doing here? I mean – come in!' She tugs me inside, looks at me in surprised amusement and gives me a hug. Not a super-close, grippy hug, but good enough for a neglectful uncle. I drop my bag and jacket to hug her back, but she is already heading down the hall.

'Mum!' she yells. 'You'll never guess! It's Sorley!'

There's a split second of silence, then a cry and a crash in the back of the house and Tess pulls me into the kitchen. In the middle of the room – painted turquoise with flying fish – stands Liana, her face drained and a smashed dish at her feet. Her hair is held up in a bun with a paintbrush, her hands covered in dough, and her small frame swamped in an apron bearing the body of a grossly fat man in tight underpants.

I burst out laughing. She bursts into tears. With a yelp, she hurls herself at me, pressing one doughy hand into my back, the other in my hair. I feel her against me, petite yet full at breast and hip, and I hug her hard, kissing her on the side of the head.

She pulls away, flustered, sniffing and fumbling around the worktop till she finds a tea towel. With her back to me, she wipes her mascara and rubs the mess off her hands. Tess passes a box of tissues.

'You beast,' Liana hisses, half-laughing. 'I beg you come for years, *hermanito*, and then – poof! – no notice at all, you walk through the door! And you ruin the supper.' She points at the broken dish with the steak and pastry splattered across the floor.

'I'll sort it,' Tess says and ferrets in the cupboard under the sink.

'Sorry,' I say. 'Communication's not my strong point. I'll order in a takeaway – my treat, of course.'

'Don't be stupid. I'll come up with something. Give that to the dogs,' she says to Tess, sweeping up the mess. 'Make sure there's no broken glass! And call your dad – tell him little brother is here. Where's Alex?'

'Owl watching. I'll call him too.'

'I'm the *only* brother. Why do I have to be *little*? I'm taller than him, anyway.'

'You always be little to us, *hermanito*,' Liana says, tweaking my cheek.

'Even though I'm six years older than you *and* taller?'

'Everyone's taller than me,' she shrugs. 'No big deal. Come.' She takes my hand and points to a chair at the kitchen table. 'Sit down, I'll get you a drink. You only been here five minutes and I scream, smash the crockery, strangle and insult you!'

'Welcome home, Unca Sorley!' Tess says, in a twangy American accent. 'Sure is swell to see fambly again.'

'You,' Liana points to her, 'shut up and call the men. You' – turning her finger on me – 'sit.'

I obey. The bossiness from one so small is disarming.

'Hmm . . . How do I shut up *and* call the men?' Tess muses, tapping her chin, eyes rolled to the ceiling.

'You know what I mean! Go!' Liana waves a hand at her and strides to the cupboard for a glass. 'Beer? G&T? Wine?'

'G&T.'

As she puts it in front of me, the outside door of the sun room shudders and there is a stomping and scraping of boots. I stiffen. The women turn towards the kitchen door.

'Hi, Dad!' Tess calls out. 'Look what the cat brought in.'

Liana shoots a despairing look at the remains of the pie on the floor and rubs her hands on the apron man's legs. I know Colvin will be changing from his wellies to his slippers, and in the seconds this takes, I slurp my drink and feel a lifetime of waiting. It's been eighteen years. At last, he pushes through the kitchen door, stooped and dishevelled, a question on his weathered face.

'Colvin!' I say, moving across, my hands rising uncertainly, ready for a hug or a handshake. He stares at me, takes my hand in his rough one and then slowly smiles, faded blue eyes disappearing into crinkles.

'Oho,' he murmurs, then crosses his arms and rocks on his heels, still looking at me with a dazed smile. 'So it's yourself,' he says and shakes his head.

A noise at the kitchen door. It's Alex. Tall and pale, he has floppy dark hair that falls over his eyes, as if he watches life from behind a screen. His figure is gaunt, shoulders already bowed like Colvin's. He wears a long green jacket and in one hand holds a notebook and pen. He pushes them into a large pocket and eyes me in silence.

'Hello, Alex,' I say, holding out my hand to him. He does not lift his and I drop mine. 'I'm Sorley – your dad's brother.'

'I know who you are. Bit impossible not to.' He points to the wall where there are several pictures of me – from the wedding, the London trip, a few childhood snaps in colourful frames.

'Right! Sorry about that,' I laugh.

'Don't think about you that much,' he says, and sits down with the jacket still on. 'Hardly ever.'

Liana is swift pulling together a second meal of omelette with local chanterelle mushrooms and melting nuggets of cheese. Over dinner we talk about Tess's music: her busy round of gigs, the competition she's won, the offer of a place at the Royal Conservatoire.

'I don't know, though,' she says, tucking her long hair behind her ears. 'I'm dead sick of school. I just want to get on the road, make music, get on with my life.'

'*Go . . . to . . . college*,' I say, stabbing my fork in her direction. She looks surprised.

'I didn't pay him to say that, *cariná*,' Liana says. 'Promise.'

Colvin glances at me, his inscrutable eyes taking me in swiftly then dropping back to his plate. Alex stops eating and stares at me.

'But why?' Tess says. 'I know what I want to do and I know I'll keep getting better just by playing lots and performing. A qualification from the Conservatoire won't get me more work or better pay, so what's the point?'

'The point is making the best start, Tess,' I say, flattered that she seems to want my opinion. 'Sounds like you've got the talent, but the right training will take that to levels you couldn't do on your own *and* it will give you contacts and credibility.' I top up Liana's glass from the wine I've brought, feeling warm and expansive in my wise uncle role. Colvin sticks to water.

'See?' says Liana, 'Is not just me.'

'*And,*' I add, 'You're far too young to hit the road.' I look round the table for approval. Tess is rolling her eyes, but smiling, Liana is nodding eagerly, Colvin's focused on his plate, while Alex's expression is a blend of disbelief and scorn.

'What d'you do after school?' Tess asks.

'Edinburgh University. Economics.'

'And see?' Liana says, carrying plates to the sink. 'Has paid off! Your uncle Sorley is very successful.'

'Well . . .' I cringe.

Then Alex speaks for the first time. 'You're very rich, aren't you?' His tone is not admiring.

'Alex.' Colvin gives a small shake of his head.

'Fabulously rich!' Tess tips back in her chair and grins.

'Tess!' Liana cries and slaps her on the shoulder. 'Enough now. Success is more than money. Sorley runs a company and employs many people, he is influential, he travels and opens his mind, he has lovely partner. University is good for all these things.'

'Quite,' I mumble, noticing how Colvin glances at Liana, then at me.

'And your partner's a model, eh?' Tess says it like I've fallen for the oldest trick in the book.

'So beautiful!' Liana cries. 'I looked her up online since our *hermanito* does not send photos. Annabelle Hickson, from Dallas, with Xandra Dean Modelling Agency.'

I wonder what else Liana has discovered digging around online. A quick search of Winglift Capital would be revealing.

'You going to bring her to meet us?' Tess asks.

'I hope so . . .'

'Wonderful!' Liana claps her hands together and Colvin nods to me. He has not met any of the women in my life nor been at either of my weddings. The first was in Sydney and he never knew about the second.

'How long you staying?' Alex asks darkly.

'Oh . . .' I shoot a look at Liana, bustling round the table, and sip my wine, hedging for time.

'As long as London can spare you,' she says, laying a hand on my shoulder. 'You never visit!'

'But you'll have to get back to work,' Alex presses.

'Yes, yes, of course. I'm taking a bit of a break and there's a fair bit I can do remotely—'

'Not here,' Tess cuts in. 'No broadband at the house, dial-up's too slow and mobile reception's shit. You'll have to go into the village.'

'Oh, I wasn't planning to stay *here*.'

'But you must!' Liana protests.

'No, no, I'll need to work, so a hotel is fine.'

'What do you do?' Alex asks.

'Ah . . . I'm in finance.'

'Like?'

'I've done lots of things, Alex.' The use of his name makes him flinch. 'The past fourteen years I've managed my own hedge fund.' I make a big noise about getting up and gathering things off the table. 'Let me do the dishes, Liana – you sit down.'

'No!' she cries, trying to shoo me back to my seat. 'Don't be ridiculous! You're a guest and this is first night.'

'Thought I was family.'

'You are, my *hermanito*, but—'

'What's a hedge fund?' Alex interrupts, as I side-step Liana's flailing hands.

'A stockpile of hedges,' Tess says, dimples appearing in her cheeks. She gets up, dragging her chair back. 'You know, privet, box, laylandei, beech.'

I laugh, a little too loudly, and grab some more dishes.

'Ha. Ha. Ha.' Alex's face is grim.

'Come on, Lex,' she says. 'Have a laugh.'

'I will, when somebody says something funny.'

She huffs and I roll up my sleeves at the sink. 'You're a comedy connoisseur, Alex.'

'Stop it now!' wails Liana, trying to drag me away. 'I won't let you wash up!'

'Well, I won't let *you* do it!' Taking her by the shoulders, I hold her at bay till she gives a little shriek and pokes me in the stomach. I yelp and hop back and she whoops.

'Stop it!' Alex yells. Everyone looks at him. 'Stop it, stop it, stop it!' His hands are clamped over his ears, his eyes screwed tight shut. Then his face buckles, his body starts to shake and a mewling cry rises up.

Liana starts towards him, but Tess raises a hand and shakes her head. Kneeling beside Alex, she speaks quietly, not touching him.

'It's all right, bud. We'll go outside.' He fights his sobby breaths. 'Find some owls.' The whimpering subsides. 'C'mon, Lex. Let's go, huh?'

After a moment of quiet, he jerks out of his chair and with hands still pressed over his ears, stumbles across the kitchen. Tess, quick as a cat, pulls open the door and slips out after him.

There is silence, then Colvin, who has made no sound during the outburst, gets up.

'I'll do the dishes,' he says.

The Hide

Alex was feeling sick again, just as he had that morning at Loch Hope. The sun-room door banged shut as he stumbled into the late summer dusk.

'Wait, Lex!' Tess called. 'Wait!'

When he got to the first tree, he pressed his head against it and dug his fingers into the jagged bark.

'What's up, eh?' she asked softly, coming up beside him.

'I hate him.' He knew Tess thought he was talking about Sorley. The way he turned up with grabbing hands and greedy eyes and made everything feel wrong. But really he meant the other man, the one with her this morning. Grabbing hands and greedy mouth and it made Alex want to howl. He ripped off bits of bark. 'I hate him.'

'He'll be gone soon.' Tess shrugged. 'Back to London in no time, I guarantee it.' Alex slapped the tree. She took a step closer. 'Walk?'

'Yeah.'

Alex was torn up, wanting to take her there, but not tonight. But yes tonight. No. Yes.

'You choose,' she said.

He couldn't. She started humming. That old song from baby days when she had hung over the side of his cot and tried to help him sleep. He listened as she hummed to the end. Then quiet. An owl.

'I'll take you somewhere,' he said at last. 'Secret place. Don't show anybody.'

'Never. I promise.'

It was up in the forest, in the cleft between the two hills where the burn twisted its way down from the moor and formed a pool. There was an old dirt track, and at the far end a pine had fallen across it. Alex led Tess in the gathering dark, showing her the best place to scramble over it and to find a trail through the saplings beyond, warning of stinging nettles and rocks. At last they stepped into a small clearing where the first stars appeared in a deepening sky and they could hear the burn. The Green Bothy loomed at the opposite side of the clearing. Inside was a cavern smelling of wood and earth, of leaves and ash. Alex struck a match and the room leapt to life: furniture, a fireplace, a silver birch rising through the floor.

'Oh my god,' Tess breathed. 'What is this place?'

He didn't answer for a moment, lighting a candle and giving it to her, suddenly unsure of what he'd done. This was not just his secret place, it was the inside of him.

'My hide.'

She gazed around. There was a rough wooden bed, a chair beside a window and a table under the other window with items arranged neatly: notebooks, pens, binoculars, some tins, an old army water bottle. And everywhere around the room were his treasures: tiny birds' nests and feathers, seed pods and strangely twisted twigs, eggshells and the porcelain skulls of small creatures.

'Oh, Lex,' she sighed, resting her hand on the ghostly white trunk of the birch tree. 'It's beautiful.' She shook her head slowly. 'How long you been coming here? When d'you find it?'

'Dunno,' he said. 'Years ago.' He didn't tell her their father had brought him here, way back when Flora the golden eagle had been poisoned and Alex was splintering with distress. Back then, the Green Bothy was so overgrown it was almost impossible to get through the door, but Colvin had said it could be Alex's special place for watching birds and he would fix it for him. They went every weekend and worked together, Colvin patching the tin roof and replacing wood panels, putting glass in the windows and heaving and hammering, while Alex gently moved nests outside before pulling away ivy and seedlings. He begged to keep the silver birch, whose leaves brushed the ceiling, and Colvin had reluctantly agreed, laying floorboards around it. Apart from these brief negotiations, there wasn't much talk because neither of them needed it. Repeatedly, though, Alex made his father promise not to tell anyone else about the hide. Colvin had agreed and watched his son – who had never shown much interest in sheep – gradually retreat deeper and deeper into the forest of birds.

'Come here all the time,' Alex said to Tess. 'Watch everything from the window, or outside. Write it down. Sketch.'

'You smart arse.' She walked to the table and shone her candle over an open notebook covered in his scrawly writing and drawings of birds. Turning back to him with a smile, her eyes held the flicker of the candle flame, and he basked in the warmth.

'I'll light a fire,' he said, piling dried twigs into the grate. As he blew on the flames, Tess lit candles and put them around the room. 'Careful,' he said. He knew it would take only the tiniest spark for the whole place to go up in smoke.

'Sit here.' He took a blanket from the bed and spread it in front of the fire. She settled down, knees tucked under her, hands reaching to the warmth while he hovered, then brought a tin from the table.

It held biscuits and chocolate. 'Help yourself.' He set it down between them, took a handful and started crunching.

'Ah, you're amazing, Lex.' She smiled and shook her head as she picked up a bar of Cadbury's. They were quiet for a moment, eating and listening. Outside the bothy there were soft rustling sounds and a bird call.

'You goin to college?' he asked.

'Oh, I dunno. Probably should. Whaddya think?'

'Don't go.'

'Why not?'

'Should stay home.'

'Stay and do what, Lex?'

'Play music. Play at Mo's.'

'What – for the rest of my life?'

'No. For a while, like. Just till . . . whatever.'

'Yeah, whatever never happens round here, Lex.' She broke off another chunk of chocolate. 'One way or the other, I'm goin. Just don't know where.'

'You can't go.'

'Why not?'

He tossed some twigs into the fire. 'Can't leave me.'

'Aw, Lex, I'm not leavin ya, I'm just growin up. I've gotta leave home and make my way. I'm nearly eighteen – that's how old Mum was when she travelled the world!'

'And ended up here. Saw it all and decided this was the best.'

'She never saw it all!'

'Saw enough. Enough to know this was "the Promised Land". She said it.'

'Doesn't think that any more, Lex.' She offered the chocolate to him.

He shook his head. 'Never leavin, Mum says. Never.'

'Yeah, cause she's married to Dad and he's married to the sheep, so she's stuck. I mean, she loves him and all, yeah, but . . . But, I'm not gonna be stuck, Lex. I've gotta go.'

'Don't want you to go.' He started snapping twigs, over and over, till they were fragments in his tight hands.

'Aw, I know that and I'll miss you, too, but it's the way life is. Be good for us both. Coupla years you can leave school and move on too.'

'Stayin here.'

'But you don't want to be a shepherd.'

'I mean stay with the birds, like.'

'And live with Mum and Dad for the rest of your life? Yeah, right.'

'Nah. I'll live here.' He looked around at his handiwork.

'Lex, you're crazy! You got no electricity, no running water, no bathroom, no nothing. How ya going to live here?!'

'I'll work it out.' A shy glance at her. 'You can live here too.'

A sputtering laugh. 'Now you really are nuts!' She leaned towards him. 'Lex, I got my life ahead of me. I've got to go and do my music and see new places and meet new people—'

'And kiss them!' His voice was a slap.

'What?'

'You're disgustin!'

'What ya talkin about? What's wrong wi you?'

'I saw you! Saw you kissing that guy today! You never seen him before! Why ya kiss him and let him put his filthy hands on you! You're disgustin!' He threw a fistful of twigs into the fire and there was a sudden blaze.

'Down by the loch?' She stared at him. 'Were you there?'

'Yeah! I was watchin the ospreys and you gave them to that strange man!'

'I didn't *give* them, Lex. I just told him about them and they're still there.'

'You gave your hands! Your kisses! You gave him everything!'

'Didn't give him *everything*, Lex, don't be stupid. It was just a cuddle—'

'Kiss, kiss—'

'Okay, and a kiss.'

'He's a stranger. Ya kiss a strange guy you don't know?'

'No. He was at the pub last night and wrote me a really nice note. So we met up this morning and we talked and talked—'

'And kissed!'

'Oh, shut up! That was only after we'd talked a lot first and we really liked each other.'

'Where is he now?'

'He's gone. Had to leave today.'

'For ever?'

She was quiet for a moment, looking into the fire. 'No, Lex,' she said gently. 'He's going back to America for a while, but we are going to write and we are going to see each other again. We . . . we're in love.'

Alex hissed.

Dreams

Liana comes out with me to the car. It is still light on this late summer evening, though much of the valley is clotted with mist. She shoots into the driver's seat, inhaling the smells of leather, wood polish and aftershave, and running her hands over the upholstery.

'Oh, Sorley,' she sighs. 'You must let me have a turn.'

'In your dreams. It's not a tractor, you know.'

'Then will be easy!' She clicks her fingers. Her hands are small as a child's, with painted nails and bright rings. Despite all these years on the farm, she maintains a style that is as rare in these parts as it is impressive. Her raven hair is always glossy, her face made-up, clothes elegant with a folky twist. She must be nearing forty, but could pass for ten years younger, whereas Colvin looks older than his fifty-four years.

'You can have a go another time. Somewhere well away from farm tracks.'

'You so silly bringing this thing all the way up here, *hermanito*.' She climbs out again. 'Don't you remember anything?'

'Oh, I do.'

She searches my face. I never know how much Colvin has told her about our childhood.

'Thank you for coming, Sorley,' she says, and takes my hands. 'We need you here. Goodnight. Sleep well.' She kisses my cheek and I know I will not sleep well. Probably not at all.

The car purrs to life and bumps back down the track to the first gate. I swear and thump the wheel and fight my way through each one, eventually pulling out onto the road that runs through Briachan. Down by the loch, the Ferryman Inn has a sign saying 'Vacancies'. It looks like it's been done up since we went for a drink there the night before

Colvin's wedding, and I wonder if it's cheaper than the Hydro in Aviemore. I can't afford any hotel at the moment but can't let on. There are still a few accounts that haven't been sucked down into the vortex of my debt, but they will all go that way soon. The light from the windows spills across the verandah and the woodpile beyond, where a couple of mountain bikes are stacked. Pushing open the door, I feel a wave of warmth, laden with the smells of open fire and fresh chips. There is music and the place gleams with polished wood and copper. I turn to the bar and am turned to stone. Leaning against it, staring at me, is Mo.

Reunion

It was him. My knees went to water, heart leaping up like a beast in a cage. Sorley, Sorley, Sorley . . . What was he doing here? He stopped dead. Certainly wasn't expecting to see me. Not in the Ferryman, of all places. Certainly not behind the bar.

He still had those raffish good looks, the fine bones and dimpled cheeks. No grey in the straw-blond hair, cut short, and no sign of the tiny perfect curl that used to appear behind his left ear. I used to trace it with my finger, on that baby-soft scented skin where I buried my nose and breathed heaven.

Seeing me, his face went white and he half turned to go, but folks had noticed him. The women having their Mums and Tots committee meeting at the corner table, the Speyside Way walkers by the fire, old Dougie MacPherson at the end of the bar. He looked at Sorley over the brim of his glass.

I murmured, 'Of all the gin joints, in all the towns, in all the world.'

Sorley scowled. I make jokes out of the most painful things; it is one of my worst habits.

He walked to the bar slowly. We both glanced at Dougie, who sipped the last of his whisky, set the glass deliberately on the counter and extended a hand to Sorley. It was knobbled and stiff with arthritis.

'Nice to see you, son,' he said, his voice brimming. 'D'ye remember me? Dougie MacPherson — Fachie's dad?'

'Yeah, I do remember!' Sorley's face was lit by a smile.

'Ach, it's so good to see you home!' Dougie beamed, pumping his hand. 'You look *so* like your—' Perhaps he saw the cloud fall over Sorley's face. 'You look so *well*, son, so well. What brings you?'

'Ah . . . just a visit, Mr Mac. Been too long.'

'That it has, my laddie, much too long. But you must call me Dougie now, just Dougie.'

They talked for a few minutes, Dougie's face a beacon, his hand often reaching out again to pat Sorley on the arm, his head shaking in soft delight. At last, he turned back to me.

'Thank you kindly, Mo,' he said, tapping the empty glass. 'Now, I really must move afore the joints rust up altogether.' And, chuckling, he eased himself off the stool, breath laboured. Taking his stick, he hobbled across to the far wall where he paused at the black-and-white photos of old shinty teams, sheep-clipping days and grouse shoots. From the back of his tweed cap, tufts of snow white hair rolled out like bog cotton.

'Can I get you something?' I said to Sorley, only meeting his eyes for a moment. 'On the house.'

'You work here?'

'I own it.'

He stared at me. One of the walkers came up and asked for another Sheepshaggers Gold and a Strathisla. I busied myself with that, humming as I always do when I'm nervous, feeling Sorley standing there like a pillar of smoke.

The walkers settled into their drinks, the mums started gathering up their notes and bags, and Dougie moved towards the coat rack.

'Beer?' I offered, pointing to the pumps. 'Nice range from Cairngorm Brewery. Or a dram?' I ran my hand along the whiskies. 'Wine?'

Turning back, I dared a glance, but his eyes were fierce. 'No, I think I'll pass.'

I looked at my hands, so big and bony and awkward.

'Bye, Mo!' the mums cried, in their sweet voices, their happy motherly, tired motherly, so bloody-damn-lucky motherly voices.

'Bye, my lovelies!' I cried and waved them off.

Silence. Sorley did not sit down.

'Something soft?' I asked, touching the fizzy drink taps. 'I've got Scotland's finest range of—'

'No, no. I think I'll just . . . head on.'

I felt panic. He was walking away.

'Wait! Are you here for long? Staying at Shepherd's Cottage? What—?'

He half turned and looked at me, as if across a chasm of a thousand years. 'I don't know,' he said. And left.

Only the walkers remained, running slow fingers over a creased map.

Broken Night

Leaving the Ferryman I drive into Aviemore to the Hydro, a sprawling complex with a leisure suite, cinema and several restaurants. At reception, a woman with garish make-up and an Eastern European accent books me in, taking the deposit from my American Express card. This time I take a standard room with a view over the back entrance and the bins. I drop my bags and head down to the bar – an uninspiring space with tartan carpet, potted palms and polished brass – and order a whisky. The Talisker is smoky and biting, and I drink slowly, scrolling through the messages on my phone: the liquidator has taken over the company email account, but the personal ones are flooding in. Mainly cries of shock and sympathy, although some are abusive. Many of my so-called friends were clients; lines had been blurred, lies told. I type an Out of Office message on my personal email account: *Sorley Munro has fucked off with your fortune and can't be found.* A bitter laugh, then change it to: *I'm offline this week but will reply soon.* Then think, *no I won't*, and start deactivating my account. Then pause again. I can't burn all my bridges; I might need these people again. Running my hand through my hair, I scratch my nails into my scalp. I just need time, need to think. Finally I type: *Thank you for your message. I am taking a short break but will get back to you as soon as possible.* I wish I could just burn every fucking bridge and run away for ever.

Eventually, in a boozy daze, I go upstairs and fall into a heavy sleep. I wake at some dead hour and lie in the dark, listening to the quiet. It is empty. In my London flat there are always sounds: vehicles, late-night revellers, boats bumping against jetties. Not always loud, but always something, always humanity stumbling on through the dark. Here, the quiet is unnerving, expectant, as though something out there – someone – is listening.

I think of Liana and her mouth against my cheek, of Colvin, wind-beaten and sad.

The night before their wedding, he met me off the train. I was a best man who hadn't seen the groom for five years and knew nothing of the bride save a sketchy and unlikely story that she was Bolivian, passing through on world travels and decided to stay. I had pictured a stocky woman, toothy, divorced, with a bowler hat and a mule. It was raining that May evening, but Liana had wanted the wedding outside, by the loch, so we had to troop down in our waterproofs and wellies for the rehearsal. She met us there, face hidden inside the hood of her bright red jacket, and when Colvin introduced us she threw her arms around me, called me *Hermanito Sorley!* and kissed me on both cheeks. Her smell was musky and mysterious, her lips electric on my cold skin, and when she drew back, I saw her face properly for the first time, pale and luminous, with large shining black eyes and a full mouth. She was tiny and the most vivid creature I'd ever seen.

And then I saw Mo.

I couldn't sleep that night and spent the day of the wedding in a blur. All I can remember is the three of them. Liana – this vision in a lace dress with a gardenia in her hair – holding the arm of my brother – a cloddish giant in his kilt with a look of dazed wonder on his face.

And Mo.

How could it be? My disappeared cousin-sister-mother. Now back again, a minister! Man-like in face and figure, recognisable by the cleft lip and the big hands, yet trembling when she joined theirs and when she looked at me. I tried not to look at her. I kept looking at Liana. Over and over again, a moth to flame.

Gathering

I stay at the Hydro for a couple of weeks, pretending to everyone that I'm running the hedge fund from afar, while in secret I trawl obsessively through the financial news and insider gossip trying to see a foothold for me. But I am a man thrown overboard. There are days when all the letters and numbers on my screen blur and I sit paralysed, suffering an internal short-circuit.

Every day I run the roads around Aviemore, and every few days I head up to Shepherd's Cottage, taking a bottle of pretentious wine or artful flowers I can't afford. I will not be reduced to cheap and nasty. Especially around Liana. She always greets me and my gifts with delight, always kisses both cheeks, always calls me *hermanito* – little brother. I search those dark eyes and wonder if her hand has rested on me a moment too long. She stirs things in me that linger through my day and long into night, but I never know if she means to.

On a mid-September day as I drive back to the farm, the world seems to be standing still. A mist fills the valley floor, shrouding the lochs and lying in drifts across the lower slopes of the hills, the sky pale and quiet. Everything is waiting.

At Shepherd's Cottage, I clamber into the Land Rover with Colvin and Liana and the dogs as we take the dirt track into the hills. She is absurdly stylish in a colourful jumper with her hair swishing around her hoop earrings and Cleopatra eye-liner. Her one concession to the conditions is a pair of sturdy knee-high boots. Colvin is in his usual saggy, faded greens, a life-long camouflage that makes him smudge into the landscape and the work, like there is no boundary. I'm in expensive kit, all breathable, waterproof and wicking, designed to withstand the environment, not surrender to it.

Bumping and heaving over the rough road makes me queasy and I wind down my window. The breeze is tainted by exhaust and I hold my nose and gulp through my mouth. Liana glances back and I can only guess at the ridiculous figure I cut: city boy in his pricey gear but with no stomach for the task.

'You okay, *hermanito*?' she asks. 'We need to stop?'

'No, no,' I say and wind up the window. 'I'm fine.' I smile and give a thumbs up.

'So good you help us,' she says and turns her smile to Colvin, whose face I can't see.

At the end of the track we pile out and a river of dogs pours from the back, sniffing and snaking around us. I have a backpack with my jacket, hat, gloves, water bottle and energy bar, and I've tucked a silver hip flask into my pocket, pretending it's just for sociability on the hill, though I know Colvin won't have any. He and Liana carry only crooks, binoculars and walkie-talkies. They've loaned me a stick for the day which I recognise as my father's. Colvin has inherited one from our grandfather, Donald.

'You go with Colvin,' Liana says. 'I head this way.' She waves towards a ridge curving off to the west.

'I can give you a hand,' I say.

'Oh no, I'm quite happy! You brothers talk.' It is an order, like her command to three of the dogs, who go straight to her heels. She kisses Colvin full on the mouth and sets off, her step light and confident, the dogs weaving through the heather in her wake. Colvin slams the Land Rover doors shut, gives a short whistle to his dogs, and with the barest nod to me, starts on a trail in the opposite direction.

He is fast, pushing up the steep slope at a strong clip, and I feel like little more than one of the dogs, only less useful. At least my running fitness means I can keep up, though my ankles twist as we contour the slope and I lose my balance on the grassy tussocks. Been a long time since I helped with a gathering. Colvin doesn't pause till we crest the ridge, and even there he says nothing to me, simply lifts his binoculars. I tug on my jacket against the breeze and take in the view. To the north and west there is nothing but humpy, treeless hills, while to the south and east, the valley is a patchwork of forest and field, scattered with houses and threaded together by road and river. From here I can see

Rowancraig House rising from her shelter of pines like a fairy-tale castle with her turrets and tall windows and the walled garden. The forest above the house stops at the deer fences, and above that is just scrubby moor.

'The estate's up for sale, I hear.' I don't mention it was Liana who told me.

'Aye.'

'No interest yet?'

'No much.' He lowers the binoculars and gestures into the distance. A whistle to the dogs and he's off again, me trailing behind. 'Away!' Colvin orders and two dogs shoot off in a wide arc to the right, while he sends a third down the slope to stop stray sheep disappearing into a gully. Once the sheep are trotting in the right direction, Colvin calls the dogs back to find the next group. As we head across the level ground at the top of the ridge I can finally walk beside him.

'Know why he's selling?'

Colvin shrugs. 'Financial crisis, maybe.'

'I imagine he lost out. Like everyone.' Nervous laugh. Colvin doesn't look at me but whistles and shouts again. 'Come by!' It's the only time there is harshness in his voice. 'Get back!' The dogs move further out, swift and responsive. Warm from the walking and the sun, I pull off my jacket and shove it in my bag, trying not to fall behind.

'What about the shooting guests?' I ask.

'None. For about three years.'

'God – why's that?'

'Bad management. Got that land agent from London, supposed to make it more profitable. But look what's happened.' I glance at him. 'Run into the ground.'

'Shame. Not good for local jobs.'

'Didn't employ many folk, anyways. Nobody working there now.'

The dogs have sent another line of sheep off down the track and Colvin pauses to look through his binoculars again. We cross a burn, him leaping easily from stone to stone and me teetering, cursing my road-runner legs. After leaving Scotland I never went back to hill running – felt too much like trudging after sheep. Colvin's walkie-talkie crackles and he speaks with Liana, looking across to a far ridge, though I can see nothing but the lines of white dots joining the exodus down the hill.

'She doing okay?' I ask.

'Aye.' We walk on, startling a grouse that launches into the sky with an angry gurgle and beating wings. Apart from that moment, nothing happens and – as far as I can see – the land is empty.

The next time we pause, I unscrew the top of the flask and offer it to him. He shakes his head and looks away. 'Where are things with the court case?' I ask, taking a sip. Liana had told me about the long-running battle with Lord Mackintosh.

'Stalled.'

'God, that's been . . . what . . . ?'

'Six years.' He starts walking again and I scrabble for another slurp before capping the flask and catching up.

'Where's it at now?'

'Lawyers pushing papers round, arguing the difference between Scots law and European law.'

'Ah yes. European law trumps everything, doesn't it?'

'Seemingly.'

We crest a peat hag and meet a strong breeze from the south.

'So . . . think you'll lose the case?'

'Probably. Then lawyers push more paper around, argue about compensation and all.'

'Will you get something back at the end of the day?'

'Doubt it.' He growls at one of the dogs, who slinks back to him.

'What if there's an offer on the estate while this is still dragging on?'

He shrugs. 'New owner inherits the problem.'

'Well that'll put people off, won't it?'

'Aye. But a family come a couple weeks ago, apparently, and viewed the house. Auntie Beulah was there. Foreigners, she said. India, I think. Or was it Malaysia?'

'God, this'll be a change for them. Old Beulah still going strong, then?'

'No really. Arthritis, angina, gammy hip, losing her marbles.'

'Never had many.'

He laughs. 'Too right. Just ask Mo.'

There it was. The name that kept cropping up at Shepherd's Cottage, the person I could no longer avoid.

'So she owns the Ferryman these days?' I try to sound casual, like I don't really care.

'Aye.'

'Thought she was a minister.'

'Was. Just runs the pub now.'

'God.'

'She's teetotal, like.'

'Really? So too good to touch the stuff herself but sells it to all the poor bastards in the village? Nice one, Rev.'

Colvin looks at me for the first time in the conversation. 'No,' he says, eyes squinting in the light. 'That's not Mo.'

Shepherd's Cottage

The night of the gathering we eat well. Liana's venison casserole, slow-cooked through the day, is now a rich brew. I have a couple of beers before the meal and red wine during it, and though Colvin sticks to orange juice, Liana and I finish the bottle between us. Tess has just departed for the Royal Conservatoire in Glasgow leaving Alex in a pit of gloom. He never said much in company anyway, but he hardly speaks at all now, at least around me. After dinner I have a dram by the fire and nod off.

I wake to Liana beside me on the couch, stroking my cheek.

'Hey, hey, *hermanito*,' she says, smiling. I want to kiss that finger, pull her in close and nuzzle my face in her neck. I am drunk. Before I do any such stupid thing, I clock Colvin sitting in the chair opposite, looking at me.

'Need to stay the night,' he says. 'Can't drive like that.'

'Oh, I've driven a lot worse,' I mumble.

'Not on my property.' He half laughs. 'With all my sheep off the hill.'

'Fair enough. I'll just stretch out on the sofa, then. No fuss.'

'Don't be daft,' Liana says. 'We have spare room. Come on – I take you.' And she jumps up and tugs on my hand. I heave myself off the sofa to follow.

The spare room, as it happens, was my old room, but now it's completely unrecognisable, covered in her wild artwork. A border of clouds run at head height around the blue walls, while stars, planets and a crescent moon dot the ceiling. Above the bed, a giant sun blazes, all sharp angles and strange features like an Inca idol.

'My god,' I murmur.

'Oh, all that from a long time ago,' she says, with a dismissive wave. 'Must paint over but no time!'

The artwork is scuffed and marked with childish scribbles appearing like alien invaders. There's a curling moustache in purple crayon on the sun.

'Family project,' I say, tapping it.

'Yeah, and I kill them for it.'

'They've recovered well.'

'Any kid of Liana needs nine lives. Minimum!'

She moves to a table where there is a sewing machine with fabric still caught under the foot. More material is heaped over the bed and a table against the wall is spread with marked-up fabric, measuring tape, scissors and spools of cotton. An ancient ironing board fills the only remaining space, a heavy iron propped at one end.

'Sorry, sorry, I'm making curtains,' she says, gathering up an armful of fabric from the bed. 'For sale.'

'No need for this, Liana,' I slur. 'I'll sleep on the sofa.'

'No, no! You are *hermanito*, Sorley. You get your bed!' She steps back into the hall and dumps the curtain pieces over the banister. 'I can't put you in Tessy's room because is a bigger mess than this.'

Follow her unsteadily. 'My fault. Drank too much.'

She puts a polished finger on my lips. 'It makes you stay. Is good.' Then pushes past me back into the room and pulls the cover off the bed, spilling threads, pins and scraps of fabric onto the floor. 'Be careful! Sharp everywhere – sorry.'

Press my finger against her lips.

'Stop saying sorry or I WILL go. *Comprende?*' I make a face of exaggerated glowering and she giggles.

'Okay, okay. I try. So much goes wrong all the time I just . . .' She fingers the air then shrugs and lays the bedcover over the machine. 'Sheets!' Opening the doors of a hulking wardrobe in the corner, she runs her fingers down a stack of linen.

'I'll make up the bed.' I open my arms to her.

'Bottom one, I think.' She tosses it to me, but when I flick it open, the middle is torn.

Liana gasps. 'Oh no! Sorry.'

My finger on her lips again. They are so full and soft. 'No sorry! It's fine.'

'It's terrible.' She bundles it up and shoves it behind the sewing machine, but the next sheet is speckled with mould and she yanks it off the bed as well, hissing.

'I don't care!' I flop on the bed. 'Grew up here, remember? Feel right at home.' Actually, I'd always hated the stained, tatty sheets, the hand-me-down clothes, the chipped crockery. It had all fuelled my determination to leave and get rich, and when I did, I'd spent filthy money on fine linen and china, designer clothes and decoration.

'I care!' she says, tugging more sheets out of the cupboard. 'What if Annabelle comes to visit?'

'Don't worry, she won't.'

'You must persuade her! We want to meet this lovely lady—'

'She's gone.'

'What?' Liana looks at me over a Cinderella duvet cover. 'Where?'

'Dunno. With someone else. I mean . . . like . . . it's over.'

'Oh, Sorley!' She takes a step towards me, reaching out.

'No, no, it's fine. Really, I'm fine . . .' I ramble on with fictions about our increasingly separate lives and amicable agreement to part ways. And ongoing friendship, of course.

Liana, sitting beside me and spearing me with her dark eyes, finally rubs my arm and says, 'Okay. One day you get your princess, Sorley.' She gets up to whip out sheet after sheet till she finds some without stains or rips. The end result is a combo of striped flannelette bottom, floral pillowcase and a Superman duvet cover.

'Alex.' She smooths it down.

'He doesn't like me,' I mumble.

'Is not you. He doesn't like . . . He just . . . different.' She looks out the window into the darkness. 'He loves Tess the most but now she's gone and he . . . he is getting worse.'

'You worried?'

She looks me straight in the eye. 'I'm always worried, Sorley. Every day I fear for my precious ones. But every day I get up and keep going. I work to the bone for them! I work and work and work, because . . . what else can I do?' She gathers up the bundle of rejected sheets and strides out the room. 'Wait for Superman?'

Happy

The night after Sorley stayed at Shepherd's Cottage, Liana came down to the Ferryman for a shift. Like a lot of folk up here she was always cobbling together work from as many sources as possible, depending on the tourist season and the demands of the farm.

'He so funny,' she said, hanging glasses in the rack above the bar. 'He comes to help with the sheep, but he looks . . . like a model, you know?'

'So do you,' I teased.

'Model for a gypsy circus only! He is like an advertisement for the most expensive sports clothes in the world, all new and no mud.'

'Well, you don't want to get that outdoor kit dirty.' I kept up a jokey tone. Liana knew the skeleton of my story but not the meat and blood, not the ferocity of love and heartbreak.

'Oh, he's dirty now, ha, ha! Baptised with sheep dip today!' She grinned triumphantly. Not, I suspected, a believer's baptism. Sorley had hated the farm; I knew that from Colvin and from the way he'd steered clear of it all these years. His return was strange. Stranger still was all this mucking in, relearning all the jobs he'd rejected. The story he told was that his doctor had ordered a break; he hadn't had a proper holiday in years and his staff were up for running the show without him. He could check in now and then remotely, but really, he just needed some time back home to recharge. Ah, the smell of fresh Highland air! The music of sheep!

None of this codswallop was offered to me, mind. He had not darkened the door of the Ferryman again, and if we crossed paths, he just nodded, said 'Mo' and melted away. I wanted to invite him for a meal or a walk, just some time alone together, but the fear of refusal defeated me.

Liana rabbited on, laughing and shaking her head at *hermanito* Sorley's sweet crazy ways. I hadn't seen her so animated since the arrival of each of her babies and it made me realise how the years of struggle had subdued her – the gnawing of debt, the shadow of Colvin's silences, the worry about one child going out into the world and the other retreating from it – how it had all seeped into her like ground water and quenched her spirit. Till Sorley, and something was ignited again.

'He so generous,' she exclaimed, wiping the bar and enumerating his extravagant presents. I knew his giving in the past had been erratic and largely misjudged. To Tess he'd sent an Edwardian doll's house when she was far too old, to Alex an electronic race track when he disliked cars, to Colvin a fancy watch he never used and to Liana designer handbags that didn't go with anything. So she just sold all his presents on ebay. The problem had always been what to send him and Colvin had always said: just a card. Anything else would be useless to Sorley and make fools of them. So Liana had complied but included photos of the children and small fragments of home: pine needles, lichen, a piece of antler, some sheep's wool.

'Because he must be missing home, no?' The Ferryman was empty by then apart from the two of us leaning against the bar. 'But at last he comes and I am so happy. Colvin is happy. *He* is happy.' She drains her wine and thumps the glass down. 'Everyone is happy.'

Lunch

I take Liana to Pierre's for lunch. She tells me she hasn't had a meal out in years; they can never afford it. I don't tell her I used to eat out every day in London, often twice, but right now I can't afford it either. I just pretend. Like I pretend I am only selling my Porsche because I fancy a 4x4 as my country wheels, not because I am scrabbling for cash. Like I pretend I moved into Shepherd's Cottage so I could be of more help to them, not because my American Express card is maxed out. Like I pretend my 'holiday' is over but working remotely is so easy I can maintain it indefinitely.

I drive into the library for a few hours every day for supposed work on the internet and disappear to distant bothies and backpackers' hostels on purported trips to London. No one questions me, no one digs around to check facts, no one suspects.

So I offer to drive Liana to Inverness for the day as Colvin needs the Land Rover and their old Skoda is broken down. She needs shoes and sewing stuff, and I told her last night, after Colvin went to bed, to wear a nice dress as we'd eat out.

Her face lit up and she clapped her hands. 'Oh, *hermanito*! You are too good!'

In the morning I go on my daily run, gradually returning to the trails I followed as a kid, then shower and shave carefully, being sparing with my French foam and fragrance as I cannot replace them. I choose a Louis Vuitton shirt, navy trousers and linen jacket and curse the lack of a full-length mirror in my room. Then I worry the look is too conspicuously dressy and change to jeans and a leather jacket. Then I remember Pierre's won't let me in with jeans, so change back to the trousers. I'm worse than a teenage girl.

Coming downstairs, I can hear Liana's rapid-fire voice in the kitchen. She is swamped in a zebra-print apron, emptying the dishwasher with much clattering and bashing, while Alex is hunched at the table, stone-faced.

'We can't do this again, *papito*, we cannot. We can't go back to all this meetings at the school and trying the tutors and the home-schooling and all. Please God, not the home-schooling! It nearly killed us.'

'You nearly killed me.'

'Yes, yes! And next time I will! And then I'll kill myself.'

'This sounds cheerful,' I say, taking a bowl to the porridge pot on the stove.

'You talk to him!' she cries, pointing an accusing finger at Alex. 'He says is not going to school again.'

His eyes slide up to me, hooded like a snake's. We both know my chances of persuading him to go to school are about as good as my chances of succeeding the Queen, so I merely raise my brows at him and say, 'Oh dear.'

When it is finally clear that Alex is, in no uncertain terms, NOT GOING to school, Liana pulls off her apron in disgust and throws it over a chair. She is wearing a red jersey dress that hugs her curves and brings out the colour of her lips. It reveals strong calves and fine ankles, her tiny feet strapped into black heels. It is the first time I've seen her in a dress since I got here.

'What you going to do all day, then?' she demands, standing with her hands on her hips.

'Dunno,' he shrugs. 'What you doing?'

'Going to Inverness to do the shopping.'

'What's he doing?' Alex doesn't even look at me.

'He's driving.'

'And carrying the bags, no doubt,' I put in, trying to sound jolly and helpful. Alex's eyes move from his mother in her red dress to me in my leather jacket and back again. You can sense him smelling my aftershave, her perfume.

'You wanna come?' I offer, trying to sound easy-going and welcoming, inwardly assuring myself it is the last thing he'll want to do.

Liana laughs. 'Alex hates cities. Doesn't even like our little town of

Aviemore much, do you, *bebe*? And he hates shopping, so I bet you won't come, huh?'

Alex looks at her steadily and back at me. 'Yeah, I'll come.'

My heart plummets.

'Oh!' Liana looks pleasantly surprised.

'Excellent,' I manage.

Of course, Alex claims car sickness, so has to sit in the front beside me, a plastic bag held open between his knees.

'Soon as you feel queasy just let me know,' I say, 'and I'll pull straight over.'

'I'll try, but sometimes it just happens.' He looks at me, taunting.

'Oh, it's terrible!' says Liana from the back seat. 'One time we're all going to a wedding and we put Auntie Beulah in the front and Alex in the back between me and Tess, and just before we got to church he is sick. All over both of us. How he managed to go both ways, I don't know, but Colvin had to drop Auntie and take us all home to change and we missed the service. But, oh, the Landy! Should have seen it. Stank to the heavens and the dogs were licking up bits for weeks.'

I shoot a look at Alex; I swear he smirks.

'Well, I've got someone giving this baby a test drive tomorrow,' I say, patting the dash, 'so make sure you speak up.'

'Guess what, Alex,' Liana says, at the end of a morning blighted by him whinging about everything and harassing her to hurry up. 'Sorley is taking us to Pierre's for lunch!' She is almost skipping. 'So generous.'

So foolish. There is only so long I can push into the overdraft on my credit cards.

'What's Pierre's?'

'Oh, is fanciest restaurant in Inverness! Very famous. Has a French chef and a view over the river. I don't know anybody that's been there and now we are going. Can't wait to tell Colvin and Mo! We must take pictures! Send them to Tess!'

'Just wanna burger,' Alex says.

'Well, we could do that instead, if you like,' I venture. 'Go to McDonald's and I'll take you to Pierre's another time, Liana?' Alex's eyes narrow. 'Some time that Colvin can come.'

'No, no!' she laughs. 'Colvin doesn't eat out, he won't come. We must go today. Eat, drink and be merry, for tomorrow we die!' She clicks her fingers in the air as if they are castanets and looks every bit the flamenco dancer with her jet-black hair and red dress, clinging at breast and buttocks, flaring at the knees. Images fill my head. 'Anyway,' she goes on, 'I'm sure they'll do burgers.'

'Probably not,' I say, 'and they may not let us in with Alex's . . . casual clothes.' He's in a shapeless sweatshirt, camouflage trousers and muddy trainers.

'You will persuade them!' she says. 'Our Superman!' And she pokes me in the ribs and laughs, like a child at the fair.

At Pierre's, a young waitress with hair glued into a high doughnut meets us with a plastic smile. Under her false lashes, her eyes flicker over Liana, then me and then Alex. The smile fades.

'Just one moment, please,' she says, and minces away.

A man in a suit appears, face a picture of professional concern. 'I'm so sorry,' he murmurs to me, 'but I'm afraid we have a dress code and trainers aren't allowed.'

'Of course,' I begin, relieved, but Liana tugs on my arm. Her eyes are expectant. Alex is staring at the floor.

'I do understand,' I continue, 'and this young man wasn't going to be with us, initially, but he—'

'Got burgers?' Alex interjects.

'I beg your pardon, sir? Do we serve burgers?' the manager asks.

Alex rams his hands in his pockets. 'What I said.'

'No, I'm afraid we don't.'

'Going then.' Alex is back out the door before Liana can grab him. '*Bebe!*' she chases him out as I apologise and follow.

Alex refuses to go into MacDonald's – too crowded and crushed with *people* – so I end up queuing and buying for the three of us as Liana stays with him outside in a park, watching the seagulls. She sits between us on the bench, keeping up a cheerful monologue with no sound from Alex and only the most clipped responses from me. I gulp a bottle of cornershop beer and think bitterly of the French wine at Pierre's. At least this torture hasn't cost me a fortune.

Driving home, I can't bear conversation and turn on the music, letting Scandinavian death metal fill the car.

'Don't like it,' Alex moans, hunched over his plastic bag, but I pretend I can't hear him and push down hard on the accelerator. In the rear-view mirror, I catch Liana's eyes, dark and unreadable. She reaches through and pats my arm. I hate the damn A9 with its miles of single lanes and twists and turns where you can't overtake, with its lumbering lorries and caravans, puttering old folks and gawping tourists. I keep pulling out and overtaking, hopping up the lines of traffic and burning the road when it's clear.

Alex says something I don't catch but I assume it's just another protest about the music.

'What you say?' Liana asks from the back.

As he turns towards her, there is a sudden heaving from him and an eruption of vomit. Right over me. In the wet explosion I nearly crash the car, lurching to the side, brakes screaming, horns blaring from the oncoming vehicles. Liana shrieks, Alex keeps vomiting and I shout as I jerk the car over to the verge and pull up so hard we are all thrown forward. I lunge out of the car, cursing, and run to the verge, ripping off my shirt. Liana shoots from the back, pulls open Alex's door and helps him out. He is retching and sobbing, bits of sick dripping out of his nose.

'Why didn't you fucking well say anything?!' I spit, shaking out my shirt.

'I did,' he says, still retching. 'You didn't listen . . . your FUCKING music.'

We drive home in silence, slowly, the windows open. The half-digested compost of Alex's lunch is all over the car: on the gearstick, the steering wheel, the dashboard, the seats, the carpet. Even the rear-view mirror got some. I glance back at Liana, who is staring out the window. Beside me, Alex is curled against the door, knees pulled up, head down.

When we get home, he bolts from the car and starts running.

'Go take a shower!' Liana calls, climbing out, but he doesn't reply and disappears around the side of the house. I get out and stand by the car, shirtless. She lets out a long, breathy sigh like a punctured tyre and shakes her head.

'Be gone for hours now. Sometimes Tess found him and brought him home, sometimes Colvin. I never . . .' She trails off and looks around her. The Land Rover is still gone. As her gaze moves back to the Porsche she winces. 'I am so sorry Sorley. This is terrible. I should not let him come but he won't go to school and is missing Tess so much and I thought for once he . . .' Her lips tremble, eyes suddenly wet. 'For once he . . . wanted to come with me.' And her face crumples, her hands flying up to hide it.

'Oh, Liana,' I say, coming around the car. 'Don't worry. It'll clean up, doesn't matter.' Without hesitation I take her in my arms, and she folds into me, letting herself cry. I hold her against my bare chest, one arm around her back, the other hand stroking her head. She is struggling to speak.

'No, no,' I murmur, my lips in her hair. 'My fault. I was driving too fast and didn't hear him. Music was too loud. My *fucking* music.'

There is a choke of laughter and I squeeze her and keep stroking, inflamed.

'Is not just the car,' she says at last, drawing back, sniffing and wiping away the mascara. I want to offer my hanky, but it's covered in vomit. 'Is . . . everything.' And she is crying again and I pull her back.

'I know, I know,' I say. 'I know.'

I don't. What do I know about everything that burdens Liana's life? 'Listen,' I say at last, when her crying softens. 'Let's go inside and change, and I'll get you a cup of tea. Then I'll tackle this beast.' I tap the car.

'No, no!' she wails. 'I will do it. My son made the mess!'

'Well, we can work on it later. You can't clean it in your best dress and I need to salvage what I can of my best trews.' She laughs a little as I steer her back to the house.

'Not my best dress, Sorley.'

'No? Well, you look stunning. I'd like to see you in your best dress, someday. That would be a sight for sore eyes.'

'Oh, *hermanito*,' she murmurs, smiling and shaking her head. 'Your eyes have seen many a fancy London lady, I know that. In best dress and without.'

I push hard on the stubborn sun-room door.

'And none of them a patch on you.' I usher her in with a grand sweep. 'In best dress, or without.'

She stops and looks up into my face, her eyes like polished stones in a river. 'You haven't seen me without,' she whispers.

My voice comes so low it is barely there. 'Then show me.'

Her face blanches and there's a sharp intake of breath. I take a step closer, everything on fire. There is the rumble of a vehicle coming up the track and we spring apart, her darting inside. I stand at the door, leaning casually against it and watching Colvin clamber out of his Land Rover. He's been at the sheep sale in Dingwall and his face is grim.

The Thief

The days pass. We move about the farm talking and working and eating as if nothing has changed. I search her face but she does not look me in the eye. We both know Colvin is travelling soon to a sheep sale in Yorkshire to buy Swaledale tups and that Alex, who is still refusing school, is going with him. Not out of any interest in the sheep but for a chance to see new birds and to get away from me, whom he now openly despises. Liana and I assure Colvin we will take care of everything and wave them off. At first she pretends I am not there; she is casual and off-hand. I am so stretched with yearning I could snap. When her eyes flicker to me, they move quickly away.

That first evening I get out a bottle of wine and fill two glasses at the kitchen table.

'Tell me,' I say. 'Tell me . . . everything.'

And she does, as I question and coax and top up her glass. She talks and talks: the Night of the Long Knives, the long-dragging court case, the plague of debt, Colvin's dark times and refusal to see a doctor, Alex's problems, Tess's independence, her own anxiety that swings her between wild hope and the grip of fear. And I ply her with more wine and she opens herself and lets tears fall and lets me take her in my arms again. Her head rests on me, my chin nestling in her hair. In a breathing sigh, my hands stroke and slide, slipping under her jumper and up her back, as her small hands roam across my shoulders and spine. Then I kiss her hair and she lifts her wet face and I kiss her forehead and down her hairline to her ear, where my tongue flicks softly and my teeth tug on her lobe and she shudders against me. Our lips trace across cheeks, hers damp and soft, mine stubbled, till lips meet and we are kissing full on the mouth, wildly, tasting wine and longing, hands groping across buttocks. We grapple with my belt buckle and jeans and tug off my shirt, shoes and socks.

'Let me,' I rasp, as she starts pulling at her own clothes. And then we go slow, so I can undo each button and catch and zip, kissing each new stretch of skin, till there is nothing but her underwear. It is not sexy and not matching. She has not planned this.

Too bad. Too late.

I peel away all that holds her back and steal my brother's wife.

The Flood

That night it rained. For the next three days and three nights it rained. With barely a pause for breath or a parting of cloud or a straggle of sun, it rained. In a tempest of wind and water, rain pelted the cairns on the mountaintops, battered the rocky cliffs and poured down on the barren hills; and because there were no trees to catch and slow the rain in their canopies, the soil was quickly drenched and overflowing; so the slopes ran with water that ribboned into small burns that became rushing currents that turned into roaring tributaries that swept like armies into the great river; and the Spey, like a mythic serpent awoken, swelled and sped and spilled her banks till she was no longer a river, but a seething lake across the valley floor.

And the rain came so quick and so hard that farmers and shepherds struggled to get to their beasts on time. Cattle stood stranded on diminishing islands, horses leapt fences of drowning fields, sheep were swept away till they snagged in trees or were pulled under. Little boats and rafts motored into the angry waters to rescue the animals. On the roof of Rowancraig House, slates were yanked away and rain fell into the attic and down through the floors. At the Green Bothy, a family of mice huddled under the boards as the forest shook and the burn fumed. On Small Isle, the osprey nest was blown off its perch. Everywhere, the water covered roads, churned across railway platforms, bumped cars away; it caught branches and litter in its brown swill and washed them across the land; it streamed into the school hall, oozed past sand bags, lapped against kitchen cupboards. The firmament that separated the waters above from the waters below was rent and the waters fell and the waters rose, and for three days and for three nights a great flood covered the face of the deep.

In Swaledale, where Colvin was inspecting new tups (and wondering if he and Alex should be talking about anything) he watched the weather news with growing alarm. He phoned Liana that first morning to get the sheep off the lochside fields, but got no answer. Each time he phoned there was nothing, and no answer from Sorley either. Finally he phoned me.

I went in search and found them in the rain. Liana and Sorley had taken the dogs out first thing and got most of the flock to higher ground. But not all. Two lambs had been swept away and one ewe. She was a strong, motherly, milky ewe who had borne healthy twins for three years and strutted round the farm with her curly horns in the air. She had two years of good lambing still to come and she was, of course, Colvin's favourite.

Liana wept.

Perhaps, deep down, I knew what had happened. But I could not bear that knowledge or what it might demand of me. The rending of loyalties, of love. And so I did nothing and said nothing; but believe me, it was not compassion that stayed my tongue, it was cowardice.

The Question

Our times together are snatched and furtive, waiting for the days when Colvin is away or up the hill. Alex has finally gone back to school, taking his dark, watchful gaze, and we steal moments in my bed under the scuffed Inca sun, or in the pastoral cliché of the hayloft, or the back seat of the Land Rover that I finally got when I sold the vomit-ridden Porsche. I keep taking us to new places where we won't be found by others or found wanting in each other's eyes.

She tried to end it after the flood, and several times since, in torrents of guilt and anguish, but I always win her round. Her life is hard enough, I say (opening a bottle of wine), she needs this comfort. I will be going back to London soon and it will all be over, so we only have now, these few days in our long lives apart; we just have to receive it with thanks (passing her a glass) and seize our passion. Of course, I add, we both love Colvin and will guarantee he never knows and is never hurt, but we need to embrace what destiny has brought us (clinking glasses), live in the moment.

I always could sell shit.

After one of those moments of fulfilling our karmic duty by tossing around in bed, while Colvin embraced his fate tossing silage into the outer fields, she slides off me and nestles into my side. An arm and leg are still slung across me, head pillowed on my shoulder, warm, slippery body pressed so close she is dissolving into my skin. Her hair spills over my arm and brushes my chin, her smell entering me at every pore. As I stroke her back, she kisses me, over and over on my neck and collarbone, her fingers trailing through the hair on my chest. I never want to move again.

'Sorley,' she murmurs.

'Mmm?'

'Do you love me?'

I hold still. I haven't expected that question, though why should I be surprised? It usually comes up at some point with women who have lingered a while and I always answer yes, though usually I am lying.

'Yes, I do.' This time it's true.

'Do you love me?' she says again.

I laugh and give her a squeeze. 'Liana! Of course I love you. Isn't it obvious?'

Somehow, it has never occurred to me that she might want my love. Loyalty to the family, yes, and this erotic pull, yes, but love? What does she mean by it?

'Do you love me?' she repeats, propping herself up on one elbow.

I shift back so I can see her whole face. Her eyes are huge, dark as a well.

'Liana, I fell hopelessly in love with you the first day I saw you, but unluckily for me, it was the day you married my brother. I have loved you ever since, and no matter how many other women have come and gone, none of them have uprooted you. I hated it because I couldn't have you. And now, after all these years, we have this and I am orbiting the stars and head over heels in love. Yes, yes, yes, Liana! I love you, I love you, I love you.'

I take her face in my hands and kiss her full on the mouth.

She draws back and there is a steeliness in her eyes. 'Then help us,' she says.

My guts clench. 'What do you mean?'

'Colvin made me vow, years ago, that I would never ever ask you for help and I have kept that promise, Sorley, all these long, difficult years. I bite my lip so hard it bleeds, but now I can be silent no longer. We need you. Please.' She presses her hand on my chest, fixes me with her intense gaze. 'If you help us we can put an end to all this nightmare. Mackintosh is desperate to sell and Aggarwal wants to buy but he won't take on the legal battle.' I know all of this already. It's what she says next that is new. 'They both agreed that if we raise the money, we can buy the farm and Aggarwal will buy the rest of the estate and the case will be closed. No more courts, no more lawyers, no more fighting. It will be ours and we will be free. But we have no money, Sorley. Only you can do it, only you can save us.'

Paradise Lost

Alex slipped out of school at lunch and cycled home. The afternoon was team project work and his group were supposed to be solving climate change. Leave them to it, he thought, pedalling hard through the late October afternoon, squinting up at the straggling group of whooper swans in the pale sky. Dumping his bike and bag well away from the house, he walked up the track to his hide, disappearing gladly into the dark canopy of trees and the sounds of bird and burn. In the pockets of his jacket he carried a new packet of biscuits and a can of Coke, his notebook and pens, and a hanky. It was a practice introduced by his father, though his mother found it amusing. He never carried a phone. If he could not be called or found or summoned, well and good. He had seen Tess once when she'd come back from college for a weekend and it had not gone well. Apparently, Glasgow was *amazing* and she was playing music *all the time* and out *dancing* and making friends and *loving it*. She was also still writing to her strange man. A bright, bubbling joy spilled out of her and sickened him. Away from home, away from him, she was so happy. He tried to forget her. There was only one happiness for him now and it was here.

He stepped into the clearing where the Green Bothy glowed in dappled light. Its wooden walls were peeling and weathered to silvery grey like the trunks of the birches around, and its corrugated tin roof was a stippling of old green paint and orange rust. As the sun's rays bounced off the pool and the leaves, there was a play of light and shadows across the bothy, painting it an ever-shifting mosaic of colour. Alex made a mental note to bring tools next time to ready it for winter, but as he walked towards it he heard sounds. He stopped. Then slowly, with the stealth of a cat, padded close. These were voices he recognised. Pressing himself to the side of a window, he inched his head round till he could see.

The fire was lit and a wine bottle and glasses were on the floor beside it. Clothes lay in a heap at the base of the silver birch. On the bed lay Sorley, with his mother. Naked. They were talking, laughing, kissing. And then things happened that made his blood turn to ice; they did things to each other and made sounds that twisted his stomach to knots; they moaned and rocked and crashed the bed till the wooden walls shook and his fists were stones and his head exploded into a million burning shards.

Fireworks

It was the village bonfire night and temperatures had dropped to freezing, with snow on the hills and a sting in the air. The first days of November had brought an icy rain and the ground was sodden, grass beaten into mud, autumn leaves lying dead. On the morning of the 5th, the rain stopped and a thick fog lay over the valley. I met Fachie on the far side of the field where the pile of wood for the bonfire sat in wet, dark layers looking as likely to burn as a shipwreck at the bottom of the sea. It put me in mind of Elijah on Mount Carmel, ordering the altar to be soaked with water before calling down fire from heaven. I wasn't convinced my ecclesiastical powers were up to the job.

Fachie stood with his fingers jammed into his jeans, his jacket hanging open. His bird's nest of red hair was spiked with grey and two deep curves ran from the sides of his nose to his mouth, lending him a gaunt, dramatic look.

'What d'you think?' I asked.

'She'll be awright,' he said. 'Won't rain today and I've got enough firelighters to blow up the whole village.'

'Excellent. Bonfire night to remember, then.'

'Aye. Everything else ready?'

'Yep. Five hundred burgers and sausages, two hundred glowsticks and a thousand pounds' worth of fireworks. Won't be able to see them through the cloud but should be fun to listen to.'

'It'll clear,' Fachie said. He could read the weather like a wizard and I'd never known him to be wrong. He had learned his skills from his dad. Though nearly ninety now and bent with arthritis, Dougie still walked every day in all weathers, in his old oilskin and flat cap, long white beard and hair tangling in the wind.

Sure enough, at five-thirty when all was dark, the cloud began to thin. As people walked towards the field in a chattering procession, the mist rolled away and the cleared air was even colder, nipping at noses and cheeks. I stood at the gate in my hi-vis jacket welcoming folks and rattling a donations bucket. The money covered costs and any extra went to a charity, this year it was MacMillan because we'd just lost the young Kiwi lass from the water sports centre to a brutal cancer. I'd seen her husband arrive earlier with a child hanging off each arm and the baby in the backpack, his face raw. He used to be one of my regulars at the Ferryman, but once he was on his own he couldn't get out in the evenings. So I got him to come up on a Friday after tea with the kids and I held the baby while he had a pint and the two bigger ones grubbed about on the floor. Then he would take them home, chuck them in bed and watch telly till he fell asleep on the couch.

They all came streaming through the gates, a lumpy, woollen flock, laughing, greeting each other, yelling at kids, losing each other in the great dark field. Fachie's ex was there with her man and their foster child in a wheelchair, the maths teacher selling glowsticks, her National Park hubby directing traffic, the fish farmer helping at the bonfire, the church ladies serving in the tea tent, one eighty-year-old farmer with a swarm of grandchildren, little boys hanging off the fire engine, a clot of teenage girls arm in arm, computer game guy standing alone with his head thrown back, looking at the stars.

Liana was there, too, with Colvin. He'd been going through a bad patch since the flood, withdrawn and gloomy, and there'd been a bust-up with Alex that day. Apparently, he'd got mad at his boy for not helping with the chores and Alex had started swearing and said he hated the sheep. Of course, Colvin knew Alex didn't want to inherit the farm and wouldn't cope, anyway, but hearing it said like that, so cold and scornful, hit hard. Like the time Sorley had said the same thing, at the same age.

So Liana had dragged Colvin out to the bonfire night and made him help her in the burger tent. Sorley was there, too, setting up the fireworks. He'd hooked up with some old school buddies and was getting involved in community things here and there, joining the Cairngorm Runners, treasurer for the shinty club. Here for over two months now, he was telling everyone how his remote management of Winglift Capital was working so well it could set a trend. His finance friends in London were envious, he claimed. Could even be the answer to repopulating the Highlands. All of this I heard second-hand, of course, as he still barely spoke to me.

Then I saw Kirat and Vivienne Aggarwal. His handsome face glowed in the light from the hot drinks stall, while she wore a furry white hat looking like a small artic fox had curled up on her head. They were standing with the Hoare-Cressingtons of Logie Estate, holding drinks and chuckling. At one point, Vivienne threw back her head in a shriek of laughter and nearly toppled the fox.

They spotted me.

'Hello, my good lady,' Kirat said. 'Good to see you again.' As I took his leather-gloved hand he kissed me on the cheek. He wore fragrance that seemed to float several tiers above the muddy ground, the beasts, the rotting leaves and earthy sweat of the rest of us.

'Rahesh tells me you know everything and everyone. Would that include Colvin Munro, shepherd for Rowancraig Estate?'

'Certainly. He's my cousin and oldest friend.'

'Oh.' Kirat's eyebrows shot up. 'Excellent.'

Then his words were drowned by the first explosion of fireworks and we turned to watch. Nearby, a two-year old wailed, and I went across to pull her inside my jacket as she pressed her hands over her ears.

When the last shower of sparks dissolved into darkness, people applauded and cheered and started streaming off the field. I gave the wee one back to her dad and headed into the burger tent where Liana was handing out leftovers to the volunteers.

'Have, have! You been so good again, so good.'

I started stacking the empty drink crates as Colvin scraped the barbecue and Sorley emerged from the shadows smelling like a smoked kipper.

'Here,' Liana said, thrusting a burger into his hands.

'Thanks. Starving.' He tore into it, smearing sauce on his cheeks.

Kirat stepped into the light of the tent and tossed his paper cup into a rubbish bin. 'That show was awesome,' he said to Liana. 'Thank you.'

'Thank him.' Her hand flicked at Sorley. 'He did the fireworks this year.'

He turned to look. Sorley froze with half a burger shoved in his mouth.

'Sorley?!' Kirat's eyes were wide.

Nodding and smiling weakly, Sorley started chewing again, quickly.

'My god! Sorley Munro – what the hell are you doing here?'

Sorely swallowed, looked around him, then pushed the back of his hand across his mouth, rubbed it on his jeans and extended it to Kirat. He still had a blob of sauce on his chin.

'Kirat!' he said, an artificial jollity in his voice. 'I could say the same thing to you.'

'I'm just visiting.' Kirat touched the hand briefly.

'Yeah, well,' Sorley mumbled. 'Actually this is my home. I grew up here.'

'God, you never! Really? Where? What did your parents do?'

'My father was the Rowancraig shepherd. Now it's my brother.' He jerked his head towards Colvin, who was watching from the back of the tent.

Kirat followed his gaze. 'Oh! Munro – of course! So *you* must be Colvin Munro!' he exclaimed, a sudden warmth flooding his voice. He strode towards him, hand outstretched. 'I'm Kirat. Kirat Aggarwal who wrote to you recently.'

Colvin slowly raised his hand and allowed it to be shaken. 'Hi, hi.'

'Well, I do hope you will take my proposal seriously. Look, my wife has fallen in love with the damn place and I'll get no peace till we've bought it, so I just want to make things fair and square for everyone and move things forward. Do give me an answer as soon as you can.'

'I can give you that now.'

'Oh, I see. Go ahead.'

'Couldn't even buy this burger tent, Mr Aggarwal, let alone my farm, so there's no point discussing it.'

Kirat's face was impossible to read, but Liana leapt into the gap.

'This is true, but we are talking as a family.' She shot a look at Sorley. 'We might find a way.'

With a sympathetic smile, Kirat turned to him. 'So have you decided to take up the crook and whistle again, Sorley? Can't say I blame you. Do you the world of good after being burned in the city.'

Sorley's face darkened and he muttered, 'Yeah, well, perhaps we should leave you and Colvin to discuss things.' He took Liana by the elbow and tried to lead her away, but she pulled back.

'What is this *burned*?' She was staring at him. We all were. 'Sorley?' She looked at Kirat. 'What you talking about?'

'Oh, the collapse of Winglift. One of the many casualties of the crash.'

'Collapse?' Her pitch was rising. 'The crash?'

'Well, yes . . . the banking crisis.' He took in a breath and looked from one to the other of us, his gaze settling on Sorley, who was looking at the ground. 'A . . . a real shame.' An awkward pause. 'Please let me know if I can help at all, Sorley.' He touched his arm and walked away.

There was silence.

'Sorley?' Liana's voice was thin.

'Ah, yep.' He threw his burger into the bin and rubbed his hands on his jeans. 'I meant to tell you. I lost my fund. And everything else.'

'Lost?'

'Everything.'

'You have nothing left?'

'No. Well, I do, actually, I do.' He squinted at the bonfire at the end of the field, billowing smoke and sparks. 'I have lots and lots of debt.'

Eviction

I get back to Shepherd's Cottage and start shoving things into a suitcase. I'm shaking. Just as I did the morning after Winglift was shut down and I got home to find Annabelle's lover in my home and my life falling apart. My stuff is everywhere and I can't think or decide. Where am I going? I shove in thick socks and fleeces. For how long? Papers, laptop, pens are scooped from the desk into a briefcase. Will I ever come back? I shove a bottle of whisky between the clothes, then scratch my scalp and turn to get my things from the bathroom.

She is standing in the door. I start. I don't know how long she has been there. We stare at each other.

'Colvin is gone to drop off the marquee.'

'Oh.'

'Let me help.'

'No, I—' But she pushes past me and yanks open the wardrobe doors, scanning my designer shirts and trousers, the bespoke jackets. She starts ripping them off the hangers and throwing them on the floor.

'Hey!'

Then she heaves drawers out of the dresser, letting them crash down, and grabs the socks and pants and rumpled T-shirts and hurls them against the wall.

'Liana.'

'Get out!' she hisses, sinking down into the litter of clothes, clutching a jumper.

'I'm trying.' I go to the bathroom and grab toothbrush, paste and a towel and, back in the bedroom, squeeze them into my overstuffed suitcase. She is still on the floor.

'I hate you, I hate you, I hate you,' she moans.

'What – because I'm broke?' I tug viciously at the suitcase zips.

'You know why, you lying, fucking cunt!'

'So I pretended I still had a company—'

'You pretended you were rich!'

I stare her down. 'And that's why you fucked me, was it?'

She hurls a shoe and I dive out of the room.

As I make for my Land Rover outside I hear the bedroom window swing open above me and then something hits me on the back. Another shoe. I get round to the other side of the vehicle as more and more of my possessions rain down. Books, clothes, a fluttering of hankies. My hat is frisbeed clear across to the chicken run where it startles the birds. All the while she is yelling, in her Bolivian Spanish, and she sounds like a lunatic in a tower. I wait till the torrent has stopped and nothing has been thrown for a few minutes, then come out from my hiding place, gather everything up from the mud and throw it in the back of the Landy. From the open window of my bedroom, I hear smashing.

Invasion

Alex heard everything. Because he so often made himself disappear, people forgot about him, or assumed he wasn't paying attention, or was stupid. But he witnessed it all from his perch in the giant Scots pine near the house. And he was glad. His uncle was leaving and was not, it appeared, coming back.

But then, instead of driving down the track towards the road, Sorley drove up it, into the woods. Alex swore, dropped down from his tree and ran after him. The Land Rover was slow on the rutted track and it wasn't hard for Alex to keep up. Sure enough, at the fork, Sorley didn't head up the moor, but continued along the gully beside the burn.

Alex's head was on fire.

By the time he caught up with the Land Rover, it was against the fallen pine and Sorley was crashing through the undergrowth beyond with a lit head torch and his two bags. Alex slipped quietly behind and into the clearing, watching as Sorley made his way into the Green Bothy. There was shuffling and then the flare of a match. Alex crept close, to the same window where he had witnessed the abomination the week before.

Inside, Sorley had lit candles on the mantelpiece and was setting the fire, using the newspaper Alex had brought, the kindling Alex had gathered. When it was going, Sorley pulled the stuff out of his bags, throwing shoes next to the door and clothes onto the bed. A towel landed on a low branch of the silver birch, toothbrush and paste onto a shelf and all the contents of Sorley's briefcase tipped out on the table as he rummaged around for his bottle of whisky. Alex's arrangements of fragile bones were bumped aside, a branch of pine cones knocked to the floor, a blue eggshell crushed.

Hell

When everything was cleared from the field I went back to Shepherd's Cottage to find Colvin and Liana arguing in the kitchen and no sign of Sorley. Apparently, he had taken his things and disappeared.

'He lied to us!' Liana was almost shrieking from her position against the counter. 'He lied to all of us!'

'Well, he barely said a word to me.' I slung my jacket over a chair.

'You know what I mean! How dare he? How dare he live under our roof and eat our food and . . . and . . . *puta madre!*'

And what? I looked hard at her. I glanced at Colvin. He was sitting, staring at the table.

I sat down beside him. 'So he's bankrupt.'

'Got nothing at all!' Liana threw her hands in the air.

'Yes, he has,' Colvin said, rubbing his eyebrow with a cracked thumb. 'Debts.'

I folded my arms. 'Come to the right place then. Debts R Us.'

Liana huffed in disgust. 'Not you. You have some goddamn fairy prince gives you pub and megabucks – just like that.' She snapped her fingers. 'You have luck, we have real life.'

Colvin looked at her and was about to speak, but didn't. His eyes flicked to me and then down again.

'So you threw him out?' I asked Liana.

'No. I never throw out family. He left. I was angry, yes, I shout, yes, but because he hurt us—' She chokes and slaps a hand over her mouth, eyes squeezed shut. 'He take everything . . . he just leaves . . . like that.' Her free hand flicks the air.

'He took . . . ?' I said. 'Did he steal something?'

'No! Yes! He stole our love. We love him as family, and he treat us like shit.'

Colvin turned to her again. 'He worked for his board here. His financial business is . . . his business.'

'You don't care he lied to you? Your own brother? He made up a big fat story and you say it only his business? Like – no big deal?!' She was shrieking again.

He shook his head and looked down at his hands.

'So where'd he go?' I asked.

'God knows.' Liana started grabbing things off the table and crashing them into the sink. 'Back to hell where he belong.'

Fire

When I finally fall asleep that night in the Green Bothy, I dream . . .

Everything is beautiful. I am walking around a vast stately home and there are elegant people drifting in and out of rooms and silent, bowing staff. Opulent carpets, chandeliers, mahogany, crystal, marble and gold. Perfect bodies are draped in silks and fine suits, jewellery glinting at ear and wrist, hair shining. As I walk I realise it is all mine and that everyone in some way belongs to me: friends, family, employees. They are a mix of people I know and people I've never seen before, and some of the strangers are my lovers and children, while some of the mute servants are my family. Moving up the grand staircase, I see the people change. Appetites rise, masks fall. A woman grabs a fistful of canapes and shoves them in her mouth, a man seizes a maid by the breast, a couple grope at each other in lust and violence. Up a flight and champagne flutes smash, dark stains spread on white shirts, make-up smears and teeth fall out. Higher and higher in the house the rooms become smaller and filthier and hotter, the people more grotesque, their debauchery unfettered and cruel. Sometimes I look on in horror, sometimes I am one of them, writhing like a maggot. I push on up, till I can barely move for old furniture stuffed everywhere, rotting mattresses and leering, disfigured faces. The heat is unbearable. Up a narrow wooden staircase in a tower, I find I am crawling through bodies that are amputated and bandaged, crushing and smothering me in their foul odours, their voices like distant, dying birds. Sweat pours off me, my clothes melt away. I reach for the door at the top and hear banging on it and shouting. As it crashes open, flames engulf me and the Devil takes my throat.

Baptism

Back in my attic flat at the Ferryman I couldn't sleep. I didn't even get into bed or change into pyjamas, but sat hunched in my big chair by the wood-burning stove. I thought over everything that had happened to Sorley – known to me and unknown – and remembered the child I had loved and left, and the adult who had returned. I held the image of him in a pillar of light and gave him up to prayers deeper and too difficult for words. And as the black quiet settled over me and I slipped into a half-dream state, I saw the pillar become cloud and Sorley vanish within it, and as I searched for his face, the pillar turned to fire.

I piled into my old van and drove it hard down the road and along the track through Colvin's farm, swearing at all the gates and the stupid sheep. There were no lights on at Shepherd's Cottage but I wasn't stopping there anyway, and continued up the track past the outbuildings and the barking of the dogs into the forested gully. Going as fast as I could, I caught flickers of light between the trees, and when I jumped out behind Sorley's Land Rover, I could smell burning. Crashing through the close-grown trees and into the clearing, I saw flames licking around the walls of the Green Bothy and up the tin roof. I ran. The heat was torture, the smoke from the treated wood stinging my eyes. I kicked down the door, dropped to my knees and crawled under the billows of smoke towards the bed in the corner. Sorley was there, unmoving. I hauled him off the bed, tangled in a blanket, and back across the room, gasping to breathe as burning flecks fell from the ceiling. Outside, I staggered with him across the clearing to the pool, laid him in the shallows and splashed his face with the cold, cold water, his head pillowed on my arm. By the light of the burning bothy, I could see bare flesh all down his body rising and blistering. I could not feel him breathe.

As I poured water over him, again and again, I cried out: *Live, live, live!*

Shroud

Alex stood in the clearing beneath a pallid sky. It was a crater of grey ash, the trees at its edges singed, the bushes and grasses trampled by the fire crew. In the middle, the bothy. It looked like a bomb had landed on it. The walls and verandah were reduced to dark stumps, the furniture burned away, sheets of metal roofing buckled from heat and collapsed onto the ground. The chimney breast remained, its stones scorched to a shocking black. There was no sign of the silver birch that grew up the middle or of any precious things – books, binoculars, birds. An acrid smell rose from the remains, filling Alex's head and stinging his eyes and nose till they leaked, his hands clutching at emptiness in his pockets.

It began to snow. Tiny motes of white drifted down, one at a time, in a slow soundless trail from the clouds above to dissolve into the mud. Then more came, and more, a thickening haze of specks that began, so quietly, to dust the ground and the dying trees and the ruin. And more and more came then, a silent mass of snowflakes in their millions, falling on the land in layers of filmy gauze till it powdered over the stinking ash and soil, and softened every brute edge and burnt skin, wrapping bandages around jagged tree limbs, spreading a blanket over the wounded earth, drawing a pall over Alex's hide.

BOOK III

BOOK III

Burnt

I wake up in harsh light, a hospital room, white sheets, tubes, noise. I sink again. I rise and fall. It could be hours, or days, or years, but finally I am fully awake and a nurse comes to explain. There will be treatment, there will be skin grafts, there will be a month in hospital, maybe more. I ask for a mirror. She says not yet.

Lie Down This Night

Mo visits every day. She brings fruit and flowers and her fumbling hands, running them through her hair, fiddling with stuff. Her face is an inland loch, shifting in colour and mood, and sometimes I see again the teenaged Mo – the big-boned, cleft-lipped, boy-girl face – that became more real to me than my mother's. I remember how she talked about Mum every day till I wasn't sure if my memories were mine or just the imaginings built on hers. She upheld Mum's traditions: the fresh hankies, the tales from the Travelling family, the prayers before bed kneeling on the floor. I resented that at the time, along with her scouring gaze when I misbehaved, or the narrowed eyes when I told tales of my own. But I forgave her each night when I clambered under the quilt and pressed my feet against the hot water bottle and threw my arms up for a hug and the kisses on both cheeks. Her face at those moments was my favourite: how it poured out light like a celebrating house, how her grin was so wide and toothy when she said *I'll eat you up!* and the way her eyes brimmed on the words *I love you so!*

And then she left us and the lights went out.

When I packed to leave home myself, I packed up my memories of her, lodged them in the attic of my mind and decided not to find them again. Till here, in the hospital, they have found me. Once again, I am lying in bed with her sitting close by, and though the hankies and hot water bottles are gone, her stories rise again, and though neither of us are on our knees, I know she prays. I wake to find her with eyes closed, hands folded on the bed. Outside it is snowing, a quiet fall of feathers. I reach across and take her hand.

Ashes

When he took my hand, it was one of those tiny shifts that shows the plates of the earth are moving, that an avalanche will fall, a butterfly change history. I began to tell him of the deeper, far-back things: how his mother became mine, how his brother became a man, how his father became maimed. Finally, quietly, I told him who I had become, why I had to leave and how much I had missed him. How much – how very much – I loved him.

But I could not say that part, as I was about to cry. I felt his hand squeeze mine and I looked up.

His face was a map, a chart of a changed country: a landscape that had grown its childhood contours under my gaze, then furrowed to adulthood in my absence and now, before my eyes again, been ravaged. Scoured as the moor, barren as the mountain. Some burning thing in the bothy had fallen on his face – a wood shaving or scrap of nest, we don't know – but enough to plough his skin raw. I wanted to wash it with sorrow, to lay cool hands on his wounds and have healing in my touch. He had lost everything. Every penny and possession, every pretence and prop. And now his face. Was there no balm in Gilead? His tears made their way down the ragged flesh like trickles across rock.

In those early days, Colvin came often. Had there been any hurt or anger at Sorley's deception, he showed no sign. He simply sat at his brother's side and waited, his giant shepherd hands resting on his thighs, his voice rare and quiet. But I knew him well enough to know that his waters ran deep and were full of care. That Sorley's return to the farm had given him hope of a bond between them and that he was not yet ready to doubt it.

It was there, in the hospital, that we first opened Agnes's wartime letters to Gid and I began to read them aloud. And there she came to us, in all her beauty and strength and laughter, her love of each living thing, her faith shining.

I Commit you to The Three in One.
The Three Who are over us,
The Three Who are below us,
The Three Who are beyond,
The Three Who are within.

Liana stayed away. The betrayal and the fire were enough to explain her tempest of emotions, swinging from anger to remorse, disbelief to distress, and she insisted her presence in the hospital would only be upsetting for everyone. She was right.

And Alex, of course, did not come. The destruction of his hide and the histrionics of his mother sent him into a dark withdrawal. He disappeared on long walks or shut himself in his room. He refused to go to school, to sit at the table for meals, to talk with anyone unless it was utterly essential. Tess dropped everything and came home for a few days, and though he let her walk beside him, he barely looked at her.

Sorley finally began to speak to me, to sketch in the years I had lost, the life he had lost. There was no pride, just a painful picking over the ashes in search of anything, anything at all, that remained.

Sign 9: Key

Nine months after Colvin disappeared, a climber found his key. It was a day in February of such radiance that the sky was an ocean of blue and the snow on the mountains shone like mother of pearl. The air was so cold it froze the hairs inside the nose, but so still, it was bearable. Deep in the Cairngorms, a small loch lies in a high bowl above the Garbh Choire and below the summits of Cairn Toul and Angel's Peak. Like many pools in the Highlands, its name, Lochan Uaine, simply means 'small green loch', but unlike most of the others, it is almost inaccessible, lying in its shelf part way up steep slopes littered with boulders and scree. A burn runs over the lip of the bowl and plummets down the cliff. It was up this waterfall, frozen into a cascade of refracting ice, that the climber made her slow route, her companion far below. Right at the top, her ice axe hit something metallic and dislodged a large key on a metal fob that said 'MacPherson'. Though it had hung on the hooks at Shepherd's Cottage, it was in fact the key to Dougie's house; the two families had swapped keys and given each other the run of their homes since Gid and Agnes were first married. But in truth, neither house was ever locked.

Penance

When I am finally out of hospital, Mo takes me home to her place, a small flat tucked into the eaves of the Ferryman. *My eyrie*, she calls it. It's the first time I've been here and she's nervous, her big workman hands pulling the zip of her fleece up and down. The place is functional and untidy, with books everywhere. Jumpers and jackets lie across the pieces of mismatched furniture, shoes litter the hall and used dishes sit on the table.

'Sorry,' she says, and starts clearing them away. 'Lunch'll be just a minute – grab a seat.' She points to a baggy sofa facing the big window at the end of the room. Following the sloping roof-lines, it is a triangle that looks out across Loch Hope to Small Isle. There's a telescope trained on the osprey nest, rebuilt by the RSPB after it came down in the storm, but empty now. This is the middle of December. Snow lies in half-melted heaps along the shore and on the bare arms of the old oak. The loch and sky are grey.

'Can I help?'

'No,' she calls from the kitchen. 'Won't be a moment.' There is pot stirring and the sharp tang of orange and ginger.

'Soup!' she announces, carrying two bowls through to the table. There is also a basket of rolls, a tub of margarine and a chopping board with a slab of cheddar. 'Come. Eat.' I take a seat and look at her. Her elbows are on the table, fingers pressed against her lips.

'Um,' she says. 'A moment of quiet first?' I bow my head. 'A prayer if you like,' she whispers.

Silence. The oven ticks as it cools; a branch brushes against the window; the smells of warm bread and soup rise to me and I feel an ache in my cheeks.

'Amen,' she says and takes up her spoon.

I eat slowly, my face hurting with each mouthful. The skin will take a long time to heal, changing colour and texture over the months, and I will always have scars. One eyebrow was burned off and there are patches on my scalp where the hair will not return. But I am told I am lucky. Any longer in that bothy and I would have inhaled fumes from the fire and died.

We have coffee, apples and chocolate over by the window, with me on the couch and her on a huge, soft chair, her thick-socked feet tucked under her. She looks nervous again.

'I've found somewhere for you to stay.'

I raise my one eyebrow. Even such a small movement pinches.

'You can't live at the Ferryman.'

'I could work for you, in exchange for board.'

She shakes her head. 'It's not good for you, Sorley, not fair.'

'How do you mean?' I know what she means.

She takes a bite of apple and chews noisily, looking out the window. Then swallows and takes a breath. 'You're an alcoholic, Sorley.'

'Been in hospital for six weeks. Not a drop.'

'Not by your own choice, Sox. This place is a disaster for you – you know that. You know the rules.'

'Those your rules, Rev?'

'Course not, you twit! You know I want you here with me, but it won't work. Common sense, right? AA. There's a group meets in the village hall Thursday nights, by the way; you should try it. Won't surprise you to know alcohol is a plague in these parts.'

'Yeah, so why you selling it?'

She looks at me, a cloud passing over her face. 'Long story, Sox, and I'll tell you some day. For now, I got you a house and a job.'

The house is a stone cottage just south of the village on Logie Estate land. The job is looking after Dougie MacPherson. A recent stroke has rendered him half blind, incontinent and unable to walk without a frame, but he's still sharp as a whip and determined not to end his days in a home.

Just push me over the cliff, he says, pointing towards the crags on An Sgiath, his old spaniel Bess at his feet. *Or throw me in the loch. Get rid of me whichever way you like, son, I really dinna care, just don't put me in that loony bin.*

He needs me for almost everything. I help him out of the sagging bed in the morning, where Bess is tucked in beside him, and onto the toilet, disposing of his heavy yellow pad. *Like a wee pishing bairn*, he says, shaking his head as he fumbles to put in his dentures, Bess sniffing around the bin. He grins at our reflection in the mirror and gnashes his teeth – *All the better to eat you with!* We make an incongruous pair: one half floppy, the other half burned, both smiles crooked. Then he sits by the sink in his dressing gown as I wipe his face with a flannel and brush his curly white hair and long beard. Sometimes I trim his eyebrows, and the hairs sprouting from his ears and nose, and I always finish with a dab of aftershave on his neck. *Steady*, he chuckles. *The lassies'll go mad*. Then he steers his zimmer frame back to the bedroom in his lop-sided gait – *Race you, son!* – with Bess and me in his slow wake, and once there he grips my shoulders as I dress him – *Shall we dance?* – lifting his carbuncled feet one at a time into his trouser legs, clinging to me as I tuck in his shirt and buckle his belt. Worn out, he collapses on a chair for the socks and shoes (he refuses slippers) and the tie (every day) and the tweed waistcoat and jacket. Together we heave him back up onto his frame and he rattles down the hall to the kitchen – *You'll beat me one day, lad, dinna worry!* In his chair, Bess curled by his feet on the floor, he watches as I make the porridge and a pot of tea and asks about my life.

He knew me as a child, though I knew him more from reputation than presence, as he and Margaret had moved to Aberdeen when I was six. But they'd come back often for visits and had always helped our struggling family, returning to settle in the strath just as I was heading to uni. By then, Dougie had become increasingly outspoken on the environment and critical of sporting estates, and frequently crossed swords with his gamekeeper son. They'd had long rifts and it was always Dougie who offered the olive branch, as Fachie was too proud. Except now, since the stroke, Fachie has softened and comes often to see his old man.

After breakfast, which is slow and sloppy, I take him back to the toilet for a quiet sit-down while I clear the kitchen. He calls when he's ready for the wiping: the smell and sight of it would be a horror for us both were it not for his jokes. *Bet you're no used to taking shit off naebody, son*. All belted and buckled again, he whistles for Bess and shuffles his frame to the back door. I put his oilskin and flat cap on him, don my jacket, which is not mine, but given by Colvin after my things were destroyed in the fire, and head out the door, holding it open for him. Come sleet, hail or snow, he always heads out, inching his frame over the threshold and down the small temporary ramp the council have installed, Bess always at his side. The worse the weather, the higher his spirits. *Awww, does you good, laddie, don't it!* He stares down the wind, his body listing to one side, hair and beard whipping round his collar, hands turning blue on the frame. Most days we only manage a short walk down the path but he always spots something new. *Hear that buzzard? Did you catch that hare? Awww, it's a storm brewing the day, sure it is. Wind about to change, lad – can you smell it? And that goose? Must have gone back for her handbag.*

Once in from his walk, it's all we can do to get him to his chair in the sitting room where he collapses, exhausted. I put the telly and the heater on, set the remote on the arm of his chair and leave him to snooze. After making the beds, tidying up and writing a shopping list, I sit and read. Dougie has published several books on Scottish land, forests and wildlife, and I discover how vast is his knowledge and how great my ignorance. He has another with his publisher, due out next year – his last, he tells me. I also delve into old Highland classics I find on his bookshelves: Neil Gunn, Robert Louis Stevenson, Sorley MacLean, the Gaelic poet after whom I am named.

And there are my mother's wartime letters, that I am gradually reading. Sometimes a childhood memory of her surfaces like a cresting whale from the deep and I am slain. In many of her letters she closes with a poetic blessing, and by way of explanation, Mo gives me an ancient, dog-eared copy of the *Carmina Gadelica: Hymns and Incantations Collected in the Highlands and Islands of Scotland in the Last Century* by Alexander Carmichael. It belonged to Mum and I discover down-turned pages and margin notes next to the prayers Mo had learned from her and spoken over me. *O God of life, darken not to me Thy light, O God of life, close not to me Thy joy.* Four months ago, the charms of Celtic monks and Hebridean householders would have been the last thing I wanted to read, but somehow it is becoming my daily companion. *Traversing corries, traversing forests, Traversing valleys long and wild. The fair white Mary still uphold me, The Shepherd Jesu by my side.*

I serve Dougie bread and soup for lunch and we repeat the routines of zimmer frame, apron and toilet. *Och, it's a wild life I lead, son,* he says, settling back in his chair. *Dinna let me lead you astray.* And he winks. I wonder if he knows how far I have strayed. Does he know he is my penance?

After lunch each day I leave him snoring with Bess and a call button and head into Kirkton or Aviemore. I do any shopping needed, I use the internet in the library, have a wound check at the doc, go to the gym. Mo often meets me somewhere for coffee, quizzes me about Dougie and my reading and AA. She asks gently what I will do next. I tell her Dougie's a survivor, that he might see me through to my retirement.

The burnt skin on my face is tight when I smile or laugh, but I don't do either very often.

I go back to the house in the late afternoon, help Dougie to the toilet again and back to his chair and start cooking dinner. I am learning to make his favourite dishes: stovies, herring in oatmeal, mince and tatties, shepherd's pie. After dinner we sit together to watch television – he loves documentaries – or to listen to what he still calls 'the wireless'. *You interested in this, son?* he always asks. *You pick us something the night.*

I rarely leave him in the evening, except for Thursday nights when someone else comes to sit with him – Mo or Fachie or Colvin, or others from the community, for he is well loved. Thursday's AA night. I dragged my feet at first, not wanting to be with a miserable bunch of losers, till I accepted I was one. And then I discovered I was wrong. About them. In those meetings there is a young mother who works hard all day as a primary school teacher and keeps her addiction deeply hidden. A university professor who houses foreign students in his rambling mansion. A windsurfer with a world record. A lawyer. Every walk of life, every weave of person, every way of being: one poison.

In those two weeks before Christmas I don't go to Shepherd's Cottage. When Colvin visited me in hospital, we never discussed what had happened and I don't know what he knows or suspects. Liana never came, nor Alex, obviously. When the police investigated, it was clear I had been drunk and fallen asleep with the fire blazing in an open grate and candles burning. But they also found the shrivelled remains of my laptop in the fireplace. I offered no leads or explanation.

One evening, Colvin comes up to the house and sits with Dougie as we talk weather and shepherding, estates and the strath. They reminisce about the overnight walk they took up into the Cairngorms with our mother and Margaret, Fachie and Mo. I heard that story so many times when I was a kid, it was like the break into Narnia, the glimpse of the Promised Land before the years in the wilderness which had been my life. *But you were there, son.* Dougie smiles. *A twinkle in your mother's eye.* I try to smile back, but my skin hurts. *One day you'll go again, so you will.*

He treads carefully around environmental topics with Colvin, knowing they will never agree about the rights and wrongs of sheep, but manages to prise out of him the latest development in the sale of Rowancraig. Since Colvin has said he can't buy the farm, Aggarwal has come back with another offer. If Colvin drops the legal battle over his lease and relinquishes any claim to tenancy, Aggarwal will purchase the estate, pay off his debts and make him an employee. That way, everyone gets a clean slate and he'll completely renovate Shepherd's Cottage into the bargain. The whole deal is spelled out in a fat document that Colvin is currently picking over with his lawyer. I can see that something very old and deep in my brother resists being bought out in this way and losing the last title claim of the Munros to the land, but I can also see he has little choice. I say nothing.

That night, unexpectedly, Fachie also drops by, and after a few minutes of awkward talk about how we're all doing – *och, fine, fine* – Colvin rises and says, *Best be getting on*, and leaves.

A Sighting

I see Liana for the first time at the small supermarket in Kirkton.
When I walk in, she's putting a bag of potatoes in her trolley, her small
frame swathed in a black leather coat, a red beret at a rakish angle.
My movement at the end of the aisle makes her glance up. I see her
shock, feel the scars on my cheeks tighten. We both stand staring, then
I turn and step out into the cold.

While Shepherds Watched

On Christmas Day morning I treated myself to a slap-up breakfast of waffles with bacon and maple syrup. I didn't go to church because I preferred the watchnight service on Christmas Eve and because I went into Aviemore straight after breakfast to start cooking the Community Care lunch. A team of us had been running a drop-in cafe for a few years, and with the recession and new amenity housing, we had quite a mixed crowd. Most of them didn't have anywhere to go for Christmas (or were better off *not* going to family) so we made a lunch for them and celebrated together. It took weeks of planning and hours of sweaty work on Christmas morning, but when you saw their faces as they walked in and tucked into the food and opened their presents, there was nowhere I'd rather be.

It was about five o'clock before every last pot and spoon was cleared away, and that was when I usually headed to Shepherd's Cottage to put my feet up and have my own Christmas dinner. The only fly in the ointment was Beulah, who – according to the eternal laws of familial injustice – had to be with us. I tell you, sometimes it's easier to love a room full of addicts and dropouts on Christmas Day than your own mother. Though she was not my own mother, of course, as she was at pains to point out when I fled the village at eighteen. The Good Lord, I believed, had given me Beulah to test my character, my patience and my capacity for forgiveness. I had yet to pass His tests, so was continually resitting them, and Christmas was the one at which I was most liable to fail spectacularly. We had long ago agreed that they would all have their sit-down dinner at lunch and I would happily scoop up leftovers when I got in, as that minimised the necessary overlap. Colvin usually tried to take Beulah home as early in the evening as possible, but she had a way of wedging herself into the armchair with the most propitious view of the television, which she shouted at, and then dropping into a sudden and deep slumber at the suggestion of heading home. I gritted my teeth.

But this year was different. This year we were all having Christmas Dinner Together.

As A Family.

That morning, Colvin went out to feed the sheep. It was no different to any other winter morning, no different to any other Christmas for the past forty years. Except for one bare fact. This was the last Christmas they would be his. He drove across the lumpy fields on his quad bike and trailer, pausing to clamber out and fork silage into a trough and toss feed rolls onto the grass, the sheep gathering in his wake. The sky hung heavy overhead, a damp quilt clotted and dripping, clouds grey like the blooming of mould. He felt the cold seep into him, through his shivered skin to the tired muscles and right down to his bones. He could never work out if he loved this life or hated it.

That morning, Lord Edgar Mackintosh went out to walk along the beach below his cottage in Cornwall. It was windy and the sea spray stung his face. He had turned down every invitation for Christmas Day and bought no gifts or special food. A stray dog appeared from the wet black rocks and trotted beside him all the way home, curling up on his back step. At last, when the storm sweeping in from the ocean had soaked the creature to a skeletal rag, Mackintosh let him in.

That morning, Kirat brought Vivienne breakfast in bed on an antique silver tray. Freshly squeezed orange juice, muesli with blueberries and yoghurt, dark coffee and a crisp white envelope. He cracked open a bottle of champagne and poured two glasses as she read the letter from the solicitor. 'Happy Christmas, my darling,' he said, kissing her on the top of the head and passing a glass. 'I bought you a little place in the country.'

That morning, Tess knocked and waited at Alex's bedroom door with her gift. A new bird book to replace the favourite one lost in the fire.

When there was no answer, she pushed the door open a crack and called to him in the fetid dark. She felt the duvet at the foot of his bed. He was gone.

That morning, Liana thought of her family in Bolivia. Her mother – hotel maid by day, whore by night. Her father – god only knew.

That morning, Beulah woke up in the Blesséd Bed in Rowancraig House.

Annunciation

The outer door of Rowancraig is half open and I can smell burning. These days, it's a smell that assaults me, even if it's just a bit of toast or the puffs rising from a neighbour's chimney. Dougie understands that as long as I am carer there are only radiators and no open fires. He never comments when I turn on the electric heater that sits like a sentry in front of the cold grate. Today he is at Fachie's where there will be a roaring fire and – once Fachie's had his one-too-many – a roaring argument.

Pushing the inner door into the hall, I see smoke and start to run. It's coming from the corridor, a smeary cloud drifting through the air like a phantom in a cheap horror film. In the kitchen, Beulah is bending over, peering into the oven while a pan on the top is on fire, pluming smoke. Yelling, I dash across and push her aside, turn off the heat and flail around for something to smother it. The kitchen is a midden, every surface heaped with junk, and there is no big lid or extinguisher in sight. I yank off my coat and throw it over the flames.

'You've ruined the sausages!' she snaps. She is wearing a long red dress, an ancient thing of crumbling velvet with scraps of lace dangling from the neck and cuffs. Her curly wig is on sideways and her face smeared with make-up. At her neck is a triple string of pearls, looking far too genuine and expensive for the ex-housekeeper.

'What are you doing here, Auntie Beulah?'

'Making the Christmas dinner, you idiot! What does it look like?'

'But Auntie, you're having your dinner at Colvin's. I've come to pick you up.'

She peers at me suspiciously. The stench of burnt fat and singed wool make me feel like vomiting.

'Who are you?' She has seen me several times since I came back and been reintroduced on every occasion.

'I'm Sorley. Your nephew. Colvin's brother.' Nothing changes on her face. 'Gid's son.'

Her eyes light up and for an awful moment I think she is going to hug me. I take a step back. 'Come on. We need to get this oven off and take you to Colvin's.'

'Don't you dare turn that off!' She presses against it. 'That's the turkey in there.'

'I see. Well, I guess they'll be needing it at Shepherd's Cottage, then. Liana said to bring it over.'

'I'm not doing what she bloody says.'

'Oh, but Colvin said he couldn't wait to taste Auntie Beulah's Christmas dinner.' She studies me through narrowed eyes. 'Best in the strath.'

She beams.

A great rummaging and tipping-out of cardboard boxes ensues and then the transfer of a shrivelled turkey and the blackened stumps of root veg, a soggy bag of defrosting peas and an evil-smelling concoction that Beulah claims is trifle. All of this goes into the back of the Landy. Beulah clambers into the front, decked in an old mink stole, its stuffed head leering at me from her shoulder. Under all her disintegrating finery she is still in her slippers.

Colvin meets us at the door of Shepherd's Cottage and while he installs Beulah in the front room with the television, I spirit her food into the bin. Then I push through the jammed sun-room door and into the kitchen. It is my first time back since I was thrown out. Liana is there, crouched by the open oven, skewering the turkey. She glances up at me and back to the bird, not a flicker on her face. I feel impaled.

Colvin walks in and heads to the fridge. 'Drink?'

'Yeah, juice, thanks.' I have been dry since the night of the fire, thanks to AA.

Step 1: *I admitted I was powerless over alcohol – that my life had become unmanageable.* Powerless over just about bloody everything.

Liana shuts the oven door, stands up and wipes her hands on her apron. It has a picture of Rudolph, with his shiny red nose, collapsed in a heap of bottles and cans. Above his dizzy face are the words 'Merry

Chri-*hic*-smash!' I don't know where she gets her aprons. As Colvin pours the juice, Liana and I look at each other.

'Sorley,' she says woodenly. There is no *'hermanito'*, no smile. 'Happy Christmas.'

'And to you, Liana. I, uh, I brought some things.' I put some supermarket chocolates and a bottle of elderflower fizz on the table.

'So kind,' she says, barely glancing at them. Never, in the past twenty years, have I been reduced to such measly offerings at Christmas. I always prided myself on exceptional taste. Now I believe there is no such thing; just money or the lack of it.

My lame offer of help is refused and I slink off to the living room to watch telly with Beulah. She talks constantly over it, pausing only occasionally to interject *What she say? What was that? You hear that, Gid?* I don't bother to correct her or to recount the lost expanses of broadcast.

I hear Mo arriving a little later, but she doesn't come in here. I find her in the kitchen regaling Colvin and Liana with tales from the Community Care Christmas lunch. She speaks with her hands, face animated and brimming with laughter.

'And then they're dancing! Wahey! And big Donnie, you know? Huge guy with the kind of monk's tonsure and the tiny terrier? Well, he started singing "Love Came Down at Christmas" and the place went quiet. Voice like Pavarotti and by the end not a dry eye in the house. Who knew?'

She sees me and throws up her hands. 'Sorley! All my Christmases have come at once!' She strides across and hugs me, then ferrets in a backpack on the floor and pushes a present into my hand. 'Open it, open it!' A book. *St Benedict for Business.* Is this a joke? She sees my face. 'Don't worry, Sox. You'll get it.'

I have no gifts for anyone.

When we sit down to Christmas dinner, Colvin guides Beulah to the end of the table furthest from the oven, seating himself and me on either side of her, though this does not prevent her steady stream of instructions and occasional efforts to heave herself up to 'help'. *Did you bring those sausages, Gid? These sprouts are too hard. But it's no Christmas without white pudding!* Liana, normally tolerant and amused by her, is strained, Mo biting her tongue. Tess loads up a plate and takes it upstairs to Alex, whom she found just before dark in the woods near the remains of the Green Bothy. She persuaded him to come home but he won't come out of his room. Doesn't like Christmas, Colvin explains. Doesn't like *people*, Mo adds. Doesn't like me, I think. And who can blame him?

When Tess is back down, Liana summons a forced jollity. *Crackers, everyone!* We cross arms and pull and snap as paper and plastic flotsam are ejected across the table. Last Christmas, the crackers Annabelle chose contained miniature birds in sterling silver. *Hats! Hats!* Liana barks, and it feels like some form of military humiliation. Only she and Tess get theirs lined up neatly on their smooth hair, while Colvin's teeters on his wiry curls, Mo's is lop-sided and mine scratches my burnt skin. Beulah fights with her yellow hat for several minutes, batting away help and finally snagging it on her wig like a bit of rubbish blown in on the wind. The jokes are read, the groans issued, the torn cracker shreds swept to the floor. Colvin pours wine for Liana, Tess and Beulah while Mo serves my elderflower fizz to the rest of us.

'Happy Christmas,' Liana says, in brittle cheer, raising her glass. We all raise and clink and echo and eat and try to make conversation. It falls mainly to Mo, with more stories about the lunch, and Tess with stories of music college, and Beulah with stories of the great and the good apparently enjoying her lavish Christmas dinner this very moment at Rowancraig House.

Colvin, who has said almost nothing, suddenly fills a gap. 'Aggarwals are buying Rowancraig.'

We all look at him.

'But it's not for sale!' Beulah protests.

No one argues.

'I'm dropping the case. End of fighting over the lease and that.' He glances up, then back to his plate, which he mops clean with a last parsnip. 'I'll be an employee.'

'Have you got a new job?' Beulah asks.

'Sorry, Colvin,' Mo murmurs.

'Is good,' Liana says, gathering up plates. 'Aggarwal is paying off all the legal expenses and he will renovate Shepherd's Cottage. Top to bottom. New kitchen, new bathrooms, new everything.'

'Who's doing this, Colvin?' There are peas caught in the fraying lace at Beulah's neck and her chin is slick with gravy. I lift my napkin and wipe it, an instinct now after my time with Dougie. She starts back and stares at me. 'Gid?'

'That's the end of a community buy-out, then.' Mo is glum.

'Never work.' Liana is emphatic as she scrapes the plates. 'Community can't agree on snacks for the Christmas party. Forget about running the estate!'

'Kirat Aggarwal –' I choose my words carefully – 'is a very astute businessman. If anyone can turn Rowancraig around—'

'Aggarwal?' Beulah has finally caught up. 'That Indian? Running Rowancraig?' She looks appalled.

'He's an American citizen, Auntie, born in Malaysia,' I explain. 'Indian heritage way back, I suppose, with a British wife, and yes, they're buying Rowancraig.'

She tries to stand up. 'Somebody's got to tell Lord Mackintosh – he'll be in the middle of his Christmas dinner – I've got to—' Colvin takes her by the elbow and tries to settle her, but it's a drawn-out affair. She is determined Mackintosh must be warned about the foreign invasion – the theft, no less – of his estate, and though she is momentarily distracted by the Christmas pudding (tactfully not set on fire this year) she keeps remembering her mission and trying to launch from her chair.

Liana looks fed up, Mo murderous.

Middle of the confusion, Tess blurts something. Whether to create a helpful diversion or out of a perverted sense of mischief, I don't know.

'What?' Liana says. Everyone is looking at her, even Beulah.

'Kirat and Vivienne Aggarwal's son – Rahesh – is my boyfriend.'

It sounds like a line from a comedy show where contestants say three outrageous things and you have to guess which is true. No one is doing any guessing. Or laughing. Just staring.

'How?' demands Liana.

'*How*?' Tess lifts her hands. 'What do you mean *how*?'

'How this happen? How – when you only see him one time? How – when he in America? How you not tell me anything? How, how, how?!' She bangs her hand on the table with each one.

'Well . . . I saw him a second time, actually, and he's not in America, he's in London and he's coming tomorrow, and . . . I'm telling you now.' She picks up her wine.

Colvin's face is grey.

Beulah leans forward, her velvety bosom skimming her custard. 'Who's coming tomorrow, pet?'

Lovers

I took Tess down to the station on Boxing Day to meet Rahesh off the London train. It was starting to snow as we stood on the platform and the flakes melted into her woolly hat and the hair on her shoulders.

'Meet you in the car,' I said, as the train pulled in.

'Thanks, Mo.' She squeezed my arm and shot me a quick, bright smile, eyes glowing.

Instead, I hid behind a pillar at the end of the platform to observe. She was the only person there, a splash of colour in her purple velvet coat, yellow boots and crazy multi-coloured scarf that had taken her three years and much swearing to knit. Only seventeen, I felt she was a baby still and I was protective as a bird of prey with chicks.

The brakes wheezed, the guard jumped out and a few doors opened. Rahesh was unmistakable, his handsome, hopeful face brightening at the sight of her, his stride quickening as he walked down the platform, small case in hand. He dropped it, and then both of them were running, and I felt a rush of fear and confusion as they flung themselves at each other and he whirled her around and around and around. Then I started sweating as he put her down and they kissed, long and close and slow. It seemed for ever before they let go and simply stood there, gazing at each other.

I felt I had invaded something sacred, and slipped back to the car. It was always that way for me, when I saw eros at work. It never stirred tenderness or passion or even a flutter of romantic sympathy, just a squirming discomfort, a wish that people would keep their love lives behind closed doors. I don't disapprove, mind, like I don't disapprove of sewage treatment or dentistry – I simply don't want to watch.

So why had I? Why had I lurked there and spied on them?

'You've stayed in touch, then,' I said, driving out of the car park with Rahesh beside me and Tess insisting on the back seat, but leaning forward so her face was between us.

'Every day,' she said, rubbing his shoulder. 'Email, texting, skype.'

'Romance ain't what it used to be,' I muttered. 'Ever written a letter?'

'Actually, yes,' Rahesh said and smiled at me. I cursed those beautiful huge eyes with their Bollywood lashes and the perfect coffee-coloured skin.

'Ever since that first note he wrote in the Ferryman,' Tess said, her finger stroking his cheek, 'we decided we wanted handwritten memories, so we've done that all along.' He put his hand on hers; I winced.

'No? Really?'

'Yep. He's Mr Orderly, so sits down every Sunday and writes a long account of his week—'

'Really boring,' he grinned.

'No! They're amazing.'

'And she's Miss Spontaneous and sends me this crazy, beautiful, mish-mash of stuff whenever the mood takes her—'

'Pile a rubbish.'

'No, I love it!'

'Like what?' I asked.

'Like her train ticket with a lipstick kiss on it, or a postcard from some dead-end town where she's been playing, some lyrics on a beermat.'

She laughed that big, joyous cackle of hers and tousled his hair. 'You better hang on to those. One day they'll be worth a lot of money.'

'Oh yeah – I could be rich!'

'You already are,' I pointed out.

'I know.' He shrugged. There was an uncomfortable pause, then he smiled at me again and said softly, 'Please don't hate me.'

How could I? He proved to be the perfect gentleman: so intelligent, polite and kind, I was floored. I kept looking for the catch, the thing to warn Tess about, but struggled to find it. All I could come up with was that he was too idealistic, too confident that the world could change and he would be part of the revolution. Was I just cynical now? Had I stopped believing when our little community lost the will to buy a piece of destiny? Just shrugged their collective shoulders so that another rich guy could take over, again? And not just any rich guy – this kid's dad.

They spent most of that week either at the Ferryman or out and about, rather than with their families. Kirat and Viv were up for New Year, staying at a Victorian hunting villa called Stag Lodge that they'd taken on as a base while renovating Rowancraig House, but when Rahesh took Tess to meet them, she felt out of her depth in their ever-shifting swirl of high-flying friends. She hadn't been to any of the places they talked about; she didn't know the orchestras, the galleries, the balls; she didn't know any of those people with titles and double-barrelled names they tossed about so casually; she hadn't watched polo, or been on a yacht, or shot game. The closest she'd come was beating on the local grouse drives and watching Colvin shoot foxes. But she didn't like guns.

Visits to Shepherd's Cottage weren't much better. True to form, Colvin said very little, Liana said too much and Alex said nothing at all, refusing to even meet the new boyfriend. Tess lost her temper and came back to me in tears, though Rahesh was philosophical and sure that everybody would be won over soon enough. I wasn't so sure.

Song

Tess and Rahesh drop in at Dougie's on their way back from walking An Sgiath on New Year's Day. I laugh at her impersonations of the Aggarwals' upper-crust crowd. *Oh, supah! Rupert and Clarabella Tiddly-Squatbottom are popping over from Balmoral for a spot of croquet! Then, what say we all go and shoot some locals after lunch?*

'Don't be intimidated, Tess,' I say. 'They're no better than you.' I hope my skin-tugging smile is more reassuring than ghastly as I pass some scones, the first I've made myself. A little doughy, but edible.

'No better? They're not half of you,' Rahesh insists, squeezing her knee. 'And whatever you do, don't try to become like them.'

I laugh bitterly. 'Been there, done that.'

'Aye,' says Dougie, shakily pushing a wad of scone and jam into his mouth. 'Thank god you've recovered.' He winks at me.

At the old man's request, Tess sings a few of his favourite tunes. 'Glen of My Heart', 'Wild Mountain Thyme', 'I Love a Lassie'. Rahesh gazes at her in rapture while Dougie gazes out at the mountains, tears in his eyes. It is the first time I have heard her sing and something about it spears me.

'My little flower,' Dougie says, 'you never met your granny Agnes, but her mark is in your ear. Her voice is yours.'

As the last notes die from the last song, we sit in silence, lost and still.

Sheep

On Rahesh's last night before flying back to the US, he and Tess came to the Ferryman for a farewell drink and Sorley brought Dougie. He still cherished his weekly visits and sat in the big armchair by the stove with his zimmer frame tucked behind and a Glenfiddich at his elbow, a straw poked in the honey-gold whisky. Rahesh took a stool near his feet and asked about the history of Briachan and the strath, indeed the whole Highlands. Dougie was a generous informant and Rahesh kept probing.

'Can I ask you a question, sir?' he said finally, leaning forward.

'Another one?'

'Has my father done the right thing – buying the estate, making Mr Munro an employee?'

Dougie looked long and hard at him, then smiled gently. 'You're a lawyer, aren't you? That's some question.'

'I know, I just want to understand. The Munros have always been here—'

'Not always.'

'No, really? Tess never—'

'Probably no one told her. The story's a wee bitty complicated.' His face was furrowed with concern on one half, slack from stroke on the other, making him appear both wise and comical at the same time.

Rahesh glanced across at Tess tuning her guitar and back to Dougie. 'Will you tell it to me?'

'Do my best, son, I'll do my best.' He settled back in the chair and sucked on his straw. 'You see, theirs is the story of the sheep in this strath and it's a long one, but dinna worry, I'll keep it brief.' A lopsided smile. 'Way back, Highlanders lived in small hamlets with cattle, pigs and a handful of sheep – just wee wiry beasts – and grew crops in raised beds called runrigs. Every summer the women and bairns herded the animals up to the high pastures, lived up there in shieling huts, then brought them back in the autumn. So it was a cycle, you see, that gave the soil at both ends fertilisation and rest.'

'Right. A good approach.'

'Aye, but life was no picnic, mind. Folk were dirt poor and often sick or starving.'

Tess started a swift, rhythmic tune and Dougie's one good foot tapped along in time.

'Their strength was in the culture,' he went on, pointing to her. 'Not just the music and whatnot, but the whole clan system of communal ownership and protection.' As she began her song, his face lit up. 'Didn't know she'd learned the Gaelic!'

'Just for singing, I think.'

'Oh, now that's a very famous one about the Battle of Culloden.' He nodded softly.

'She took me there yesterday. Pretty bleak place.'

'Och aye, still haunted they say.' He gave Rahesh a wink.

'Yeah, I could almost believe that, especially on a freezing January day blinded by mist!'

'Well, it's the authentic experience, laddie. We aim to please.'

They laughed and sipped their drinks.

'What did you learn, son?' Dougie turned a keen gaze on Rahesh as the young man related a well-remembered account of the Jacobite rebellions and the notorious final battle on British soil.

'But what really struck me was the aftermath,' Rahesh said, shaking his head. 'The violence of the Crown's troops right across the Highlands, the rape and destruction. Like, even the stripping of weapons so people couldn't defend themselves.'

'And far worse: the stripping of culture.'

'Yeah, I'd never realised bagpipes and tartan were banned, and the whole Gaelic language.'

'Oh yes. It was the ripping out of a tongue, my son, of a people's soul.' He turned to listen to Tess, as she started picking a gentle tune, her head bobbing with eyes closed. 'And I'm not sure we've ever recovered. In this very strath, the bairns were beaten in school for speaking Gaelic. I was beaten! Now they're desperate to teach it to them again!' He waved his glass towards Tess, then took a long pull on his straw. 'Ach, it's no the same!' he said, scowling at the object. 'But it's that or waste half of it doon me beard.'

'No Scotsman would waste whisky.'

'No Scotsman should waste *anything*.' Dougie winked at him again.

'Yeah, I love that. Wish Americans could say the same. But, hey, you were telling me about the sheep.'

'Oh aye! Actually, Culloden is part of the story cause with the loss of their weapons chiefs lost their fighting men, you see. So then they began to shift their loyalties from the humble clans to the upper crust of Edinburgh and London. Got fancy titles and the deeds to clan land, then wanted houses and the high life to match. Didn't need their clansmen any more, but needed money.'

'And sheep?'

'Drum roll, my laddie. We're there at last! The money, you see, was in the sheep – the big new breeds from the south, Cheviot and Blackface, the 'Great Sheep' they were called. So from the middle of the eighteenth century Highland chiefs started bringing flock masters up from England and the Borders and turning the land into sheep walks. The peasant farmers with their raggedy beasts and poor harvests were moved off.'

'Right. The Clearances. Tess has a song about that, as well.'

'Oh aye, there are many! Where would folk music be without tragedy?'

They laughed again and Dougie had a small coughing fit, Rahesh holding his glass till it was over. 'I'm coming apart at the seams, I'm afraid,' Dougie rasped, with a watery smile. 'But no, the Clearances were terrible. Course, there were folks refused to leave and found their homes burned down before their very eyes. Some were dumped on bits of poor land, while others gave up and went to the cities or overseas. The Americas, Australia.'

'Where, if you'll forgive me, some became land-grabbing oppressors themselves.'

'That they did. Another scar on our history, I grant you. Far worse.'

Rahesh nodded and spoke slowly. 'My ancestors have done it.'

Dougie studied him. 'My own are guilty, too, son. Oh, you'll get folks round hear swearing black and blue that *their* people never did such a thing, but of course they did. Our dear Mackintoshes of Rowancraig were notorious, as was the MacPherson chief. Some clan loyalists won't speak to me because I tell the truth, but in one way or another all the chiefs round here became lairds and moved the people to make money.'

'Tess took me up one of the valleys and we saw the ruins of the old villages, barely there under the grass.'

'Aye, aye! There were hundreds of souls up these glens once. Almost all gone. It's why most of the towns in this strath were built – to house the cleared peasants, because the lairds still wanted *some* people for the forest plantations and cannon fodder for their regiments. And of course the flock masters from the south needed a few under-shepherds.'

'Were Tess's' forebears hired then?'

'Tess's' forebear, my son, was not a Highlander. He was a flock master.'

Rahesh looked up, startled. Dougie met his gaze. 'Told you it was complicated.'

The young man's brow furrowed and he glanced across at Tess. She was singing a Gaelic waulking song, knocking the rhythm of the moving tweed on her guitar. 'I didn't realise . . .' he murmured. 'I thought . . .'

'Sure, he was like any other man, needing work. But it wasn't just the people who suffered. The old cycles of fertilising and resting disappeared and those vast flocks mowed the grass down, nibbled away at the seedlings and trampled the soil. Even their shit wasn't good enough, if you'll pardon my French. And though it pains me to say it, for Colvin is like a son to me, sheep are a plague of white locusts and we won't get good earth back or forests – *or enough people* – till we deal with them.'

Rahesh looked crestfallen.

'Ach, it's not just the shepherds' fault, laddie. Most of them are like Colvin – just struggling to make ends meet and to keep their rights over the land. It's the field sports that are the bigger problem. Hundreds of thousands of acres kept as a playground for the wealthy at the expense of the environment and the local people. Ours is a devastated landscape.' His eyes were on fire, cheeks inflamed, the glass trembling in his hand.

'I'm sorry, son. I've had too much of that,' he muttered, nodding at his glass, 'but if I keep quiet the stones will cry out.' Then he heaved himself forward in his seat and leaned into Rahesh, fixing him with a steely gaze, his whisky voice a passionate rasp. 'Trees and people have been decimated in our Highlands, son, and it's time for justice!'

Heart Failure

After Beulah nearly set fire to Rowancraig House that Christmas, Colvin, Sorley and I took it in turns to visit her every day, usually needing to extract her from some corner of the Big House and take her back to her own. I was never sure how much was dementia or how much was just the deliberate denial of reality that had marked so much of her life. Either way, Rowancraig was *hers* and we were dragging her away – from her job or her home or her family, depending on the current flight of fancy.

We got a place for her in a local care home where she stalked the corridors directing the staff and inspecting the housekeeping, and finding it all wanting. Every day she asked for Gid, or Archie, or Lord Mackintosh. On any given day, any one of them could be the laird or the keeper or the shepherd, or her husband or brother or son, and any one of them my father.

And then she died. A heart attack and it was all over.

I got someone else to do the funeral and stood there with my hands rammed in my pockets. She had never, ever, said she loved me or wanted me. She'd never said sorry, or well done, or asked if I was okay. She'd never said *You're mine*. So why do I not feel free? Instead of lifting the weight off me, why does her death only push it down harder? Why am I crying?

Two mothers gone. Where is the third? (Who was actually the first.) I have never tried to find her, but I cannot forget her. Can I forgive her? Does she ever think of me?

Easter Lamb

The road to Logie Castle runs past the Kirkton golf course, round the back of Ben Bodach and a few miles up the narrow Logie glen till it opens at Loch Glass. The castle sits on the far side of the loch, its stern face patched with pebble-dash, like a hard man staunching his shaving nicks with bits of tissue. Usually shrouded in mist and myth, that April day the castle was glowing in the sun and skirted with daffodils.

As the Aggarwals parked their Range Rover on the gravel drive they could see Lady Hoare-Cressington setting a vase of tulips on a garden table. Shielding her eyes, she peered across at them, then waved and came over.

'Hello, hello!' she fluted, her hands open, the sleeves of her chiffon dress wafting around her elbows. She was late seventies, thin and heron-like, with silver hair swept back in a french roll. 'Isn't this lovely!' She gripped Viv's hands and kissed her on both cheeks.

'Wonderful, Miranda!' Viv fluted back.

'So good to have you,' Lady Miranda continued, turning her hands and lipstick to Kirat.

'So good of you to invite us,' Kirat said. 'This is our son, Rahesh.'

Lady Miranda beamed and he gave himself to her papery hands and soft pecks. He was back from America to see Tess and had spent a few days swept up in the whirl of her Glasgow life with her young musician friends, classes and rehearsals, gigs and late nights. At first her circle treated him with polite distance and he felt as foreign amongst them as she did with his parents' set. But when they discovered he had turned his voracious hunger for learning to all things Scottish, including its music, they let him in.

One night as he walked Tess home after she'd been playing with her folky trio at a pub, he stopped her in the street, the city lights playing on her face. 'I could never take you away from here, Tess, not while you're still studying and carving your career. Not ever, if you don't want to leave.' She stared at him, uncertain of his meaning. He tucked a strand of hair behind her ear. 'But I would come. Do you want me in all of this?'

The next day, they came up to the strath for Easter, she to Shepherd's Cottage and he to Stag Lodge where his parents were staying for a week of holiday.

The long table in the Logie Castle dining room was overflowing with decorations: small baskets of eggs and fluffy chickens, vases of daffodils and chocolate bunnies on every plate.

'I've always splashed out on the Easter table,' Lady Miranda said, almost apologetic. 'The children loved it so much and now the grand-children do.' Her gaze ran across her guests, finding their place cards. She had a daughter and two sons, but only one was here, with his three children, new partner and her teenagers. All her children had messy lives – divorces, disgraces, debts – and all had children of their own whom she would have fought duels to protect. Except the main danger in their lives seemed to be their parents. *Her* children. Whom she'd brought up to do better than that. Perhaps the schools had gone soft, or perhaps it was not living through war, or not having her start in life: she was a fishmonger's daughter when she'd met the young Walter.

Whatever it was, they never came together as a whole family any more. Ever. The disputes had become too bitter. So the great (late) Hoare-Cressington Family Easter Sunday Lunch had become a friends-and-neighbours affair with an appearance from one branch of her own tree or, if she was very lucky, two.

After lunch, everyone gathered on the front steps for the commencement of the annual Logie Castle Easter Egg Hunt. Lady Miranda gave out cane baskets with long handles and pastel ribbons and explained that all the eggs were either in the walled garden, the topiary or the Italian terrace. The children set off screaming, the teenagers quickly overtaking them, and the adults yawning after the big lunch and eyeing up the garden chairs. But no, everyone had to join in; Lady Miranda was very strict on that point, just as she insisted that no chocolate was to be eaten during the hunt but shared equally at the end.

'You must come with me,' she said, looping her delicate hand through Viv's arm. 'I want to give you the tour of my garden. Will you indulge me?'

'Of course! I have so much to learn about gardening up here. I gather it's quite an art.'

Lady Miranda led her round the back of the house. 'An art, a science, yes – a kind of black magic, maybe?' Through a small gate they stepped into a grassy space where a scattering of young birch trees stood, buds still furled. At their feet, a carpet of purple and gold crocuses nodded in the breeze. Viv gasped and Lady Miranda beamed.

'Rather special, aren't they?'

'Ohhh . . .'

'But I tell you, this is a battlefield. Doesn't look it, but that's what gardening is up here, Vivienne – it's a battle.' She led her into the walled garden. 'Against the weather, the rabbits, the deer, the soil, the sheep, the dark: the list goes on and on!'

'Oh, but you've won, Miranda. Look at this place!' Viv waved her hand at the neat beds, the fruit trees, the climbers trained over walls and archways.

'No past tense, Vivienne, it has no end. Like everything about running a Highland estate, really. The victory is just in carrying on.' Then she laughed, a light tinkling sound, like glass chimes.

They continued through the garden arm in arm, Viv listening intently to Miranda's advice, Miranda quizzing her on their plans.

'Complete regeneration, top to bottom!' Viv said. They had already started by appointing an estate manager based in Perth, who would have oversight of the entire project. 'We were advised to avoid a local.'

'Oh, I would agree. Too bound in with everybody else. You need outside eyes.'

Then they'd appointed an architect and a building firm to restore the house to its former elegance, but with new roof, insulation, plumbing, wiring and glazing.

'And not just Rowancraig House, either,' Viv said. 'All the estate infrastructure – roads, fences, ditches, walls, you name it. And all the tenant properties, too. My god, there's been no refurbishment for years – it really is a travesty.'

'They'll love you, then.'

'I doubt that, Miranda.' Viv smiled wryly. 'No one loves the laird. But that shouldn't stop you from being a good one and we're really quite determined to do the right thing. We're terribly lucky to have wealth, but we know it comes with responsibilities.'

'That's exactly it, Vivienne. Owning all this land is a privilege, but we do it in trust. We are beholden to look after it wisely for all who live here now and in the future. And of course, that includes the environment and the wildlife. I am absolutely passionate about that.'

'Oh, *snap*! And about maintaining heritage. We're definitely going to revive the traditional field sports. We both absolutely adore them, and really, that's what Highland estates are all about, isn't it? Getting up on those moors with your guns and dogs, the sight of those regal stags, the shots ringing out and, oh, the gun smoke!'

'I know, there's nothing quite like it!'

'And then coming in to roaring fires and whisky and feasting. It's what Scotland does so well and we're absolutely having all that romance and tradition again, absolutely!' Her eyes glowed. She and Kirat had been guests on many a shoot and relished comparing notes afterwards, dissecting everything from the small talk of the host to the wines, and they knew *exactly* how they would do it themselves. 'So, even though the house won't be ready for another year, at least, we appointed a head keeper straight away to start preparing the moor. Now he *is* a local.' Kirat had asked around, got the word on the street, the whisper on the moor, as it were, and heard that Fachie MacPherson was the best there was.

Lady Miranda agreed. 'A bit of a brooding character,' she said, brushing leaves from a stone cherub's head, 'but god does he know the land!'

'So I hear, and no one blames him for Rowancraig's decline. Everything down to Mackintosh, apparently, or circumstances beyond his control.'

'I'm afraid so,' Lady Miranda sighed. 'He really got into quite a bad way, did poor Edgar. Never really recovered after his little boy Freddie died – their little boy – and then Clarice so soon after. Terribly sad. Took all the fight out of him.'

Meanwhile, Kirat, who had been oiling the wheels with his new neighbours throughout the lunch, joined Major Hoare-Cressington in the topiary.

'So, you'd advise just getting rid of the sheep, major?' He plucked a pink foil rabbit from a bush.

'As quickly as possible, my good man, and you must call me Watty. Everyone else does – when they're not calling me something unrepeatable. There's no money in wool and not much in lamb if you're trying to farm it up here. Too bloody cold. All your profits get lost in extra feed and wintering them away. We make it work by mixing it with cattle and using the sheep as tick mops on the hills for the grouse, you know?'

'And the payments from the EU.'

'Oh god, yes, there's not a farmer in the land could turn a profit without the EU subsidies, and yes, especially up here.' He unwrapped a silver egg and popped it into his mouth. 'But they do keep chopping and changing the policies, so you've got to be flexible and ready to diversify. Your man's just a shepherd – and not a very good one at that.'

'Really?' Kirat saw an egg in a birdbath and dutifully put it in his basket.

'I'm afraid not. Too traditional, too stuck in his ways, too stuck in the fifties, frankly.'

'Seems to keep the sheep well. Doesn't lose many.'

'Yes, but doesn't breed many, either. His return's too small, Kirat.' The major pounced on a chocolate chicken and started peeling off the foil.

'From what I can see,' Kirat said, suppressing a smile, 'between him and Lord Mackintosh there hasn't been investment in the farm for years, so his equipment and buildings are in a sorry state.'

The major didn't let a mouthful of chocolate hold him back. 'That's because that fool Colvin's wasted all his money fighting a lost cause. If he'd just accepted the limited partnership at the outset he'd be in a much better place now, and so would poor old Edgar, I dare say. So what are your plans?'

'Depends which member of the family you ask, but I definitely want to get the shooting back to a high standard so I'd like to utilise the sheep more for tick management, I think.'

'Well, you don't need your own. Let our lot graze your hills and you're sorted.' He pinged a creme egg into his basket.

'There's a thought.' It was not a new one. Kirat had heard it already from his estate manager who had drawn up a plan, complete with grazing leases. Rowancraig did not need its own sheep. Nor, it followed, a shepherd. It would have been quite straightforward if it wasn't for the complicating factor of Rahesh being, it seemed, besotted with the shepherd's daughter. They'd had no idea anything was going on till his blunt announcement at Christmas dinner. Kirat and Viv had been incredulous, though quickly tripping over themselves to staunch any suggestion of criticism or, worse still, class bias. Alone together, they had shaken their heads and rolled eyes. *Utterly bonkers.* A summer fling they could understand. A romp in the hayloft with a country wench – why not? But a *relationship*? The whole thing was completely ludicrous. Viv had taken to referring to Tess as Rahesh's *little shepherdess* (only to Kirat, of course), perhaps to reassure herself the girl was just a plaything, a passing fancy from a pastoral folk tale, of whom he would soon tire. Neither discussed it with any of their friends and family because, apart from being faintly embarrassing and something of a slur on their son's judgement, who was, after all, at the beginning of what was supposed to be an illustrious legal career, acknowledging the affair might give it solidity, a definite quality that could not be so easily erased, and erasure was the plan.

Unfortunately, things were not going to plan. Kirat entertained no illusions that Rahesh had flown all the way from America to spend Easter with his parents. Clearly, this girl was very important to him and so, by extension, was the shepherd.

To his chocolate-gobbling host he simply said, 'Let's explore things, major.'

'Watty, Watty, Watty! Can't be doing with pomp and ceremony in my own back garden.'

'Oh, but you know us Americans. We love it. That's why we come here.'

'Yes, of course – why don't you buy yourself a title off the internet or something? What do you fancy? Duke of Briachan? Earl of Rowancraig?'

'Nawab of Neverland?'

Watty roared with laughter. 'Here,' he said, paddling his big hand into Kirat's basket. 'Let me have some of yours or I'll get into trouble with her ladyship again. You wouldn't believe ... she's always accusing me of cheating!'

Bonding

'Sir?' Rahesh said, turning an anxious face to Colvin.

'Aye?' Colvin stood, hands on hips, watching the ewe with her twins. They were in one of the in-bye fields in the early days of lambing, a day of shifting sun and cloud and a nipping breeze.

'When I came to Briachan last year I had no idea how much it would change my life. I totally fell in love with this place . . . These people.' Rahesh gestured around him, taking in the whole valley and the surrounding hills. 'I particularly fell in love with Tess.' Colvin kept his eyes fixed on the sheep. 'Fortunately for me, she has returned that love. During our time apart we have written to each other and phoned – every day – and come to know one another very well. My visits at Christmas and now Easter have confirmed our love and . . . our desire to be together.' Colvin still said nothing. He did not move. Both lambs had found their mother's teats and were tugging happily. 'So . . . sir, I respectfully ask your permission to marry your daughter.' Silence. 'I have a good job in an international law firm and can transfer to the Glasgow office next year so Tess can finish her course. I earn enough to support us both so she will always be free to pursue her music. She deserves that. She is very talented.'

There was a long pause till Colvin said, 'She is also very young.'

She had turned eighteen that February. The same age Liana was when Colvin married her. Rahesh knew this but didn't mention it. 'Yes. I understand that will be of great concern to you; it is to me, also. But sometimes . . .' He talked on about all the provisions and arrangements, trying to find the vital piece of information that would win him over, but Colvin neither spoke nor looked at him and seemed more interested in a pair of large crows stalking along the fence near the lambs.

'Sir?' Rahesh said after a strained silence. 'Do I have your permission, sir?'

At last Colvin's eyes flickered to him briefly, then away again. 'Didn't think young folks asked for that any more.'

'I wanted to. And Tess agreed . . . Sir?'

'I take it she's said yes.'

'Yes, sir.'

'That's that, then, isn't it.'

Another pause.

'May we have your blessing, sir?'

Colvin squinted across the field. 'There's a yow needing help,' he muttered and walked away.

Boats

'Married?!' Viv stared at him over her glass of wine. 'To Tess?'

She laughed. At first a kind of cough of scorn, and then a full-bodied cackle that hit hysterical notes at the end. Kirat joined her. Rahesh felt his face burn, his fists tighten.

'Don't be ridiculous,' Viv said, pulling herself together with a sniff.

'I'm not. I'm deadly serious.'

'Oh, darling!' She turned her face full on him, her expression a blending of mirth and sympathy, much the way she had greeted the hare-brained schemes of his early childhood, the plans to explore Mars or be the next Jay-Z or run for president. 'Really now.'

'My choice is not good enough for you?'

'It's not that, Rahesh,' Kirat said. 'Of course we have no objection to Tess, personally, but you're too young. Both of you.'

'I'm twenty-five. The age Mum was, and you were only a year older.'

'Yes, but Tess is still a teenager and still a student, for godsake!' Viv protested. 'Honestly, sweetheart, have some sense!'

'You think I'm a fool?'

'Of course I don't think that, my darling, I just think you are terribly in love and that is the most wonderful thing and I think you should absolutely enjoy it, for however long it lasts, but just not worry about marriage! Not yet. Not for years! There's no rush.'

'We're not rushing. We aren't setting a date for the wedding and we aren't moving in together, but we are getting engaged and I am moving to Glasgow as soon as the company can organise the transfer. I've already applied.'

Viv opened her mouth, then shut it again and slid her eyes to Kirat. He put down his cutlery.

'Why, Rahesh? Why the move?'

'Because I have met the love of my life. We both know it. We cannot imagine being apart, so we have pledged to be together.'

Viv let out a long sigh. 'I remember feeling that way, too, darling. Several times. I was just the same, I—'

'You are not the same.' He pushed back his chair, dropped his napkin on his plate and left the room.

Later, as Rahesh stood outside contemplating the vast sky of stars, Kirat came out to join him. They stood in silence for a time. There was a rustle in the forest.

'Rahesh, I can't find the right way to say this, but I have to. I owe it to you.' Somewhere in the house, Viv switched off a light. 'Marriages may start with love. Or that thing we call love. That thing that knocks us over, makes us feel more alive and overjoyed and passionate than ever before. But that thing is like a gust of wind. It rises and falls, it changes direction, it disappears. Sometimes it destroys.' He puffed on his cigar and blew out a slow curl of smoke. 'It never sustains. For marriages to last, you can't cling to a sail and expect the wind to carry you across the sea. You need to build a boat together that you can steer and row and repair, over and over again. And that is work, Rahesh, not passion . . . And it is better if you know the same boats, if you get my meaning? A steamship and a canoe are too different.'

'You and Mom came from different boats.'

'Our childhoods, yes, but we had lived in the same world since our teens.'

'Her world. You lost yours. Or did you reject it?'

'That is too harsh. My family were never very traditional and neither practised their religion—'

'Because they came from different ones. Different boats.'

'And it cost them dearly, Rahesh.' His father's Muslim family had cut him off completely and his mother's high-born Hindu family were always unhappy about the marriage. As a result, Kirat grew up in a fiercely atheist home in which the prevailing religion was Advancement with daily sacrifices made to the chief deities of Discipline, Education and Acquisition. Kirat gaining US citizenship was the Promised Land; this and his business successes and strategic marriage were all evidence that the sacrifices had paid off, that the gods had delivered. Success had usurped salvation, material gain trumping spiritual surrender. And through it, his sense of himself as Malaysian was elusive, at times precious to him, at other times forgotten. It was surprising and uncomfortable to him that Rahesh cared more about it than he did, insisting on visits and learning about his heritage.

'But it was worth it, wasn't it?' Rahesh interrupted his thoughts.

'What was?'

'For your parents. The cost of coming together from different backgrounds.'

Kirat said nothing at first. There had never been any question of his parents' marriage not lasting, perhaps merely out of pride, to prove their point. But love? He had witnessed little affection between them, no shared laughter.

'They had other things in common – like your mother and I—'

'Money,' said Rahesh.

'That is not what this is about.'

'Class?'

'Why do you scorn me, Rahesh? Do you not believe I want what is best for you? That this is love?'

Farewell

Colvin and Tess were leaning against the cairn at the top of An Sgiath. It was a spring day of unusual stillness: the light brimmed the bowl of the sky and spilled into the strath in arcs. The sun stirred the fragrance of the hill – the ling and grasses and peat – and gave warmth to the stone at their backs. Below them, two buzzards circled above the woods, their high mournful call ringing through the air. Tess sat tucked into his side, with her arms around his middle and her head resting against his collarbone, her hair smelling like rabbit pelt. She had done this since she was tiny, this curling up so close she was almost inside him, and when she'd left for college he'd felt his ribs laid bare to the wind.

'Dad,' she said at last. He made a sound so quiet it was just a hum in his chest. 'Whatever happens, this is home.'

He squeezed her. Her hands tightened around him. And then she said those words that were hardly ever spoken in their family, certainly not by him. They seemed a foreign language, a foreign way.

'I love you.'

He couldn't speak.

Benedict

Dougie has suffered another stroke and lies in a hospital bed, vacant and dribbling. It is a cruelty I can hardly bear to witness but I visit often and read aloud from his favourite books. I found his old field notebooks with the spidery hand recording each sighting and I read out the longer passages from these. Sometimes, there is a rare personal comment, as if the binoculars were turned suddenly on himself.

Glen Feshie, June 1939. A pair of golden eagles circling above Mullach Clach a Bhlair. The first I have seen for many years and I think I know where their nest is. I enlisted yesterday but because of my forestry skills, they want me here in the Timber Corps. Disappointed not to be going out with the boys, but know I must serve where I am needed.

There is no change on his face, but I keep reading.

February 1940. Terrible destruction of the woodland. It grieves me to see these old giants crashing to the earth and the forest a wasteland. How on earth will the trees return? Where will the birds and beasts go?

He blinks and I wonder what his mind's eye looks upon.

June 1941. We have built for us a little hut in the woods on Rowancraig Estate, nicknamed the Green Bothy. It is rough and bare, but when the fire is burning and we are eating our rabbit stew, it is fit for kings! Some weekends one of the villages holds a ceilidh and the lumberjills come in from Glenmore, and what a fine evening we have of it. The pick of them is a Traveller girl with a sweet way and the voice of an angel – Miss Agnes Stewart. But I know she waits for Gideon, and though we all fear he is lost, we hold out hope. Until it is dashed, I will make no move.

I wonder at this life of principle and conviction. What would he have said to me if he'd known all I had done? Strangely, I wish I had told him.

In the weeks after Christmas, as I gradually healed from my burns, Mo nudged me to make plans. It was strange how my life had flipped, how I stood looking back on a trail of destruction and was unable to see ahead, when *before* – before the fund crashed and I ran away – everything in my life had always been about the future. Probably ever since I was eight and realised Mo wasn't coming back, I'd become obsessed with getting out and getting ahead, always driving, always pressing on. It's why I was so good at the stock market, because it's all about the future. And why I was so bad, in the end. Because it's all about the past. The wise ones know their history, and learn from it.

'You are not finished,' Mo says. 'You are purged. Now begin again.'

'I have. Caring.'

She gives me a sharp look. 'Financial consultancy?' she offers, casually, over a flask of coffee on a hillwalk.

I nearly choke on mine. 'Who would want to listen to me? *Do as I say, not as I do.*'

'Not as you *did*. That's the whole point. You understand how it all works and why it crashed. You wouldn't do it the same way again.'

'I wouldn't do it at all.'

'Why?'

'It's corrupt, twisted. All about greed. I'm not going back.'

She spoke slowly. 'Are you saying nobody should save or invest? Ever? Nobody should lend?'

'No, obviously, but . . .'

Silence.

'Why do you think I'm running this pub, Sorley?'

I begin to get in touch with my financial contacts again. I write some of the first honest emails for a long time. Not trying to pretend or persuade. Not trying to get anything, or anywhere, or anyone. Just telling my story. And fulfilling AA Step 8. *Made a list of all persons we had harmed, and became willing to make amends to them all.*

The answers blow me away. So many have lost so much. People are struggling, lonely, ashamed. I am telling their story, they say. People ring up and talk for hours, they ask to meet, they ask for help.

The burned leading the burned.

And then there are those who didn't get blown up – many, in fact – but they are interested in listening. They want to hear what I learned. They want their staff to hear it. I have finally started reading *St Benedict for Business* and am surprised at what a sixth-century monk can offer the twenty-first-century financial sector. Ethics, leadership, the value of people. I start scribbling thoughts, and there are meetings, consultations, some training. They offer expenses. A fee.

'See?' says Mo.

Even Kirat is interested. You can't make a Highland estate profitable on field sports alone, he explains, so how about a place for company retreats, courses, seminars and significant collaborations? *The Rowancraig Centre for Business Excellence.* Would I like to toss around ideas?

'Told you so,' says Mo.

Messenger

Fachie came to see Colvin one night, when the sky was turning dark green and Venus hung like a jewel in the west. In the past six years they had shared few words, but the same hurt of friendship lost. That night, they stood outside the lambing shed, the bleating and sheep smells behind them. Once again, Fachie came with bad news, but this time not at the behest of his employer. This time, behind his back.

Just that day, Kirat, who didn't know the history between these two families or how loyalties shift in small communities, had told Fachie his plan. A secret plan, of course, because 'hire slowly, fire quickly' was the motto, and he still wanted to keep Colvin on till the September sales when all the Rowancraig flock would be sold. But after that he would make him redundant.

'I argued for you,' Fachie told Colvin. 'I said we should keep you and this flock as tick mops, but he wasn't having it. Said he already had an arrangement with Logie, decision made. I'm sorry, Colvin. I tried.'

Colvin stood perfectly still. A family of swallows burst out of the shed and into the sky.

'Why are you telling me, then?'

'I'm not supposed to, but I wanted . . . I thought maybe if you had a bit of time . . . bit of warning.'

'Then what?'

'I dunno – talk to your solicitor, find out some other options, like. Make your move before he does.'

There was a long silence, Colvin staring into the dusk. 'You happy working for him?'

'Naw, I'm not *happy*, I just . . . I need the work, Colvin. I haven't had my own job for three years, been getting bits and pieces on other estates but mainly just shit. Doing gardens, building walls, picking litter, for fuck's sake—'

'That'll be me now.'

'But not because of me! It's not my job that's taking yours. God, I'm only trying to help, Colvin, can't you see that? If Kirat finds out, I'm back on my arse.'

Colvin squinted into the darkening sky, gnawing on his finger stump. 'That's that, then,' he said, turning back into the shed. 'Work to do. For now, anyway.'

Fachie watched him disappear, stood staring into the space, then walked away. Neither saw Alex, on his branch in the great Scots pine, listening.

Man of Sorrows

At the end of April the weather turned cruel. The wind came from the north and brought a freezing rain like darts of iron. The birthing ewes stood shivering in the fields, pressed against walls or under trees, their lambs sodden and thin. And then the rain became sleet and snow, scraping the face and stinging the breath. For three days, Colvin pushed through the blowing sheets of ice, watching the mothers, checking their young, bringing the suffering into the shed where straw and lamps gave warmth. Four times a day, he made his rounds, starting at five and not falling into his bed till after eleven, aching in every limb, cold as stone. And each day he got up to start again.

Liana tried to help but he refused it.

'Just the food is good,' he mumbled, as if that was all he now hoped from her.

And so she fed him with all the love and remorse that filled her. She added cream to his porridge and extra meat to every meal, turning out scones and cakes and pies like it was an army of farm hands she fed and not one lone shepherd.

Even Alex offered help, emerging slowly from his prison of rage, but Colvin refused that, too. The boy was beginning to settle into a small tutor group with others who hated school, but even getting him there each day was a challenge.

'Just you make a go of that new group,' Colvin said. 'Go for your exams, like.' He didn't know Alex had no intention of sitting exams and that the tutor let him spend all day walking and peering through binoculars and looking at bird sites online.

On the third day of the storm, when the snow blew sideways and stung his eyes, Colvin struggled across a field like a blind man. He found a ewe lying awkwardly, a new lamb bleating a few feet away and the hooves of another one sticking out of her. The mother was dead. Pushing his hand inside, he found the lamb's head pushed back, and with slow twisting and straining, managed to work it forward and draw the creature down. It, too, was dead. One of his hands was slimy and bloodied, the other frozen white; his face was frosted over, snowflakes massing in his eyebrows and lashes, lips blue. With the wind railing at him, he scooped up the living lamb, now so cold it no longer bleated, tucked her inside his jacket and drove home.

That was where Liana found him: kneeling on the floor of the shed in his sopping waterproofs, kneeling beside the pen of orphaned and rejected lambs, kneeling in a pool of muddy water. In his arms was the lamb he had just brought in, silent and stiff, its small head cricked to one side.

And Liana saw and heard something she had never witnessed before. An unearthly dry hacking sound, a shuddering all down his back, a gasp on the intake of breath.

Colvin was weeping.

A Time to Leave

She woke early with the sun shafting through the gap in the curtains. The bedroom was still, floating in liquid light. Squeezing her eyes shut, she rolled over towards Colvin. He wasn't there. The duvet on his side of the bed was not thrown back in the usual heap but neatly drawn up to the pillow. The mattress was cool and there was no sound, anywhere. The clock by her bed said 5.47 a.m. He didn't normally get up this early when lambing was over. But then, he hadn't been sleeping well lately and she'd been aware of him rising at strange hours or lying awake on his back, staring into the half-dark of the late May night. Sometimes, out of compassion and guilt, she had tried to make love to him, but he had pulled away. Once, he had held her at arm's length, his big rough hands on her shoulders, and stared at her, as if seeing her for the first time. Then she remembered that in the middle of this night she'd woken to find him standing at the window, looking out at the deep green sky.

She got up, pulled her old frayed dressing gown around her and went to find him. He wasn't in the bathroom or the kitchen or the living room. In the sun room she saw that his jacket and shoes were gone, so she dressed quickly and went out to check the barns and byres. There was no sign of him, but in the dog shed where she was greeted with the usual barking, she saw one of the cages open. Tiree was gone.

Strange. Had he woken early and seen – or sensed – that sheep had strayed, and gone out to find them? Going for his binoculars, she noticed that his usual pair – cast off from Alex – were missing. She found another pair and went out to scan the fields. All the sheep were scattered across the grass as ever, dozing, ambling, munching. If Colvin had been anywhere near, they would be trotting after him in hope of feed. She turned the sights up to the hills and traversed them slowly.

The morning light made everything glow, every rock and blade of sedge sharp and clear. No sign of him.

By now it was nearly seven and she was hungry. Back in the kitchen, she saw crumbs on the chopping board and a butter knife in the sink. In the bread box she noted that almost half the loaf was gone. A new block of cheese in the fridge had lost a large chunk and there was an empty ham packet in the bin. Opening the tin on the table, she was greeted by the rich, sweet smell of fruit cake, but only a scattering of currants. The cupboards revealed absent oatcakes and flapjacks, and apples were missing from the bowl. And the big flask.

It made no sense, because today they were supposed to be marking lambs, starting at 9.30. Maybe, she thought, clutching at straws, it was just a packed breakfast and he'd gone out for an early walk. But she knew that wouldn't happen. Colvin had so much walking to do for his work, he rarely did it for leisure. He never did anything for leisure, in truth, except flop exhausted in front of the television at night and fall asleep.

Sorley was coming to help with the marking. Dougie was in hospital, so he'd made the offer. *Old times' sake.* Colvin had tried to refuse but Sorley had insisted. He'd been back at Shepherd's Cottage a few times since Christmas, brief, uncertain visits. When Alex saw Sorley for the first time after the fire – saw the scars and the twisted cheek and the bald patches, saw the shadowed creature and the shabby clothes, mostly passed on from Colvin – his face went white. After that, he still didn't speak to him, but neither did he grip inside his pockets or go crashing out of the house. As for Liana, there rose between her and Sorley a painful blend of formality and gentleness, apology and side-stepping, an avoiding of eye contact and never being alone. They moved as if the air itself was fragile, that with a snap there would be nothing left to breathe.

When Liana phoned me shortly after 9.30, I came straight away. Colvin's mobile was sitting on his cluttered desk, so there was no way of calling him. Bizarrely, the wallet that normally lay untouched in a top drawer for days on end, was missing. Had he gone somewhere he would need money? Then why go at the crack of dawn and why walk? His crook was gone, too, which suggested he was looking for sheep, but why take all the food? He'd gathered the ewes and lambs into the enclosure by the barn the night before; he couldn't have forgotten marking. The three of us checked the house and outbuildings again, none of us speaking our fears, and then the in-bye fields. That was when I found the knife. Agnes's knife, lying beside the gate of the stone fank in the furthest field. So strange for him to leave it.

Throughout the morning we phoned around to see if anyone had seen him or knew anything, but when there was nothing, we phoned the police.

The search went on for nearly a week, with police and dogs and mountain rescue and most of the village involved, especially Fachie, who would not rest. Tess came back from college the day after he disappeared, and she and Alex walked the strath and the forest and the moor till their feet were blistered and their faces raw. Neighbours came to help on the farm, Sorley became the centre of communication for the search, while I coordinated the flow of food and people and cursed God for making me go through this again, in this same kitchen, for another dearly beloved. Liana shifted from rapid-fire instructions and blind ploughing on with chores to sudden collapses into sobbing. After two weeks, Rahesh flew from America and Kirat came up from London.

It was Kirat's first time in Shepherd's Cottage, and in the chaos and grief he seemed to lose all his self-assurance and sat perched on a kitchen chair folding and unfolding his hands. He assured Liana she did not need to worry about the farm: he would employ temporary labour till . . . and she could stay in the house till . . . and he would continue to pay Colvin's salary till . . . There were too many unfinished sentences. None of us could bear to contemplate the endings. And none of us, apart from Alex, knew then what Fachie had told Colvin a few weeks previously, though I discovered later that Kirat had feared it was known. We all feared so much and hid our guilt.

All that was discovered that first week was the knife and then the hip flask on An Sgiath. In the weeks and months that followed, his other belongings appeared, in a strange meandering trail that never brought us any closer to him, but gradually told his story.

Our story.

This story.

Sorley – After

The great torment is hope. We keep believing. Keep imagining there will be a call – *He is found!* Keep thinking he will walk back through that kitchen door. Keep looking to the line of hills to the north and – *There! On that ridge!* Once I was so sure, I broke into a run. A man with a stick and a dog. My shout of joy, arms flung out. And then the stranger passing by. The polite nod. And I'm on my knees in the dirt.

Inventory

Kirat insisted that Colvin's family should stay on at Shepherd's Cottage rent-free for a year, at least. How much was because of his guilty conscience or because of Rahesh's love for Tess or because of inherent decency I didn't know. Nor, I suspect, did he.

Liana took in more sewing work and added catering to her meagre sources of income, selling cakes to local cafes and doing events. As far as I could see, she worked all her waking hours, and from the look of her, that was most of them.

Alex dropped out of the tutor group and spent nearly all his time outside. Whether looking for birds or his father, no one knew.

Tess moved back home and spent the summer working with Liana or me, trying to be the strong one of the family.

Rahesh got his transfer to the Glasgow office early and spent every weekend here with Tess.

Kirat and Viv came and went between Stag Lodge and London. They pushed on with renovations at Rowancraig House but were subdued. They were learning more about the complex web of connections here and the history between Fachie and Colvin.

Fachie denied telling him about the redundancy plan.

Sorley moved into a tiny bedsit in Kirkton and cobbled together odd jobs doing just about anything as he slowly built up his consultancy. Mending fences one day, flying to London the next. Missing a few AA meetings, but still dry.

Dougie died.

I stood behind the bar at the Ferryman and listened to them all. Even Dougie. I felt his presence when the place was quiet and there was nothing but the shifting of logs in the fire. Once, I am sure I heard him speak.

Wish you were here.

But Colvin. My brother, my beloved, my Colvin.

That rare, quiet voice I craved but never heard. That absence. That unknown.

He was never found.

Sign 10: Gun

Ten months after Colvin disappeared, Fachie found his shotgun. It was an overcast March day and he was managing the muirburn on Rowancraig, setting light to the heather where it was long and woody to stimulate fresh growth for grouse chicks. As he walked with his blowtorch, smoke billowing around him, he nearly trod on the gun. He knew immediately it was Colvin's, as he'd helped him choose it years ago in the Inverness gun dealer's, though Colvin only ever used it to kill foxes or suffering sheep. The gun was empty, and after so long in the elements, the wood was splitting and the barrel starting to rust.

Beating

Sorley

Middle of October, 2010. When I arrive at Stag Lodge at 8.30, the party is gathering in the front drive, all trussed up in tweeds and kilts and breeks, gun dogs snooping around their feet, 4x4s parked nearby with doors wide. I have been here many times now, as the Aggarwals have been insistent in their welcome and Kirat has bent over backwards to help me develop my consultancy. They could have retreated into frosty indifference to our tragic family, but perhaps because of Rahesh and Tess they can't. And, of course, because of Colvin. When the Aggarwals saw how the community rose like a great wave in the search for him and the standing with us, they must have known their reputation depended on their response. One way or another, they are saddled with us. And we with them. Whenever they are up, they have me round for a meal or drinks, and Kirat took me on a shoot on an estate in Sutherland in August, on the Glorious Twelfth, the start of the grouse season. In my wealthy days I went shooting quite often; it was a good way to win clients. It's why, with deep ambivalence, I am here today. Dougie, I imagine, would have his head in his hands.

Kirat throws out an arm to me as I approach across the gravel. 'Sorley! Thank god you're here – we need someone who can count.' He slaps me on the shoulder and steers me towards the others. 'Hey, everyone, this is Sorley Munro. Last time I went on the moor with this sharpshooter he was like Clint Eastwood, I tell you!'

'Hello, cowboy,' says a large man with a bristling white moustache and a deerstalker.

'Major Walter Hoare-Cressington,' Kirat explains. 'Logie Castle.'

'Oh, Watty, Watty!' the big man cries. 'Just call me Watty.' His fleshy hand pumps mine up and down as his piggy eyes gleam.

'He gets called a lot worse,' says a tall thin man by his side, extending a hand. 'Francis.'

'Hello. You local as well?'

'No, no. I'm at Lochmully over the mountain. Popped across last night – can't resist a grouse shoot, or Kirat and Viv's hospitality.' He smiles; his accent is posh Scots and beautifully oiled.

'Francis Deveraux is our man in Scottish Land and Estates,' Kirat says. 'What he doesn't know about land law isn't worth knowing.'

'And there's never been a more critical time to know it,' snorts a man gnawing on a pipe a few feet away. Stout and bald, he wears a pale green kilt and bright green socks with orange flashes. 'Bloody Bolsheviks trying to ruin the place.'

'Sorley, let me introduce Lionel MacLeod, Earl of Balgarry,' Kirat says, and the man removes his pipe and stands up to shake hands.

'Grew up here, I gather?' he asks, smiling at me.

'On the sheep farm.' I nod.

'Well, as long as you shoot the birds and not the beaters, I don't give a damn where you come from. Welcome aboard!'

Mo

The beaters meet at Snowberry Cottage, where Fachie lives with his new partner, who runs it as a B&B alongside her efforts to sell her paintings, button jewellery and crochet work. The honeysuckle and roses over the door have died back and there are only late blooming flowers left in the beds. About twenty of us have gathered for the day, mainly local teenagers earning pocket money, but also some keepers from the neighbouring estates: Logie to the south and Glenfarr to the north. I am a late recruit.

We pile into the 4x4s with the dogs at our feet, the air thick with the smells of leather, canvas and damp wool, gunpowder and diesel, dogs and bodies. Fachie leads the way in the front vehicle and I'm happy for him. This is his first shoot as head gamekeeper on Rowancraig since Mackintosh laid him off four years ago. Today is the inaugural shoot, a family-and-friends affair, with Kirat and Vivienne playing their cards well, strengthening bonds with neighbouring estates and some very high-placed landowners in the Highlands. There's an invisible web connecting them all, spun over hundreds of years with the threads of boarding school, Oxbridge, the Northern Meeting, the peerage, balls, banquets and business deals. They occupy the same physical landscape as the rest of us, but move in entirely different territory.

Of course, Rahesh has made a tear in the fabric by getting engaged to the daughter of the failing shepherd. Now the lost shepherd. He is not the first, nor will he be the last, to threaten the system by falling in love outside the net, but it never seems to change anything. The upper tiers repair the hole and close ranks. He should have been with his parents today, hobnobbing with the guns and furthering his prospects, but he wanted to be with Tess and she wanted to be with the beaters. There was a tense conversation with Kirat and Viv and a compromise: they would beat in the morning and shoot in the afternoon.

Liana is also part of the grand expedition. Vivienne commissioned her to provide the lunch for the guns and she span into orbit, going over her menu with me countless times, practising her quiches and vol-au-vents, experimenting with crumble fillings, concocting wild mushroom soup and quail egg whatever. The owners of all the neighbouring estates would be there, so potentially a lot of work. Must impress.

Tess and Rahesh came to the Ferryman on Friday night to meet with Fachie and the other keepers so he could talk them through the plans for the day. Alex tagged along. Which was strange. He avoided social spaces at the best of times (particularly if Rahesh was there) and we all knew he hated the shooting of birds, especially driven grouse, which he called orchestrated slaughter and the cause of raptor persecution. But there he was, hunkered by the stove, repeatedly snapping twigs and firing them in as the others sat round a table with a map. Then Fachie and the keepers left and Alex blurted out that he was coming. There was shocked silence. Tess asked why and he shrugged and just said *Because*. We tried to reason with him. He would hate everything about it: he hated shooting; hated following orders; hated groups (hated *people*). The dead birds would distress him, the bumpy drive make him sick, and the guns infuriate him.

And then he explained, staring into the fire as he shredded a twig. 'I dropped out of school and I don't earn anything. Everyone else is working hard. I have to . . . make an effort.' We fell over ourselves to commend this laudable attitude. It was the first time he'd shown any sign of emerging from his private darkness. But it didn't have to be a grouse shoot, we urged. There was other work around. He could chop wood for me if he wanted, or wash up.

'Everyone else is doing *this*,' he said. 'The whole family. I need to join in.'

We insisted he didn't, but then he delivered the fatal blow.

'For Dad.'

There was no logic to it but no arguing either.

Fachie, when he found out, was wary. A lot was hanging on this shoot for him. This was his first chance to prove Kirat had been right in reappointing him, and he didn't want anything, least of all a surly Alex, getting in the way. But when I explained that Alex felt this was for Colvin – a gesture of family solidarity – he sighed and relented. Of course Liana, already stressed and feverish in her preparations, nearly erupted. The prospect of Alex in this high-stakes day was too much. But it was when my dear strong Tess confessed her anxiety, that I agreed to go along.

'He'll lose it at some point,' she said. 'He'll just go crashing off into the wilderness and I won't be able to help him.'

'But you've always been the person he needs at times like that. You can steady him like no one else.'

'Not any more. First it was me going away to college, and then Rahesh, and now Dad . . .' She tried to speak but could only wave her hand vaguely at the hills, eyes squeezed shut.

'Okay, baby,' I said, rubbing her arm. 'I'll try to keep him calm. He'll probably want to leave pretty quickly, anyway, so I'll just drive him home and it'll all be over.'

Sorley

I'm ushered into Kirat's 4x4 with Lady Miranda in the front seat, Captain Robert Eccleshare, heir to Dunbeattie Castle, on my left and Joseph Anokhin, laird of Glenfarr Estate, on my right. I can't help smiling at the thought of getting them round for drinkies in my bedsit. But Joseph is unpretentious and his deep black eyes are full of interest as he asks about my growing up in the area and my life since. I am honest about the finance, but guarded about the family. Everyone local knows about Colvin's disappearance and Kirat, at my request, warned his guests not to mention it. Joseph, who looks a bit like Rasputin after a haircut, has owned Glenfarr for over ten years now and I have heard mixed reports. Accounts of his wealth are eye-watering, possibly exaggerated, but he does own property and businesses all around the world as well as his vast Highland estate. Some people despise a Russian owning so much Scottish land and paying very little tax in this country.

'But that's not his fault,' Francis Deveraux – our man in Scottish Land and Estates – tells me, later in the day. 'That's just the law as it stands and he's doing everything by the letter. And, look, if some foreign bugger wants to pour his money into this blasted heath then he's welcome to it, I say. You don't make money on a Highland sporting estate, you merely contribute to the local economy, and he's doing a jolly good job of it. More power to him.'

It looked to me like he was making rather a lot of money from his estate and certainly the Earl of Balgarry wasn't so supportive.

'He's a greenie! Culled that many deer there aren't enough left for his neighbours to have a decent stalk. It's outrageous.'

With an almost religious reverence for trees, Joseph had committed to extensive reforestation and largely dispensed with deer fences for protecting seedlings, choosing instead to cull large numbers and allow the forest to regenerate naturally. His estate was a model of diversification, with a caravan park, holiday accommodation, wildlife tours, a farm and events programme as well as some of the traditional sporting pursuits. He paid his staff well, improved their accommodation and got to know them, and they respected him. At the same time, others in the community resented him for being rich and progressive and successful and foreign. It was hard to know which of these crimes was worst.

Up on the moor we head to the first line of butts, stone hollows built into the ridge and facing north, completely hidden by turf at the front. Mine is right at the top, with views across the moor on all sides and little protection from the wind, so I'm glad of the thick jacket Colvin had passed on to me and Dougie's old flat cap, tucked over the tops of my ears. Fachie had lent me gun and sheath, cartridge pouch and ear defenders. He'd also insisted I wear a tie.

I set up the marker sticks at either corner of the butt and load the gun. Far across the valley to the south east I can see the Cairngorms, their curved flanks in shades of rust and brown, crowned with the year's first dusting of snow.

Mo

A sharp breeze trembles the heather on the moor. The forests on the lower hills are glowing orange and gold, and wisps of mist rise from the loch. We spread out in a long line, about ten metres apart with the flankers at either end and Fachie in the middle. Alex is half way down our side with Tess on his right and me on his left, while Rahesh has tactfully placed himself far down the other end. The wind tangles Alex's long hair and his pale, spot-ridden face is almost hidden behind it. He's said very little today, but has complied with every instruction. At Fachie's signal we walk forwards at a strong pace, flipping our white plastic flags and adding the occasional call. Alex makes an eerily exact imitation of a grouse cry.

A covey of them catapult into the sky and shots ring out.

Sorley

The grouse spear through the air at over seventy miles per hour, above us and behind us in a flash. We shoot and reload and shoot and reload and shoot. Birds twist and plummet. Dogs run. The sky is punctured by shots, the air pungent with gun smoke, the moor thrumming. Then comes the call to stop

The beaters and the pickers-up appear, trudging across the uneven ground. Rahesh, courteous and interested, Mo joking, Tess watching Alex, Alex watching the ground. The guns point out where their kill fell, the dogs retrieve, and the birds are counted and loaded onto the argocat. There is chat and laughter and sharing notes, and we all return to our vehicles for the next drive. After that one, Vivienne passes around rich coffee and Liana's cakes, and I remember how easy it is to enjoy this world. Along with seven brace of grouse, I have also bagged a wealth management consultation with the heir to Dunbeattie Castle and an after-dinner speech for Scottish Land and Estates.

Mo

The gunshots send a jolt through Alex's body. I'm looking right at him when they ring out. He walks on, pushing through the sedge, his face tilted up now to the birds in flight. When each one plummets to the ground, he shuts his eyes. I give him a cup of tea at morning break and notice his hand is trembling.

'Time to go home,' I whisper. 'I'll take you.' He just shakes his head. 'C'mon, Alex. Why you doing this, pal?'

He doesn't speak for a while and when he does, his voice is harsh. 'For Dad.'

'How?'

What has any of this got to do with Colvin? Sure, he went beating as a kid, and some of his sheep were tick mops on the grouse moor, but he had no real interest in the sport. From what Tess said, he never suggested Alex go beating. Never even mentioned it.

'How is this for your dad?'

He shrugs, squints off at the horizon, then his eyes slide to me and I see something in them that fills me with dread.

Sorley

After two more drives we stop for lunch at Crow's Roost, a wooden bothy far up the moor and near a burn. Liana is already there and has lit the wood stove and the Rayburn and laid the table. She is in chef's whites with her hair held back by a white band. She looks nervous and so thin. But painfully beautiful. I see the sculpture of her face: the dark eyes and sensuous mouth, the ridges of her cheekbones flushed with pink. Since Colvin's disappearance we have circled each other warily, relieved to witness the other's grief, refusing to admit in our gaze what passed between us, though in my mind it is a growing torment. With her now, I am possessed by longing, a physical ache from behind my ribs to the flaring in my groin, and it is hard not to watch her every move as she smiles and greets the guns, passes out hot fruit punch and settles us at the table.

Tess enters with Rahesh and there are cries of welcome from some and polite nods from others. She hugs Liana and takes the vacant seat beside Lady Miranda, who smiles at her and squeezes her hand.

Mo

During lunch I offer Alex cheese sandwiches, crisps and chocolate but he won't have anything and won't sit down. He keeps circling the argocats piled high with dead grouse and then walking away, muttering and clutching in his pockets. Every now and then he climbs into a 4x4 and fossicks about and then gets back out and takes off walking, then returns again. People watch him and glance at me; Fachie gives me a hard look.

'That's enough now, Alex.' I sidle up to him. 'This is just killing you. We're going home.'

He walks away.

Sorley

Liana's lunch is a triumph, from the forest mushroom soup and herb rolls, through to the warm smoked salmon quiche and salads, to the rhubarb and ginger crumble with whipped whisky cream. I am about to refuse the wine but as Liana moves round the table offering the bottle, somehow, with breath-taking ease I think *Why not? Just one.* And so I drink, and more than just one. It's all washed down with dark coffee and home-made pralines, and by the end I am swollen with food and alcohol and pride and lust. As we rise, I brush against her, my hand trailing her thigh. Her eyes flicker to me.

Watty, who has drunk more than anyone, pushes between us. 'That was a tour de force, darling!' He takes her hand and kisses it noisily. There are cheers and applause from all. *Oh yes, absolutely delicious! – A feast! I shan't be able to walk, far less shoot! – We'll get your number off Viv, my dear, you could be very busy!* All the men kiss her, on the hand or the cheek or both cheeks, as they head outside. I am deliberately last. I pull her close so she can smell the wine on my breath and feel my excitement. She looks me straight in the eye, leans forward and kisses the scars on my cheek. Then her lips drift to my mouth and we are lost, seizing each other in a deep, desperate kiss. It might have gone on for ever but for the shouting outside.

Mo

One of the young beaters yells and points. Far up the burn where the ground opens in a shallow basin of long grasses, a pair of stags are squaring up for the rut. We gather to watch, the guns appearing from Crow's Roost and joining us, Major Watty glassy-eyed and burping. The stags eye each other with heads high, antlers draped with moss and bracken, nostrils flared, while behind them on the brow of the hill a party of hinds watch, motionless but for the occasional twitch of an ear. One of the stags roars, a sound that makes my hair stand on end. The other roars in return, louder, fiercer. Then at some invisible signal, they charge at each other and crash heads, antlers locking, hooves digging and pushing into the ground as they circle.

Watty cheers and a few people run to the vehicles for cameras and binoculars.

Near me, Fachie sidles quietly up to Kirat. 'Sir.'

'Fachie!' Kirat turns and claps a hand on his arm. 'What an awesome day you've put on for us! How'd you get those stags lined up right on cue?' He is laughing, glowing, full of bonhomie. Things couldn't be better.

'All in a day's work, sir,' Fachie says, with the barest nod.

'Well, you sure know what you're doing, my friend. Glad I listened to everybody.'

'Thank you. Eh, excuse me for saying it, sir, but I don't think the major is fit to shoot this afternoon.' They both look across to where he is doing an impersonation of a stag, all stumbling steps and bawdy roaring with plump fingers rising from each side of his head.

'I see what you mean. But I think that's more high spirits and horsing around than too much drink, don't you?'

'Perhaps, sir, but I am concerned.'

'Don't be, Fachie. He's been out shooting since he could walk, he tells me. Very experienced, and yes, drinks like a fish, but he's a big man. He can handle it.'

Fachie stands in silence for a moment, watching the major trip on a tussock of grass, catch himself on Robert Eccleshare's arm and erupt with laughter. The head keeper of Rowancraig nods curtly and turns back to gather the beaters.

Alex

I see it now. The vision in my head. The call.

The guns are there, laughing, patting their stomachs. Kirat in the middle, then a fat man with a pipe, then Rahesh, joking with the old lady. Then a thin man, with his hand on Tess's back.

This is what I must do. I see it, I see it:

Walk to the nearest 4x4, back doors open, take out a gun and walk towards them.

Mo will shout my name and they will all turn to look. Point the gun at Kirat.

This is the time to kill.

'Alex?' cries Kirat, lifts his hands to the side.

'You drove my dad to death. You took his farm, you took his job. You left him with nothing!'

Everyone stares. Sorley and Mum come out the bothy door.

'Give that to me, Alex,' Fachie says, moving towards me.

'Get away!' I yell and swing the gun on him. 'You're no better! Supposed to be his best friend and you served him notice to quit.'

'Alex, I didn't—'

'Night of the Long Knives! You betrayed him!'

'Put it down, Alex.'

'And all of you!' I sweep the gun across the lot of them, their ugly faces gaping. 'You kill and kill and kill! These birds today – and the raptors! The eagles and hen harriers and kites – so they won't take the grouse chicks, just so youse can kill em!'

'Lex.' It is Tess, walking slowly towards me, hands stretched out. 'Lex, no.'

'And you!' I swing the gun to her. I try to be strong but my voice is breaking. 'You betrayed me! You broke your promise!'

'What?'

'You promised – all your life – to look after me – and you left – and you betrayed our whole family – to marry him.' I turn the gun on Rahesh.

'Lex!' She starts running towards me.

'Stop or I'll shoot him!' I'm looking at Rahesh, his hands up at his shoulders. 'You don't belong here. Your family has destroyed my family. You've driven my dad to his death. You've stolen my sister – she's not one of you! I'm going to fucking kill you!'

'Lex.' Tess is on her knees.

'Alex!' It is Mum this time, pushing her way past the others. 'Bebe!'

'You?!' I point the gun right at her face. 'Don't you dare call my name! You destroyed Dad more than anyone!'

'Alex?' She is crying.

'*You fucking bitch!*' I can't stop crying now. '*You fucked his brother right under his nose, you fucking whore!*'

'*Alex!*' Sorley now.

'*And you! You deserve to die first, you motherfucker! You didn't give a damn about us when you were rich and then when you lost it you came and stole everything from us! You told my sister to leave home. You fucked my mother. You burned down my hide. You drove my dad away – from his farm, his family, his life! You come here today to be one of them, not one of us, and now you steal the birds out of the sky, you cunt – you stole everything and you will die!*'

Sorley

Rounding the back of the vehicle for my camera, I almost walk straight into Alex. He's fumbling with a gun. We both startle.

'Alex?'

His face is white and he is trembling. 'You?'

'What are you doing, Alex? What's wrong?'

'Everything! Can't you see? I have to do this!' He waves the gun.

'Do what? Join the shoot?'

'I have to . . . for Dad.' His face clenches.

I raise a hand slowly, careful not to touch him. 'No, Alex. Your dad wouldn't . . . You don't have to—'

'I have to kill!'

'Kill? You mean the birds?'

'You!'

My breath sucks in. But he doesn't point the gun at me. He grips it side on, making no eye contact.

'Let it go, Alex.' I speak low and quiet. 'Lay it down.'

He shakes his head and clutches the gun to his chest, the barrel pointing to the sky. I spread my hands open in front of him, repeating my words.

Then, teeth chattering as if he's freezing cold: 'You ruined *everything* – Mum . . . my hide . . . Dad . . . You should *die*—'

His whole body is shaking, face contorting.

'Yes, Alex. You're right. Do you want to kill me?'

He nods, then shakes his head. 'Want to kill myself!' And he sobs, his hands groping at the gun.

'Alex, Alex . . .'

'I never wanted to follow Dad. I didn't help. I hated sheep. I made him go . . .' His voice splinters, lost in the crying. 'Kill myself!' he howls, and tries to swing the gun to point at his own heart, fumbling for the trigger.

I throw myself at him and we fall together, wrestling and rolling on the ground. As I wrench the gun away, a shot fires.

The Tenth Plague

There is an explosion of screaming and running.

Alex stops struggling in my arms. The gun lies on the ground beneath us, cold. The firing and the outburst is from somewhere else. I jump up, grabbing the gun away from him, and feel a searing pain down my left leg. He scrambles to his feet and follows me round the vehicle, but any fight between us is forgotten when we witness the scene below.

People are crowded around a body on the ground, some running to the vehicles or Crow's Roost. A woman's voice wails. Major Walter Hoare-Cressington stands at the back of an open Land Rover, eyes wide and mouth slack, a shotgun in his hand.

The body is Rahesh.

Confessions

In those first raw weeks, they come to me at the Ferryman, one at a time, when all is quiet and they can be alone.

Fachie comes and tells me – over and over again – that he warned Kirat, and look what came of it? Then one night he tells me about the other warning, the one he gave Colvin during lambing, and look what came of that? Why was he doomed to always be the bearer of bad news? The harbinger of ruin?

'Even had to tell my own kids when their mum left. Why did I have to do that? What did I do to deserve this?'

He isn't sure how long he will have his job. There are no more shoots scheduled on Rowancraig for the time being. Possibly ever.

And he misses his father. When he speaks of Dougie, there is a twitch in his cheek. By the very end, they'd given up arguing about land use and talked about what they both loved: Fachie's kids, shinty, dogs. Oh, they both loved the land, right enough, but when they looked at it, they saw different things.

Kirat comes, drawn and fearful, everything unknown. He orders whisky but doesn't drink it. Just turns it in his hand as he tells me about his son and all the plans he and Viv once had for Rowancraig, good and ill. He confesses the plan he had not shared with Rahesh: removing the shepherd. 'Do you think Colvin knew? Is this my punishment?'

Viv comes, sitting by the stove and staring into the fire. I take the chair near her, put a wine on the table at her knee. She tries to speak but starts to cry. My hand rests on her arm and she grips my fingers as she pushes a tissue into her eyes, smearing her make-up. 'Why?' she gasps.

Liana comes, she's helping in the kitchen a lot now. No catering requests arose from that grouse shoot after all. 'What's the point?' she mutters, slamming oven doors and washing pots like she is beating the devil out of them.

Tess comes, burdened and brave. 'Where to now?'

Even Alex comes – after hours, when absolutely no one else is here – and confesses in a few stark words his vision on the grouse moor. What he had wanted to do, but could not. The violence of it. 'Who am I?'

Sorley comes, hobbling. He never sits at the bar, just finds a chair in a far corner, avoiding the smell of alcohol and the heat of the fire. I take him a lemon, mint and ginger cordial, and if no one else is around, we talk. He tells me what happened that day – between him and the wine, him and Alex. Doesn't mention Liana. 'Why am I back to square one? Step One.'

'What about Step Three?' I ask. *'Made a decision to turn our will and our lives over to the care of God as we understand Him?'*

'I don't understand him.'

'Same here, but you know what it means.'

'I'm not doing the steps in order. Got stuck at two and the Higher Power.'

'Maybe that's why you're back at one, then.'

He takes a breath but says nothing.

I have never seen his face so sad. Touching his hand, my voice comes soft. 'How about five? Leave God out for now, but . . . *admitting to ourselves and to another human being the exact nature of our wrongs?'*

The silence seems to last for ever.

Finally, he speaks. 'My name is Sorley MacLean Munro and I am the shepherd boy made banker. The younger son, with a hand on his brother's heel.'

Recovery

When Alex and I fought on the ground, he was crying so hard it was like he was breaking apart, and for the first time I felt compassion for him. He was writhing and kicking, but not so much to hurt me as to make me hurt him. To stop me from stopping him shoot himself.

'Alex!' I panted. 'Your dad loves you! Wants you to live!'

And then the gun fired. The other one.

Alex's gun, I discovered later, was never even loaded.

But something happened to my hip as I wrestled with him and I am always in pain now, always limping. Sometimes it wakes me at night and is like fire from my groin down though my leg.

Strangely, the fight seems to have cleared the air between us. Alex now speaks to me and looks me in the eye – without hatred – and I am straight with him. *Get counselling or I'll tell the police what happened.*

He is straight with me. *Get away from Mum or I'll tell everyone what happened.*

Fair enough. *For now or for ever?*

He just stares at me.

But he does go for counselling. With Mo. She suggests all the sessions are outdoors or in hides and Alex can be staring down his binoculars the whole time if he wants.

I stay away from Liana and she makes no contact with me. I do not trust myself – why would anyone else? So I avoid her, except in my dreams. All day I remember her, imagine her, desire her. At night all the delights and deviances of my life parade themselves in a contorted bacchanal, a circus of the macabre in which the trapeze artists fall, the clowns dismember themselves and the lion devours a child.

Unexpectedly, Tess becomes a friend. Doesn't drive, so I give her lifts when Mo or Liana can't, biting my lip when a gear change sends pain knifing down my leg. After the shooting, most of the journeys are because of Rahesh.

No, he wasn't killed. The shot sprayed the side of his head, puncturing his jugular, and if it hadn't been for Fachie's swift first aid, he would have died on the moor. But instead he was airlifted to a hospital in Aberdeen where a surgeon operated for three hours, sealing the burst vein, removing shot from his neck, face, ear and skull, but was forced to leave behind the fragments that had pushed into the edge of his brain. His head was shaved, swollen, bruised, scarred and stitched. He looked like a monster.

Coming round, he was subdued, almost submerged. He said nothing for a few days and after that only a few words and only in response to direct questions, as if the answer was being dragged out of him. But he recognised Tess immediately, his eyes lighting up when he saw her, fingers curling around hers. Any resistance or jealousy Kirat and Viv may have felt was quashed by their greater desire for him to recover, and any fool could see that if he could muster the strength to live, it would be for her. So they insisted she stay with them at a hotel near the hospital. She accepted their offer, though found the potent brew of emotions – the revelations and recriminations, suppressions and outbursts – almost unbearable, and was relieved when Rahesh was transferred to Inverness and she could move back home. The emotional cocktail with Liana and Alex was not much easier, but at least she was used to them and had Mo nearby. And now me.

On those hour-long drives up and down the A9 she talks to me and I learn things about my big brother that I hadn't known. He loved slapstick American sitcoms, he was the one who had got up for the kids at night, and it was his side of the bed she had slipped into after a bad dream. She tells me how – when she was tiny – he lay flat on his back so she could fall asleep on his chest, and how he'd taught her our mother's songs. His voice was ragged but his pitch was good. I tell her some of my childhood memories, trying to focus on the happy ones, the early ones, when Mo was still with us. I describe a game when Colvin carried me on his back pretending to be my horse as we galloped in pursuit of her, jousting with brooms, and how I could feel the laughter through his ribs. Sometimes, after one of our stories, we both fall quiet, looking out at the moorland: in opposite directions neither daring to voice the questions that still haunt us.

Rahesh surfaces, drawn up by Tess's hand and the enfolding net of her voice as she sings softly in the ward, an anti-lullaby to pull him back from sleep. Soon he can speak and sit up and walk, soon those parts of him return and reassemble and begin to tick. But not like before. The hearing is lost from the injured ear and sometimes the memories hit him like a freight train and he can be on the floor, whimpering. Some tiny shards of bone and shot must have fused parts of his brain in strange ways, sometimes fearful, sometimes funny. He forgets names and the most basic information but spouts monologues from high school plays; he doesn't always recognise people he knows well and occasionally mistakes a stranger for an old friend; sometimes he is lost for words, and when he finds them, they can be the wrong ones or hitched together in odd ways.

Shall I wear this dictionary, or the red one?

Oh, that man came to fix the lobster.

Look! Breaking through the clouds there: the rainboat!

A return to law seems unlikely.

He moves into Stag Lodge while he recovers, getting speech therapy and letting the scars heal. Viv is there permanently now, Kirat coming when he can, and Tess as much as possible given her various jobs and fragmented family. Rahesh starts reading about Scottish land reform, talking to Mo about the failed community buy-out and grilling his parents about their vision for Rowancraig. He makes them and their guests squirm. Has the bird shot in the brain loosened his inhibitions, or is it just a convenient excuse? Either way, no one dares challenge him.

Tess recounts these conversations to me, laughing. 'I love him even more now he's a little bit crazy. And because of him, they all have to be nice to me.'

'I think you're winning them in your own right, Tessy. Kirat speaks very highly of you. Says he's never seen such strength and sense in someone so young.'

She blushes and looks away. She has given up on her course at the Conservatoire but not on her music; she's still writing new songs and playing gigs around the strath.

As for me, I carry on with my absurd combination of odd jobs and high finance. Most of the local work is manual – stacking supermarket shelves, painting sheds – and I have to limit some of it because of my damaged hip. Discussions with Kirat about the Rowancraig Centre for Business Excellence are on hold, so I focus on the consultancy, which is growing. The hardest part of the work is the socialising. It was the bit I revelled in before, but I can no longer afford the expensive restaurants and I'm fighting with every fibre of my being to avoid alcohol. But it's all over the place and pressed on me at every turn. Especially in the City.

How do you do it? How do you make your way in that world when the deals are done over fine dining and sealed to the clinking of glasses? Even if I plead some silly diet and only have a bowl of soup and a tap water I can still end up splitting the bill – or footing it. I now know how it feels to hate the rich. Know what it must have been like to be around me when I was at my wealthiest and my worst. *Step 4: Made a searching and fearless moral inventory of myself.*

London has lost its shine for me. Each journey feels more and more like a descent into a forsaken world, a reshouldering of a shed skin, and I am less and less comfortable. Till the day I got honest again and told my clients that I'm still paying off debts and I'm in AA, everything has to be alcohol-free, and if we're doing lunch it's cheap and cheerful or it's on them. A few people disappear, but most find it refreshing and a relief. Some of them even confess their own addictions. We stop pretending to have it all.

But I am always glad to get home. Each return to the Highlands is like surfacing again to breathe. I've taken to using the train and feel a growing excitement as we crest the pass at Drumochter and press on through the bleak hills to the sudden green of the strath.

Whenever I can, I walk the land, taking my father's crook and Colvin's jacket. It still smells of him. Of sheep's wool and waxed cotton, of straw and dogs and farm, of his sweat and skin. I start with the trails he walked as a shepherd, in the footsteps of our fathers, our family as hefted to the hill as the beasts. My sore hip means I am slow and have to stop often to rest, but gradually the frustration fades. For the first time since childhood I notice things. An otter's splash, the fragrance of peat, the textures of bark and lichen on an ancient tree.

Dougie bequeathed to me his maps and field guides, all annotated in his fine hand, so that I sense he accompanies me as I walk. As does my mother. Her letters have revealed this landscape like a treasure that was never buried but always hidden. And her words reveal love. It is an inheritance I am only just beginning to claim.

Father

It is February and the Ferryman is quiet. A north wind is blowing, and outside, snow is heaped around the walls in bulky drifts. I clear up, lock the door and move over to the stove with a peppermint tea. It is my sacred time of the day, when everything settles into a hush of prayer and I take down the big leather Bible from the shelf. Not many pubs have a Bible, but this one is looked over and laughed at. And loved. I rest it in my lap and hold Colvin before God, because I cannot hold him any other way.

May the everlasting Father Himself take you
In His own generous clasp,
In His own generous arm.
May God shield you on every steep,
May Christ keep you in every path,
May Spirit bathe you in every pass.

I wait in silence and firelight.

It is broken by banging on the door and the apologetic voice of Kirat, his coat and scarf up round his ears, hat low.

'I'm so sorry to disturb you,' he says, seeing my wet eyes. 'I thought you would still be open.'

'Normally am. It's just that everyone left, so I shut up shop. Come in.'

He won't have a drink, but agrees to sit with me by the stove for a moment. We exchange the customary preamble about the weather — always safe ground, common experience. In truth, Kirat and I have talked much over the past months, as he has been harangued by Rahesh and heard about my dashed hopes for the community buy-out. There is a longing in his eyes but he can't yet find a way to reconcile the competing aspirations within his own family, let alone the community. We have that in common, too.

'I've got something for you,' he says, lifting his bag onto his lap. 'Now that the renovations at Rowancraig are finished, we're moving the furniture back in. Some of it we bought with the house, you see, and has been in storage. Lord Mackintosh cleared out his personal effects first and then, of course . . . well, there were your mother's things.' I shake my head at the memory of all Beulah's possessions squirrelled away into every nook and cranny of the house. Sagging nylon dresses next to Lady Clarice's fur coats, fag packets buried in sofa cushions, lottery tickets stuffed into Lord Edgar's desk.

'The other day,' Kirat goes on, 'Vivienne was looking through an antique secretaire that used to be in Lady Mackintosh's private sitting room and she noticed it has a secret drawer, right at the back. But it was locked. She went through every key we were given in the sale, including the big ring of housekeeper's keys your mother had, but none of them were right. Then today we unpacked the silver candlesticks that were in the dining room. We told you that story . . . well, anyway, we're getting rid of them . . . but when we took out a stump of candle in one of them we found a tiny key underneath, in a puddle of wax. It was the key to the drawer. Inside, we found this.'

From his bag he draws out a battered cigar box with faded lettering on the front; it looks vaguely familiar.

'We think it's yours.' He passes it over.

'Mine? I never went anywhere near Lady Mackintosh's secretaire.'

'I know. But it's quite likely your mother did.'

'Ah, I see. Good old Beulah.'

I lift the lid. There is an envelope, speckled and yellowing, with *Maurabelle Donaldina Euphemia Duggins, When Eighteen* written in a heavy hand. Under it are war medals and a pocket watch and a pair of cufflinks, and under that a tattered postcard from Whitby and some old black-and-white photographs. A young man at the seaside with an older lady, wind-tossed and laughing. The same man in uniform, then at his wedding, then holding a baby with a lace shawl over her mouth. And that is when I realise the man is Archie and these things are his.

I feel memory like a sudden toothache and a pricking in my eyes. It doesn't take much to bring tears these days.

'Oh,' I murmur, lifting the letter. 'Nearly forty years too late.'
Then I see the rip along its edge and look at Kirat.

'Yes, it has been opened, I'm sorry. But not by us, Mo, I assure you.
We haven't read it.'

I nod and run my finger along the tear, knowing exactly who had.

'I'll leave you to it,' Kirat says quietly, and touches his hand to my
shoulder before slipping out.

The letter is dated 5 May 1955, a month after I was born.

To my dear little Mo,
I hope you never have to read this as I want to explain
everything in person. Also, I am not very good at handwriting
and grammar and such, so is better if I can speak in my own
voice. But, in case the Lord takes me too soon I have asked
your Auntie Agnes to keep this letter and give it you when you
turn eighteen. Really, I pray to be with you on that proud day,
but just in case, you understand.

First of all, I want you to know that your mother – Mrs
Duggins, that is – and I are very pleased to be your parents.
You are God's gift to us at our time of need. Secondly, we are
not your parents. Not in the Biblical sense, if you know what
I mean. We took you in and will bring you up as our own, but
you didn't start with us.

The truth is your mother – your bodily mother that is –
was a young lass who worked here at Rowancraig House as a
maid. Nellie Pegg was a good Christian girl, with a nice nature
and very hard-working and so forth. You can be proud of her.
The difficulty is that she was unmarried when she had you and
your father would not take responsibility and her own family,
being strict Catholics and all, didn't want to know. She had to
pass you on. I am sorry to say that your father treated her very
badly. Not only did he desert her in a terrible situation, but
seemingly he forced himself on her in the first place.

That is why your mother – Mrs Duggins, that is – and I
have decided we will bring you up believing you were born to
us. It is the best way, so you feel you belong. You've a hard
enough time ahead with all the operations on your mouth and

whatnot without knowing your sorry start in life. Mrs Duggins, I must say, does not know the identity of your father. I know it because I found you with your birth certificate and Nellie's letter in a grouse basket in the stables.

Your father, she said, is Edgar Mackintosh.

As he was only twenty and off at Cambridge when you turned up, I felt duty bound to report the matter to his father, Lord Staines Mackintosh, who was resident in the house at the time. He received me in his study and was fair taken aback by the sight of you. But when he read Nellie's letter and saw your name on the birth certificate – Dolores Pegg Mackintosh – he laughed.

'Doesn't prove a thing,' he said. 'Claimed your mother was a gold-digger. And, can you believe, he threw both documents in the fire.'

I was that angry I could barely speak, but I managed to ask respectfully if we could keep you.

'Do what you like,' he said. 'It's nothing to do with me.'

But as I left he slipped me a wad of cash and warned me not to say a word to anyone. Said it was all nonsense but that rumours like this would hurt all of us. You understand?'

I understood perfectly. Which is why I didn't tell Mrs Duggins as I feared she might let slip. We both had jobs at stake.

However, I think when you're eighteen, all finished school and ready to go into the world, you should know the truth and decide for yourself who to tell and what to do. You see, as much as I want to make you my very own, I've decided only to foster and not to adopt you. That is so you keep your legal right to inherit from the Mackintosh family and get some just recompense for Nellie and yourself. You are the grand-daughter of a lord and you have a right to as much wealth, land and power as any of them. I cannot prove your descent, but perhaps you will find a way.

In any event, I wish you to know that I will do my level best to be a good father to you and I count it my honour to treasure the pearl of great price that the mighty have rejected.

Your loving father (by gift),
Archibald (Archie) William Duggins
Head Keeper
Rowancraig Estate

I sit till the fire dies and there is nothing but embers and the quiet dark. A letter from my father. About my father. And my mothers. (All three of them.) This letter was given to Agnes, so why . . . ? And then I remember: Beulah stripped her room before any of us got a chance. And Beulah would have torn open this letter and read it straight away, being Beulah. *She knew, she knew.* And even when I turned eighteen she never gave it to me and even when I fled she never told me the truth. Nor when I returned and met him again.

Lord Edgar Mackintosh – my father. By rape.

I picture the last time I saw him. He came for a final visit to Rowancraig in the December just after the sale was confirmed, and asked me to deal with Beulah, who had all but moved in. He met me on the front drive, looking beaten and old.

'I had hoped to pass it on, to keep it in the family,' he said, staring at the house. 'But I have no children and . . . well, there was a time when I loved it very much . . . but it's become a millstone. There is a time to turn away.' There was a glitter in his eyes. 'I have lost so much, Mo.' Then he turned a steely look on me. 'And I suspect you will say it is my own fault.'

I was not quick to answer, for once. We held each other's gaze until something softened. 'What do *you* say?' I asked.

He looked back at the house and sighed. 'A lot of it, yes, but not all. Was I so very bad? Did I deserve to lose my wife and my only child? Or is it the sins of the fathers visited upon me? The accumulated sins of generations of fathers? Forty generations, is it not? That's what your God calls justice, isn't it, Mo?'

He has not been back. Rumour has it he has sold all the family properties and assets apart from the cottage in Cornwall, where he lives in solitude with a dog. There will be a stash of money, then, from all those sales. I have a legal right to inherit, and according to Archie, a moral right. But do I? By what right does anyone inherit? Is it justice that wealth is passed on to heirs, thereby hoarding it within a family? It is unearned privilege. And unearned misfortune in the case of others. But regardless of the law or anyone's wishes, we all take on the legacy of our parents. Genes, social world, reputations, affiliations and prejudices, their nature and nurture, along with their money – or lack of it. Fair or not, we turn up in a certain family and are saddled with everything they give us. For generations. More than forty.

And in my case, it is a very complicated inheritance, having arrived in one, passed through another and ended up in a third. Should the Mackintosh money be part of it, by the mere fact of a sperm cell planted over fifty years ago? Though there was nothing 'mere' about it in my mother's experience, or indeed mine, when you consider the fallout. At least I exist. Had all this happened a generation later she might have got rid of me. And I would not judge her for that. But here I am. So would the inheritance right the wrong of my mother's rape and my abandonment? Nothing can right it, but perhaps the money could bring a better future out of a bad past. I don't need it, but I know plenty who do. Is it worth the fight? Do I even want Mackintosh to know?

I look back down at the letter. As old Lord Staines Mackintosh said, nothing can be proved. Unless I chase Edgar for a DNA test, which I won't. It's likely I am not Edgar's only child, regardless of what he knows or claims. Perhaps we kids should try and find each other and have a family reunion. An illegitimate family reunion. Maybe trace our mothers and get them along and invite Edgar and they can all reminisce.

My mother. Nellie Pegg. Is she still alive? Does she want to meet me? Do I want to meet her? Do I forgive her? The forgiving of mothers seems to have become my life's work.

And who am I, anyway? Dolores Pegg Mackintosh? Maurabelle Donaldina Euphemia Duggins? Mo Smith? Bastard, orphan, heiress?

All of the above.

And more.

Sign 11: Ring

A year after Colvin disappeared, a fisherman found his wedding ring. He had caught a salmon off the Moray coast near Spey Bay and when he gutted it, the ring fell out. The fish, called a grilse, as it was returning to its breeding grounds after a year at sea, was silver and speckled with tiny black dots. The ring, which he handed to the police, was gold and set with a small sliver of semi-precious stone. A blending of purple amethyst and amber-coloured citrine, it was called ametrine and came from Bolivia. According to legend, the stone was first brought to Europe as a conquistador's gift to the Spanish queen after he was given a mine in Bolivia upon marrying a local princess. According to online sources on crystal healing, the dual nature of ametrine unites male and female forces, opens the third eye of the chakra and sustains one in astral travelling. According to Liana, Colvin never wore it.

Wedding

Everyone is invited.

To the upside-down wedding of Tess and Rahesh. Where the bride has lost her father – for two years now – but found a man who will love her as deeply, and where the groom has lost a bit of his head and all of his heart to her and her home. Where they arrive at the church early, before everyone else, to give thanks and let the maverick minister (lucky me!) pray for them. *May the Father take you in His fragrant clasp of love*. Where she wears a dress of gorse yellow and he wears a Malaysian kurta and they both have wildflowers in their hair. Where they greet all the surprised guests at the door with hugs and the orders of service, designed by Liana with her crazy, curly art. Where the pews are decorated with fallen leaves, pine cones, feathers and flowers, gathered by Alex, who watches everything through the leper's peep in the vestry, which feels like a bird hide. Where the music is played by a raggle-taggle band of Tess's friends on fiddle, accordion, guitar and bodhran. Where Kirat and Vivienne are surprised by joy. Where there is no bride's side or groom's side of the church, but everyone is mixed up and muddled about, especially after the passing of the peace in the middle of things where you have to swap a feather for someone else's pine cone, a flower for a leaf, and wish them *Deep Peace of the Flowing Wave* or *the Shining Stars* or *the Tree of Life*.

Where the rejoicing in the kirk spills out to the shores of Loch Hope where we gather for the wedding picnic, and on to the bar of the Ferryman, where the music floods the whole village and everyone is up dancing, and our hands are joined in the binding and the blessing.

Where everyone is welcome.

Even my mother.

Mother

We finally found each other, my mother and I. The first mother – who became the last – and her firstborn child, who was also the last.

The year after I was given Archie's letter, the reception bell at the Ferryman rang and I went through to the front desk to find a very elegant lady clutching a map. She was in her late sixties, with a tailored linen trouser suit, grey hair in a sharp cut and perfect make-up. At the sight of me, her eyes widened and all the colour drained from her face.

'Helloooo!' I beamed. 'And how can I help you, madam?'

She looked down in confusion, struggling to speak. Her hands were large but perfectly manicured and sported striking rings. She finally squeaked something about directions for viewing the osprey nest.

'Hey, hey! You've come to the right place!' I took her out to the bench under the old oak with its view across the water to the nest on Small Isle. It was April, gentle with sunshine, and both birds were just returned from Africa. Giving her the guest binos, I told her all about their astonishing separate journeys and how the young would go back all alone. She kept turning to me in a kind of dazed wonder, so I kept on talking, about all the other birds of the loch as well, the swans and geese and ducks, the curlew and heron.

At last, looking across the water through the binoculars, she said, 'Forgive me.'

'Sorry?'

'Forgive me.' She lowered the glasses and her gaze. 'I'm not really here to see the birds.'

'Oh . . . sorry. That must have been boring, then.'

'No, no, I could listen to you for hours.' Her grey eyes searched me. 'I'm your mother.'

I sat dumbstruck.

'Forgive me,' she murmured again. I half opened my mouth but couldn't say a word. Then she shook her head and jumped up, dropping the binoculars and snatching up her bag as she spoke in a rush. 'I'm so sorry. I wasn't going to say anything. I just – I just wanted to see you and hear your voice and – and then go away again. I'm so . . .' She almost ran across the lawn, gasping another *sorry!* as she got to her black Volvo and dived in.

I stared as she roared the ignition, squealed into reverse and knocked over a bird bath. Then she killed the engine and collapsed onto the steering wheel. I picked up her map that had fallen to the ground and walked slowly across. After standing there watching her motionless, head over her arms, I opened the door and squatted beside her.

'Are you Nellie Pegg?' The head nodded. 'I think you left something.'

She lifted her face, tight with emotion, saw the map I extended and made a funny coughing laugh which wobbled into a sob. Her hand flew to her mouth and the other arm gripped herself around the ribs as she forced her breathing to slow.

'Don't go,' I whispered. She looked at me again, her face brimming with fear. Mine felt struck by lightning. Voice a croak. 'You – you came back. You can't just go. Again.' A flush in her cheeks as she nodded. I stepped back, and she climbed out of the car, holding onto her bag with both hands and staring straight ahead. As we walked back to the bench she looked like a criminal being escorted to trial. There was a terrible tightening in my throat as we sat down again, an uncertain space between us. Down at the loch, the ducks were upending in the golden rushes.

I broke the silence. 'You want to start from the beginning?'

A pause.

'My name is Eleanor Pegg. Here they called me Nellie. I . . . what do you know?'

I told her about Archie's letter and the burned documents. Her face pinched.

'The world has changed so much I wonder if you can even begin to understand . . .' Her eyes followed a flock of gulls rise and swoop. 'Before your birth I was sent to the Sisters of Charity in Inverness. They said your conception was my fault.' A bitter laugh. 'And that you would be given to deserving parents. I denied the first charge, of course, but I did believe that adoption was best for you. I was only fifteen, Mo. I had nothing and no one. I—'

'I know.' She looked at me. I gave the tiniest nod. 'I know.'

Her gaze fell to my mouth. 'Till you were born and I saw your face. I'm sorry, I was so afraid no one would want you . . . and you'd be left with the nuns.' Her head turned back to the loch. 'So I decided to force Mackintosh to take responsibility. I slipped out of hospital, registered your birth and got the bus here. But I made sure Mr Duggins would find you, because I knew he would guarantee you were cared for, one way or another.' A light breeze swept like an ocean wave through the trees around us and her voice dropped to a whisper. 'Then I caught the next bus down the road. It was the worst day of my life, Mo. Even worse than . . . worse than . . .' Her hand made the slightest gesture and she took a deep breath. 'I cried the whole way. And I was still bleeding and my breasts were leaking and it felt like . . . like my whole life was draining away.'

I said nothing. The surface of the loch moved, stippled and strafed under the wind's fingers.

'But I resolved I would never be so powerless again. I was going to spurn men, get rich, and give the orders, even if it killed me. And in a way it did. I worked myself to a rag and I did get wealthy and powerful and I got everything I wished for. Except the most important thing. The only thing . . .' She looked back at me, her eyes glittering and fierce. 'Believe me, Mo – I thought about you every day and wished somehow, *somehow*, I could have you back.'

I nodded and ran my big hand over my wonky mouth, for once in my life completely at a loss for words. I gripped my chin to stop the shaking.

'A few years ago I came back to Briachan and slipped into the church.' She pointed to the white bell tower, almost hidden in the trees on the far side of Loch Hope. 'I don't believe in God or anything, but I sat there and stared out the window with the Celtic cross. It was so quiet. So beautiful. I asked for you to be healed of all that harmed you. I asked forgiveness.'

The sunlight caught the wings of a grey heron making its slow, flapping flight along the loch and we watched till it disappeared down the river. My throat burned.

'On my way out I saw the noticeboard with all the photos of the kirk session. That was when I saw the Reverend Mo Smith. In a colourful cap and denim jacket, that squashed nose and lop-sided smile, Mackintosh's ears. My eyes. I cried and cried.'

She heard the shudder in my breath and turned to me, just as my face crumpled. Then my mother threw open her arms and I was in them, sobbing like a baby on her linen shoulder as she wept in my hair. At last, in a sniffling mess we pulled back, her burrowing in her bag for tissues, me in my pocket for a hanky. She dabbed as I honked and when it was quiet again, her hand took mine and held it on her knee. Our knuckles were the same shape.

'I came here to the the Ferryman for a coffee and the old owner told me all about you. How the people loved you, Mo, even those who didn't go to church.'

'Well—'

'Because you loved them. And he told me you wanted to buy the pub, because more people came here than to church. So I bought it for you.'

My breath sucked in and she squeezed my hand.

'I stayed anonymous because I was ashamed and afraid. Could you forgive me? Could you like me? Would you reject me as I had rejected you?'

I watched her as she watched the osprey circling above the nest.

'But then I finally realised I was letting Mackintosh keep robbing me and that I could no longer bear to live in fear and regret. I wanted to see you, just once, and then . . .'

'Then?'

She lifted my hand and cupped it in both of hers. 'I don't know, dear heart. That's up to you.'

Sign 12: Crook

On Dougie's maps I've marked the locations where each of Colvin's possessions have been found – in a strange trail first heading north then curving back east across the river and up into the Cairngorms. With the discovery of each one, I have gone to the place where it was left and searched for more signs, clues – answers.

Three years after my brother disappears, I find his crook. Despite my hip that still clicks and grinds in strange ways and aches at the end of a day, I make my slow way up the walk they took when I was just a light in my mother's eye, up through the pass of the Lairig Ghru in the Cairngorm mountains and into the Garbh Choire. It is midsummer's day and the smells of moss and peat rise around me in the warm air, cotton clouds drifting in the high blue. Stones shift under my feet and hands as I pick a route up the rocky slope to the Lochan Uaine and the waterfall where the MacPhersons' key was found. Hip throbbing, sweating, I pull off my pack and ease down onto a rock, enjoying the cool air on my damp back and hair. Above me rise the twin summits of Cairn Toul and Angel's Peak, together forming a curving wall of steep cliff and scree slope that shelters me from the full force of the wind. Stretched out between me and the foot of the cliffs, the lochan is a vivid blue-green, deeper than the sky. Its surface is lightly brushed with ripples, edges lapping on pebbles that all look grey at first, but gradually reveal their colours, from pearly white to peach and pink, mottled mauve and black.

As I can no longer run, I have taken up swimming in the lochs and rivers of the strath, gradually toughening against the temperatures. Barely thinking, I strip and wobble into the shallows. The icy water and hard stones make pain shoot up my legs, but at last I am deep enough to strike out and swim, shouting at the fierce cold and hearing my echoes bounce around the laughing cliffs. I plunge my head under and rise up gasping, sure I am seized by death, thrashing and kicking. Slowly I feel my blood flow return and my limbs buzz as I crawl out on the sun-bright shore, head open as a glass bowl, hairs standing on end. Every cell of my body is singing.

I lie that night on a mossy ledge beside the lochan, the hood of my bivvy bag unzipped so I can stare at the sky. It never quite gets dark but glows a deeper, lovelier green by the minute, drawing me into drifts of light sleep and welcoming me back as I wake to the sound of a bird or a voice in my dream. Each time, I find the moon has travelled, a silver canoe rowing the deep. In the very early hours, with the sky softening to pink, I see a deer a few feet away. She is young and delicate, one hoof lifted, her eyes fixed on me. We watch each other, barely breathing. Then her ear twitches and she shoots away, so swift and quiet it seems she is spun from light.

It's 3 a.m., but I get up, drink from the cold lochan and climb the curving north ridge beside it to the summit of Angel's Peak. It is slow and painful, and I am light-headed from hunger and lack of sleep. By the time I get to the top, the sun has risen and washed the whole of the Cairngorms in gold. The peak rises in a triangular spur with a green slope falling away to the south and two steep cliffs dropping to the east and west. I collapse onto my stomach at the rim of the summit and look out at the humps and ridges of the mountains, cut clear and sharp in the early light. A sudden dizziness floods me and I close my eyes, dropping my face to the ground. I don't know if I pass out or fall asleep, but when I look up, the sky above me is humming and someone has called my name. Still stretched out on my front, I peer over the edge of the cliff to the lochan, hundreds of feet below. An eagle launches from the rock wall and takes the air in radiant silence. And that is when I see it. Just below me, caught in a crack in the cliff beside a solitary tuft of mountain willow, is my brother's crook. I know that long, honey-coloured hawthorn stick with the curved black handle of buffalo horn, the surface worn smooth and shiny as jet, the small acorn at its base. Pushing myself forward I reach down till my fingers touch the handle, and stretching a bit further, I manage to grasp it. But however hard I pull, I cannot release it.

'Colvin!' I shout and draw my arm back, my face falling into my hands. I don't know how long I lie there crying, but finally I am silent. Perhaps I sleep. Then the wind is rushing up the slope and over my back. A bird calls. I feel a sudden and powerful sense of presence, both terrifying and joyous. A shaking seizes me and I sit up, searching. There is nothing below me on the cliff now but empty space. As the tears sting again, something lifts my eyes and there, far on the rim of Cairn Toul, I see a man. He is walking to the east with a collie trotting at his heels, crook in hand.

At his side a figure appears, with streaming white hair, who embraces him in laughter. And then another, shining. And with them, the wind.

On a far mountain at daybreak,
> where the veil is thin,
>> the Three.

Blessing

We are gathered here today on the shores of Loch Hope in the presence of God, in the worshipful company of birds and beasts, on the hallowed ground of the Earth, to give thanks for the life of Colvin Munro.

I did not try to tell his story alone. All were invited to share, and Liana made a book for folks to write their thoughts if, like Colvin, they weren't much for talking. Fachie was not much for words in any form, but wanted to honour his lost friend. 'Just one story,' I told him. 'From when you were kids. How bout the shinty?' He nodded. Hint of a smile. And he made everyone laugh. Tess made everyone cry with her song for her father, in spite of Rahesh joining in on the whistle. Or perhaps because of it. And everyone sang together: 'How Lovely is Thy Dwelling Place', 'Caledonia' and 'The Lord is My Shepherd'. Except Alex, who doesn't sing, but at least he came. Shepherds were there, from far and wide (with a dog each, as requested); as were keepers, stalkers and ghillies; hotel owners and cleaners; ramblers, environmentalists, tree loggers and tree huggers; skiers, bikers and wild swimmers; artists and activists; poets and plumbers; the landless and the landed. Kirat and Viv stood among us quietly, forever changed. And Sorley. My brother, born upon my knees, returned to me in body and spirit, gave a tribute to break and make every heart. But at last, he did not steal the show. That honour went to Tess and Rahesh's four-year-old twins, who danced.

So now, my precious family – like it or not, that is all of you – it is time to close.

There is a time for everything. A time to bind and a time to let go, a time to search and a time to cease, a time to weep and a time to laugh.

We remember with thanks how Colvin lived and with sorrow why he left. We have known guilt and sought forgiveness; we have lain down in remorse and longed for release. But, if we have learned anything in these seven years, it is that we do not move on by forgetting history, nor do we heal by denying the wound.

If we are to honour Colvin, we must walk with him. Not to disappear into the land, but to claim it; not to lose a people but to liberate them; not to relinquish, but to redeem. For I tell you, the vanished are not gone; the dead have been seen alive.

And now, may you go out in joy and be led forth in peace; may the mountains and the hills break forth into song before you, and all the trees of the field clap their hands.

For this is not
The End

Acknowledgements

It takes a village to write a book, and in my case, an international one. I am indebted to the many people who gave so generously of their time and expertise through the years of weaving this story. All the characters in the novel are fictional and do not represent the people I interviewed or the groups to which they belong. I have sought to be faithful to history and contemporary realities, but any inaccuracies will be mine and not those of my informants. A list of reading that was invaluable to my research, as well as a glossary and a list of characters, can be found on my website: www.merrynglover.com. Some of the following people have moved on from the organisations listed here or have, sadly, passed away. In every case, it was my privilege to learn from them.

For a novel about a shepherd I could not have found kinder or more knowledgeable guides than Campbell, Sheena, Archie and Cathy Slimon, representing several generations of shepherding in Laggan, who let me trail along on their rounds and answered my endless questions. I believe they even named a burn after me when I was the lost sheep on a memorable gathering. Special appreciation also to Campbell and Sheena for helpful feedback on a draft and the wealth of information in *Stells, Stools, Strupag*. Thanks also to shepherds Vic Watson of Alvie, the late Donnie Ross Snr of Leult, and Graham Grant of Gaskbeg. For further information on farming, tenancies and crofting, thanks to: Malcolm McCall, Willy Hamilton and Christopher Nicolson. I was moved to write this story partly because of the life and loss of local shepherd, Duncan McBain.

My deepest thanks to all the following for information and help:

On the workings of Highland estates both for sport and regeneration: Thomas MacDonnell, Wildland Ltd; Donnie Ross, Glen Feshie Estate; David Kinnear, Alvie Estate; Jamie Williamson, Alvie

Estate; John & Marina Forbes-Leith, Dunachton Estate; Sam Sutaria, Alladale Estate; Drew MacFarlane-Slack, Scottish Land and Estates; Murray McCheyne, Murchison Law; the late Ann Williamson, Alvie Estate. On land use, ecological regeneration and trees: Eileen Stuart, Scottish Natural Heritage (now NatureScot); David Balharry, Rewilding Britain; Nicol Sinclair, Forestry Commission; Alan Watson-Featherstone, Trees for Life; Will Boyd-Wallis, Cairngorms National Park Authority. On Highland and local history: Joe Taylor, fount of local knowledge; David Taylor, historian; Professor James Hunter, historian, University of the Highlands & Islands, who also gave feedback on a draft. On fostering and adoption: Kathryn Cox, Barnardos; Margaret Hood, Senior Registrar, Inverness; Mike Hancock, PAC-UK; Alison Gordon, Head of Service, Adoption & Fostering, Highland Council; Steve Bruce, Adoptions Officer, National Records of Scotland. On local wildlife: the late Mark Denman and Duncan MacDonald, who also gave feedback on a draft. On investment banking: Paul Bayton, John Duncan and Russell Hogan, who also gave feedback on a draft. On Highland Travellers: Rachel Chisholm, Highland Folk Museum; Essie Stewart, Highland Traveller, who also gave feedback on a draft. On cleft lip: Professor Khursheed Moos, maxillofacial surgeon. On the Queen's Own Cameron Highlanders: Lieutenant Colonel George Latham, The Highlanders' Museum. On questions of crime and punishment: David Higston, Procurator Fiscal; Neil McIver, Police Scotland. On Highland Games: Ian Grieve and James Brown, Scottish Highland Games Association. On the *Carmina Gadelica*, Dr Domhnall Uilleam Stiùbhart, Sabhal Mòr Ostaig. On fire-fighting: Alison Murray. On Bolivian Spanish: Andrew Irvine. On all things medical: Dr Alistair Appleby, who also read drafts, edited, and held the author together.

Heartfelt thanks to all the following exceptional people: my agent, Cathryn Summerhayes, for making things happen and always being there, editor Jamie Groves for a strong steer, and Jess Molloy for kind help. To the team at Birlinn/Polygon, for believing in this and birthing it, especially Alison Rae, for championing and laser-sharp editing, and Edward Crossan for insight, patience, unflagging support and everything else. You are the knee-woman!

I acknowledge, with thanks, the support of Emergents/XpoNorth for a manuscript appraisal, Creative Scotland for funding towards time to write, the Society of Authors, for everything you do, and the writing community near and far who never fail to share help and kindness. Your number is legion.

Love and deepest thanks to my dear friends who have listened, encouraged, prayed, waited and walked with me. Your spirits fill this book. Special appreciation to John Ross, for the use of your home by the sea when I needed a writing retreat, to Debbie Sawczak for thoughtful reflection, Karen Hodgson Pryce for feedback on a draft, and, once again, to the incomparable Kathy Hoffman, teacher, reader, wise one and soul friend, who has coaxed this book through its several lives. Gratitude, also, to the interwoven villages of this strath, for demonstrating how communities can be close-knit and open-hearted. To my extended family, who live like everyone is family, especially Mum and Dad, for unfailing love. To Sam and Luke, for being the best reasons to stop writing each day. And most of all, to Alistair, for making everything possible. Without you, I cannot imagine.

For the Three in One

A note on the author

Merryn Glover was born in Kathmandu and grew up in Nepal, India and Pakistan. Her first novel, *A House Called Askival* was published in 2014. She has written plays for BBC Radio 4 and BBC Radio Scotland and numerous short stories. Australian by citizenship, she lives in the Highlands and has called Scotland home for over twenty-five years.